unhuman

Inspector Hobbes

and the Curse

unhuman II

Wilkie Martin

The Witcherley Book Company
United Kingdom

Published in United Kingdom
by The Witcherley Book Company in 2017

First published in paperback and ebook (Kindle)
by The Witcherley Book Company in 2013

British Library Cataloguing in Publication Data.
A catalogue record for this book is available from the British Library.

ISBN 9780957635128 (paperback)
ISBN 9780957635135 (ebook)
ISBN 9780957635173 (ebook)
ISBN 9781910302064 (hardback)

.

1

When I drew Hobbes's attention to the unpleasant, if somewhat underwhelming, article on the front page of the *Sorenchester and District Bugle*, neither of us could have foreseen the deadly and bizarre events it heralded. The next few weeks were to prove among the most painful, frightening and horrific of my life, taking me to dark places I would have given almost anything to have avoided.

I was, at the time, having to live at Hobbes's, sleeping in his spare room, jobless, broke and pretty low. Mrs Goodfellow, his housekeeper, had left us to fend for ourselves while she attended a dental conference in Norwich: she wasn't actually a dentist, merely obsessed by teeth, having amassed a collection of several thousand. To start with, things had been fine, for she'd prepared meals to heat up, but we'd devoured the last one the previous night and I'd volunteered as stand-in cook, having made a passing study of the old girl's culinary technique during the months I'd been staying there. Admittedly, my experience had been mostly confined to hanging around, getting in her way and eating whatever she prepared, yet I'd been quietly confident I'd absorbed enough and could cope so it had seemed only fair that I, as a non-paying guest, should help out. Hobbes, to his credit, had let me get on with it, on a trial basis. Breakfast had been a doddle, there being little I could do wrong with Sugar Puffs and marmalade on toast; my first big test was lunch.

Since we'd been surprised by a burst of intense summer, I had opted, as a first attempt, for simplicity. I threw together a salad and cold meats, using up a few leftovers and adding some green stuff from the garden. Unfortunately, it hadn't looked sufficient for me, never mind for Hobbes's vast appetite, and so I'd decided to make a nice gazpacho, using a recipe I'd spotted in *Sorenchester Life*. This, I thought, combined with our remaining bread, would fill the void.

Taking advantage of the fine weather, I served the meal beneath the fractured shade of the knobbly, old apple tree in the middle of the luxuriant, flower-scented back garden. After Hobbes, according to his custom, had said grace, his voice competing against the buzzing of countless bees, I handed him the salad, which was, in my opinion, not bad. Certainly, he ate his without fuss, seeming not to mind the big green caterpillar on the lettuce, and he even complimented me on its freshness. He did, however, point out that the potatoes in a potato salad are better when cooked.

Then, proudly, I ladled out the gazpacho, its blood-red hue and tingling aroma of herbs and spice a promise of excellence, yet, from my first spoonful, it was obvious something had gone terribly wrong, resulting in a weirdly unpleasant meaty flavour that, combined with a nasty grittiness, caught the throat and turned the stomach. Hobbes only got as far as sniffing his before, aiming a puzzled frown in my direction, he headed towards the kitchen.

Sitting on the garden bench, watching the ants avoiding a spot of soup I'd spilled, I tried to figure out where I'd gone wrong, following a recipe the magazine claimed to be foolproof. So far as I could remember, I'd followed the instructions precisely, using only fresh vegetables, and, being short of tomatoes, a big squirt of tomato purée. Although my soup had come out considerably redder than the photograph, I'd put it down to the printers saving on red ink.

When Hobbes returned, carrying an immense slab of cheese and pickle sandwich, he tossed the tomato purée tube in front of me with an amused snort, except it wasn't tomato purée at all but the dog's meat-flavoured toothpaste. Hobbes, grinning at my shudder of revulsion, my look of despair, took a big bite from his sandwich and sat chewing.

On finishing, he suggested it would be better if we ate out, or bought in takeaways until the old girl got home. I didn't argue, merely taking myself to the kitchen to make a pot of tea, a task at which I'd become reasonably adept.

I'd just picked up the *Sorenchester and District Bugle* when Hobbes, sauntering in from the garden, helped himself to a steaming mugful of tea from the pot I'd made. Chucking in a handful of sugar, he stirred it with his great, hairy forefinger, relaxed into the battered, old chair next to mine, stretched out his thick legs, took a quick slurp, and placed his mug on the kitchen table.

'Let's hope,' he said, grimacing, 'that the lass returns before you finish both of us off.'

I shrugged, trying not to feel more inadequate than usual, for I was really doing my best in the absence of Mrs Goodfellow and, pointing at the front page, changed the subject. 'Umm ... According to this, there was blood everywhere.'

'Whose blood?'

'The sheep's I suppose. What d'you reckon did it?'

Frowning, he scratched the side of his bull neck. 'The very beginning is a very good place to start. About what are you talking?'

'This.' I pushed the paper towards him.

Taking it, he scanned the article, his bristling eyebrows plunging into a scowl. 'You want *me* to tell *you* what killed it, even though you've got all the information I have?'

I nodded. 'Well, you are a detective.'

He smiled. 'Alright, I'll do what I can, though there's precious little to go on. First point: yesterday morning, a farmer found a dead sheep in a field just off the main road to Pigton. Second point: its throat had been torn out. Third point: it had been partially eaten. Those are the facts; the rest is filler.'

It was, I thought, a good summary, though the reporter had managed to inflate the story to cover half the front page, while hinting at dark mysteries. Still, 'Sheep Killed' was not among the snappiest headlines Rex Witcherley, the editor, or Editorsaurus as I called him, had come up with and the blurry photograph of a sheep in a field, entitled 'A Sheep in a Field' that occupied most of the rest of the page, was not the most creative idea he'd had. To be fair to the Editorsaurus, it wasn't always easy to find hot news in a small Cotswold town like Sorenchester. Furthermore, he'd been going through a tough time since his wife got herself locked up in a secure unit for attempting to murder Hobbes, me and others the previous November, and wasn't yet back on form.

Hobbes, taking another swig from his mug, continued. 'I suspect a dog might be to blame, possibly a stray, because when pet dogs run wild they are less likely to eat what they kill. Anyway, there's nothing I can do about it, unless there are further incidents.'

Dregs, Hobbes's delinquent dog, padded in through the open back door, his long pink tongue snaking out to lick a blood-red globule dripping from his shaggy black muzzle. He slumped onto the cool red-brick floor with a sigh, wagging his tail as if he'd just done something clever.

'Look!' I cried, my finger trembling as I pointed, 'It was him, but he's always well fed.'

Hobbes's laugh rumbled round the kitchen. 'You'd be hard pressed to make the charge stick, since he was with me at the station at the alleged time of the incident. Furthermore, if you observe more closely, you'll notice that it's not blood but your … interesting tomato soup round his chops. You shouldn't jump to wild conclusions.'

I flinched and said nothing, wallowing in a familiar sense of failure. It was worse that, this time, I had really tried.

At length, draining his mug, he got to his feet. 'I'd better be off,' he said, 'Superintendent Cooper asked me to have a word with Skeleton Bob Nibblet. Do you fancy a trip out?'

'Umm … Yeah. Why not? What's he been up to this time?'

'Same as usual – poaching.'

'Well,' I said, 'you can't blame him; he looks like he needs the meat.'

Bob's hollow eyes, sparse frame and skull-like head were familiar to *Bugle* readers, his frequent appearances before the magistrate providing the crime desk with a constant trickle of small news. His offences, always petty, usually detected early in their inception, meant he would never be regarded as a criminal genius, yet he had a reputation as an excellent poacher and, according to pub rumours, supplied many respectable people with illicit game.

Hobbes led Dregs and me from number 13 Blackdog Street towards his rusting blue Ford Fiesta. As we got in, I wondered why I was always relegated to the cramped back seat whenever the dog travelled with us. In a way I was glad of this inferior position, for Hobbes's maniacal driving, showing no signs of abating, meant I enjoyed a slight sense of security when cowering in the rear, reasoning that the chances of him reversing into a tree at breakneck speed were considerably less than those of smacking into one at full speed ahead. Dregs, on the other hand, showed every confidence in Hobbes's abilities and, to give him his due, the facts backed up his nonchalance, for no one I'd asked could recall Hobbes ever being involved in a road accident. Apparently, the time to worry was when he went off road; more than one vehicle had allegedly disintegrated about him while he was hot on some miscreant's trail.

The engine growled into life. Dregs growled back in challenge, barking madly until we yelled at him to shut up. The ritual complete, we hurtled along Blackdog Street, screeched round the corner, flew along Pound Street and Spittoon Way, ignored the red traffic light onto the main road and sped in the general direction of Pigton.

Despite the open windows directing a hurricane of

miscellaneous insects into my face, sweat was soon trickling down inside my loose white shirt and pooling around the belt of my khaki chinos, which, like all my clothes, had once belonged to Mrs Goodfellow's husband, last heard of attempting to set up a naturist colony on Tahiti. Dregs's long tongue was lolling like a pink snake as he stuck his black head out the window, enjoying the jet stream. Hobbes, though apparently unaffected, still wearing his usual heavy, bristly tweed jacket and baggy flannels, making me sweat even more whenever I glanced at him, had, as a concession to the heatwave, ventured out without his battered gabardine mac.

At least with him driving, it only took a few desperate minutes before we were turning off the main road into a tree-shadowed lane. After a couple of hundred yards and a sharp turn, we bounced onto a track, stopping in a fog of dust. Back home on the kitchen wall, Mrs Goodfellow had put up a calendar showing glossy images of romantic cottages, all black and white walls, thatched roofs and roses round their doors, but Bob's cottage would never have got anywhere near the long list, though, what it lacked in roses it more than made up for in brambles. It was, in fact, a crumbling, red-brick hovel amidst a small yard overflowing with rusting bits of car, and mysterious remnants of machines that might once have had an agricultural purpose. In the corner, a rotting shed slouched against a crumbling brick wall and next to it stood a cage, shiny and clean and looking well out of place.

As we got out the car, Skeleton Bob, filthy string vest drooping from bony shoulders, was perched on an upturned beer keg in the porch. A faint, musky odour tainted the breeze.

Hobbes nodded. 'Good afternoon, Bob.'

Bob grunted.

'Who is it?' asked a woman's breathless voice from inside.

'It looks like the circus has come to see us,' said Bob grinning, displaying a spectacular set of discoloured and broken teeth. 'Leastways, we've got the strongman, the lion and the clown.'

A spherical, red-faced woman immersed in a billowing purple tent rolled from the cottage, coming to rest beside Bob, her hands on where her hips might have been.

'Good afternoon, Mrs Nibblet,' said Hobbes, touching his forehead.

'Oh, it's you. What's he done this time?'

'I've done nothing,' said Bob.

She frowned. 'You can shut up!'

Bob shrugged.

'It's been brought to my attention that someone's been poaching in these parts,' said Hobbes, shambling towards the Nibblets.

Mrs Nibblet sniffed. 'Oh, is that all? Can't a poor man take the odd rabbit to feed his starving family?'

'If,' said Hobbes, 'only the odd rabbit had been taken, I very much doubt I'd be here. Unfortunately, there's been a sudden and dramatic reduction in the pheasant population. Colonel Squire has been objecting. In fact, he's been objecting very loudly to Superintendent Cooper, demanding action. He says there's a lot of money in pheasants.'

'In which case,' said Bob, 'the odd one or two going missing won't hurt him.'

'Keep quiet, you,' said Mrs Nibblet, glaring at her husband, turning back towards Hobbes. 'Look, Bob only takes the odd bird or two that he comes across. Loads more get killed on the roads.'

'However many he takes, poaching is still against the law. Yet, in this case, Mrs Nibblet, dozens of young birds have vanished without trace, while a similar number have been found without heads. Do you know anything about it?'

Bob and wife spoke together, 'Dozens?'

'Yes, dozens.'

Bob shook his skull head. 'Honestly, Mr Hobbes, it's got nothing to do with me.'

Hobbes frowned. 'Fair enough, but perhaps you know something about it?'

Bob glanced at his wife as if seeking permission.

'We know nothing,' she said before he could open his mouth.

'Nothing,' said Bob after a moment's hesitation.

Dregs yelped and I turned in time to see him leap away from the cage, blood oozing from the black tip of his nose and dripping onto the grass.

'You ought to keep that dog away from my ferrets, or he'll get hurt,' said Bob, shuffling off his beer keg, approaching Dregs.

'Careful,' I warned, 'he's fierce.'

Bob ignored me, taking Dregs's head in his hands and examining the injury. 'That's no more than a love-bite,' he said, reaching into the pocket of his threadbare jeans, pulling out a battered tobacco tin and handing it to me. 'Open it, please.'

I screwed off the lid. The waxy brown goo inside stank of garlic and stuff. I wrinkled my nose. 'What's in this muck?'

'Garlic and stuff, but it's not muck.' Scooping up a globule with a bony, nicotine-stained finger, he massaged it into the wound.

To my astonishment, Dregs, after a faint whimper, allowed the indignity. I knew I'd never let the gunk get any closer to my nose than arm's length.

'Won't he just lick it off?'

'Would you lick it off?' asked Bob, his grin exuding his habitual good nature.

'Thank you,' said Hobbes. 'He'll not do that again. I doubt he's ever seen a ferret before.'

Dregs's tail thumped a staccato beat as Bob stroked him; I wondered how he would have reacted six months ago when Hobbes had first brought him home, a savage, vicious, malevolent creature. It had only been a few days after I'd moved in and, without exaggerating, I'd been in fear for my health and safety, if not for my life. In fairness, Dregs had only nearly killed me twice and neither time had it been on purpose. Since then we'd become friends.

'We'd better be on our way,' said Hobbes. 'Sorry to disturb

you, Mrs Nibblet.' Again he touched his forehead in an old-fashioned salute.

She nodded, waddling back into the cottage as Hobbes turned, strolling towards his car, gripping Bob's arm. Dregs and I walked beside them.

'Right, then, Bob,' said Hobbes, 'you want to tell me something.'

'Do I?' asked Bob, biting his lip, looking shifty, which was normal for him.

'You do. I saw the look you gave Mrs Nibblet.'

'I try not to look at her.'

'You can tell me in confidence,' said Hobbes. He chuckled, his arm encircling Bob's skinny shoulders, like a python round a fawn.

Bob squeaked and found himself in agreement. 'OK, OK, I'll tell you … just give me a moment to catch my breath.'

Hobbes releasing him, Bob talked. 'Look, don't think I'm going funny or nothing and I don't really know if it's important or not, but I did see something the other night … something strange.'

'Go on,' said Hobbes, slowing to snail-pace.

'I was out for a quiet walk in the woods a couple of nights ago.'

Hobbes raised his eyebrows.

'And you'll never guess what I saw.'

'What?' I asked.

'A big cat.'

'A big cat?'

'Yes, a big cat.'

'How big?'

'Andy, shut up a minute,' said Hobbes. 'How big was it?'

'Much bigger than this dog of yours but it was black like him.' Bob glanced around as if hidden ears might be listening. 'I reckon it was one of them panthers.'

'So,' said Hobbes as he reached his car, 'you reckon a big cat's been taking the pheasants?'

Bob nodded and then shook his head. 'Yes … no … er … could be.'

'Go on,' said Hobbes.

'Look,' Bob whispered, 'I didn't see it do anything; it was just slinking through Loop Woods, that's all. It might just be a coincidence.' He stopped and frowned. 'You don't believe me do you?'

Hobbes looked thoughtful. 'Let's say I don't not believe you. Thank you for your help and if you see anything else you know where to get hold of me. By the way, I'd lay off the night-time excursions on Colonel Squire's land for the time being if I were you. I'd hate to hear you'd been eaten by a stray cat. Goodbye.'

With a nod, he squeezed into the driver's seat and, as soon as Dregs and I had taken our places, started the engine, waving as we lurched and bumped back down the track. Bob was standing still, rubbing his shoulders, wearing an anxious frown on his bony face.

'What d'you make of that?' I asked.

'I don't know yet,' said Hobbes. 'There have been plenty of reports of mysterious big cats over the years, so it's not out of the question, but Bob's never been the most reliable of witnesses.'

'I reckon he was just trying to cover his tracks,' I said. 'It's hardly likely that a big cat would eat loads of pheasants.'

'It depends on how hungry it was and, if we allow the possibility that one big cat's on the loose, there's a chance there may be others. And don't forget that dead sheep; that could conceivably have been the work of a big cat.'

'It's a bit far-fetched. Surely, you don't believe him?'

'As I said, I don't not believe him. In fact, it wouldn't be the first time there've been big cats on the loose around here.'

'Really?' I said. 'I don't remember.'

'It was a few years ago, just after I'd been made up to sergeant, and it all happened up by the Elms estate, which in those days was a quiet, pretty place with lots of beautiful elms and very few houses. It was, by all accounts, a lovely spring day and no one could have anticipated the terrible events. Do you want to hear it?'

'Yes.'

'I wasn't there, being on holiday in Rhyll at the time, and only heard the story when I got back. Apparently a small travelling circus had come to town, featuring among the usual acts, a pair of lions in the charge of Claude the lion-tamer.' He paused, frowning. 'Actually, that might not have been his name, but he was definitely clawed, and had to be taken to hospital with multiple lacerations, leaving the other circus folk to look after his animals. They didn't do a very good job.'

The car bumped along the track, stopping at the end of the lane, the bleating of nearby sheep drifting in through the window.

'Go on,' I urged, meaning to continue his story, not to pull out in front of the lorry that was powering towards us. Brakes shrieked, the engine roared and somehow we were still alive.

He continued. 'They forgot to feed them for a few days and, when they remembered, both lions lay limp in their cage, as if dead. A juggler and a clown went in to check – the clown had nicked himself shaving and was bleeding. Anyway, to cut a long story short, the lions weren't dead; they'd merely been sleeping and woke to find two men in their cage and the door wide open.'

'Gosh,' I said. 'That must have been scary, especially for the bleeding clown.'

'Language, Andy. As it happens, the lions, ignoring the clown, went straight for the juggler, who was in front of the door, and knocked him to the ground. Yet, the lure of freedom proved stronger than hunger and they fled without harming him. The circus folk contacted the police, who organised a big search but found no sign of the beasts.

'They turned up on Sunday morning. Back then there was a pleasant little church on the estate and a service was in progress when the lions walked in. The story goes that the vicar looked up to see them bounding towards him down the aisle. "Oh Lord," he prayed in his terror, "turn these ravenous beasts into Christians."'

'What happened?' I asked, agog.

'Well,' said Hobbes, 'on hearing his words, the lions stopped, bowing their heads before the altar. The vicar rejoiced, certain a miracle had been granted to him, until he heard what they were saying.'

'The lions could speak? What did they say?'

'For what we are about to receive ...'

I laughed. 'No! I don't believe you.'

Hobbes chuckled. 'Oh well, you're learning. Actually, most of the story is true, just not that last bit. In reality, old General Squire, Colonel Squire's grandfather, shot them both in the apse. A pity as they weren't doing any harm.'

'What next?' I asked.

'I think we should pay a visit to the Wildlife Park and have a quiet word.'

'You do think there's a big cat on the loose.'

'I would merely like to eliminate the possibility from my enquiries.'

2

The road to the Wildlife Park, being quiet, presented Hobbes with an opportunity for some brutal accelerator crushing. I clung to my seat, sweating, wishing I could be as cool as Dregs whose head was stuck out the window, ears flapping like bats in a hurricane. Now and again, Hobbes insisted on looking over his shoulder to talk to me, allowing the car to swoop wildly across the road, taking the shortest route. Responding only encouraged him; keeping quiet only made him turn to check nothing was wrong.

Fortunately for my well-being, the ten-mile journey could only have lasted five minutes, since the more I got used to his driving, the more frightening it became. Turning into the Wildlife Park, we slowed down, having, as always, made it without harm to ourselves or others. A small herd of antelope stared at us, acting skittishly as if we might be predators. To the left, half a dozen two-humped camels lounged in the shade of a mighty tree, watching the world with total disdain.

'I'd best keep well away from that lot,' said Hobbes, a look of concern on his face.

'Why? They're not dangerous are they?'

'Not as such, but unfortunately I have an allergy to camels; at least they're not dromedaries, because they can make me really bad.'

'Well, at least you're not allergic to something common, like dogs or cats. You can't run into camels very often.'

'You'd be surprised.'

The car park was guarded by a broad, red-faced man in a

narrow, green booth. Standing up, he emerged, ticket machine swinging from his bulging neck.

'Be careful,' I said, 'he's going to charge.'

Hobbes, stopping the car, smiling, held out his ID. 'I'd like a word with the manager.'

'Very good, sir. Try the main office in the big house, but dogs aren't allowed.' He pointed to a large sign confirming his statement.

'It's alright,' said Hobbes, 'he's with me.'

'But …'

'He's with me,' said Hobbes, his tone leaving no room for argument.

'Fine. In that case, you'd better leave your car by the coaches,' said the poor man pointing vaguely behind him, mopping his forehead with a red handkerchief, 'because the parking by the house is rather limited at the moment. We're expecting delivery of a kangaroo.'

Hobbes thanked him and parked and we piled out of the oven. I felt as limp as a month-old lettuce and even Dregs was drooping.

'You two look like you could do with a drink,' said Hobbes, parting the flock of excited school children loitering in front of the kiosk, deciding which sweets would rot their teeth best. He returned with a large lemonade for me and an ice cream carton filled with water for the dog. Dregs lapped it up, splashing almost as much as he drank.

'We'd best find the manager,' Hobbes said when I'd drained my paper cup and Dregs had licked the carton dry. 'Come on. And quickly.'

We headed towards the house, an impressive, turreted, stone edifice with fine mullioned windows and ivy draped around the porch, where a sign directed us inside to the main office. Going inside was almost like stepping into a cave, the coolness coming as a blessed relief, the shade delightful. The problem was my eyes, taking a few moments to recover from the glare, failed to spot the sign advising visitors to mind the step.

I didn't mind it. Stumbling down, struggling to regain my balance, I might have succeeded had it not been for the rug slipping beneath my feet. My legs began a desperate race, trying to keep up as my upper body lurched headfirst towards a door that was, fortunately, ajar. Bursting through, sprawling full length, skidding across the marble floor on my belly, I came to rest a few centimetres from a pair of elegant ladies' shoes. On pushing myself to my knees, I couldn't fail to notice the equally elegant pair of legs, clad in sheer black nylon. An intoxicating, powerful perfume filled the air.

I'd never had much luck when meeting attractive women, somehow never appearing at my best, as if cursed to be a buffoon, a klutz. Yet, as I looked up, the smile on her face suggested amused sympathy, rather than the horrified contempt I'd expected.

'Are you alright?' she asked, her voice soft and gentle with rather a posh accent, suiting her look of quiet sophistication. She wore a black skirt and a pale-green silk blouse, which clung around her. My eyes, briefly meeting hers, stared at the carpet, yet I retained an image of full red lips, sleek, dark hair surrounding a face suggestive of Mediterranean ancestry, eyes flashing green like northern seas in the sunlight, beneath fine quizzical eyebrows, and ...

'Andy?' Hobbes arrived in a more conventional manner, his voice bursting into my reverie like a hippo into a paddling pool. 'Are you hurt?'

'Umm ... er ...'

'Do you think we should call an ambulance?' asked the woman, sounding concerned. 'He might have hit his head.'

A great muscular paw dragged me to my feet. An electric fan whirred, blowing cool air into my back.

'He probably should get his head examined,' said Hobbes, 'but I don't think he's hurt himself.' He sniffed, rubbing his nose.

'I'm alright,' I said. 'I ... umm ... fell.'

When the woman smiled at me, my knees came close to giving way.

Another woman spoke. 'Can I help you?'

An older woman, flecks of grey in her short, gingery hair, wearing round, red-rimmed spectacles, sat behind a desk. I had found the main office.

'Forgive me,' said Hobbes in his official voice, showing his ID, 'I'm Inspector Hobbes and this young oaf,' he patted my back, 'is Andy.' He sneezed. 'Excuse me.'

I flinched, but not from the suddenness of the sneeze. Being labelled an oaf in front of such a beautiful woman was not good for the ego, especially when the accolade was well deserved. Yet, she smiled again before turning to the other woman.

'Thanks, Ellen,' she said. 'I can see you'll be busy with these two gentlemen so I'll come back later.' She walked away, with an elegant swing of the hips.

'Good afternoon, Inspector,' said the older woman, rising from her chair, 'I'm Ellen Bloom, Mr Catt's secretary. How can I help you?'

She smiled at him; I still wondered how he managed to conceal his otherness behind his policeman's façade.

'It's merely a routine enquiry. I wondered whether you might have lost any big cats recently?'

'I wouldn't have thought so. We are not in the habit of losing animals, especially big ones.'

'No, I thought not,' said Hobbes, nodding. 'However, I needed to check. I wonder if I might have a word with your boss?'

'Mr Catt is not in his office. I'll find him.' Sitting back in her chair, picking up a walkie-talkie, she pressed a button and spoke. 'Mr Catt? It's Ellen.'

The walkie-talkie crackled and buzzed in response but Mrs Bloom seemed to understand it.

'I have an Inspector Hobbes here, who wants to talk about big cats ... OK, I'll tell him ... goodbye.' She released the button, looking up at Hobbes. 'Mr Catt is in the reptile house attending

16

to the crocodiles. Go out the front door, turn left and left again. You can't miss it.'

'Thank you,' said Hobbes as we left.

'Wasn't she gorgeous?' I murmured.

'Mrs Bloom?'

'No, the other lady. I wonder what she's called?'

He grinned. 'It's like that is it? And there was I thinking you'd thrown yourself at her feet by accident.'

'I did ... D'you think I made a fool of myself?'

'No,' he said with a chuckle, 'almost certainly not.' Pulling a handkerchief from his pocket, he blew his nose like a foghorn. 'I think the rug you slid on must be made of camel hair. It's good to get some fresh air.'

I nodded, unable to take my mind from the woman, who, though she must have seen me as a clumsy oaf, had smiled at me. It had been a smile of sympathy but it had shown off her perfect white teeth, lovely lips, the way her eyes crinkled at the corners ...

'Where's Dregs got to?' asked Hobbes, looking around.

He'd definitely been with us when we'd entered the house but I couldn't recall seeing him since. There was no sign of him.

'We'd better find him,' said Hobbes, 'and quickly. Otherwise he'll end up in the lion's den – or worse.'

He loped away in a crouch, his hairy hands nearly brushing the dusty concrete and, though he looked awkward, I had to jog to keep up. At least I could keep up for a short while. When I'd first met him, I wouldn't have stood a chance, but Mrs Goodfellow's good food, combined with running after him and Dregs, had lifted me to a level of fitness that was still a novelty. Nevertheless, I was puffing and sweating like a Turkish wrestler when we found the dog, cowering under the car, trembling, showing the whites of his eyes, licking his lips. He seemed pleased that we were there and crawled out, whining like a frightened puppy. I'd never seen him like it before and it came as a shock, for I wouldn't have believed anything could scare him.

'What's up with him?' I asked, stroking his hairy head.

'I don't know but something's obviously given him a fright.'

'Perhaps it's the scent of all the animals round here?'

'I doubt it. He normally likes that sort of thing.'

'I suppose so. Perhaps my fall upset him?' Even I was sceptical about this theory for, judging by past experience, Dregs regarded any trip or pratfall with great, tail-wagging amusement.

'Who knows, but whatever was up with him, he's better now.'

It was true, for Dregs's whiplash tail was working overtime and he was now bouncing around us as if nothing had happened.

Hobbes shrugged. 'Oh well, let's find Mr Catt.'

As we headed towards a long, low-slung building, my stomach started turning somersaults because I'd always had a thing about reptiles, and particularly snakes, even the little ones. I had a moment of hope on spotting a sign saying the reptile house was temporarily closed to the public, but it didn't deter Hobbes or Dregs who plunged inside, while I dithered, scared to enter, yet unwilling to miss out on whatever transpired. At length, screwing up my courage, I ran after them. It was bad, as bad as I'd feared. There was a boa constrictor slithering in my direction in the first tank and a pair of anacondas, sleeping but sinister in the second. Then came smaller tanks, writhing with all sorts of venomous serpents but the worst was a massive reticulated python, its belly swollen to the size and shape of a small pig. I shivered, avoiding eye contact, trying to hurry past, while Hobbes peered at it, obviously fascinated, and Dregs bounced, barking in excitement.

'This fellow's enjoyed a good lunch and no mistake,' said Hobbes, 'and it's obviously not the snakes that frightened Dregs.'

'C'mon,' I urged, 'let's find Mr Catt.'

'There's no hurry,' said Hobbes, putting his great, hairy paw up to the glass and waving. 'Hello, Mr Python, curling round a tree.'

The snake, responding, slithered towards us, making me feel sick and wobbly, scarcely able to breathe, as its unblinking gaze locked onto me, following my every movement. Though my rational mind knew it was safely behind the thick glass, I couldn't help myself wondering what would happen if the glass broke, or if some careless keeper had left the door open.

'Can we go now?' I asked, backing away.

'I think she's got a crush on you,' said Hobbes with an evil grin.

Turning, I fled towards a walled pen at the rear, where a pair of crocodiles lurked. Hobbes followed, chuckling.

The larger of the crocodiles raised his head as we drew close. 'Ah,' it said, 'you must be Inspector Hobbes. I'll be with you in a moment.'

I was so startled that, forgetting my panic, I stood still as a statue, gaping like an idiot, until a chubby, little man, red-faced, dressed in a dishevelled safari suit, stood up abruptly from behind the wall, seized the smaller croc by the tail and plunged a syringe into it. The beast thrashed and snapped but the man had moved on.

Sauntering away, he climbed back over the wall, dropping the syringe into a yellow plastic box. 'A jab well done,' he said, rubbing his hands together, chuckling at his own joke. 'I'm Francis Catt, the director. How may I help you?'

'I'm sorry to disturb you, sir,' said Hobbes, 'but have you lost any cats?'

'Felines, nothing more than felines,' Mr Catt sang in a wavering tenor and grinned. 'No, we haven't lost any. Have you found some?'

'Possibly,' said Hobbes, 'according to Mr Nibblet.'

'Would that be "Skeleton" Bob Nibblet?'

'Yes,' said Hobbes. 'I take it that you know him?'

'Oh yes. He's turned up here several times recently, fretting that we'd lost a black panther. We haven't of course. The only thing we've ever lost is a grass snake.'

I couldn't stop myself from looking around, preparing to run. Grass snakes, I knew, were mostly harmless, but they were still snakes.

'Do you think,' asked Hobbes, 'that he was making it up?'

Mr Catt thought for a moment. 'I wouldn't go so far as to say that but he always seems to run across big cats on Friday nights and Ellen – you've met my secretary? – she lives not far from him and says he's usually rolling drunk on Friday evenings.'

'I see,' said Hobbes.

Mr Catt continued. 'I'm not saying he's lying deliberately but I wouldn't rely on him. He's not so bright at the best of times and with a skinful of beer, well, I think it's likely that he's just seen a normal black moggy and blown it up out of all proportion.'

'That would seem likely,' said Hobbes, nodding. 'Still, while we're here, would you mind if we take a look at your big cats. What have you got?'

Mr Catt, escorting us from the reptile house, took us along a dusty path, past groups of happy visitors, heading for the cats. 'We've got lions,' he said. 'Tony, the lonesome tiger, and a pair of leopards – you might find them interesting. Zoologically speaking they are synonymous with panthers, the so-called black panthers, merely being melanistic variants. We have a couple of fine specimens but they're safe in their pen. Anyway, even if they did escape, they wouldn't get far; leopards are always spotted.' He sniggered like a schoolboy. 'By the way, did you know lions are so called because they're always lion around?'

'Huh!' I said and, to distract him, pointed towards a pen where some white birds with long beaks were standing round a pond. 'Are those storks?'

'No, they're Egrets. Egrets, I've had a few, but then again too few to mention.'

I sighed. We were passing the rhino enclosure when Hobbes stopped walking. I continued, chatting to Mr Catt.

'What's a melanistic variant?' I asked, more as an attempt to halt his little 'jokes' than because of a thirst for knowledge.

'It's merely an animal that possesses an increased amount of black, or dark, pigmentation. Interestingly enough it can occur in many felines and, it's not generally known but …'

'How dangerous are rhinoceroses?' asked Hobbes, frowning.

Mr Catt looked puzzled. 'The rhinos? They're not really dangerous at all, so long as they're confined to their enclosure and we're safely out here. Why do you ask?'

'I wondered if that little girl was safe,' said Hobbes.

'What? Oh hell!' Mr Catt groaned.

The child was running through the enclosure, presumably having squeezed under the wire and clambered across a ditch. She was heading for her sunhat which must have blown off. One of the rhinos raised its head, staring, ears twitching, ambling towards her. The other, looking up, trotted after it.

'If something startles them, they might charge,' said Mr Catt, his ruddy complexion having turned the same greenish colour as the dried mud caked on the rhino's backside.

'Then I'd better get her out,' said Hobbes, 'because she's public and it's my job to protect her.'

'No!' said Mr Catt, his voice almost a shriek, 'you might alarm them and ...'

But Hobbes, vaulting the high steel gate into the enclosure, was already speeding towards the girl. Then a tall, thin woman, unmistakeably a schoolteacher, even at a distance, noticing her charge, called out a sharp command. The child, running towards the wall, was pulled to safety and given a stern rebuke. Mr Catt and I had barely moved, understanding how it felt to be rooted to the spot.

Hobbes, slowing to a jog as he saw the girl was safe, bent to pick up her hat.

Both rhinos charged.

Mr Catt and I yelled in unison. 'Look out!'

Though the rhinos' massive feet were kicking up dust and turf as they pounded the dry pasture into a thundering rhythm, like a troupe of Japanese drummers, Hobbes didn't appear to have noticed. Cold horror clutched my insides, for surely not even he could withstand a direct hit from a pair of three-ton rhinos. The first one lowered its horn and I shuddered, imagining the scene when I told Mrs Goodfellow of his untimely and messy end.

Then, straightening up, brushing the dust from the hat, he sprang into a twisting somersault, carrying him straight over the first rhino. Landing with a gymnast's poise in time to meet the second one, he vaulted it, as if playing leapfrog, his teeth glittering in a grin of pure exhilaration. Before the bewildered creatures had skidded to a halt, he'd hauled himself from the enclosure and was handing the hat back to the little girl, touching his forehead in salute as she and her friends goggled, open-mouthed. The rhinos, seeing no sign of their target, obviously assuming they'd pulped him into oblivion, swaggered back across their field. If they'd exchanged high fives, I wouldn't have been surprised. Actually, I would have been, but, there was no denying, they were exuding an air of smug achievement.

The grin was still on Hobbes's face when he rejoined us. 'You can have a lot of fun with rhinos,' he said, 'but we're here for a look at your leopards.'

'Oh, yes, alright,' said Mr Catt, rubbing his sleeve over his face. 'That was a remarkable thing you just did.'

'Not really. The child needs her hat on such a hot day. Anyone would have done the same.'

'Of course they would,' I said, nodding my agreement.

Hobbes chuckled, patting me on the back. I picked myself up, brushing down my trousers, following as he propelled a shaking Mr Catt towards the leopard enclosure. Dregs, who'd been investigating a lamppost, appeared not to have noticed anything out of the ordinary.

'You should have seen that,' I told him. 'Who'd have thought a big bastard like him could do a backward somersault in mid-air? From a standing start, too!'

Dregs wagged his tail to indicate he'd have thought it.

Mr Catt was in lecture mode as we caught up. 'Of course,' he said, 'leopards are by far the most adaptable of the big cats, being equally at home in forests, savannahs, semi-deserts and mountains. If any big cat could survive in this country I feel it would have to be a leopard, but I'm sure they'd leave signs. I can't believe they'd go undetected for long.'

Hobbes nodded. 'I agree. Most of England is too crowded to shelter large wild beasts. It's a shame there's no room for animals these days.'

'Well,' said Mr Catt, 'I, for one, am pleased. No one would pay to come here if they could see the exhibits roaming outside for free. Anyway, it'd be dangerous. Our male leopard weighs as much as the average man and can easily overpower prey much larger than himself. He could kill or seriously injure someone.'

'There is that to consider,' said Hobbes thoughtfully, as if the idea hadn't occurred to him. 'Human beings are annoyingly fragile and it's a good job they've got good brains.' He glanced at me. 'Most of them, anyway.'

Mr Catt smiled at my affronted expression but I was playing along with Hobbes's joke. I assumed he'd been joking.

'Our leopards,' Mr Catt continued, 'are particularly fine specimens and we're hoping they'll breed soon. The female has already had a couple of litters at her previous zoo but, for some reason, our male doesn't seem capable of making her pregnant, appearing to prefer cheetahs.' He sniggered. 'We think he might be trying to pull a fast one. Anyway, we've got the vet coming here next week. We're hoping he might be able to do something to get her in cub.'

'Will she let him?' I asked, smirking.

Mr Catt rolled his eyes. 'Don't be silly,' he said, as if talking to an imbecile. 'The vet's going to check if there are any physiological or nutritional reasons for their failure to copulate.'

'I was joking. But … where are your leopards?'

The pen appeared empty apart from trees and stumps, a variety of wooden platforms at different levels and tufts of tawny and grey fur, blowing in the breeze.

'Eh?' said Mr Catt with a look of wide-eyed panic.

'Up there,' said Hobbes, pointing to the topmost platform where two pairs of furry ears twitched in the shade. 'They're having a lie down.'

'Of course,' said Mr Catt, regaining his composure, 'they spend about twenty hours a day sleeping and lounging and prefer to do it at height. Unfortunately, it's not so good for the visitors but the animals' welfare must come first.'

'Of course it must,' said Hobbes.

The walkie-talkie crackled and Ellen's distorted voice informed Mr Catt that the kangaroo had arrived.

'I'd better go and see to it,' said Mr Catt. 'Bruce, our marsupial keeper, is laid up in a coma after Rufus the red kangaroo jumped on him during his first day with us.'

'How did that happen?' I asked.

'It's actually a very sad tale. Rufus, who was our alpha-male, was an orphan who'd been hand-reared at Walkabout Zoo where he was born. It turned out that Bruce had started his career at Walkabout, one of his first jobs being to hand-rear young Rufus. Apparently, he used to wear a sort of apron with a pouch for Rufus to jump into. When he started work here, he didn't recognise Rufus but Rufus recognised him and tried to leap into the bag of food Bruce was carrying. Being hit full on by two hundred pounds of solid kangaroo is not good for a man.'

'I understand why Bruce isn't here,' I said, 'but why do you need another kangaroo?'

'Because, before uncovering the full story, assuming Rufus had just gone berserk, we thought it best to shoot him. Ellen ordered a sane one on eBay.'

'That's really sad,' I said. 'Poor Rufus.'

'True, but every cloud has a silver lining. The leopards did rather well out of it.' He pointed towards the clumps of fur.

'Well, thank you for your time,' said Hobbes. 'It has been most instructive. Do you mind if we look around on our own?'

'Be my guests.' Mr Catt bustled away.

We strolled round the park for an hour or so, Hobbes studying each animal with keen interest, now and again licking his lips and swallowing, as if hungry. Dregs slouched alongside with an expression of acute boredom that only lifted when he saw the tortoises; they caused great and noisy excitement. He obviously held the opinion that rocks should stay put and should not sprout legs and lumber around. Hobbes had to grab him by the scruff of the neck and drag him away. Otherwise, I think he'd be there still. Other than that, we came across nothing of great interest, though Hobbes appeared to be deep in thought about something. I contented myself with walking at his side, occasionally kicking stones for Dregs to chase.

A barbed-wire fence eventually indicated the limits of public access. I noticed one or two matted tufts of brown fur snagged on the barbs, as a pair of Bactrian camels, appearing from the shade under an oak tree, began pulling at a bale of hay.

'I'd be a bit careful if I were you,' I said. 'That could be camel hair.'

My warning came too late. Hobbes had already plucked a tuft from the wire and sniffed it. He looked up. 'I wish I hadn't just done that.' He reached for his handkerchief.

He sneezed so violently that Dregs fled a hundred yards up the path, loping back towards us suspiciously, growling. Hobbes sneezed again. And again. He blew his nose, which, I swear, though prominent enough at the best of times, was growing and ripening.

'I've got some stuff that helps in the car,' he said, snuffling. 'I'd better get back there ... and quickly.'

By the time we reached the car park his eyes had swollen shut as if he'd come off worse in a punch-up and his nose shone like a baboon's bottom. I had to guide him as he groped for the car.

Reaching into his pocket, he handed me the keys. 'Look in the boot. There should be a black bag. I'd be obliged if you'd open it for me.'

I did as he asked. The bag contained a bottle of Optrex, half a dozen handkerchiefs and an assortment of glass vials filled with a coloured liquid.

'Could I have one of the green ones, please? And a fresh

handkerchief. This one's ripped.'

Ripped wasn't really the word: it had been blown to shreds. I handed the things to him. Between explosions, he bit the top off the vial, tilting back his head, gulping down the contents. Then he sneezed again. Then he howled like a wolf. Then he collapsed like a factory chimney that had been dynamited.

3

Though Hobbes came down with a thud, a desperate dive saved me from being completely crushed. Even so, I ended up flat on my front, my legs trapped beneath him. As I pushed myself up on my elbows, Dregs ran up, nosing me, wagging his tail, as if it was all a jolly game.

'What do I do now?' I asked.

He made a strange snicker that I interpreted as, 'You're the human. You do something.'

'A great help you are.'

Neither education nor experience had prepared me for how to act when my legs were pinned beneath a hefty, unconscious police inspector. Groaning, wriggling and straining proved to be of no avail; I might just as well have tried to break free from the stocks. Yet, most of all, I was worried about Hobbes. Unable to tell how sick he was, though able to feel the rise and fall of his chest, I felt utterly helpless, not to mention ridiculous. Dregs, thumping his tail on the ground, eager for further entertainment, sat by us, expectantly. I had a great idea.

'Go and fetch help,' I said in my most commanding voice.

He listened, his head on one side, his tail beating faster and then, to my amazement, ran off, as if on a mission. 'Good dog!' I cried, impressed.

Sadly, he had not turned into a latter-day Lassie and, returning, he dropped one of the chewed rubber balls he kept in the car in front of me, bullying me until I threw it. As soon as I did, he bounded after it with a joyous bark.

Fearing rescue would not come until I gave up on dignity, I decided to call for help, though the car park was deserted.

'Excuse me, anybody,' I cried, at a polite volume. 'I could do with a little help here.' Since there was no response, I concluded a more effective option might be to scream with all the force of my lungs. For me, to think was to act and so, throwing back my head, opening my mouth, I sucked down air in preparation for a titanic bellow. As I did, Dregs, scampering back, dropped the ball. My mouth wasn't big enough to take it in, at least not in one bite, but it stuck between my upper and lower teeth, gagging me. Spluttering, I spat it out, wiping my mouth in a frantic bid to remove any dangles of dog drool, as a low, rumbling groan emerged from Hobbes.

'Are you alright?' I asked, continuing to wipe away with the backs of my hands, while Dregs, barking excitedly, stared at the ball, waiting.

'Ugh,' said Hobbes, pushing himself into a kneeling position.

Pulling my legs to safety, I rubbed the life back into them.

'Are you alright?' I repeated.

He turned towards me, his face pale, skin glistening like moist putty, eyes damp and red, though, at least, his nose had shrunk to its normal dimensions. He nodded and we helped each other up. Then he leant against the car, every breath bubbling and popping, as if he were sucking through a part-flooded snorkel.

'Optrex!'

I handed him the bottle. His hands shook and he must have spilled half of it as he filled the bath to rinse his eyes.

'That's better.' He sighed.

Maybe he really did feel better, but he still looked as if someone had scooped out his eyeballs and filled the sockets with overripe strawberries. It was a most striking effect, causing my own eyes to water in sympathy and a small group of respectable elderly visitors strolling by to gasp and hurry away.

'Andy,' said Hobbes in a loud, nasal voice, 'a word of advice. It's never a good idea to let the dog drop his balls into your mouth; you don't know where they've been.'

The blood boiling in my cheeks, all I could do was nod and grin inanely.

The pensioners departed even more rapidly, muttering, shaking their heads.

'I'd like to go home now,' said Hobbes, 'but I can't drive like this. I wonder if Billy's free?'

Billy Shawcroft was a binge-drinking dwarf, who, for reasons I'd never fathomed, drove a reconditioned hearse and claimed Hobbes had once saved him from the clutches of a witch. Whether or not his grasp of reality could be trusted, he seemed to like Hobbes, often providing valuable information and other help. There was no point in asking me to drive; the last time I'd tried I'd demolished a Volvo while creating the 'Leaning Tree of Fenderton', as the *Bugle* dubbed it. Not that it leaned anymore; last January, having decided enough was enough during a storm, it had lain down across the main Fenderton Road, holding up the rush-hour traffic for several hours while the chainsaws reduced it to bite-sized chunks. Hobbes had since offered me driving lessons, but I'd declined. It seemed wisest.

Pulling his mobile phone from his pocket, he handed it to me. 'See if he can pick us up. His number's in the menu under "D".'

'OK. "D" for dwarf.'

'No, "D" for driver,' said Hobbes and attempted a smile. 'You're under "D" too.'

'Eh?'

'No, not "A"; "D" for don't let him drive.' His attempted chuckle turned into a soggy cough. Those pensioners didn't know how lucky they were to be out of earshot.

As I phoned Billy, who was available, didn't sound as if he'd been drinking and reckoned he'd be with us in about half an hour, Hobbes slumped in the shade of a tree, groaning that he wished to be left alone.

As we waited, I chucked the ball round the field, keeping Dregs entertained, mostly thinking about the wonderful woman, kicking myself for not asking her name, though my father would, no doubt, have pointed out that she was way out of my league. I had to admit he might have been correct, but I could dream and hope, which are two things I was rather good at. After all, there was no accounting for taste and, one never knew, she might have fallen under a curse, compelling her to fancy an out-of-work, crap journalist. I might have been just her type. These things can happen … really. In fact, at the very same moment, she might have been feeling similar regret at not having asked for my name and telephone number. My hand feeling the smoothness of my chin, I was grateful for Hobbes's Christmas gift of an electric razor, something I used nearly every day. I wished I'd managed to buy him a little more than a bumper bag of walnuts, which had been all I could afford. Still, he'd appeared rather pleased and had eaten them all, though I would have preferred it if he'd removed the shells first.

The image of the woman's loveliness, having burned into my brain, I knew I'd never forget her face, her eyes, her hair, her figure, her clothes, her everything. She'd smiled at me and moved with such grace, her voice as warm and soft as a kitten's purr, and I realised with stomach-churning certainty I'd never see her again, unless, of course, I could persuade Ellen Bloom to give me her name and number, an act of bravery that would risk embarrassing myself further. Remembering the old saying that faint heart never won fair lady, time and again, in between throwing the ball for Dregs, I tried to revive my fainting heart and had probably nearly succeeded when Billy's hearse showed up.

He waved, sitting atop the pile of cushions he needed to see over the steering wheel, operating the pedals by means of long wooden extensions. It must have been illegal but no police officer had ever brought him to book, which I suspected was something to do with Hobbes's influence. Even so, Billy was an excellent and careful driver, who retained enough sense never to try when he was on a bender. On those occasions, he might sometimes be seen flailing down The Shambles on a pair of roller blades that scared him silly when sober. I had long suspected that at least part of the reason for his headaches after a night on the booze was because he'd fallen over so often, but at least he didn't have far to fall.

He chugged towards us, stopped and jumped out. Dregs bounded up to him, an old friend, greeting him exuberantly, jumping into the front seat, chewing his ball.

'Hiya,' said Billy, in his high-pitched, piping voice. 'How ya doing? You don't look so good.'

'Thanks,' said Hobbes with a grimace.

'Have you been messing with camels again?'

Hobbes nodded.

'I've told you before they're no good for you,' said Billy, with a stern frown.

'I made a mistake.'

'You're telling me? Oh well, I'd best get you home. You'll have to pick up your car tomorrow.'

Billy helped Hobbes stand, trying to support him as he struggled to the hearse, the pair making an entirely ludicrous tableau. I helped get Hobbes into the back, where he lay flat, groaning, and joined Dregs and Billy in the front, there being plenty of room for three to sit abreast. Following a brief scuffle, I had to take the middle seat, so Dregs could stick his head out. An elderly gentleman raised his sunhat respectfully as we pulled away at a speed in keeping with the vehicle's original use.

'Has he taken one of the green bottles?' asked Billy.

'Yes,' I said. 'What on earth is in that stuff?'

'Mysterious herbs from the East, so I was told. Mrs Goodfellow makes it and it's powerful stuff, though the side effects can be alarming.'

'I've seen them,' I said, nodding.

'Did he howl?'

'Yes. It didn't half give me a turn.'

'Not as much as it gave me,' said Hobbes and coughed

horribly.

'At least he's compost mental again,' said Billy.

'That's compos mentis,' said Hobbes.

'Which proves my point.' Billy chuckled.

Hobbes didn't speak for the rest of the journey, except for a snuffly complaint about a headache. I wondered about the green stuff he'd taken, alarmed that its side effects were presumably better than not drinking it. On reaching Blackdog Street, he rolled from the hearse with a brief word of thanks and went straight upstairs to bed. I checked on him from time to time but he was fast asleep, still bubbling like a cauldron on the boil.

I was, therefore, by default, back in charge of catering and, despite the lure of the pubs, I decided it wouldn't be fair to desert Hobbes. Besides, I had no money. Dregs's dinner was not a problem; opening a tin of dog food, I spooned it into his bowl and watched him wolf it down in half a dozen noisy bites, before taking himself upstairs to lie at Hobbes's door. Next came the important thing: my supper. A rummage through Mrs Goodfellow's cupboards revealed surprising quantities of tins, mostly ancient ones. I was amazed she kept so many for I'd hardly ever known her use one – except for tins of pears, which Hobbes liked with his Sunday tea. None of them appealed.

Then I had a brainwave. A jacket potato with cheese would taste great and be highly nutritious. Selecting a brick-sized spud from Mrs Goodfellow's store, scrubbing it clean, I sliced it down the middle. Next, taking a nice chunk of the wonderful, crumbly Sorenchester cheese from the pantry, grating it with a potato peeler, I heaped a generous amount onto the potato halves and shoved them under the grill. After lighting it, reckoning they'd take about half an hour to cook, I sauntered into the sitting room and turned on the telly. As I sat down, the regional news came on, making no mention of dead sheep or big cats.

However, one item caught my attention, a report on the First Annual Great Sorenchester Music Festival. I watched with increasing interest, despite the inane and annoying presence of Jeremy, a reporter who clearly imagined himself the epitome of cool. He might have been twenty or more years earlier, though I doubted it and his three-minute slot showed him to be a patronising, smug, ignorant twit. He interviewed the festival's organisers, a pair of local farmers, clearly not gentleman farmers but genuine, horny-handed sons of the soil, though I couldn't imagine how they'd managed to get so encrusted in mud when it hadn't rained for weeks.

Why the report piqued my interest so much mystified me for, although I had attended the occasional music gig over the years, I'd not really enjoyed them and the last time I'd gone out to see a band had been quite painful when a careless, or vindictive, person had dropped a full drink from the balcony and, though I'd been fortunate a safety-conscious management had replaced glasses with plastics, it had left a deep impression on the bridge of my nose and a bloody mess down my shirt.

The acrid stink of smoke in my nose, my eyes were already running with tears as I leapt up, running to the kitchen, where heavy, yellowish, greasy smoke was billowing from the grill. I was coughing like a sixty-a-day man, my potato and cheese belching fumes like a pair of miniature volcanoes, erupting into orange flame as I tugged the pan from under the heat. I tipped the whole lot into the sink, spinning the taps to full throttle, watching as, with a sad hiss, the fires dying, the potato halves collapsed in on themselves, leaving a blackened, soggy mess. Throwing open the back door and window, I flapped a tea towel to disperse the smog, dreading what Hobbes would say when he woke up, for it wasn't the first time I'd nearly set fire to his kitchen and, since the reason I was staying there was because I'd accidentally burned my old flat down, I feared he might regard me as a liability.

Though I was fortunate there were two closed doors between him and the kitchen, I was sure he'd notice the smell, unless I cleaned up as well as possible. Finding a bucket and cleaning stuff, I scrubbed every surface I could reach until I was dripping with sweat, and then spritzed air freshener all around; it turned out to be fly spray but it did mask the pong quite effectively.

Afterwards, my culinary confidence dented beyond repair, I resorted to cold baked beans à la tin, eating in the garden, resolving to pay much more attention next time Mrs G was cooking. Then, before turning in, and much to Dregs's disgust, I splashed bleach around, hoping the pungent fumes would mask any underlying odours and that Hobbes would think I'd merely decided to clean up.

As I lay in bed that night, thinking of the music festival, I hoped I'd find a way to get there, despite what had happened at the last one I'd sort of been to as a schoolboy. It had started when my mate Baz, spotting a poster for a free festival, grew really excited at the bands listed and, though they'd meant little to me, I'd allowed myself to be dragged along in the slipstream of his enthusiasm. I'd agreed to go with him, providing I could get father's permission, something I'd thought unlikely with the festival taking place during term time, albeit over a weekend. To my surprise, he'd said yes.

Just after tea on the Friday evening, Baz's mum had given us a lift to the farm hosting the event, dropping us off with our rucksacks and a tent we'd borrowed from Baz's sister. We'd been surprised – and not a little proud – to be the first arrivals. Tramping across a squelchy field that had quite obviously been home for many cows, we found what we considered a suitable spot and set to pitching the tent. The sky was already darkening when we started the argument about which one of us should have brought a torch and, by the time we'd called a truce, we could really have done with one, if only to read the instructions. Instead, opening the tent bag, tipping everything out, we used the grope, stumble and curse method, taking an hour at least to contrive something tent-like.

Then, while I held it together, Baz, picking up the rubber

mallet, attempted to knock in the pegs. Taking a massive overhead swing, he struck the first peg a mighty blow, bending it in half, as the mallet, rebounding, gave him a fat lip. Our strained friendship could have done without my heartless laughter. Still, in the end, we succeeded in pegging it down. We then spent another half-hour discussing whether we needed the flysheet; Baz, insisting that we wouldn't since it was too cold for flies, won the argument on the grounds that it was his sister's tent. We were well past the tetchy stage when, at last, we chucked our gear inside and set out for a recce.

Still no one else had arrived and we slipped and squelched through mud that would have been ideal for a First World War movie, searching with increasing desperation by the flickering light of a match for a signpost, or anything to direct us to the facilities. I'd begun to get a very bad feeling by the time we were forced to pee in a hedge.

The downpour started as we groped our way back to the tent, where we discovered what a flysheet was for, how badly we'd put up the tent and how thin were our sleeping bags. That night had been the longest, the most uncomfortable and the most miserable of my life, up to that point.

Having finally got to sleep in the dawn's grey light, we were woken by a grinning farmhand who, roaring up in a tractor, told us, through tears of laughter, that we were a month too early. By the time Baz and I managed to get a lift home, a tedious process in the days before mobile phones, we were no longer on speaking terms.

I sighed. I've never been very good at keeping friends, or making them for that matter. In fact, by then, my best friend was either Hobbes, or Dregs, something I didn't like to dwell on. Nevertheless, hope was prevailing over experience and, having recently seen a film clip on telly about Woodstock, the idea of sitting in a sunny field with a few beers amidst friendly, peace-loving fans appealed and, maybe, my lovely woman would turn up.

Waking next morning, after a sweaty night of broken sleep and hot dreams, I washed, dressed and strolled down to the kitchen. Hobbes was already up. His eyes had lost their strawberry look, though they still retained a delicate pink tinge. He was growling to himself, eating Sugar Puffs straight from a large bowl with 'DOG' written on the side. Sometimes I wondered how much of his weird stuff was done for effect.

'Morning,' he said, still snuffling.

I felt some guilt at my relief when he didn't mention the stink of smoke or fly spray or bleach. 'Good morning,' I said. 'Did you sleep well?'

'Yes, thank you and thanks for helping out yesterday. I really should take more care with camels.'

'You should.' I nodded. 'Umm ... what was in the vial? It seemed to have a terrible effect.'

'Mysterious herbs from the East: Norfolk, I think. The lass makes it, and it does me a power of good, though it tastes vile.'

'It didn't appear to do much good.'

'You haven't seen what I'm like without it. You should see what happens to my ...' He paused.

'To your what?'

'You're sure you want to know?'

'Yes ... umm ... probably.'

He shook his head. 'I think it best that you don't.'

After breakfast, he led Dregs and me to the car. I'd climbed into the back and put on my seat belt before it struck me that it shouldn't have been there.

'How did this get back?' I asked

'I expect the car fairy brought it,' he said, with a strange grin.

I think he was joking but I wasn't entirely sure. One day, I probably would meet a car fairy and many things would become clear. The thought had occurred more than once that I was stuck in a dream, for there was no way someone like Hobbes could exist and, yet, there he sat, as solid as a pile of bricks.

We left town, heading roughly in the direction of Skeleton

Bob's place, but Hobbes said he was planning to ask around some of the farms and cottages in that area and see if they'd noticed anything out of the ordinary.

'Are you still worried about the panther?' I asked.

'I'm not worried. I want to know if there is any truth in Bob's story – and I still need to find out what happened to those missing pheasants.'

The odd thing was that, though he was driving, I could talk with him, look about and enjoy the ride since he was driving safely, within the speed limit, keeping an eye on the road. In a way, I almost found it more disconcerting than his usual maniac style.

We stopped at several farms and homes in the area; no one claimed to have seen any big cats or, indeed, anything unusual at all, most regarding the suggestion with amused scepticism. I, for one, didn't feel in the least surprised.

Then, a couple of miles beyond Bob's place, we visited a small farm bordering the woods where he'd claimed his sighting. It was Loop's Farm, according to a blue enamelled sign by the entrance. Rattling over a cattle grid, we bumped along a dusty drive towards the lichen-encrusted walls of an old stone farmhouse, where two men were leaning against a gate into a field, dotted with Sorenchester Old Spot pigs. We pulled up next to them.

The younger man nodded. 'G'day.' A length of orange twine substituted for a belt round his mud-spattered moleskin trousers, his bare chest was nearly as hairy as Hobbes's and he was wearing a tatty, broad-brimmed straw hat.

'Good day,' said Hobbes as he got out.

The older man smiled. He was dressed like the first one, except for a red-checked shirt with the sleeves rolled up. He gave the impression of being even muddier, as if he'd been rolling in muck with the pigs. 'What can we do you for?' he asked.

Hobbes was introducing himself as I slithered from the car. Dregs, who had fallen asleep with his bottom half on the front passenger seat, his top half in the footwell, awoke with a resounding woof and bounded into the yard, upending me as he sprang towards the farmers. I sprawled in the dust, fearing he was going to attack, but his tail span like a propeller as he danced around them, as if meeting old friends.

'Nice doggie,' said the older man, patting him. He held out a big, grey-haired hand towards Hobbes. 'Bernie Bullimore and this is my son-in-law, Les – Les Bashem. Now, how can we help you?'

Hobbes shook hands. 'I have a few routine questions.' He hauled me to my feet. 'There have been reports of pheasant poaching in these parts and I wondered if you'd had any problems?'

'No, not really,' said Les, 'but, then, we're not a shooting estate and there's not much for 'em to take. Bob Nibblet takes the odd rabbit now and again but we don't object to that.'

'Does he have permission to be on your land?'

'Not as such but we know he does it and he knows we know and we know he knows we know, if you know what I mean. It's an informal arrangement. Old Skelly Bob don't do much harm.'

Hobbes nodded and I brushed the dust and dung from my trousers. Dregs was rolling on his back at Les's feet, like an excited puppy.

'Funny you should mention Mr Nibblet,' said Hobbes, 'because he reported seeing what might have been a big cat in Loop Woods. I don't suppose you've seen anything out of the ordinary?'

'No,' said Bernie, shaking his head so emphatically that his hat spun away like a Frisbee. I thought he glanced at his son-in-law.

'Mind you,' said Les, 'we was wondering what'd killed that sheep, 'cos we ain't seen no stray dogs around here, not this year anyhow. And it was found on Henry Bishop's land and that's right close to Loop Woods. Of course, Henry's not the sort to let dogs get at his beasts. He's always ready with his shotgun – a bit too ready if you ask me.'

'That's right.' Bernie nodded. 'He damn near blew my head off once, when I was picking nuts in the woods by his hedge.'

'Why?' asked Hobbes.

'Because I like nuts.'

Hobbes chuckled. 'No, why did he shoot at you?'

'He said he mistook me for a stray dog.'

'But dogs don't pick nuts.'

'That's what I told him.'

'How did he respond?'

'He said, "Get off my land" and popped in another couple of shells. Of course, I wasn't actually on his land, but Henry's not one to let facts get in the way of a good catchphrase. He enjoys having something to moan about.'

Hobbes looked stern. 'Did you report the incident to the police?'

'No. The way I saw it, there was no harm done, but I make sure the kids keep well away from him.'

'That's right,' said Les. 'The nippers can go where they like on the farm, except near that old bugger's place. It's best for everyone. He's not the easiest of neighbours.' He grinned. 'Mind you, he might say the same about us when we hold our festival.'

Only then did the recognition circuits in my brain connect. 'I know you!' I said, 'I saw you talking to that twerp on the telly last night before I set f …' I glanced at Hobbes. 'That is … umm … before I … umm… set the table for my tea.'

Bernie took a bow. 'That's right. Me and Les are celebrities now. You can have our autographs for a fiver.'

I smiled. 'I'll remember that when I've got one. I would like to see the festival though. Unfortunately, I'm skint.'

'Quiet, Andy,' said Hobbes. 'We're here on police business, if you remember?'

'Sorry.' I shut up.

The festival's appeal was growing, though money would be a problem. Since losing my job at the *Bugle*, I'd been unemployed, except for a disastrous two weeks as stand-in waiter at the Black Dog Café. They gave me a uniform but the trousers, being very much on the tight side, I'd had to wear them with caution and much stomach sucking. Though the memory was as painful as the trouser squeeze, by the end of the second week, I'd believed I was getting the hang of things. Then, one busy lunchtime, came a moment of explosive release, a feeling of freedom, which lasted until a lady started making a fuss about flies in her soup. Since the teeth of my zip were grinning up from her bowl and my predicament was obvious, there'd been no point in denying ownership. I hadn't regarded it as my fault but the manager, taking a different view, had sent me on my way.

I could perhaps have got another job since then, but Hobbes seemed to need my help and, despite everything, I enjoyed being out with him and Dregs. It was far more exciting than working as a not-very-good journalist or as a waiter and, thanks entirely to Hobbes's and Mrs Goodfellow's generosity, I lived better and healthier than ever before. I just wished I had some money.

Hobbes and the farmers were now discussing the forthcoming event. 'So,' he said, 'it's all happening over the last weekend in July? What's your security like?'

'It should be fine,' said Bernie. 'It's not as if we're trying to compete with Glastonbury or anything, we're just getting in a bunch of local acts and the Kung Fu club are willing to act as stewards. We were willing to pay normal rates but the lady I spoke to didn't want paying, so long as we allowed her to keep any teeth she found.'

Hobbes nodded with a grin that almost made him look human. 'Ah, yes,' he said. 'I think I know the lady.'

Of course he knew her. Mrs Goodfellow, besides looking after us and collecting teeth, taught Kung Fu and gave instruction (as a result of a printing error) in the marital arts.

'It sounds like you've got it sorted,' said Hobbes, 'but I think it would be a good idea for me to be here, in an unofficial capacity. It's not the big cat that worries me so much as Henry Bishop's short temper and shotgun.'

Bernie smiled. 'I really don't think it's necessary but we'd be happy to have you here.'

'I'll want Andy and the dog with me, if that's alright,' said Hobbes.

'Fine by us, Inspector,' Les said. 'He's a fine dog.'

'We'll bring a tent,' said Hobbes, 'mingle with the crowd and I'll keep myself inconspicuous.'

I suppressed a grin. Hobbes in a crowd was about as inconspicuous as a gorilla in the ballet. Still, he had solved my problem of how to get in, though he was not a regular fairy godmother.

'That's sorted then,' he said, rubbing his hands together. 'Will I know anyone taking part?'

'We're expecting No One You Ever Heard Of,' said Les.

'Excellent. I read about the jig they did at the Feathers.'

'The *gig* they did,' I corrected. He knew of course; it was all an act, almost certainly. And it had, reportedly, been some gig: never before in Sorenchester had a band generated so much raw emotion, never before had so many instruments been smashed in such a short time. The band really should have asked 'Featherlight' Binks, the landlord, before starting to play. If they had, he wouldn't have said no; he'd have said a whole lot more, though the meaning would have been much the same, but asking would have saved a great deal of suffering. Featherlight had only got away with it because the magistrates refused to believe the band's injuries had been caused in a brawl and assumed they must all have been in a car crash or two. Presumably, since the band had been booked, they'd been discharged from hospital.

Les continued. 'There's gonna be all sorts of bands and singers for every taste. So far we've booked Tiny Tim Jones, Mad Donna, the Delius Myth, Lou Pole and the Lawyers and Stink – you might remember him – he used to be in the police.'

Hobbes nodded. 'Yes, I know him. He wasn't, in fact, a police officer. He worked in the canteen for a while, but never quite mastered basic hygiene.'

'There are more bands and singers that haven't yet confirmed and we're also going to have fire-eaters and jugglers and magicians and lots of things.'

'I can see you've got it all running smoothly,' said Hobbes, touching his forehead in salute. 'Well, you must be busy so we'll leave you to get on with it. If you do see any big cats, you know where to find me. Goodbye.' He turned away. 'C'mon you two.'

Dregs was reluctant to leave but I managed to coax him into the car with half a biscuit I found in the glove compartment. As we pulled away, I looked back. Les and Bernie had returned to business. Leaning on gates must have been a vital part of farming.

Our next stop was at Henry Bishop's overgrown smallholding, outside the house, a house that looked as if it was still in the process of falling on hard times. So did Henry Bishop who burst from his tumbledown barn, an open shotgun over the crook of his arm, his unshaven face as red and as dirty as the handkerchief round his short, thick neck. His nose might have been mistaken for a giant blackberry.

Dregs, I noticed, was staying close to Hobbes. I couldn't blame him. I was keeping pretty close myself.

'Get off my land!' Henry shouted. 'I'll have the law on you!'

'I am the law, sir,' said Hobbes with what passed for a pleasant smile as he showed his ID. 'I'd just like to ask you a couple of questions. I take it that you are Mr Henry Bishop?'

Henry glowered. 'That I am. Now, get on with it. I haven't got all day.'

'Firstly, do you have a valid certificate for that shotgun?'

'What? Of course I do.'

'May I see it, sir?'

'I'm not sure where it is. Somewhere inside, I expect. It may take some time.'

'We're not in a hurry,' said Hobbes, his smile broadening. 'I can help you find it.'

Henry scratched his bald head, frowning in thought for a moment. 'I'll get it myself,' he said, spitting, slouching away, and closing the front door behind him.

'I don't think he's pleased to see us,' Hobbes remarked as we waited in the shade of a worm-eaten, old apple tree.

Henry's furious shouting penetrated the door, though I couldn't make out any words. He reappeared, thrusting a plastic wallet into Hobbes's great paw.

Hobbes, opening it, nodded. 'Thank you, sir. That appears to be all in order, except for the date. This expired two years ago. You shouldn't try to amend it with a biro, it doesn't work.'

'Well, I forgot,' said Henry, spitting again. 'It happens. I'll renew it tomorrow. I never use it anyway.'

'Very good, sir,' said Hobbes, 'but I'd better take the shotgun for the time being. I'm sure you don't mind and it will stop you from inadvertently breaking the law any further.'

'Very well.' He handed it to Hobbes.

'And I'd better take the others.'

'What others?'

'The ones in your cabinet. I really ought to check that, too. Do you mind if I take a look inside?'

'Yes,' growled Henry, his ruddy complexion darkening like an impending storm, 'I bloody well do mind.'

'I'm sorry to hear that, sir,' said Hobbes, shrugging, pushing open the front door, stepping into the house.

With another spit and a curse, Henry followed.

Dregs and I looked at each other, agreeing to keep out. Henry Bishop was a nasty piece of work and both of us were happy to keep our acquaintance with him to the minimum. Mopping the sweat from my forehead with a handkerchief, I lounged against the tree, contemplating lunchtime, thinking of the pleasant little pubs that weren't far away, hoping Hobbes would decide to stop at one or other, relishing the prospect of a nice, cold lager and a bite to eat.

The sudden commotion inside the house made Dregs bark and retreat and made me quake. The front door jerked open. Henry ran through with a terrified howl. He hadn't gone more than a couple of steps when Hobbes burst out, catching him within a couple of loping strides, seizing his collar and swinging him off his feet. Henry's legs kept moving, his eyes bulging like a rabbit's, as Hobbes twisted him round and dropped him. He fell to his knees but Hobbes lifted him by the lapels on his jacket, shaking him like a duster.

'I'm not going to do anything to you now,' said Hobbes, speaking slowly and at terrifying volume, his face showing a rage I'd never seen before, 'but if it comes to my attention that you ever do anything like that again, I will dismember you. Is that clear?'

The front of Henry's trousers darkened and he moaned as a wet patch spread down his leg. I felt some sympathy for him, no matter what he'd done, because Hobbes was at his terrifying best and, even as an innocent bystander, the collateral fear almost overwhelmed me, making my legs shake. God alone knew what Henry was feeling.

'Is that clear, sir?'

A squeak emerged from Henry's bloodless lips. His flour-white face looked as if he'd suffered an extreme vampire attack. 'Yes. Yes. It's clear. I won't do it again, I swear I won't.'

Hobbes, increasing the ferocity of his glare to force twelve, released the hapless man, who, dropping to the ground, lay in a quivering foetal position, sucking his thumb like a baby.

'You'd better not sir, because I mean what I say.'

I, for one, didn't doubt it. Hobbes, turning his back on the human detritus, returned to the house, remaining inside for a few minutes. I could hear his voice rising and falling gently. He reappeared, carrying three shotguns.

'If you obtain a valid certificate and behave yourself,' he said, looking down, 'I may let you have them back. Right, my next question is, have you seen any big cats around here?'

Henry, still lying in the dirt, shook his head and whimpered.

'Thank you, sir,' said Hobbes, walking back to the car, dropping the guns into the boot. As Dregs and I crept in, he started the engine and moved off. Looking back, I glimpsed a woman at the upstairs window. She was pale, thin and grey-haired, her most outstanding feature being the grotesque swelling of her right eye. Understanding, I shared Hobbes's anger. We drove away in silence, broken only by the sound of Dregs licking himself.

Despite the angry feelings, I was extremely pleased when Hobbes pulled up outside The Crown at Dumpster. He ushered us into the cool gloom of the bar where horse brasses gleamed and the smell of cooking made my mouth water. 'A double lashing of ginger beer for me, a pint of mild in a bowl for the dog and a pint of lager in a glass for the lad.'

The rosy-cheeked barmaid poured out our drinks.

'And I'll order three steak and kidney pies with all the trimmings and one for the dog too. Do you want anything, Andy?'

I sipped my lager. 'I'll have the same.'

'Same as me or same as Dregs?'

'Same as Dregs.'

He smiled. 'That'll be five steak and kidney pies then please, miss.'

4

Both outside and in, The Crown gave the impression of unchanging permanence. Hobbes and I took opposite seats on a pair of creaking, old settles in the corner, while Dregs stood on the timeworn flagstones, lapping at his bowl of mild. Though Hobbes smiled, commenting on the horse brasses around the bar, the bunches of hops hanging from the beams, there was something tense in his hunched posture as if he was not quite at ease. That, combined with his strange feral odour, always there, but seeming suddenly stronger, made me nervous and I was relieved that, when the barmaid served our meals, he thanked her with his normal gentle, old-fashioned courtesy. For the next few minutes as he shovelled down his three substantial, steaming pies, I ate mine with quiet appreciation. Though it wasn't up to Mrs G's standards, it was good – and hunger adds relish to any meal. Dregs, wolfing down his lunch and licking his bowl dry, took himself out through the open front door. A few moments later, there was a furious, imaginative and prolonged outbreak of swearing from some man in the garden.

Hobbes, a semi-circle of empty plates in front of him, ignored the commotion, mopping up any remaining gravy with his fingers and sucking them clean. He drained his glass in one long, slow movement, putting it down carefully on a beermat. The rank, feral taint in the air grew stronger.

'That sort of thing makes me angry,' he said, his voice rumbling. 'In fact, it makes me very angry.' He thumped the table and a plate, bouncing off it, hitting the stone floor, exploded into jagged splinters. He grimaced, glancing apologetically at the barmaid. 'Sorry, miss, it was an accident. I'll pay for it.'

She stared at him, as if at a diabolical manifestation.

'What does?' I asked, in case it was something I'd done, fearing he was going to blow his top because I'd nearly set fire to his kitchen again, coming over all sweaty and breathless. It brought back a memory of how I'd felt as a ten-year old when I'd been summoned to the headmaster's office to explain why I'd broken the windows in the gym. Although, I'd had absolutely nothing to do with it, someone had reported seeing me in the vicinity and, despite all my denials, I was forced to take the blame, all my pocket money for the next few months going to pay for the repairs. It still rankled.

'Bullying,' said Hobbes.

I was able to breathe again. I'd never done anything like that. 'Do you mean what Henry Bishop did?'

'I do. He hit Mrs Bishop in the face just because she had to stop and think where he might have put the key to the gun cabinet. It was such a casual thing, even with me standing there, and her eye was already bruised. If he's like that when the police are with him, what's he like when they're on their own?'

'Worse?'

'Damn right!'

He'd never before sworn in my presence and, though it was mild by most standards, the shock hit so hard I struggled to breathe, having to force myself to speak.

'You won't really dismember him if he hits her again, though?'

'Won't I?' His scowl was as deep as the ocean.

'You scared him pretty well. He'll behave himself, won't he?'

'Oh yes, he will for a while, a few days, maybe for a week or two, but bullies like him don't change. Still, having their arms and legs torn off usually slows them down.'

His laugh was deep, long and wicked. The barmaid, dropping a tray of glasses, scurried, wide-eyed towards the kitchen; a man walking in, an empty glass in his hand, turned, heading straight back out.

'Right,' said Hobbes, his hands twitching and clutching, as if they were already squeezing Henry's throat, 'I think a visit to the butcher's is in order. And quickly.'

I nodded. 'Are you alright to drive?'

'Never better.'

Indeed, having stopped snuffling, his eyes, no longer retaining the pink tinge, having instead turned a furious, burning red, he appeared fully recovered from his allergic attack. Despite being reasonably confident that he wouldn't harm me, I felt like a kid in the tiger's den. Standing up, dropping a handful of money onto the bar, he dragged me from the settle, to which I'd become quite attached, and dumped me in the back of the car. Dregs jumped into the front, his panting almost as loud as the engine.

I closed my eyes, clinging to the seat as we accelerated away from the pub onto the road, realising just how wrong I'd been to suggest his careful driving of the morning might have been more alarming than his usual style. I knew we were going fast, overtaking in places where no one in their right mind should overtake but, when the car seemed to jump, landing heavily, my head banged the ceiling and my eyes opened involuntarily, I saw he was taking a short cut through what I guessed was Barnley Copse. Trees and shrubs whizzed past only millimetres away, as we plunged into hollows, leaped over mounds, swerved past fallen logs. But we didn't hit anything, not even Bob Nibblet, who was staring open-mouthed, a sack over his shoulder, as we skirted the hulk of a vast, rotting trunk.

After a few minutes, a stomach-churning bounce and the wail of car horns, we left the bumps and ruts behind, meaning my teeth were only chattering with terror. When he stamped on the brake, stopping the car, I cannoned into the seat in front, sprawling back, stunned, into the footwell, wishing I'd got round to doing up my seat belt. As Hobbes got out, slamming the door behind him, Dregs stuck his head between the seats to snicker at my predicament. By the time I'd extricated myself and had struggled back into a sitting position, Hobbes was striding back, a bulky parcel wrapped in white paper and string balanced on his shoulder. Slinging it down beside me, he started the engine, and the nightmare journey continued. Fortunately, it didn't take long to get home and as I clambered from the car I reflected, not without a degree of horror, that I did regard 13 Blackdog Street as home.

Hobbes was already bounding up the steps to the door, the parcel tucked under his arm, Dregs very attentive at his heels. At the top, he turned, tossing me the car keys. I caught them – on the bridge of my nose, which didn't half smart. After wiping away the tears, I retrieved the keys from the gutter, locked the car and prepared myself for the sitting room. I knew what was happening and intended keeping out of the way.

As I entered, Hobbes having already spread newspapers in the corner of the sitting room, lobbed his parcel onto the paper, springing after it, like a lion onto a wildebeest. The bag disintegrated, spilling a dozen or so cow tails, as, shutting the front door behind me, edging past, I fled towards the kitchen, cringing at the sound of his great jaws crunching hide and bone. Dregs prowled round the edge of the paper like a jackal hoping for scraps. When he'd first joined us, he'd refused raw meat in favour of gourmet meals, but acquaintance with Hobbes had broadened his horizons.

Hobbes's face was already slathered with blood and hide and bits of bone, the hairy end of a cow's tail protruding from his mouth, as I made it to sanctuary. I shut myself in the kitchen until it was all over. Though I'd seen him the same way several times and no longer experienced the same paralysis of horror as on the first occasion, I did my best to keep out of his way whenever he was enjoying one of his 'little turns', as Mrs Goodfellow described them. She reckoned it was just his way of ridding himself of built-up anger and frustration and it seemed to work, for he was always most affable after a good session of bone crunching. Frankly, the whole procedure turned my stomach and

I couldn't rid myself of the fear that, one day, having run out of bones, he'd start on me.

I shuddered, turning my attention to tea: hot, sweet tea being unbeatable in times of stress. Sitting down at the table, clutching my mug, I pondered where Hobbes put it all, for he'd polished off three large steak and kidney pies and within half an hour he was stuffing his face with cow tails. Yet he wasn't fat, though there was a hell of a lot of him. I put it down to his unhuman metabolism.

He was still a mystery. I'd only known him a few days when I came to the unlikely, if undeniable, conclusion that he wasn't actually human, yet I'd never quite worked out what he might be. Sometimes, on waking in the night from disturbed dreams, I'd felt close to a great revelation but it always slipped away before I could grasp it. One thing was certain, I'd never met anyone like him, even in Sorenchester, a town with more than its fair share of individuals who were different, though none of them seemed different in the same way that Hobbes was different. During my time with him I'd nearly been buried alive by ghouls, had tea and crumpets with a troll and been told about a witch, but what other types of being might be lurking on the edge of perception, I couldn't guess. Sometimes I feared the vague, hazy images that haunted my nightmares might not be far from the truth.

I'd just finished my second mug of tea when I heard Hobbes's footsteps walking upstairs and, a couple of minutes later, the new shower starting. He was very proud of the shower, having installed it himself, like most of the plumbing in the house. Never before had I seen anyone crimp copper pipes with his fingers, but it appeared to work, for nothing dripped. Having only used the shower once, coming within an inch of drowning as alternate blasts of icy and boiling water flattened me, I now stuck to the bath, in a manner of speaking. Though he would roar as the hot and cold torrents found their mark, he always emerged from the bathroom with a happy grin.

It wasn't long before he strolled into the kitchen, clean and glowing, dressed for work, as if nothing unusual had happened. 'I ought to go into the station for a couple of hours,' he said, helping himself to tea, 'I have some paperwork to catch up with, worse luck. Do you want to come?'

I shook my head.

'OK – I'll get a takeaway on the way back. What d'you fancy?'

'Fish and chips, probably.' After the cow tails, I didn't fancy burgers.

'Right. Oh, would you mind clearing up?' Pointing to the sitting room, he quaffed his tea. 'Cheerio.'

He strode away, Dregs walking obediently to heel, behaving well as he always behaved for Hobbes and Mrs Goodfellow, while doing what he liked with me. Not that I really minded, for we were on friendly terms, quite accustomed to each other's roles, and I'd come to enjoy taking him for walks, his zest for living being infectious. Walking with him in the park or out in the countryside offered a rare kind of freedom, allowing me time to think and reflect on life, though, for the most part, my brain ticked over in pleasant idleness. Apart from that, his exuberant behaviour meant other dog walkers, even women, sometimes talked to me. It was as if I'd joined a club, with the advantage of not having to pay for the privilege.

Taking a bin liner from a cupboard, I went to clean up the sitting room, which didn't look too bad, considering; apart from the torn and bloodied newspapers and the occasional cow hair, little evidence remained of what had gone on in there. As I stuffed the papers into the bag I shuddered, with a sudden fear that Henry Bishop could go the way of the cow tails, should he dare to transgress Hobbes's law again. I don't know what put that in my mind, for Hobbes had not, to my knowledge, killed anyone, apart from those in the First World War, who didn't really count.

Yet, there'd been this guy called Arthur Crud, who, a few months ago, having got off a rape charge on a technicality and having celebrated his lucky acquittal with a few beers in the Feathers, had never made it back home. My suspicions had been raised earlier that same evening when Hobbes had phoned to tell Mrs Goodfellow he wouldn't be home for supper. As the only other time I'd know him miss his evening meal was when he'd been trapped in a hole, I'd wondered what was up. Since then, no one had found any sign of Arthur, though I doubted anyone had bothered looking and, though I supposed he might have just left town or been abducted by aliens, I couldn't quite rid myself of the absurd notion that Hobbes had, not to put too fine a point on it, eaten him.

After tidying up and disposing of the bag, I switched on the telly, sprawling on the sofa, relaxing. Nothing grabbed me, so I watched some awful chat show until my head drooped. I must have fallen asleep, for I dreamt of bone-crunching, hairy terrors creeping up on me, while I groped with increasing urgency for the fly spray that would defeat them. Finally, my fingers chancing upon the can, I jerked up with a roar of defiance and, still half asleep, rolled off the sofa.

Hearing a slight movement, I looked up, straight into a jawful of huge brown teeth, only a few inches from my face. I gasped, recoiling, trying to squirt the fly spray, finding it wasn't fly spray at all but the telly's remote control. The jaw pulled back; it was attached to a skull, appearing to float in mid-air.

'Hello, dear,' said Mrs Goodfellow, 'did I wake you?' Her smiling, wrinkled face came into focus next to the monstrosity. 'Look what those nice dentists let me have.'

Holding the skull aloft like it was the World Cup, she leaned over me, exuding the peculiar, sweet scent of dental surgery, a smell I hated, for not only did it unlock memories of pain but it reminded me of my father's surgery, a place I'd spent many a miserable day while he tried to interest me in his profession.

'Hello,' I said, climbing back onto the sofa, fighting to control my breathing and racing heart. 'You're back early. I thought you were finishing tomorrow?'

'Yes, dear, that was the plan but the hall was overrun with flies, so we called it a day.'

'Flies?'

'Yes, dear, there were horrible, buzzing bluebottles everywhere.'

'Umm … Where'd they come from?' I asked, awake but still confused.

'From the air conditioning. There was a dead cat in it.'

'Oh, well. It's good to have you back.' I meant it, for apart from her unnerving habit of appearing from nowhere, scaring the shivers out of me, she treated me with enormous toleration and kindness and cooked like a goddess.

'Thank you, dear.'

'That's a very fine skull,' I said, trying not to make it too obvious that I was humouring her. 'Whose is it?'

'It's mine.'

'But … umm … where did you get it from?'

'The dentists said I could have it. They were using it in a seminar to demonstrate the effects of a rare dental condition. Just look at these.' She pointed to the malformed canines. 'Don't they look like Dregs's?'

'Yes, very nice,' I said, 'but didn't they want to keep it?'

'No. Just after I told them my opinion, the chairman asked if someone would have the goodness to get rid of the old relic. So, I did.'

'I see.' I smiled.

'Where's the old fellow?' She polished the dome of the skull with a delicate, lacy handkerchief.

'At the station, doing some paperwork. He's just eaten a bag of cow tails.'

'I expect he needed them. Shall I make you a nice cup of tea?'

'No thanks. I'm going out for a walk. Umm … By the way, he said he'd bring fish and chips back tonight, so there's no need to cook.' I spoke with some regret, for fish and chips, though delicious in their way, just didn't compare to a Mrs Goodfellow special, or even to a Mrs Goodfellow ordinary, if such a thing existed.

I needed to get out; the skull had unsettled me. Something didn't look right about it; it wasn't just the horrible, discoloured canines, though they were bad enough, but the shape was all wrong. It looked nearly human, in some way reminding me of Hobbes and yet it was almost completely unlike him. I wondered if it might have belonged to another 'unhuman' being, though, I guessed it was more likely to have come from an unfortunate human with a nasty dental condition.

Leaving the house, I walked towards the centre of Sorenchester, trying not to think about the skull, happy for it to remain a mystery, insoluble and forgotten, except by Mrs G and possibly the dentists. One more mystery wouldn't make much difference to me.

The sun was dazzling as I left the shade of Blackdog Street for the broad stretch of road known as The Shambles, where it occurred to me that I had no idea why it was called The Shambles; there was nothing shambolic about the neat rows of Cotswold-stone shops or the hulking tower of the parish church. Turning down Vermin Street, I headed for the bookshop, hoping to find a local history book – not that I could buy it, of course, but a little browsing wouldn't hurt.

Going into the smart, modern, airy interior, it only took a couple of minutes to find *A Concise History of Sorenchester* by local historian, Spiridion Konstantinopoulos. According to this, Shambles was an ancient term for the meat market or slaughterhouse which had occupied an area in the centre of town until the early nineteenth century. I nodded, appreciating Spiridion's scholarship, flicking through a few more pages until chancing on a selection of black and white photos. In one, dated 1902, I spotted Hobbes, lurking behind a luxuriant moustache. He was in uniform, standing as stiff as a fence post, his hand resting on the shoulder of a wide-eyed, grubby-faced schoolboy in a too-small blazer and a too-big cap. In the background, a building, the 'derelict Firkin public house,' said the caption, lay in ruins. The boy, Frederick Godley, had been playing inside when it had started to collapse and only the timely arrival of Constable Hobbes had saved him from being crushed.

'Do you intend to buy that book?' asked a severe man, in a rainbow bow tie and a brown woollen cardigan.

'Umm … no. I was just browsing.'

'Well, this is a bookshop, not a public library. Either buy it or get out.'

'I'm sorry. I was only looking.'

Grabbing the book, he thrust it back onto the shelf. The cover, catching against another book, creased.

'Vandal!' cried the man, pulling the book back out, shaking it in front of me, its cover flapping like a broken wing. 'Look at the damage you've caused. You'll have to pay for it.'

'But …'

'It'll cost you fourteen pounds and ninety-five pence.'

'But I didn't do it and, anyway … umm … I haven't any money.'

The small group of bibliophiles who had gathered to watch the fun stared at me with deep loathing.

'I didn't do anything,' I insisted.

'Just look at it,' cried the man, holding up the book like exhibit A.

There was a collective intake of breath and much shaking of heads among the jury.

'It wasn't my fault.'

'I'm going to call the police.'

The man's hand gripped my shoulder and the jury murmured with intent. As far as they were concerned, I'd been caught red-handed, though I could feel my face was even redder. The injustice was horrible.

I evaluated my options: I could run for it, though a couple of blokes in the crowd looked big and fit, like rugby players, I could feign a sudden, severe illness, or I could await my fate with equanimity and contempt for the mob. In the end, I dithered and gibbered, letting myself get hauled towards a side office.

A deep, authoritative voice rang out from the back of the crowd. 'Release that man at once.'

'I will do no such thing,' said the man in the brown cardigan.

'You are laying yourself open to a charge of assault and false imprisonment if you choose to continue this ridiculous charade.'

Twisting free, I turned to face the voice.

'He damaged this book and refuses to pay for it,' said the man in the cardigan.

'No, he didn't. I chanced to see what really happened,' said a tall man, with sleek, dark hair and striking, green eyes, parting the mob. 'You took the book from this unfortunate man's hand and damaged it yourself before putting the blame on him.'

I nodded. The man in the cardigan, his face as red as I imagined mine was, backed away. 'That's a lie. He did it.'

'No doubt you have security tapes,' said the tall man. 'Can we perhaps examine them and see who's telling the truth?'

'Oh. Well, perhaps I was mistaken. Perhaps it would be best to say no more about it then,' said the man in the cardigan, retreating behind his counter, breathing hard, his face now white.

The crowd dispersed, disappointed.

'Thank you,' I said to my rescuer.

'Don't mention it,' he replied, turning away, walking towards the exit.

Although I knew with absolute certainty I'd never seen him before, for some reason he seemed extraordinarily familiar. I watched him leave the shop, impressed by his easy walk, the cut of his black suit, how he looked so cool despite the heat and, most of all, by his confident manner. I envied his elegance, something to which I could never aspire, for even if the cream of Savile Row tailors had poured their expertise into a suit for me, I'd still have looked like a sack of potatoes with a belt round the middle. Then, since the man in the cardigan was giving me the evil eye again, I walked out before he could rally and launch a fresh, unprovoked attack.

My feet, with little input from my brain, carried me to the recreation ground just off Moorend Road, where, sitting on a bench in the shade of a conker tree, I watched two guys knocking a ball around on the tennis court. I paid them little attention, since my mind was circling in a galaxy far, far away, trying to work out why my benefactor in the shop had seemed familiar. I returned to earth with a bang as a tennis ball struck me on the nose, exactly where the car keys had hit earlier. Putting my hands to my face, I felt no surprise at the smear of blood as I pulled them away.

A harsh voice bellowed from the tennis court. 'Oi, Caplet, you dozy git! Wake up and chuck the ball back.'

There was no hint of apology and though my eyes watered so I could only see blurs, I knew it was Len 'Featherlight' Binks, the gross landlord of the Feathers public house. I would never have suspected him capable of playing tennis, or of engaging in any physical exertion, other than raising a glass or brawling with his customers; Mrs Goodfellow had picked much of her tooth collection from the floor of his establishment. Pulling a handkerchief from my pocket, I clamped it to my nose.

'Come on Caplet, shift your lazy arse.'

My vision clearing, I found the sight of Featherlight in pink, flowery shorts almost as disconcerting as the blood pumping from my nose. I picked up the ball, throwing it back, staring in horror. His shorts, obviously designed for a person of considerably inferior girth, had perhaps fitted him a quarter of a century ago, when such garments had briefly and inexplicably achieved fashionable status. In addition, he was wearing a pair of mildewed plimsolls and his habitual stained vest, through which gingery chest hairs protruded. His opponent, by comparison, was a young, athletic man, clad in the sort of gleaming whites that detergent manufacturers often promise but rarely deliver.

If ever there was a mismatch, this was it. Featherlight, his belly swinging low, twirling a warped wooden racket between sausage fingers, was puffing and wheezing, looking done in even before they'd completed the knock up. At last they started. He served, tossing the ball high into the air, raising his racket, swinging like a professional, giving his opponent no chance; the match was over before the ball even hit the ground. He'd won by a knockout. Raising his massive, mottled arms to the sky in triumph, picking up the ball, he lumbered to the other end of the court to retrieve his racket. It was lying beside his fallen opponent. Squatting, he removed a ten pound note from the man's top pocket, grunted and strode away, without looking back.

As I hurried to the victim to see if I could be of assistance, he sat up, spitting blood and groaning. We made a fine pair.

'Umm … Are you alright?' I asked.

'Do I look alright?'

'Sorry.'

He held out his hand and I shook it.

'Actually,' he said, 'I was hoping for a hand up.'

I helped him to his feet. 'Why were you playing Featherlight?'

'For a bet.'

'You should never bet against him,' I said. 'You can't win. One way or another, even if he loses, he comes out on top. I once got lucky and beat him at darts and won a fiver. When he actually paid up, I felt pretty pleased but, when I was taking my darts from the board, he threw one of his, and pinned my hand to it. Then he charged me ten pounds for cleaning off the blood.'

The man snorted and packed his kit away into a smart leather bag bearing a crown symbol and a King Enterprises logo. 'Binks might have won the bet but he won't win in the end. Mr King wants to take over his pub and Mr King always gets his way.' With a curt nod, he walked away, holding a tissue to his mouth.

He left me with a puzzle. Why would anyone wish to buy the Feathers? It had a reputation as far and away the nastiest, most dangerous pub in Sorenchester, though it retained a loyal clientele. In addition, Featherlight, to the despair of the council, had become a sort of unofficial tourist attraction, with people visiting the Feathers because they couldn't believe the rumours. Few left disappointed, for Featherlight really was the vilest slob of a landlord you could hope never to meet. He kept his beer badly, refused to serve wine or soft drinks and his spirits were 'interesting', and I knew of one customer who, having asked for a glass of his best malt, had been given malt vinegar. The fun really began if anyone complained; few dared and fewer dared a second time. The really intrepid even ate there. No one had died yet.

By then my nose had stopped bleeding, so I decided to head home and clean up. Though the sun had dipped well into the west, the afternoon's heat continued to build. If I'd had any lager money I would have visited the Feathers to find out about the take-over. However, I was broke and it wasn't wise to ask for credit. There was a hand-written sign over the bar with the legend, 'If you ask for credit, you'll get a punch in the mouth'. It wasn't a joke.

When I got home, it seemed very still, so I assumed Mrs Goodfellow had gone out and that Hobbes and Dregs weren't back. I went upstairs, washed my face, came back down and poured myself a glass of Mrs G's ginger beer, which she made in the cellar but stored in the fridge. I made a point of avoiding the cellar, because the old girl had a tendency to lock me in. According to Hobbes, this was a result of a childhood trauma and I wasn't to take it seriously. It was, he claimed, just a sign of affection but it didn't stop him moaning whenever she did it to him. Besides, there was another reason for avoiding the cellar: it contained a hidden door that Hobbes had warned me against opening. He gave good warnings and my stomach still quaked when I remembered it. I reasoned that, if I kept away, I wouldn't be tempted to explore, but sometimes, waking at night, I lay and wondered about its secrets.

The ginger beer, tingling on my tongue, cooled my throat. Emptying the glass, I refilled it and sat at the kitchen table with the *Sorenchester and District Bugle*, amazed to see the image of the man who'd helped me in the bookshop smiling from the front page. It was millionaire Felix King, head of King Enterprises, who, according to the report, was looking to develop properties in the area. He had already acquired the old cinema, intending to demolish it to make way for luxury flats and claimed the scheme would provide plenty of jobs for locals and that no one would miss the cinema since everyone preferred to watch DVDs at home. In truth, the article interested me less than Felix King himself. He was a remarkably good-looking man in his late thirties, I guessed, impeccably dressed, slim and masterful. I stared at his picture, perplexed. Something about his face was definitely familiar but what was it? Resting my chin on my hand, I dug through layers of memory.

'Did you have a nice walk, dear?'

An involuntary leg spasm launching me upwards, my knees struck the bottom of the kitchen table, knocking it at least six inches into the air before coming down hard, as if retaliating. Missing my chair on re-entry, I sprawled on the red-brick floor, gasping like a fish. Ginger beer dripped onto my stomach.

'Did I surprise you, dear?'

I nodded, puzzled, unable to see her.

'Sorry.'

I sat up. 'Where are you? I thought you'd gone out.'

'No, dear, I've been cleaning the tin cupboard.'

Smiling happily, she was kneeling on the shelf, half-hidden behind the cupboard door, a bucket and a sponge in front of her.

'From inside? Why?'

'Why not? Would you clean a room from outside?'

It was true but, then, I probably wouldn't clean a room at all, if I could help it.

'It's the best way to reach into those awkward little corners. And someone had messed up all the tins.'

I climbed to my feet.

'Anyway, dear, I'd best get the kettle on. The old fellow will be home soon.'

Clearing up my spillage, I helped her set the table. When, at half-past six precisely, Hobbes returned, bearing fish and chips, Dregs insisted on a five-minute dance of tail-wagging welcome for Mrs G, while Hobbes engulfed her in an enormous bear hug that had me worried. She emerged red-faced and beaming a vast toothless smile.

As always, when eating at home, Hobbes said grace. Then we could tuck in – and about time too – my walk and the shock having left me ravenous. The fish was fragrant and flaky, the chips crisp and hot and liberally vinegared. It was nowhere near as good as what Mrs G would have produced, but still pretty good.

Afterwards, Hobbes picked up the newspaper. 'This chap on the front,' he remarked, 'must be related to the lass who took your fancy at the Wildlife Park. They've got the same eyes. I'd guess they're brother and sister.'

He was right.

Mrs Goodfellow gave me a gummy twinkle. 'You've found yourself a lady-friend then? It's about time, too.'

I shook my head. 'No, I'm afraid not. She's lovely.' I could feel a blush coming on. 'But if that really is her brother and she's a millionaire too, she's never going to be interested in someone like me.'

Leaving the kitchen, I sat and moped in front of the telly.

5

The evening, bringing in heavy cloud, wind and rain, conspired with my feelings of hopeless inadequacy, to push me into a dark, moody place where I spent the next two days. The fact that the woman's brother was super-rich had, I knew, only reduced my chances of getting to know her from next to none to none, but it had slashed through a slim thread of hope, a thread I'd been holding onto. I brooded on my life, raking up embers of failure and misery from the ashes of cold despair, wondering how much I could blame the misfortune of my birth date for my situation. Why, I thought, had I, a man seemingly incapable of being punctual for anything, allowed myself to be born precisely on time? If I'd only held on for a few more hours, I wouldn't have been an April fool, wouldn't have been such an object of derision to my schoolmates.

That April I'd celebrated, if that was the word, my thirty-eighth birthday. By that age, a man should have achieved something: a decent job, a home, a wife, perhaps a family, whereas all I had I owed to Hobbes. Despite my enormous gratitude for his kindness, I was scared resentment might erupt from the seething magma chamber of my past failures and make me say something I shouldn't. I kept to my room, only emerging for meals, toilet breaks and long, damp walks in long, damp grass with Dregs.

On the third day, the wet weather having apparently doused the nefarious schemes of local villains, Hobbes joined us as we headed to Ride Park. When I let Dregs run free, he set off like a guided weapon, targeting a small white cat, rubbing its whiskers against a holly bush, apparently daydreaming until, spotting the incoming dog just in time, it leapt into a tree. Dregs's momentum carried him, scrabbling madly, well above head height, until gravity, realising what was up, pulled him down. The cat mewed from the topmost branches.

'I suppose,' said Hobbes, looking up, 'that I should rescue it.'

He jumped, grasping a branch, pulling himself into the tree, swinging from arm to arm like a great ape, disappearing among the greenery. I did what I could to calm Dregs who, thinking we'd started a wonderful game, was making bounding attempts to join him. From above, came rustling and the occasional creak and, now and again, Hobbes's grinning face emerging from the foliage.

'Here, kitty, kitty,' he called in a voice that would surely have driven even a fierce creature further into the canopy. There was a pause. 'Aha!' he said, as something cracked. 'Oops.'

A drum-roll of thuds and crashes coincided with a shower of leaves, twigs and drops of water. Then came Hobbes.

'Oof!' He chuckled as he lay on his back in the grass, the cat clamped in one hand, a broken branch in the other. Tossing the branch aside, he sprang to his feet. 'Make sure you've got hold of Dregs,' he said, 'and I'll let kitty go.'

'Umm,' I said, grabbing Dregs's collar, 'wouldn't it be better if ...'

Too late. Putting the struggling cat back onto the ground, he released it. It hissed, bolting straight back up as Hobbes, brushing moss from behind his ear, laughed. 'Kitty appears to like it up there.'

'Are you alright?' I asked, shaken. 'I suppose you must know how to fall?'

'I'm fine and any fool knows how to fall; the trick is in knowing how to land. It's not the first time I've fallen from a tree.' He glanced upwards. 'In fact, I fancy it's not the first time I've fallen from this one – and I dare say it won't be the last.' He coughed and spat into a patch of nettles. 'It clears the tubes out most wonderfully. You should try it, but start with a small tree, because you need to build up your resistance and make sure there's a nice, thick layer of leaf mould in the landing area.'

I nodded, taking a decision to ignore his advice. 'Are you going to get the cat down again?'

'No, she can look after herself.'

'Then why fetch it down in the first place?'

'I needed the exercise.'

The shock of his plunge did, at least, jolt me from my brooding, and, though I still felt the ache of thwarted desire, I continued living. Unfortunately, this meant I had no excuse for getting out of St. Stephen's Church Fete when Hobbes asked me, saying he'd be showing off his King-Size Scarlets. These he declared were a sort of delphinium and nothing to snigger about. As I couldn't tell the difference between lavenders and lupins, I had no reason to doubt it and, assuming they were the ones he'd been growing for the last few months, they were eye-catching plants, their vivid scarlet spikes standing up to my shoulders and adding ranks of regimented colour to the exuberant scruffiness of the back garden.

Waking early on Saturday morning, I drew back the curtains and was greeted by sunlight glinting off the damp street and the roofs opposite and, despite my impending fete, I was filled with an unexpected sense of well-being. My feelings had been very different the previous year, when, as a very badly paid reporter, I'd attended the fete, which alongside pet shows and beetle drives had been my speciality, since Editorsaurus Rex had rarely trusted me with real news. I remembered arriving and shaking hands with the new vicar of St. Stephen's, before a downpour of biblical proportions forced us into the refreshment tent.

When, somehow, I made it back to the office, my recollection of the event was hazy, possibly on account of the farmhouse cider stall I'd discovered, I had nothing to report and Editorsaurus Rex was on the rampage. However, always resourceful in a crisis, and working on the theory that all church fetes were basically the same, I wrote a few inconsequential words about rain and then cut and pasted an article my colleague, Phil, had written the previous year. If I'd read it first, I might have remembered that not all fetes were the same, for that particular one had been remarkable for the untimely and, indeed, unlikely, death of the old vicar who, having just awarded first prize in the flower show, had been struck down by a bolt from the blue. Though some had considered it a sign of the wrath of God, it turned out to have been debris from an ex-Soviet satellite. Obviously, this meant my subterfuge didn't pass unnoticed and I had to endure a most unpleasant and prolonged showdown with the Editorsaurus. Still, the event summed up my life at the time: a succession of lousy assignments, failures, drunkenness and apoplectic editors.

Such problems hadn't afflicted me since the fiasco of my last mission, which had been to report on Hobbes. Since then, life wasn't bad at all, though it might have been better, and very soon did get better, the scent of frying bacon greeting my nostrils as I hurried downstairs.

After breakfast, I helped Hobbes as he worked in the greenhouse, a structure he'd thrown together from odds and ends picked out of skips, but it wasn't long before he suggested that I might try getting under someone else's feet for a change. So, grabbing myself a glass of ginger beer, I sat on a bench, enjoying the sun, watching his pest control procedure. Refusing to use chemicals, he examined each plant from leaf to stem, removing any aphids and harmful bugs by hand, his patience amazing me. Still, it looked like he would produce a bumper crop of aubergines.

When satisfied, he left the aubergines and felled a small forest of King-Size Scarlets, sticking them into a black plastic bin, filled with water. Then, after a mug of tea, he prized me from my seat, ready to go to the fete. Grasping the bin to his chest, he set off for St. Stephen's. Mrs Goodfellow held the back door for him, while I rushed to open the front door. Though I doubted I'd be able to move such a weight, never mind carry it, I could still barely keep up with him as he marched through the centre of town, down Vermin Street, weaving through the Saturday shoppers, as if he wasn't carrying a flower shop. Sweat dripped off me but he looked just as cool as ever in his tweed jacket.

Although the sun was high and hot as we reached St. Stephen's, I couldn't suppress a shiver, for the last time I'd been there, on a dark and stormy night, a pair of ghouls had tried to bury me alive, until Hobbes intervened, dissuading them with a spade. Taking a deep breath, I followed him into the marquee, where the noise and migrations of herds of roaming exhibitors drove the horrifying memory back to its dark recess. He found a space, marked W.M. Hobbes, and set about arranging his blooms while I, finding I was superfluous, wandered off to take a look around. Apart from the bustle in the marquee, loads of other people were setting up all sorts of stalls, including one where customers could bowl for a pig. What the lucky winner would do with a pig, I hadn't a clue.

I moved on, fascinated by a small brown wigwam staggering from place to place until it found a spot to settle near the front gates. A woman, magnificent in purple and lace, emerging like a butterfly from a chrysalis, erected a cardboard sign that read, 'Madame Eccles, palms read, fortunes told, medium.' She looked more like a large, or even an extra-large to me. I looked like a customer to her.

'Can I read your palm, love? Or would you prefer to talk to loved ones who have passed over? Cross my palm with silver – or paper money would be better – and all proceeds to charity.'

'I'm sorry ... I'm ... umm ... skint.'

'Never mind, love. Step inside and I'll give you one for free.'

It was an offer I couldn't refuse.

I followed her inside. In actual fact, since she occupied most of the interior, I perched on a three-legged stool in the entrance as she, forcing her ample backside into a fold-up chair that groaned most piteously, drew a small crystal ball from deep within her robes and placed it on her lap.

'Palm reading? Divination? Or would you prefer an encounter with the spirit world?'

'Palm reading.' I said; it sounded safest. I held out my hand.

'Oh no,' she said, shaking her head, 'that's not right.'

'What's the matter?' I asked, feeling a lurch of fear, though I knew it was all bunkum.

'Wrong hand, love.'

I gave her the other one.

'Let's see. Aha! That's interesting … But that's not so good. Do you know, I've never seen such a varied fate line.'

'What's going to happen to me?'

'You will live an unusual life. I see fear and laughter, delight and horror. Love may be on the horizon but, beware, something wicked this way comes.'

Though I normally had no truck with this kind of nonsense, a sudden cold sensation up my spine made me shudder. The feeling persisting, I looked behind me. It was Dregs, his nose stuck where my shirt had rucked up, looking sheepish, as well he should have been, for Mrs Goodfellow had harnessed him to a small cart loaded with bottles of ginger beer. She'd brushed his wiry black coat till it shone and, as a final indignity, had garlanded him with ribbons. He looked at me with mournful eyes and, though I sympathised, I couldn't help; he was in the clutches of a far greater power. I was glad the old girl was there though, because she was helping out with the refreshments and I hoped I might be in for a few freebies.

'Hello, dear,' said Mrs Goodfellow, as I jumped up, tucking my shirt back in. 'Has he been pestering you, Edna?'

'Not in the least,' said Madame Eccles. 'He's a very interesting young man and is going to lead an eventful life.'

Dregs sighed as I made my excuses and left them talking.

I looked in on Hobbes who'd completed his arrangement. It

was breath-taking for, as well as his King-Size Scarlets, he'd worked in daisies, producing a flower sculpture of a sheep with its throat torn out. There was blood everywhere. 'That's amazing,' I said.

'Thanks.' He blushed.

Although he had a superb eye for detail and his great paws could work with amazing delicacy, he seemed to think that art wasn't quite manly. I wished I had a fraction of his skill, even though his creations gave me the creeps.

'Let's get some grub,' he said, before I could embarrass him any further. 'The fete opens at two, so we've got about an hour. We could try the Cat and the Fiddle. I haven't dropped in for ages and I hear they've got a decent menu.'

'Great,' I said, already feeling hunger pangs.

We left the marquee but never made it to the Cat and the Fiddle. 'Just-call-me-Dave', the vicar, approached. He was a pale and nervous man at the best of times and I could tell that times were not the best.

His voice trembled. 'Excuse me, Inspector, I wonder if I might call on your expertise?'

'Of course, vicar. What's the matter?'

'It was like this … A group of young men bumped into me in town. They apologised and I didn't think anything of it, but I'm afraid my wallet and car keys have gone. The worst thing is that I'd picked up a load of cream cakes for the cake stand and now they're locked in the boot of my car. The cream will go off in this heat and they'll all be spoiled.' He wrung his hands. 'Can you help me?'

'Of course,' said Hobbes. 'That's my job.'

'Unfortunately, my car's parked in town.'

'That's not a problem,' said Hobbes. 'I'll give you a hand. C'mon, vicar. And quickly.'

As he turned to go, he paused. 'Sorry, Andy,' he said, 'the pub's off.' Reaching into his pocket for the small, hairy and deeply disturbing pouch that served him as a wallet, he removed a twenty-pound note, thrust it into my hand and loped away with Just-call-me-Dave.

It was a heady feeling to once more have money in my pocket. I headed for the Cat and Fiddle, intending to spend it wisely on food and a pint, or possibly two, of lager. However, I hadn't gone far, the pub still out of sight, when my nostrils detected the scent of frying onions. It was like a Siren song, luring me down an alley towards the lurking burger van, a greasy little man with a stained white coat and discoloured grin watching me approach.

'What can I do for you, squire?' He stirred the onions.

The sizzling overcame any remaining resistance. 'I'll have a jumbo hotdog,' I said, 'with mustard and loads of onions.'

'Good choice, squire. That'll be three-fifty.'

Handing over the money, I gloated as I received my change, sixteen pounds and fifty pence, money to spend on refreshments. I'd noticed a keg and several crates being loaded into the beer tent and could believe it wasn't going to be a fete worse than death after all.

Carrying my hotdog back, I sat on a low wall overlooking the road in the shade outside the church. Saliva flooded my mouth as I inhaled the aroma. However, on taking a bite, the bun, aided by a sausage with the texture of cotton wool, sucked up moisture, leaving my mouth as dry as blotting paper. It became a struggle to force the stuff down my reluctant throat and I had to spit out a couple of mouthfuls of gristle. Still, the hotdog served two purposes: it filled me up pretty well and made me appreciate Mrs G's cooking even more. I'd just finished and was beginning to wish I hadn't started, when a skinny young man in shorts, t-shirt and trainers shot past, breathing hard, going like a whippet down the road. Shamed by his commitment to fitness, I wondered how he motivated himself.

A moment later, Hobbes loped into view, a couple of hundred yards behind, catching up, despite having a cursing youth tucked under each arm. They didn't look like they were enjoying themselves.

'A couple of bad lads,' said Hobbes with a grin as he passed.

I stepped down, running after him to see what was happening, until the hotdog made its presence known. I slowed to a jog and then to a brisk walk. I wasn't following to offer my assistance – he only had three to deal with – but to see how the hunt ended. I was far too slow. Within a couple of minutes, I met him coming back, lecturing his prisoners, who were walking in front, hanging their heads like naughty three-year olds. One of them appeared to be crying.

'I'm just taking these boys to apologise to the vicar,' said Hobbes. 'They picked his pockets and were trying to steal his car. They might have got away with it if the vicar had remembered to fill up with petrol. They didn't get very far.'

I followed them back as far as the church wall where, indigestion claiming me, I sat back down, stomach churning, watching them out of sight. A few minutes later, Just-call-me-Dave reappeared, driving his little red car at a sedate pace, as fast as the sweating lads could push it. Hobbes ambled behind, offering encouragement and good advice.

'Right, boys,' he said as the vicar parked by the kerb, 'I hope you've learned a good lesson today. Crime does not pay, especially when I'm around. However, it's far too nice a day to go inside and mess with paperwork, so I'm going to let you go away and reflect on what you've done. If you behave yourselves, there'll be no need for me to pay any unexpected visits, which, I ought to point out, you wouldn't enjoy at all. Now, give the vicar a hand with his cakes. Then run along, and mind how you go.'

After profuse apologies and some serious grovelling, they hurried away.

The church clock striking two, the vicar opened proceedings with a speech that must have been a contender for the most boring ever, still rambling on twenty minutes later, by which time almost everyone had left him to it. The stalls began to get busy and, by three o'clock, the fete was swinging as well as any fete swings.

A pushy old man in a striped, multi-coloured waistcoat and a straw hat persuaded me, against all reason, to bowl for the pig; my attempt was humiliating, painful and best forgotten. Afterwards, I headed to the refreshments tent, still suffering from the hotdog, needing a drink to take away a lingering taste. Mrs Goodfellow's ginger beer stall, conducting a brisk trade, I bypassed it, since I could enjoy it for free back home, and went to the bar for a lager. They only had the bottled kind, and since the bottles were small and expensive, and the day was hot and humid, I changed my mind, heading for a table where a red-faced, tubby woman was selling Brain-Damage Farmhouse Cider, kept under restraint inside a large plastic tub. Ordering a pint, I was delighted to find it considerably cheaper than the lager, with a fruity, rich, refreshing, innocuous taste. I had another and a third, by when the world was taking on a golden haze of well-being. I began to enjoy the fete, exuding a sort of paternal benevolence, a smile for everyone.

A young lady walked up to me, carrying a tray loaded with ginger beers. Her friendly smile was, I thought, a good sign, even if she failed to live up to the woman at the Wildlife Park's standard, being a little plump and disfigured by tattoos. However, I wasn't fussy: I couldn't afford to be.

'Hello,' I said, trying my best to look interesting.

'Oh, hello,' she said. 'Would you mind moving aside? You're in my way.'

'Oh ... umm ... yes, of course.'

As I stepped back, a man yelped and swore.

'Sorry,' I said, moving my foot.

The cider chose that moment to show off its strength. Co-ordination failing, I stumbled into the young lady, knocking the tray from her hands.

'Sorry.'

As I squatted to pick it up, I found my legs wouldn't work properly. Rocking backwards, slightly overcompensating, I lurched forward. Next thing I knew, I was lying across the young lady, who was face down in a sticky puddle of ginger beer.

'I really must apologise,' is what I wanted to say, but it came out slurred and incomprehensible. Anything I attempted seemed to require considerable concentration. I pushed myself upright, vaguely aware of my hands pressing on something soft.

'Take your filthy hands off my arse,' she said.

Her words were a little crude for a lady, but making allowances for the circumstances, I did as she asked, as hands grabbed my shoulders, pulling me up. Considering it a diabolical liberty, I wriggled free and, slumping forward, found I was lying across the young woman again, who made such unpleasant remarks I could no longer think of her as a lady. Somebody shoved me and I rolled off her onto my back. A big hand grabbed my shirtfront, jerking me to my feet, so I was looking into the face of a burly man, his head shaved as smooth as a hard-boiled egg.

'I'd be obliged if you'd leave my wife alone,' he said.

'Don't you tell me what to do.' I wagged my finger in his face.

'Look mate, I can see you've had too much to drink, so I'm not going to make a fuss. Just leave her alone, walk away and try to sober up.'

He had a dotted line tattooed round his neck above the words, 'cut here'. It struck me as rather amusing and I giggled.

His frown deepened. 'D'you think I'm being funny?'

It deepened even more when my wagging finger found its own way up his nostril.

'Right, that's it.' He raised his fist, 'love' tattooed across the knuckles.

The realisation that I was in for a pasting almost sobered me up. I squealed like a snared rabbit, cringing, anticipating pain as the fist drew back. The punch never came. Hobbes was holding it in his own great hand.

'Calm down, sir,' he said with a shake of his head, 'there's no need for violence. We're all friends here. Andy, get your finger

72

out. And quickly.'

'Sorry.' Freeing it, I wiped it down my trousers.

'Now,' said Hobbes, 'what's going on here then?'

The woman got to her feet. 'He knocked me over, spilt our drinks and pinned me to the ground.'

'Is that true, Andy?'

'No. Well ... umm ... yes. It's sort of true but it was all an accident. I stepped back to get out of her way like this ...'

A man yelped and swore.

'Sorry.' The cider still had me in its grasp. Stepping off his foot, I stumbled, the edge of a table coming up at me.

I came to, lying on my side on a hard bench somewhere cool and gloomy, my head throbbing, women's voices echoing as I tried to sit up. It appeared I was inside the church. I shook my head to clear the fuzziness, a bad mistake, only amplifying the pain, slumping back as waves of nausea overwhelmed me.

'How are you?' a woman asked.

'I'm going to be sick.' Sitting up abruptly, I threw up.

Someone thoughtful had placed a bucket next to the bench. I missed, distributing my hotdog and cider over the stone floor, splashing a pair of elegant ladies' shoes.

'I'm sorry,' I said, encoring with another deluge. Closing my eyes, I held my head in both hands, hoping the pain would subside. Someone had tied a rag round my forehead. It felt sticky.

'The ambulance will be here in a minute. How are you feeling?' asked Mrs Goodfellow.

'Awful,' I groaned.

'I'm not surprised. I'll go and find a mop and something to wipe your shoes.'

'What's wrong with my shoes?'

'Nothing, dear, I was talking to this young lady.'

I was intrigued, though everything seemed to be very distant and getting further away. 'Umm ... good. Who's the ambulance for?'

'For you,' said a woman with a soft, comforting purr that made me think of rich velvet.

'For me?' It sounded unlikely. All I needed was a rest and maybe a new brain.

'Yes. You banged your head.'

She sounded like the beautiful lady at the Wildlife Park. I risked opening my eyes. It was her. Again, I retched, the hot, sharp taste of vomit stinging my throat. 'I'm so sorry.'

'Mind yourself, dear,' said Mrs Goodfellow, clattering a metal bucket, wielding a dreadlocked mop. I lay back, groaning, as she swilled away my mess. What would the beautiful lady think of me now? It had been bad enough throwing myself at her feet but throwing up on her feet was such a horrible thing to do. I wondered if I was cursed. I always messed up with women.

The church doors opened and a man and woman dressed in green entered. The light hurt my eyes and blurred my vision.

'Hello, sir' said the green man. 'What's your name?'

'It's …' I said, 'it's on the tip of my tongue.'

'How are you feeling?'

'I have a headache but I think someone's had an accident.'

'How many fingers am I holding up?'

'Yes. Why not?'

'I think we'd better get him to casualty,' said the green woman.

I wondered about whom she was talking. 'Has there been an accident?'

'Yes,' said the green man, untying the rag round my head. It came away red.

'Someone's cut themselves,' I said. 'You'd better make sure they're OK.'

My recollection after that is fragmentary. They wheeled me to an ambulance and a pigeon flew overhead, while a man with a bald head said 'sorry.' I couldn't imagine why. When they loaded me into the back, the beautiful lady looked in, looking worried. It felt good until Mrs Goodfellow's voice impinged.

'I wouldn't worry about him too much, he's got a good, thick skull. Do you think they'll give him a brain scan? I wonder if they'll find anything?'

'Poor man,' said the lady.

The doors closed.

6

The rocking motion would have put me to sleep had the green man, who seemed to think he was in an ambulance, not insisted on talking to me. When, at last, everything went still, the door opened and they wheeled me into an echoing building with a white ceiling. Now and then something bumped and pain jolted through my head, making it spin, yet, on another level, everything seemed a long way away, as if I were drifting like a balloon. A Casualty sign hanging from shiny chains above my head, it dawned on me that there'd been an accident and, since my head was hurting, I wondered whether I might have been involved.

A thin lad in a white coat, a stethoscope dangling around his neck, appeared above me. 'Hello,' he said. 'Don't I know you?'

He was familiar, though last time I'd seen him he'd been less blurry and there'd been only one of him. My head throbbed, throwing up a memory. 'You're Dr Finlay and you've heard all the jokes.'

'That's correct and you're Mr Andrew Caplet. I remember meeting you after the fire. Nice to see you again. Now, I want you to lie still while I take a look at you. A nasty bang on the head, wasn't it? I'm sure you'll soon be on the mend.'

Flashing a torch into my eyes, he asked loads of questions. I answered those I could but he seemed to think I should know something about a fete, when all I wanted to talk about was a beautiful woman. Apparently, I spent the afternoon and evening under observation, though I slept through most of it when my headache allowed, for they wouldn't let me take anything for the pain. I was told I also underwent a CT scan and that I cheered when Dr Finlay said it showed absolutely nothing wrong with my brain that a couple of days of rest and quiet wouldn't cure. I asked him to let Mrs Goodfellow know.

Next morning, still delicate, though feeling much better, I lay in a white bed behind curtains, a pretty nurse with a sympathetic smile and a scent of soap, checking up on me from time to time. At some point, with a clattering and a nauseating smell of burned grease, my breakfast, charred bacon and leathery eggs, with bread that had been toasted just enough to dry out, without browning, arrived. I made an attempt at it but didn't much fancy staying for lunch. However, Dr Finlay, looking in, allayed my worries.

'Good morning,' he said. 'How are you today?'

'Not too bad, apart from a sore head and feeling a bit confused.'

'That's perfectly normal after a minor head injury, though I expect it feels like a major injury from your side. Tilt your head, please ... good. You have a magnificent goose egg on your forehead, or it would be magnificent if we hadn't put a couple of stitches in – they'll drop out in a few days.'

Nodding, I yawned. I couldn't remember being stitched, which was good because I'd always feared needles. The lump, beneath a sticking plaster, was very tender.

'You'll probably notice that you tire easily in the next week or so. Listen to your body and take plenty of rest. How's your vision?'

'It's ... umm ... fine now. It was all fuzzy yesterday, I think. Like my memory.'

'Excellent. And your speech patterns are normal. You were perseverating yesterday.'

The blood rose to my cheeks. 'Oh God, I wasn't, was I? I'm ever so sorry, I didn't know what I was doing ... Umm ... What was I doing?'

'Perseverating – you had a tendency to repeat yourself – a

classic symptom of a concussion.'

'Oh, is that all?'

'Yes. Well, Mr Caplet, in my opinion you'll be fit enough to go home in a couple of hours. Will there be anyone to look after you?'

I nodded, cheered by the prospect of getting home for Sunday lunch, wondering what the old girl was cooking, hoping there'd be plenty for me.

'Excellent. Remember, plenty of rest and quiet and don't go back to work for at least five days.'

I smiled, approving Dr Finlay's instructions, the sort I could agree to follow without hesitation or guilt. His bleeper sounding, he left me to doze.

Just after twelve o'clock, Hobbes stomped into the ward, his head appearing round the curtain. 'The hospital called to say you can come home. How are you?'

'Much better, but the doctor says I need rest and quiet.' I was hoping to influence his driving.

I needn't have worried. On leaving the hospital, I found he hadn't come in the car, instead bringing Dregs and the little cart, to which he'd fitted a three-legged stool from the kitchen. Dregs, taking it all in his stride as I sat down, set off, trotting by Hobbes's side. At first, I squirmed with embarrassment, though few people were out and about in town, but after a while, to my amazement, I began to enjoy the ride, feeling safe and comfortable, if eccentric. The town glistened with the sprinklings of an overnight downpour, the streets steaming under the sun's power.

'It's a fine cart,' I said.

Hobbes agreed. 'It is. If you'd hung around a little longer yesterday, you'd have seen him giving rides round the fete in it. The children loved him and he raised more money than any other attraction, though the lass might have matched him if she hadn't run out of ginger beer.'

'She makes good stuff,' I said. 'I wish I'd stuck to it. That cider was lethal.'

Hobbes chuckled. 'It nearly was, wasn't it? They're talking about renaming it "Dozy Headbanger" in your memory.'

I grimaced. 'How did you get on in the flower show? Did you win?'

He shook his head. 'I'm afraid not, though they awarded me a certificate for the most original use of delphiniums, which was nice of them.'

'Shame. Umm ... by the way, have there been any more big cat sightings?'

'Not as such, but a bird watcher reported a large paw-print in Loop Woods. I took Dregs up to have a look this morning but, unfortunately, some lads had been motor biking and everything was churned up. There were no signs of cats and the whole place stank of two-stroke.'

'If there really was a big cat on the loose, would they get someone to shoot it?'

'Not if I had my way,' said Hobbes.

'What would you do?'

'Catch it.'

'How?'

'With stealth, cunning and a big sack.'

'Then what?'

'Find it somewhere to live where it can't be hurt by anyone and where it can't hurt the public.'

His answer came as some relief, for I'd got it into my head that, if he found one, and caught it, he'd bring it home. Having a panther in the house would not be good for my state of mind, especially when I needed to rest.

All went well until, reaching Blackdog Street, Hobbes, pulling the keys from his pocket, strode up the steps to the front door. Dregs, forgetting what he was doing, bounded after him. The cart's wheels bounced and skipped and, though I grasped the stool with desperate hands, I tipped out backwards with a yelp, bracing myself for a heavy fall. I never hit the floor. Hobbes, diving full length down the steps, caught me.

'Sorry,' he said, standing up, setting me down. 'That wasn't much of a start to your course of peace and rest. Are you alright?'

'I'm alright, but what about you?'

The knees of his baggy, old trousers were torn and his elbows, poking through the sleeves of his tweed jacket, were dripping blood.

'I'm fine,' he said. 'The odd scrape won't do me any harm. Mind you, I'll need to get these clothes fixed.'

Springing back up the steps, he opened the door and let us in. A delicious scent of roasting meat welcomed us.

'It's good to be home,' I said, with some difficulty for my mouth was flooding.

'Good,' said Hobbes, 'and now you need to take yourself up to bed.'

'But I'm alright … and hungry.'

'Doctor's orders. Up you go. And quickly.'

Arguing with Hobbes never worked, so I went up to my room, undressed, climbed into bed and hoped the old girl wouldn't forget me. The next thing I knew, I'd woken up. From the light outside, the emptiness of my stomach, I guessed it was late afternoon. As I stretched and sat up, still a little weak, I became aware of soft breathing. A little man was sitting cross-legged on a stool in the window, sewing. He had a big head and a long, thin nose, supporting a pair of half-moon glasses. Looking up, he grinned and nodded.

'Good afternoon,' he said, the guttural tone of his voice suggesting he was foreign. 'I am not, I hope, disturbing you?'

'No.'

'That is good.'

As he returned to his sewing, I closed my eyes, convinced I was dreaming, but when I looked again he was still there.

'Who are you?'

'I am the tailor, sir.'

'What are you doing in my room?'

'Stitching a rent in your trousers,' he said, holding them up with long, spindly fingers. 'You tore them, so I am told, at the fete.'

'Did I? Thank you.'

'Don't mention it.'

I must have dropped off again because the light was fading when my eyes opened. As I stretched and sat up, I became aware of soft breathing.

'Hello, dear,' said Mrs Goodfellow, folding my chinos, hanging them in the wardrobe. 'Did you sleep well? Would you like something to eat?'

'Yes to both questions. What time is it?'

'Half-past nine. Would you like a cold beef sandwich?'

'I'd love one ... Actually, I'd love some. I'm starving. With mustard would be nice.'

'Shall I bring them up here?'

'No, I'll come down.'

She left my room and a few minutes later, still in my pyjamas, I followed her into the kitchen.

She cut a freshly baked loaf into mouth-watering slices, spreading them with mustard, piling on the beef.

'Where's Hobbes?' I asked, detecting no signs of his presence; I could usually tell if he was in, even if he was being quiet.

'He's out with Dregs. He took Milord home and went to investigate another dead sheep.'

'Right,' I said. 'Umm ... Milord?'

'The tailor. He came round to fix the old fellow's clothes and I got him to stitch the tear in your trousers that you made when you fell on the railings.'

'I fell on some railings?'

'After you'd put your head through the cider counter. Here you are.'

Handing me a plate of sandwiches, she poured me out a mug of tea. I sat at the table, chewing in confusion, with no memory of railings, then or ever. After I'd defeated the worst of the hunger, a thought occurred.

'Is he a lord, then – the tailor?'

'No, dear, whatever gave you that idea?'

'You called him Milord, didn't you?'

'It's his name: Milord Schmidt.'

'That's a strange name.'

'A strange name for a strange fellow, but his given name was Villy; he changed it when he settled here after the war, thinking it would impress people.'

'Did it?'

'Not really, dear. Still, he is a most excellent tailor and is always happy to look after the old fellow's clothes. They come in for a lot of wear and tear. He's especially good with trousers and zips – the old fellow calls him the Milord of the Flies. Not to his face, though: he's very highly strung.'

I nodded. Despite my rest and the wonderful sandwiches, my brain did not feel up to a long conversation with Mrs G. Still, another thought occurred.

'Did you say there was another dead sheep?'

'Yes, dear, out on a farm off the Pigton Road.'

'Do you know any details?'

'Sorry, you'll have to wait till he gets back.'

As I finished my sandwiches and tea, to my astonishment, I felt sleepy again and having yawned and stumbled upstairs, I slept until late the next morning. By then, I felt more or less better, though the previous couple of days remained hazy. It was almost like trying to remember dreams, when all that remained were flimsy, unconnected threads.

I washed and dressed, taking my time. On going downstairs, I found I was alone, which was fine; I needed peace and quiet. Having made myself tea and toast with marmalade, I sat at the kitchen table, munching and slurping with great pleasure, until, finishing, I picked up the *Bugle* from the table. The headline, 'Another Dead Sheep', was printed above a censored photo of the dear departed animal, whose throat, according to the article, had been torn out and who had been disembowelled. Local resident, Mr Robert Nibblet (42), had apparently stumbled across the gory remains when returning from an evening out. It took a second or two to register Skeleton Bob's real name and to realise he'd let the cat out of the bag, so to speak, having blabbed about his sightings. I couldn't blame him for wanting his moment.

'There have been,' the article continued, 'hundreds of big cat sightings across the country over the last few years. While some may dismiss them as fantasies, the evidence of this, a second mutilated sheep, suggests a truly terrifying wild beast may be at large in the vicinity of Loop Woods.'

I sniggered, reckoning he'd hit the nail on the head; Hobbes fitted the description perfectly, though I doubted he'd really dismember a sheep, unless he was extremely hungry and then he'd make sure to pay for it. However, if the victim had been Henry Bishop, I'd have had few doubts as to the perpetrator.

I flicked through a few more pages, finding only a short piece, about the music festival, of interest. It said that, although Tiny Tim Jones had, reluctantly, been forced to drop out because a court appearance had not gone according to plan, the organisers had managed to fill the gap with the Famous Fenderton Fiddle Fellows, or 4F to their fans. I was amazed they had any fans, having seen them once, when they'd played a New Year's dance in the Corn Hall, playing so atrociously that they'd cleared the place well before midnight. As most of the punters didn't have press cards like I did but had paid thirty pounds a head to get in, the consensus was that they'd suffered robbery with violins and the band had to be smuggled out the back to prevent a riot.

I cleared up my breakfast things, wondering what to do with myself until lunchtime, for, though I was feeling so much better, I was too lethargic to go anywhere.

The doorbell ringing, I walked to the front door and opened it.

The beautiful lady was standing at the top of the steps.

'Hello, Andy,' she said, smiling.

The unexpected apparition made my jaw drop, my legs lose rigidity, my heart pound, as I struggled for breath.

'Are you alright?' she asked.

Dancing black spots got in the way of the lovely vision as, head spinning, I made an idiot noise, feeling as if I'd fallen back into dreams, feeling the touch of her cool, soft hand on my wrist, smelling her warm, heady perfume, as she guided me to the sofa and sat me down. I remained there, confused, amazed, almost fainting, until she pressed a glass of water into my hand. When I bent forward to take a sip, sweat, dripping from my nose, rippled the surface.

How could she be in Hobbes's sitting room?

'I thought,' she said, 'that I'd come round to see how you're getting on. You had me worried at the fete but I bumped into Mrs Goodfellow in town and she said you were much better. I can see you're still poorly, though.'

'I ... umm,' I mumbled.

'Would you like more water?'

'Eh?'

'More water?'

I shook my head. 'How did you ... I mean ... what do you want?' I felt I was not at my articulate best.

'Oh, sorry,' she said in her soft purr, a slight blush, making her even more striking, 'you probably won't remember me. We met briefly at the Wildlife Park? And at the fete?'

'Umm ... fete ... yes.' Of course I remembered her. It would take more than a mere brain trauma to drive her from my mind. Unfortunately, memory also threw up an image of what I'd done on her shoes.

'I'm sorry,' we said together and paused.

'Go ahead,' she said after a long few seconds.

'Umm ... I'm sorry I was ... umm ... sick on your shoes. I hope you managed to clean them alright?' At the back of my mind a seed of worry was growing: had she come for compensation? Why else would she want to see me?

'Don't worry about those old things. You couldn't help it. I hope you are feeling better now. I've never seen anyone knocked out before and you looked so pale and ill.'

I nodded and, the conversation halting, she smiled again. Her teeth were white and regular. Mrs Goodfellow, I thought, would covet them.

'Would you like a cup of tea or coffee or something?' I asked, trying to stop the silence growing uncomfortable. 'Or ginger beer? It's home-made.'

'A cup of tea would be lovely.'

Dazed, I walked into the kitchen and put the kettle on. She *had* come to see me! My sense of confusion lifting, I grinned like a loon, performing an idiot arm-waving dance around the stove.

'No sugar, please, Andy,' she said, standing in the kitchen doorway, her eyebrows arched in amusement.

Feeling a blush flooding my cheeks, I made as if I'd been swatting a fly.

'Missed,' I said. 'Damn these bluebottles!'

I doubted my acting was very convincing, yet she smiled while I tried to stop staring at her like a fixated owl.

'You called me Andy,' I said. 'How do you know my name?'

'Mrs Goodfellow told me. We had a little chat while we were waiting for the ambulance. Oh, I'm sorry but I haven't introduced myself. I'm Violet. Violet King.'

'Oh, right. You must be related to Felix King. He helped me out when I had a spot of bother in town. Of course, I didn't know who he was until I saw him in the *Bugle*.'

'Felix,' she said, with a hint of grimace, 'is my big brother.'

'He seems very nice.'

'He is. Most of the time. At least, when he's not working.'

The kettle whistling, I made tea and carried it through to the sitting room. She sat down on the sofa and, so that I wouldn't appear too pushy, I pulled up one of Hobbes's old oak chairs.

'Would you like a biscuit?' I asked before sitting.

'No, thank you.'

'It's very nice of you to call round and see me. I'm feeling very much better now.'

'That's good … Andy?'

'Yes?'

Her handbag suddenly chiming, she pulled out a mobile, answering it, with an apologetic smile. 'Hi Felix … When was that? Oh … That's unfortunate. Can't it wait?' She sighed. 'Right, I'll go straight round and sort them out … OK … bye.'

She rose to her feet. 'I'm ever so sorry, but I must go. It's business; I work with Felix.'

'What about your cup of tea?'

'Sorry.' Standing up, she walked towards the front door, stopped and turned round. 'Look, I'm sort of new to the area and I hardly know anyone. I wondered if you'd mind having dinner with me some time? Or lunch?'

'Umm,' I said, 'I don't know.'

'Oh. If you don't want to, I understand.'

'No. It's not that … I wouldn't mind … I'd love to … only, well, I'm a bit short of money at the moment.'

'That's OK. I can pay – if you don't mind.'

'Of course not. I'd love to have dinner with you … or lunch … or breakfast, if it comes to that.'

As she raised her eyebrows, another blush burned my cheeks.

'Sorry, I didn't mean to imply I want to spend the night with you, I just meant I'd love to go out with you at any time that's convenient.' I had a feeling my response hadn't come out right. 'Umm … it's not that I don't want to go to bed … umm … I mean I ….'

I wished I could rewind and start again.

To my amazement, she laughed. 'When you're in a hole, it's best to stop digging. I'll tell you what, how about if I pick you up tomorrow evening at eight?'

'That would be great.'

'You can decide where we go; I don't really know any places round here. Bye, Andy.'

'Bye.'

She walked away, closing the door behind her. Shortly afterwards, hearing a car's engine, I peeked out the window, watching as she drove away in a red, open-topped Lotus.

Sitting down, I poured myself a cup of tea and held it, watching it grow cold, my brain, having gone into overload, unable to cope with frivolities. I could hardly believe Violet King wanted to take Andy Caplet out to dinner. No one had ever done anything like that before. Might it be possible, I thought, that my concussion was causing hallucinations? Had the last few minutes all been a wonderful dream? Yet, I could still feel where she'd placed her hand on my wrist, still smell her perfume in the air.

'Wow,' I said at last, putting my mug down on the coffee table, standing up.

Mrs Goodfellow, arriving home a few minutes later, didn't seem surprised to see me dancing and emitting whoops of amazement and joy.

'Hello, dear, how's your head?'

'It's wonderful.'

Waltzing towards her, I hugged her, taking care to be gentle, for she looked all skin and bone, fragile as a dried twig, yet she'd once knocked me out with a single kick, having mistaken me for a ninja.

'I like it when you smile, dear,' she said, staring up at my mouth, 'you've got lovely teeth.'

'Not as lovely as hers,' I replied.

'Hers?'

'Violet King's. She came to see me and is going to pick me up and take me out for dinner tomorrow. She's lovely.'

'Ah, the charming young lady from the fete, the one with beautiful teeth? Well, if she's coming round again, I'll have to tidy up a bit after I've put the shopping away. I'd better get cracking.'

In the circumstances, I felt I should show willing. 'How can I help?'

'By keeping out of my way. You still need your rest, dear.'

Considering this a most satisfactory answer, I took myself upstairs for a lie down, ensuring I couldn't overdo things. I had not yet come to terms with the idea that Violet, what a lovely name, wanted to take me out for dinner and a cynical part of my brain kept suggesting that she was just playing a cruel joke. Awful thoughts stampeded through my mind. What if she never turned up, leaving me waiting on the doorstep? What if she took me to a swanky foreign restaurant and, unable to understand the menu, I ordered a dish of raw liver … or something worse? What if I chose somewhere that wasn't good enough and she walked out on me? My fears, overwhelming the euphoria, I sat on the bed, chewing my fingernails, fretting until Hobbes returned and Mrs G called me for lunch. Pulling myself together, I went downstairs.

The sitting room, smelling of bleach and polish, everything that could gleam gleaming, I doubted even the tiniest speck of dust had survived the onslaught, though the room had been spotless even before. I made my way through to the kitchen, where Hobbes was waiting at the table. When he'd said grace, Mrs Goodfellow served a wonderful mixed salad with the remains of yesterday's roast beef before vanishing. In all the months I'd been living there, I'd yet to see her eat anything, other than a taste to ensure whatever she was cooking was up to scratch.

I ate my lunch with great relish, something she made from onions, tomatoes and spices, something that, had she ever decided to sell it, would have made her a fortune, though I doubted she'd know what to do with the money. So far as I could see, she was happy looking after Hobbes, teaching Kung Fu and collecting teeth.

Hobbes, finishing, dabbed his lips with a napkin. 'I hear you've got a date tomorrow evening.'

'Yes.'

'Good for you, but I advise taking it easy on the alcohol. I must warn you, though; you'll miss a vindaloo.'

Normally that would have upset me for Mrs G made the most wonderful, aromatic, perfectly-spiced curries, but the prospect of being with Violet overcame everything else. Still, I couldn't pretend I didn't have a lingering regret.

'Anyway,' said Hobbes, 'there's been another big cat sighting, this morning. This one made the curate come off his motorbike.'

'Is he alright?' Kevin Godley, Kev the Rev, having helped me out on a number of occasions, I almost regarded him as a friend.

'He's fine, though his bike's a write-off. He says a big cat with a pheasant in its mouth ran from Loop Woods, straight across the road. He swerved, trying to miss it, but thinks there may have been an impact before he came off. By the time he'd stopped skidding and had climbed from a ditch, it had vanished.'

'So does that solve the mystery of the vanishing pheasants?'

'Possibly, though the cat would have to enjoy a fantastically healthy appetite to have eaten dozens of the birds in a matter of a few weeks.'

'Maybe,' I said, 'but, when I was a boy, our cat, Whisky, was forever bringing birds home. They were mostly sparrows and finches, but once he came back with a duck. The thing is, though he loved to hunt, he hardly ever ate them; he was too well fed.'

'That's an interesting thought,' said Hobbes. 'Are you suggesting the big cat is someone's pet? It's certainly a possibility. Perhaps someone lets it out at night, like a normal house cat. That could explain why it's not been found and why the pheasants keep vanishing. You might be onto something, well done.'

'Thanks,' I said, pleased, since he didn't often dish out compliments and their rarity gave them added value. 'Whisky used to torment the birds before killing them. Once, when I'd managed to get one away from him, Father made me give it back. He said it was natural for cats to play with their prey.'

'He's right,' said Hobbes, 'but pet cats aren't natural.'

'That's what I thought, so I tried to release them whenever I could, which wasn't easy, since Whisky soon realised what I was up to and, if he saw me sneaking up when he'd got a bird, he'd scarper. I spent many hours chasing him round the neighbours' gardens.'

Hobbes laughed. 'I suspect it might prove even more difficult to take a pheasant from a panther.'

'I guess so. But what about the dead sheep?'

'There's really no more information than appeared in the *Bugle*. By the time I got to the last killing, the rest of the flock had trampled the area, leaving no scent or trail. It's bad enough that sheep have been killed, and that some of the farmers are getting angry, but what if it attacked a member of the public? It's worrying.'

We went through to the sitting room, where Mrs Goodfellow brought us tea. I'd just taken my first sip when I noticed Hobbes stare at something and frown. I couldn't see why, the room looking the same as always, if possibly a little shinier. Then I noticed she'd placed her new skull on the mantelpiece as a rather gruesome centrepiece.

'What is that?' asked Hobbes, bounding over the coffee table to take a look.

'It's a skull.'

'I can see that. Where did it come from?'

'Mrs Goodfellow.'

Picking it up, he examined it, his frown appearing to be one of concern, rather than anger. 'Would you mind stepping in here, lass?' he shouted.

She came in from the kitchen, wiping her hands on her pinafore. 'Yes?'

'This skull,' he said, 'do you know what it is?'

'According to the dentists, it's from a man with an unfortunate dental condition. His teeth aren't pretty but they are most unusual.' She smiled, patting the dome.

'Most unusual,' he agreed. 'It's not from a man, though.'

'A woman's?' I asked.

'I don't believe it's human at all: not exactly.'

'Umm ... What do you mean by not exactly?' I asked.

'I'm not quite sure,' said Hobbes, 'but it reminds me of something from years ago.'

'What?'

'A werewolf.'

7

Whereas Mrs Goodfellow merely nodded, I, my mouth dropping open, stared at Hobbes, dumbstruck for a few moments, thinking that he'd played cruel jokes on me before. I wasn't inclined to fall for this one, at least not without a fight.

'A werewolf?' I said at last. 'Come off it!'

'It's unusual, I admit,' said Hobbes, 'and I'm not absolutely certain, because it's so many years since I've seen one wolfifesting and, of course, he had his skin on at the time.'

'What the hell do you mean wolfifesting?' I asked.

'Language, Andy. Wolfifesting is the process whereby a werewolf transforms into wolf form; it's the opposite of manifesting.'

'No it isn't, you'll not get me this time,' I said, well aware that he'd proved himself adept at making me fall for ludicrous tall stories. The trouble was, some of the tallest had proved to be true.

'I'm not trying to.' Turning the skull round, he sniffed it. 'This one doesn't look quite right. I wonder if maybe he was killed mid-transformation.'

'Are you telling me that there really are werewolves?'

'Oh yes, dear,' said Mrs Goodfellow, 'of course there are, but I haven't seen any since old Wolfie Tredgrove passed away, and that must be over thirty years ago.'

'More like forty years,' said Hobbes. 'Poor old Wolfie. He grew very deaf in his final months, becoming more of a "what? wolf". Still, he was getting on, being well over ninety – I'm not sure what that would be in dog years – and it was the mange that got him in the end, an uncomfortable place to get it. Unfortunately, werewolves have grown scarce and increasingly shy since the invention of the gun. Many people are so intolerant of anything different and, in fact, this poor fellow was shot. See this?' He pointed to a small round hole towards the base of the skull.

I almost believed him. 'Umm … would you use silver bullets on a werewolf?'

He frowned. 'Of course not. Bullets can be very dangerous, even silver ones. You might hurt somebody.'

'I mean, would you use them if you wanted to kill one?'

'Why would I want to kill one?'

'Well, it if attacked you.'

'It'd hardly be likely to do that; wolves are shy creatures, werewolves doubly so. If one ever did get a little frisky, then a short, sharp rap on the nose with a rolled-up newspaper would do the trick.'

'But aren't they really dangerous?' I asked. 'I mean to say, I don't know much about them, only what I've seen in films, where they're usually portrayed as bloodthirsty monsters …' I paused, realising suddenly how completely I'd swallowed his story. Nearly completely, anyway.

'I'm afraid most people only see what they want to,' said Hobbes, shaking his head. 'They have a regrettable tendency to justify themselves when they've acted shamefully, such as trying to portray the wanton killing of a harmless creature as somehow heroic. I've never understood how using a high-powered rifle to kill an unsuspecting animal from a safe distance makes some feel courageous and manly. People can be very strange, but, getting back to your point, you are partly right, in that werewolves can be fierce when cornered.'

'So what would you advise then?'

'I'd advise not cornering them.'

I made a decision: should an opportunity arise, I would not, under any circumstances, attempt to corner one.

'You should see the pups,' said Mrs Goodfellow with a smile.

'They are adorable.'

Hobbes nodded. 'Though they can give you a playful nip if you get careless.'

'Would you turn into a werewolf then?' I asked, fascinated, despite the occasional twinge of scepticism.

'No.' He chuckled. 'You're confusing them with the silly old tales. With werewolves and I believe with vampires, it's genetic. However, should you chance to get bitten, I would recommend a course of antibiotics; they've never been keen on baths and you don't know what they might have been eating, or where they might have been. I wouldn't worry; there haven't been any round here since Wolfie.'

'That's a pity,' I said, though really I was glad. Whatever Hobbes said, I hoped never to meet one.

'Right,' he said, replacing the skull, 'I ought to get back to work. I intervened in an attempted mugging on the way home and the bad lad's probably had enough of hanging from a lamppost.'

I looked at him, shocked. 'You shouldn't have hung him from a lamppost,' I said.

He grinned. 'I didn't put him up it. He bolted up while attempting to evade arrest and refused to come down. Since I didn't want to be late for my dinner, I left him there.'

'I expect he's run off by now.'

'I doubt it. I left Dregs on guard. He knows his stuff.'

'Can I come with you?' It was always fascinating to watch Hobbes dealing with law breakers.

'No, you're still under doctor's orders and need rest.'

'Yeah, right. But I am going out tomorrow. I'm much better now.'

I went upstairs for a nap and fell asleep immediately; werewolves and panthers, red in tooth and claw, pursued me through dreams. Awaking, hot and sweaty, soft breathing tickling the back of my neck, I leaped up with a bellow of alarm.

Sleeping dogs, I discovered, can perform vertical take-offs. Dregs, rocketing from the bed, crashed to the floor, giving me such a reproachful look I was embarrassed, though my heart was going like the clappers.

'Sorry,' I said, patting his head.

The house shook as Hobbes, pounding upstairs, burst through the door. 'What's going on in here?'

'Umm …'

'Have you been teasing the dog?'

'No. It's just that, when I woke up, there was something breathing on my neck. I … umm … didn't know it was him. I thought it was a werewolf.'

Hobbes snorted with laughter. 'I suppose we need to make allowances for that bang on the head. Never mind, it'll soon be supper time.'

'I've slept right through the afternoon?'

'Yes.'

'Was the mugger still up the lamp post?'

'Of course and he'd drawn quite a crowd. He wouldn't come down and became quite obnoxious. In the end, I was forced to borrow a tin of pink salmon from an onlooker and knock him from his perch.'

'Was he hurt?'

'Apart from a small bump on his noggin, he was fine, but he didn't enjoy going to the station for a little chat.'

Having been present at a number of his little chats, chats that, even though they'd been directed at the suspect, had reduced me to gibbering terror, I understood. In fact, suspect was the wrong word. When Hobbes decided to arrest someone, he was never a mere suspect; he was a definite.

'When I was sure he'd seen the error of his ways,' Hobbes continued, 'I took him home and made him a cup of tea. I had to go out and buy him tea and milk because everything in his fridge was green.'

'Was he a vegetarian?'

'No. It was mainly sausages.'

'That's horrible,' I said, screwing up my face, trying to ignore the fact that the fridge in my flat had sometimes contained similar pestilential relics. I'd since grown accustomed to a more gracious standard of living.

Supper, a simple macaroni cheese, confirmed my opinion that Mrs Goodfellow possessed astounding alchemical skills, being able to transmute the basest ingredients into pure gold; I wished I knew the secret.

Afterwards, I washed up, since the old girl had gone to her Kung Fu class. I'd once considered joining, getting as far as listening outside the church hall, the sounds of screaming and thumping turning me into a quivering jelly, making me chicken out. Next day, I discovered I'd got the wrong part of the hall and that I'd been listening to the philately group's AGM: passions could evidently run high in stamp collecting. Since then, I'd never summoned sufficient courage to go back and, besides, I didn't need to know self-defence if Hobbes was around.

He was sitting at the kitchen table, finishing the crossword, as I scrubbed the last pan. 'Featherlight's in the cells again,' he said, putting down his pencil with a satisfied smile.

'What's he done this time?' I asked, turning the pan upside down to drain, reaching for a tea towel.

'He assaulted an assistant at the garden centre.'

'What was he doing in the garden centre?'

'He works there.'

'No, I mean, what was Featherlight doing there?'

'He said he'd decided to carry out some improvements to the pub.'

'Really? Well, I suppose it's about time,' I said, suspecting little had been changed, or cleaned, in the last fifty years.

'He's thinking of turning the back yard into a beer garden. At the moment it's full of cracked slabs, weeds and rubbish. He went to the garden centre looking for ideas.'

'But why assault the assistant?'

'I was coming to that,' said Hobbes, his mouth twitching. 'He says he was wandering innocently round the store when, in his words, a "spotty herbert" approached asking if he could be of assistance. Featherlight explained why he was there and the youth apparently said, "you need decking, mate". Featherlight decked him first, claiming self-defence, although he's twice the assistant's size.'

'If,' I said, 'anyone else had come up with such a lame reason, I wouldn't have believed it. In his case it could be possible.'

Hobbes nodded. 'I believe him, though it doesn't excuse him.'

'Is the spotty herbert alright?'

'Apart from a black eye, a thick lip and a mild concussion. I had to arrest Featherlight, though.'

'Did he come quietly?'

He shook his head. 'He never does anything quietly. He cursed and swore all the way to the station.'

I could believe it for Featherlight, as far as I could tell, was unique in lacking fear when confronting Hobbes. I had an idea this did not attest so much to his courage as to his stupidity.

'What'll happen to him?'

He shrugged. 'He'll go to court tomorrow and probably get off with a fine, as usual. I fear that one day he'll really get himself into trouble – and he'll deserve it, though he'll not have set out to cause any harm. He never does. I'll have to have a long chat with him sometime, when he's sober.' He sighed and stretched, 'Ah, well, sitting here and wagging chins won't get the dog walked.'

He took Dregs out and I, having Violet to consider, forgot about Featherlight's misfortunes. My main problem was where to suggest she might take me. While it couldn't be anywhere too expensive, in case she thought me a freeloader, it couldn't be anywhere too tatty, in case she thought me a low-life. The trouble was I didn't know many eating places not on the tatty side of the register; besides pubs, and the Greasy Pole, I hadn't a clue about dining out. There was the Black Dog Café, of course, but I feared

I was still persona non grata there.

Resorting to careful study of the *Yellow Pages*, finding loads of restaurants but no inspiration about their suitability for dining with a sophisticated lady, a millionaire's sister, I was, after an hour, no nearer to a decision. Taking out my frustration on an innocent cushion, I punched it with great zeal, until it exploded, a soft cloud of feathers encircling my head, getting into my mouth and nose. I was spluttering and choking when Hobbes and Dregs returned.

Hobbes stared at the carnage and frowned. 'What's wrong?'

Fearing I was in trouble again, I tried to explain but only spat feathers.

'A little down in the mouth, eh?' he said with a chuckle.

Dregs bounded through the mess in great excitement, a white plume plastered to the black tip of his nose, sneezing.

'I had an accident,' I said and coughed.

'I'd never have guessed. What were you doing?'

'Looking for a suitable restaurant for Violet.'

'And why does that require a room full of feathers?'

'Umm … Sorry. I got fed up and punched a cushion and it burst.'

'I see,' said Hobbes. 'So did that give you any hints? Presumably, you're not going to take her to the Feathers?'

I shook my head. 'I don't know anywhere that's good. Do you have any ideas?'

'That depends on what you fancy. If it's a bit of curried Irish stew, why not try Bombay Mick's? Some people like it. Or Pavarotti's is excellent if you prefer spaghetti.'

'I want something a little more sophisticated – not overly expensive but still up-market.'

'In that case, Le Sacré Bleu might be your best bet. It's French and it's highly recommended by the Fat Man.'

'The Fat Man? Who's he?'

'The *Bugle's* food writer. Don't you know him?'

'Oh, yeah, but I've never read any of his stuff,' I said,

remembering his occasional appearances at the *Bugle's* office. He was a tall, bearded man, a little doughy around the middle perhaps but not fat as such. With his battered leather coat and hunter look, he ought to have been a crime writer.

'You should, he's very good. He has a most inventive and ludicrous turn of phrase but, once you cut through that, he's a reliable and honest critic. He's brave too. About five years ago, having lunched at the Feathers, he wrote a scathing, though truthful, review of Featherlight's cooking, refusing to recant even when Featherlight dangled him from the church tower.'

It says something about Featherlight that I was more surprised to hear he'd squeezed his great bulk up the narrow, twisting staircase of the tower than that he'd dangled a man off it.

'What happened?'

'Featherlight dropped him onto the slabs below, where he made a splendid splash of colour on what would otherwise have been a rather grey winter's morning.'

'Did he?'

'Of course not. I managed to convince the lump that passes for Featherlight's brain that dropping the Fat Man would result in even worse publicity, so he put him down and went back to the kitchen. Of course, when the *Bugle* printed the story, people queued up for hours to enjoy the Feathers' experience.' He shook his head.

'So,' I said, trying to get back on track, 'you'd recommend Le Sacré Bleu? Have you ever eaten there?'

'Twice, when I've had work to do around there.'

'Where is it, exactly?'

'Out on Monkshood Lane at the bottom of Helmet Hill.'

'Oh right. That's near Loop Woods isn't it?'

'Yes.'

'D'you think it'll be safe? I mean with this panther about?'

He sucked his teeth. 'I shouldn't think so. Panthers are notorious for attacking customers in smart restaurants.'

'You're joking ... aren't you?'

He sighed. 'Look, panthers are shy beasts and, though it's possible one might lurk in the woods, it's hardly likely to lurk in a restaurant. Now, I think you ought to clean up your mess before the lass gets home.'

I nodded, reassured and pleased now I had somewhere suitable to take Violet. Strangely, I quite enjoyed picking up the feathers and stuffing them into a bin liner, since it seemed an age since I'd felt able to do anything. I still went to bed early and slept until late.

I awoke, refreshed, to a bright, warm morning. As consciousness returned, I grinned the smug grin of a man who, in a few hours, was to be taken out by a beautiful woman and wined and dined and … I didn't dare consider any further possibilities. I knew so little about her, other than that her voice had a lovely, silky purr, that she was beautiful and sophisticated and that her brother was a millionaire. It wasn't long before my stomach contracted, for a nasty little voice in my head kept niggling, saying I didn't deserve her, I was nowhere near good-looking enough, I was pathetically lacking in dynamism and success. Nothing about me could possibly attract a woman like her: it was obvious she had other motives. Another voice, not so nasty, but equally insidious, suggested she only wanted me for my body and that, having used me, she'd discard me, broken-hearted. Although, for a moment, I wished I could call the whole thing off, hanging around with Hobbes had awakened my sense of adventure and I was determined to see it through, to accept whatever fate had prepared for me. Besides, I didn't know her phone number.

After breakfast, I just wished the day would get a move on. I spent my time pottering round the garden or loitering in the house, trying to avoid Mrs Goodfellow, who insisted on twinkling and digging me in the ribs. In mitigation, she did, at least, feed me with a world-beating pea and ham soup at lunchtime.

Afterwards, she helped me sort out some clothes for the evening: smart-casual was what she had in mind. Ferreting through cupboards, chests of drawers and wardrobes, she dug out a crisp white shirt, a silk tie bearing a crest that meant nothing to me, a navy-blue blazer with gleaming buttons, and a pair of white deck shoes. It all looked pretty good, though I did rebel, not wishing to appear foppish, when she produced a straw boater.

Apart from a brief encounter at breakfast, I didn't see Hobbes until he returned for his supper. Mrs Goodfellow's curry had been steaming and bubbling and enticing me with mouth-watering aromas for hours, and his evident delight as he devoured it proved too much to bear. I had to go and sit in the garden with Dregs until it was all over.

Then it was time for a bath, to get dressed, to ensure I was presentable. When, finally, reasonably satisfied with the results, I went down to the sitting room to fidget. Hobbes, who having finished the Demon Sudoku, was preparing to go out, told me that Henry Bishop, having dug out another shotgun, had taken a pot shot at one of Les Bashem's kids before running away. Though, fortunately, the child had not been hurt, he had decided to arrest Henry. Despite being more focussed on how long the clock was taking to reach eight o'clock, I felt a twinge of pity for the hunted man, who wouldn't, I suspected, get very far before retribution took him. Still, I thought as Hobbes left, the bastard deserved everything that was going to happen to him.

A car pulling up outside, I leaped up, looking out the window. It was a middle-aged couple in a Volvo. Sitting back down, I tried to keep still, watching the clock's hands, working in slow motion, at last reach eight o'clock and creep on to five past. I knew she wasn't going to turn up, knew my fears had come true; it had all been a cruel joke and she'd diddled me out of an exceptional curry. Sighing, I got to my feet, intending to hide my dis-appointment in my room.

The doorbell ringing, Dregs burst into the sitting room, barking madly.

'Shut up!' I yelled.

Since he hadn't quite forgiven me for shocking him the

previous day, he retreated to the kitchen with a martyred look as I opened the door.

'Hi,' said Violet.

'Hi,' I said.

She looked stunning in a simple red dress, her smooth, tanned shoulders glowing in the evening light. Her hair was up and the soft curve of her neck took my breath away.

'Hello.' She smiled over my shoulder at Mrs Goodfellow. 'Shall we go, Andy?'

'Umm … yeah.'

'Make sure to have him home by midnight,' said Mrs Goodfellow. 'The lad needs his sleep.'

'Of course.' She waved goodbye, and led me to her gleaming red Lotus, parked a few yards down the street.

She started the engine. 'Where are we going?'

'To Le Sacré Bleu.'

I suddenly realised it was my responsibility to tell her how to find it and, though I had been out that way with Hobbes on many occasions, I'd mostly had my eyes shut: fortunately, the car had a satnav. Violet liked to drive fast but only when the road conditions permitted and I felt quite safe. The wind, the growl of the engine and the blare of the classical music she was playing meant conversation was impossible, which was just as well, because I couldn't think of anything to say.

After about fifteen minutes and one nearly wrong turning, when the satnav suggested a short cut via the River Soren, we crossed a bridge into the car park of Le Sacré Bleu.

Stopping the engine, she unbuckled her seat belt. 'Nice place,' she said.

It was. Before us was an ancient manor, its mellow, honey-coloured stone, clad in an ivy gown, snuggled in a hollow at the foot of Helmet Hill. The little River Soren, fringed with dancing reeds, dotted with jerky moorhens, wound past on the edge of a daisy-strewn lawn. A lazy heron flew above and sheep murmured in the surrounding fields. It looked idyllic, except that the car park was worryingly full.

'Shall we go in?' she asked. 'I'm starving.'

'OK.'

I gnawed my lip as we followed our long shadows down the stone-paved path to the entrance, cursing myself silently as an idiot for not having thought to book a table. A familiar, cold feeling had gripped my stomach and the memory of all those parked cars was twisting my insides. Still, I had no choice; I had to go through with it.

Violet ushered me inside into a pleasantly cool room, with dark beams, white tablecloths, sparkling glasses and gleaming silver, a room where rich aromas tempted all taste buds. Noticing every table in sight was occupied, I swallowed, trying to look suave.

'This is obviously the place to be,' said Violet. 'It's a great choice.'

I attempted a nonchalant smile as a tall man in a white shirt and bow tie approached.

'Bonsoir, monsieur, mademoiselle. Welcome to Le Sacré Bleu. How may I help you?'

'Umm ... a table for two, please?'

'Have you booked, sir?'

'Umm ... well ....'

The man sucked his teeth and glanced around him. 'I'm afraid we are rather busy tonight.'

'There's no problem is there, Andy?' asked Violet.

'Umm ....'

'Andy?' The man smiled. 'Ah, so you must be Monsieur Andy Caplet?'

'Must I? Umm ... yes, I suppose I must be.'

'Excellent. Then we have a booking for a table for two persons at eight-thirty. Follow me, please.' Picking up a couple of menus, he led us to a table by an open window, letting in a refreshing breeze and the scent of flowers.

'I see you have influence,' said Violet.

I nodded, trying to keep it together, dazed by what had just happened, ridiculously afraid another Andy Caplet would turn up, demanding his booking.

The man seated us and handed out the menus. 'Would you care for aperitifs?'

'No, we've brought our own.' I said, not thinking straight. 'Oh, you mean drinks?'

Violet laughed. 'Very funny. I'd like a pastis, please.'

'Very good, mademoiselle. And for monsieur?'

'A pint of lager … umm … on second thoughts, I'll have the same.'

As he departed, I smiled across at Violet, who smiled back. I smiled again and sent my gaze to wander round the room, searching for something to say.

'This is really nice,' she said before anything occurred. 'Isn't the view delightful? The river's lovely.'

'It is. I've never been here before but Hobbes reckons it's good.'

'He scares me,' she said. 'I don't know why.'

'He scares me a bit, too, sometimes – but he's been very kind.'

The introduction of Hobbes, coinciding with the arrival of our drinks, breached the dam and conversation began to flow. Suddenly, I was chatting to her like to an old friend, explaining about Hobbes, what he'd done for me, about his crime-busting, but I couldn't bring myself to expose his dark side or to mention the really odd bits. I didn't want to present him in a bad light. After all, he could do that well enough for himself.

When, a few minutes later, a waitress arrived to take our orders, we had to send her away as neither of us had got as far as opening the menu. When I did, my heart sank for most of the words, except for ratatouille and meringue, were in French.

'This is inspired,' said Violet. 'I think I'll start with the Pieds de Cochon Farci au Foie Gras et aux Langoustines. How about you?'

'Umm … I might have the same.'

'Really? It's not everyone who likes pigs' trotters.'

'Oh ... I didn't think ... Sorry, but my French isn't very good.'

'Mine is.' She smiled. 'When I was a little girl we used to holiday in a chateau by the Rhone. I'll help you.'

It felt weird to admit my ignorance and not feel stupid about it, for something about her made me secure and I felt no awkwardness as she translated and explained. I even felt secure enough to tell her about my holiday on the Algarve, when I'd ordered chocos, expecting something chocolaty, instead being presented with a plate of cuttlefish. I'd put a brave face on it, forcing them down, bones and all. She laughed, seeming to find me very amusing. In the end, with her help, I settled for 'potage du jour' followed by 'Fillet of Venison and Confit of Shoulder with Dry Fruits Sauce'. She went for 'Shank of Pork Confit with Lentils Sauce and Bacon' and ordered a bottle of Château something.

The food was superb, nearly matching Mrs G's, though it felt disloyal to think so. Nevertheless, I didn't appreciate it as much as it deserved because Violet was taking so much of my attention. For some reason, and it wasn't the wine, because I was being sensible, I felt utterly relaxed in her company, absolutely comfortable. She laughed or offered sympathy in all the right places, smiling whenever our eyes met. In my opinion, and realising I'd only just met her, we were right for each other. If I'd have had time to think, I would have been amazed.

At length, excusing herself, she headed towards the Ladies. I watched her walk away, appreciating the sway of her hips, the way her dark hair gleamed in the candlelight, noticing with some indignation and, I admit, a touch of smugness, that she'd not gone unnoticed by other men. While I tried to look cool, as if accustomed to dining with a beautiful woman, I still found it unbelievable that she'd picked me and had to keep on trying to quiet the niggling part of my brain warning that good things didn't happen to me and that, if they did, the price I'd pay would be terrible.

Once she was out of sight, I permitted myself a sip of wine, savouring the smooth, mellow fruitiness for the first time. She obviously knew her wines, for even I could tell it was a cracking good one, nearly as good as Hobbes's.

Outside, a cow bellowed, a little owl yipped, and a couple of muffled pops suggested a farmer was waging a vendetta against the wood pigeon population. Inside, I was revelling in how much I was enjoying the evening, smiling complacently at other diners, occasionally peering out into the garden, which was already filling with dusk. Across the road, I could make out part of Loop Woods, which, beyond the shadow cast by Helmet Hill, glowed bright and brittle in the red light. In that moment I felt a chill, as if something was watching me. Perhaps, deep under the cover of the trees, a panther really was lurking. Taking a gulp of wine, I tried to ward off my foolish fears. Violet seemed to be taking her time doing whatever women do.

As I looked back into the restaurant, I glimpsed a movement from the garden, as if something had slipped from light into shadow. I jerked back, staring, unable at first to see anything out of the ordinary, nearly convinced my mind had been playing tricks. Then, without a doubt, there was a movement. Something darker than twilight was heading my way. It was nowhere near tall enough to be human and, though, it might have been as big as a panther, its lurching, uncoordinated movements were anything but feline. As it moved from my field of vision, I wished, for the first time that evening, that Hobbes was with me. I tried to persuade myself that I was being ridiculous. What danger could there be inside a crowded restaurant? But where was Violet? Feeling a sudden cold horror that she'd decided to step outside for a moment, I heard a cry from the garden.

I stood up and ran towards the door, side-stepping an astonished waiter, his arms full of plates, and jerked the door open. A hunched figure grabbed my blazer, whispered 'Help me' and fell face forward onto my feet. A woman screamed and the restaurant was in turmoil. Blood had splattered the stone floor, spotting my trousers; the figure, a man, making a low, bubbling groan, lay still.

'What's happening?'

Violet's voice, coming from behind me, I breathed a sigh of relief. The situation seemed to have paralysed everyone, except for her. Pushing through the gawping diners, brushing me aside, she knelt by the body and rolled it onto its back.

It was Henry Bishop, his shirt front dripping with the blood that gushed from a jagged wound in his throat.

8

Henry Bishop lay in a spreading pool of his own blood, as Violet, pressing her slim white fingers to his neck, fought to stem the dreadful flow. It was to no avail. He twitched, gurgled and her hands were drenched by one dreadful, final haemorrhage. His life had ended and, though he'd been a violent, wife-beating bully, no one deserved to die like that.

Everyone in the restaurant was standing in a wide, staring semi-circle around us: not quite everyone, for someone was vomiting.

'Is he alright?' asked the headwaiter, his face as white as his shirt.

'No, he's not all right,' said Violet in a quiet voice.

'Oh, Lord!' The headwaiter waved his hands in the air like a man distracted.

'Do you think he's dead?' asked a fat man in a too-tight dickey-bow. 'Have you checked his pulse?'

I doubted Henry had enough throat left to check.

'What are we going to do?' asked the headwaiter, teetering on the verge of hysterics.

Violet looked up, the hem of her dress dark with blood. 'Could someone get help?'

Nobody moved, all of them paralysed, shocked.

'I'll do it,' I said, 'if someone can lend me their phone?'

A young woman, looking horrified, scared, rummaged in her handbag and handed me her mobile. Calling 999, I requested an ambulance and the police before trying Hobbes's mobile. He didn't answer so, giving the phone back, I knelt to help Violet.

The headwaiter was clutching his head, moaning. 'We'll be ruined. What will become of us? What could have done such a thing?'

'Perhaps it was that panther,' said a bald, red-faced man.

Panic ensued, diners running, grabbing handbags and jackets. A plump, middle-aged couple headed towards the door, as though intending to paddle through the blood.

I stood up, feeling I had to do something. 'Everyone stay where you are,' I shouted. To my surprise, the stampede ceased, as all eyes looked to me for leadership and, though I could feel my cheeks reddening, I knew the procedure.

'No one else must touch the body, or leave the building until the police say so. We don't know what killed him yet and they may require statements.'

Some nodded, a few frowned but no one moved for the door. The woman whose phone I'd borrowed began to cry.

'If it's the bloody panther that killed him,' said the red-faced man, pushing towards me, 'it's not murder and there's no reason to stay. I want to leave.'

'We don't know a panther did it,' I said. 'Besides, if it did, who's to say it's not still outside?'

My argument striking home, the red-faced man returned to his table, where, to my astonishment, he sat down and carried on eating his steak. 'Shame to waste it,' he said.

Although some, agreeing with him, returned to their meals, most sat, grey-faced, waiting for the police.

'Andy,' said Violet.

She was still kneeling and, despite everything, I couldn't help admiring the sparkle of her eyes, her brave attempt at a smile, the hint of cleavage as I looked down.

'I need to wash,' she said.

I helped her to her feet, trying not to recoil at the sticky, congealing blood on her trembling hands, supporting her towards the door of the Ladies. 'Will you be alright?'

She nodded and I turned away, wiping my hands on a napkin before covering Henry's corpse with a white tablecloth. As it turned red, I had to fight the urge to throw up. People were looking at me as if expecting that I'd take charge but, having done my bit, I knew what had to be done next.

Beckoning the headwaiter, I asked him to fetch me a brandy.

For all the comprehension I saw in his eyes, I might have been speaking Swahili. 'Get me a brandy,' I said in slow, measured tones, 'a large one. Now!'

At last, he nodded, staggering to the bar. As he reached for a glass, his hand was shaking so much he shattered it. Though his second attempt was better, he still slopped more onto the counter than into the glass before finally filling it, handing it to me, and pouring one for himself. I took it back to our table, sipping, comforted by the fiery liquid searing its way to my stomach. Hearing an approaching siren, I glanced out into the garden.

Something large was moving in the deepening darkness, something stealthy, something approaching the restaurant. I gasped as Violet returned to her seat.

'What's up?' she asked in a small voice, 'is something out there?'

'I think so, but I'm not sure what.'

She was pale and trembling as I reached out to hold her hands.

'It'll be alright,' I said, 'the police will be here soon and, anyway, I'm sure we're safe inside.'

'Thank you,' she said, squeezing my fingers until I yelped.

Another movement caught my attention, much closer than before, caught in the beam of a car's headlights. A hefty figure, more ape-like than cat-like, was loping towards the window. I groaned.

Violet gazed into my eyes. 'What's the matter?'

I shook my head, unable to speak. Hobbes was out there, with blood on his face, a feral look in his dark eyes.

A few moments later, two policemen entered and took charge. I was soon too busy relating what I'd seen to think about Hobbes, except to avoid mentioning him. In my defence, I'd assumed he'd walk in to help with the investigation and could give an innocent and reasonable explanation.

Some paramedics, a pair of detectives and men in white suits turned up but Hobbes never showed.

After we'd all given our names and addresses, and an ambulance had taken away its gory cargo, we were allowed home. It had just gone midnight.

I was dazed as I left. I held Violet's hand while she led me to the car and strapped me in.

'You certainly know how to show a girl an interesting time,' she said with a grimace as she drove me home.

When at last we reached Blackdog Street, I asked her in for coffee, feeling a mixture of relief and sadness at her refusal, for my eyelids felt heavy, as if coated with lead, and I couldn't stop yawning. I'd known all along that the evening would end in disaster but could hardly believe it had gone so spectacularly wrong.

'Good night,' I said, though the words didn't sound appropriate. 'Thank you for dinner and I'm ever so sorry for everything.' I got out of the car.

'It wasn't your fault, Andy,' she said, her voice calm and flat. 'I'll call you.'

She drove away as I scaled the steps to the front door and went inside. Having dreaded telling Mrs Goodfellow what had happened, I was glad she'd already turned in. I went into the kitchen for a glass of water, finding Dregs dozing in his basket; he acknowledged my return by blinking and giving a single wag of his tail, which suited me, for I wasn't in the mood for enthusiasm. I hurried upstairs, washed and got ready for bed, terrified Hobbes would turn up so I'd have to talk to him, relieved when he hadn't appeared as I curled up in bed.

How could he have done it? I knew that, for a policeman, he took a somewhat personalised view of the law, but surely killing someone, even Henry Bishop, was murder. Certainly, the man had deserved punishment but not death. Though I tried to convince myself I'd imagined what I'd seen, that there'd be a reasonable explanation, the image of Hobbes with blood on his face and that wild look in his eyes would not go away. I lay in the dark, jumping at every noise, fearing his return, wondering if I dared challenge him, wondering if I should just tell the police, afraid they wouldn't believe me, scared what he might do if he learned what I'd witnessed.

Even more worrying was what he might do to Violet, if he thought she knew anything. I felt so sorry for her for, though I'd had little experience with women, I couldn't help feeling the killing must have quite ruined her evening, not to mention her beautiful dress. Still, I admired her courage. She'd been the only one trying to help the dying man and it wasn't her fault he'd already been beyond hope. Would I ever see her again? I doubted it, unable to escape from the fact that I'd only met her four times, three of which had been total disasters.

The last thing I expected happened. I fell asleep, sleeping well into next morning, waking in a sweat, all the blankets piled on top, as if I were an animal in its den. Since I'd not got round to drawing the curtains, I watched the dust-dancers twinkling and scintillating, living their moment in the sun's spotlight. From the kitchen came the rich scent of baking bread: from the roof, a blackbird's honey-throated singing. Life felt great until a deluge of memories swept all before it.

By the time I'd forced myself downstairs, I'd made a decision to say nothing to Hobbes – until the time was right.

Mrs Goodfellow was chopping vegetables at the table. 'Good morning, dear. How was your evening?'

'Not very good,' I said, wondering how much she knew. 'It started pretty well but then … well, umm … a man got killed, which rather spoiled things.'

She raised her eyebrows. 'I'm not surprised. What happened

to him?'

'He had his throat torn out. Violet tried to help him but it was no good.'

'That's not nice. Did an animal do it?'

'I don't know. I suppose so.' I couldn't tell her what I was thinking.

'Was he anyone I know?'

'Henry Bishop.'

'Henry Bishop? No, I don't know him. I never will, now. Hold on, though, isn't he the one who hits his wife?'

'He used to. Didn't Hobbes tell you about it?'

'No, dear. He must have got up early and was out before I came down. He's taken the dog, too. He had Sugar Puffs for breakfast, so I suspect he's busy but, of course, he's bound to be busy if someone's been killed.'

'Of course,' I said, sitting down.

'Oh, well. Would you like any breakfast?'

'Just toast and marmalade. I'm not that hungry.'

'If you're sure.' She sliced some bread and put the kettle on.

The way she looked after me, though I did enjoy it, often made me feel uneasy, for she was Hobbes's housekeeper, not mine; I could, in theory, have looked after myself. With a shrug, I awaited service.

'We don't get many killings round here,' she said, buttering a thick slice of toast. 'The old fellow won't stand for them and he'll be in a right grumpy mood until he catches the killer, whatever it is.'

'He might be in a bad mood for some time,' I said.

'Why's that?'

'Oh, well, this time, he mightn't want to. He might think Henry deserved it; when he saw what he did to poor Mrs Bishop, he was more furious than I've ever seen him.'

'He'll still want to clear things up. He always has done, and he's good at it.'

I nodded, wondering how much had now changed. As I

munched my toast, I again tried to work out how to proceed, for the police might just laugh at my suspicions; alternatively, if they took me seriously and came to arrest him, I doubted he'd go quietly. I wasn't even sure I could betray him after everything he'd done for me. Furthermore, I couldn't imagine how the old girl would take it. She idolised Hobbes, treating him with a peculiar mix of motherly pride and schoolgirl crush. Another important consideration was that, if I did turn him in, I'd have to move out and fend for myself, a prospect far from pleasant, yet, wasn't it still my duty, as a responsible citizen, to report what I'd seen? I couldn't do it, though whether through loyalty, fear, or selfishness, I couldn't decide.

Wondering whether the *Bugle* had reported the incident, I asked where the paper might be.

'I expect the old fellow took it. But, never mind that, did you get on well with your young lady?'

'Alright, in the circumstances I suppose. She's ever so nice but she's hardly going to forget an evening like that. It's all over before it's even started.'

'Did she say that?'

'No. She said she'd call me.'

'There you go. It couldn't have been so bad if she's going to call you.'

Putting on a brave smile, I nodded, finishing my breakfast. I'm sure the old girl would have loved me to talk more but I wasn't in the mood, responding to her questioning with grunts and one-word answers. My stock of optimism had run out and all that remained in store was a glut of gloom and misery.

'I need some air,' I said, wiping toast crumbs from my hands and heading for the street.

We were in the grip of a scorcher and, though the church clock showed it was not yet eleven, the town was oppressive as if it had been superheated. Rolling up my shirt-sleeves didn't make me any cooler, just allowing the sun to scorch my forearms.

I went into the library, which offered welcome shade, picked up the *Bugle* from a rack by the door and took it to an armchair in the corner. Though Henry Bishop's grisly death having made the front page wasn't a surprise, I was amazed the lead story was about Felix King's plans for the town. I ignored it, reading Phil Waring's article about Henry, which, to my astonishment, made no suggestion that Henry might have been murdered. The police, it reported, were keeping an open mind but there was a suggestion that a panther might have done it.

It seemed Hobbes had committed the perfect crime.

Except, it wasn't quite perfect; I was a witness, even though I hadn't actually seen him do the dirty deed.

Thoughts swirled through my head like snowflakes in a globe: images of Hobbes covered in blood, Henry's frightened face, Violet kneeling in his blood, the faces in Le Sacré Bleu. Unable to clear the dying man's last gurgle from my head, my brain felt full, as if it would explode. I fought to remain calm, to think rationally as I concentrated on the reported facts, sketchy as they were. According to the article, Henry's shotgun had been found by a tree. For a moment I tried to work out how a tree was capable of finding anything. Realising I wasn't making sense, that I needed air and space, I ran from the library.

I don't know what would have happened had I not stumbled across Billy Shawcroft, lying on the lawn outside.

Crying out in alarm and pain, he knelt up, rubbing his back.

'Sorry, I didn't see you there,' I said. 'Are you alright?'

'I was better before you trod on me. Can't a guy sunbathe in peace?'

'Sorry, I was distracted. I saw someone with his throat torn out last night.'

'What? That bloke in the paper that got done in by the panther? You were there?'

'I was.'

'They say he was a right bloody mess.'

'Yes.'

'But,' asked Billy, looking puzzled, 'didn't it happen up Monkshood Lane at some posh restaurant?'

I nodded.

'So, what were you doing there?'

'I was having dinner with … umm … a … lady.'

Billy's eyebrows going into orbit, a big grin split his face. 'You lucky bugger!'

'Not so lucky. The murder rather spoiled everything.'

'I suppose so, but it wasn't murder, was it? It was a panther.'

'Was it?' I asked, shaking.

Billy stared. 'You'd better come with me. I start work in ten minutes and you look like you could do with a drink but, take it easy won't you? I heard what you did at the fete.' Getting to his feet, slipping his shirt back on, he took me to the Feathers.

I walked with him, dizzy, swaying as if I'd already had a few, gasping in the midday heat. He led me inside, sitting me by the door, where a breeze ruffled my hair.

'What can I get you?'

'Umm … I've no money.'

'My treat. Whisky?'

I nodded. 'And a lager, if you don't mind, I'm very thirsty.'

The drinks appearing before me, I swallowed half the lager and knocked back the whisky, which, as always, had an odd flavour. According to rumour, Featherlight's spirits were distilled in a disused warehouse in Pigton. It burned like liquid fire, melting my throat, numbing my brain, making me feel better, despite a burning sensation and a sour affliction of the stomach. Lost in my own thoughts, I lingered over the remnants of my lager until, the hands on the clock showing a quarter to one, it was time to go home for dinner.

'Cheers, Billy,' I said to the top of his head, all I could see of him as he poured a glass of cider for a man in a pinstripe suit.

Walking back to Blackdog Street with my stomach gurgling, I was unsure whether to blame the whisky, or the prospect of having to talk to Hobbes, something I'd have to do sometime, if I had sufficient nerve to confront him. If I hadn't, I wasn't certain I could stay with him, knowing what I knew.

From a purely intellectual viewpoint, I knew it would be better to do it sooner rather than later but cowardice was strong that afternoon and suggested silence would be easier.

Relieved on opening the front door to sense he hadn't yet returned, I found the fresh tang of salad and baked bread soothing. The church clock chiming the hour, the front door opened as I took my place at the table. A moment later Dregs was jumping all over me and Hobbes walked into the kitchen with a slight limp. Despite that, he looked remarkably cheerful, if a little weary. He grinned at me.

'I understand,' he said, 'that you took charge at the restaurant last night. Well done.'

I mumbled something non-controversial.

'I'm famished,' he said, washing his hands in the sink, 'and parched, too.' He sat at the table and poured a flagon of ginger beer down his throat. 'That's better. How was the Feathers?'

'How do you know I've been there?'

'Elementary, Andy. You reek of lager and the stuff he calls whisky and your forearms are stained with that unusual blend of old beer, cigarettes and general filth that only exists on tables at the Feathers.'

I glanced at the orange-brown stains. 'I see. Billy bought me a drink because ... umm ... I trod on him. Featherlight wasn't in.' It was hardly an adequate explanation, but Hobbes was distracted by the vast plate of salad and meats the old girl was carrying.

'Thanks lass,' he said as she laid it before him.

I received a similar, if smaller offering and, after the usual delay for grace, we tucked in, treating the meal with the reverence and deep appreciation it warranted. The only words he spoke until we'd finished were when he asked me to pass the pepper. After we'd finished every last morsel, I expected he would enjoy a mug of tea in the sitting room, as usual, giving me an opportunity to ask how he was getting on with the investigation. I gulped, because, at the appropriate time, I intended voicing my suspicions.

To my relief, things didn't go as expected. Instead of going through to the sitting room, he picked up his mug, threw in a fistful of sugar and said, 'I'm going to take forty winks.' Having stirred the scalding liquid, he licked his finger dry and turned to Mrs Goodfellow. 'I'll be out early tonight, so I'd be obliged if you'd prepare my supper for five o'clock.' He yawned.

'Of course,' said Mrs Goodfellow. 'I was planning beef rissoles.'

'Thanks, lass. That will be splendid. Make plenty of 'em; it may be a long night.' With that, he retired to his bedroom from where, a few minutes later, a series of bone-shaking snores emerged.

Taking my tea into the garden, I sat beneath the old apple tree as the afternoon grew still and humid. Surrounded by the hum of bees and the soporific, heavy scent of flowers, I, too, nodded off, awaking to the sound of thunder. The sky was leaden, the first fat raindrops were shaking the leaves, as I grabbed my mug, still half-full of cold tea, and fled inside. The kitchen clock showed five-thirty.

I was mostly pleased to see the old girl washing up Hobbes's dishes, to know he'd already gone out, despite realising that delay would only make accusations more difficult.

Dregs was dozing in the doorway to the sitting room. Stepping over him, switching on the television, I sat on the sofa, waiting for the news. Henry Bishop hadn't made the national headlines, only coming in third on the local news, behind reports of a political scandal in the council, and a devastating fire in a warehouse near Pigton.

'Good evening,' said Rebecca Hussy, a pretty, fresh-faced reporter in a crisp white blouse, addressing the camera outside Le Sacré Bleu. 'Last night, around ten o'clock, Henry Bishop, a respected local farmer and businessman, was discovered bleeding in the doorway of the exclusive restaurant behind me. Despite staff and customers battling desperately to save him and paramedics rushing to the scene, Mr Bishop died. According to unconfirmed reports, he had suffered severe injuries to his throat, injuries consistent with a vicious attack from a large predator. Terrified local residents say a big cat, probably a panther, has been sighted on numerous occasions recently. Red-faced officials admit they have not taken the reports seriously.'

So, the big cat story was holding up; Hobbes was not even a suspect. Rebecca went on to interview Mrs Bishop, who appeared distraught at the death of her husband, describing him as 'one in a million, the sort of man who would never have hurt a fly.' There was hardly anything new, except for one fact that made me gasp; both barrels of Henry's shotgun had been fired. Might that, I wondered, have explained Hobbes's limp? Flinching as a rumble of thunder rattled the windows, I dived deep into a dark pool of worry.

'Rissoles!'

Mrs Goodfellow's voice ringing in my ears, I jumped up, barking my shin on the coffee table. Her constant sneaking up on me could not be good for my heart.

'Your rissoles are ready,' she announced. 'You'd best eat them while they're hot.'

'Thank you,' I said, following her into the kitchen where she dished up a plate of rissoles and good brown gravy with a selection of nicely steamed vegetables. After the first bite, I decided, once again, to forgive her pretty much anything, so long as she continued to feed me, for although I hadn't been much looking forward to supper, having unpleasant memories of Mother's dry, tasteless cannonballs, the old girl's take on the humble rissole would have delighted the fussiest gourmet.

Later, relaxing in the sitting room with a nice, fresh mugful of tea while the old girl dusted the spotless room, my thoughts returned to Hobbes. 'Did he say what he was doing tonight?' I asked.

'No, dear, I expect it's something to do with the panther. He said he'd got a scent of it last night, so he'll probably try to catch it.'

'On his own?'

'I expect so. He wouldn't want anyone getting hurt.'

'But what if Henry Bishop wasn't killed by a panther? What if someone had murdered him and the panther was getting the blame?'

'Then, I'm sure the old fellow would have mentioned it,' she said, rubbing the television screen with her duster before returning to the kitchen to wash up.

I was neither convinced nor comforted. First, it had been Arthur Crud. Now, it was Henry Bishop. Who would be next? Furthermore, how many others might he have murdered in the name of justice? Though somewhere, in a dark corner of my mind, a vigilante was applauding what he'd done, the rest of me couldn't help but feel that the two men should, at least, have had a fair trial with a proper, human jury. I couldn't blame him for detesting rapists and wife-beaters but he held strong views on thieves and dangerous drivers (except himself) and I wondered where it might end. He had no right to act as judge, jury and executioner.

I wished I had someone to talk to. Violet would have been best but I could see no hope after what I'd put her through. Though I knew it hadn't been my fault, if I'd let her take me somewhere else, somewhere less swanky, she wouldn't have spent the evening kneeling in a dead man's blood. Yet, maybe, I reasoned, it had been for the best; I'd have screwed things up anyway, sooner or later. Some things were inevitable. The rain beat against the window, thunder crashed overhead, I jumped and unplugged the telly, sitting in the gloom, until the storm passed. When the rain stopped just before nine o'clock, I slipped out for a walk.

The evening air cooling my heated brow, I revelled in the fresh smell of the town's air, washed clean of car fumes and stagnant drains. As I stepped over a puddle, I thought, what the heck and jumped and splashed my way down The Shambles, going wherever my fancy took me, sometimes striding out, sometimes dawdling, or looking in shop windows. I half wished I'd taken Dregs, but having been asleep under the kitchen table, he didn't look like a dog that wanted to be disturbed.

After a while, the evening fading towards dusk, I realised, having walked in a near circle, that I was approaching Ride Park. The last time I'd been there, Hobbes had fallen from the tree, a time seemingly long ago, when I'd mostly trusted him. Grimacing, pushing through the gates, ignoring the path, I kicked through the sopping grass, enjoying the rich scent of damp earth, the fluttering and piping of birds getting ready for sleep, feeling pretty good. Perhaps, I thought, life wasn't so bad. It had its ups and downs and, admittedly, there were too many downs, but the compensations were great.

After half an hour or thereabouts, as I turned for home, I remembered noticing a sign saying that the park gates were locked at dusk. Yet, there was no need to panic, for, if all else failed, I could knock on the door of the park-keeper's cottage. He would let me out, I was certain, but only after I'd suffered a torrent of his pent-up frustrations about life and the idiocy of members of the public who ignored clear notices about closing times. I didn't fancy any aggravation of that sort and had an idea there was a side gate that might still be open about half a mile along a path through the woods.

The last glimmers of sunlight having all but faded, myriad stars twinkled in the velvet blackness, a faint glimmer of silvery light heralding the rising of the moon. A slight breeze blew up a mist, concealing my legs below the knee as I hurried on, with a shiver and a yawn, keen to put the park behind me, to get home, to get into my comfy bed.

I stepped beneath the canopy of the trees into what seemed utter blackness. Beneath my feet, a twig cracked like a shot in the stillness. Small woodland creatures going about their nocturnal business rustled and squeaked and, in the distance, a pair of owls hooted.

A deep growl nearly stopped my heart. Although I tried to convince myself it was a fox, or the park-keeper's dog, something about it chilled my blood. As I hurried on, not quite daring to run, far too scared to stop, the growl came again, closer and, surely, in front of me. Hesitating, half-turning to run, I tripped over my own feet and thudded into the soggy leaf mould. I lay still, my eyes wide open yet, with the dark and the clinging mist, I might just as well have been blind.

A faint hiss – the wind? Or soft breathing over sharp teeth? Whatever was out there was getting closer and all I could do was to stay still, to hold my breath, my heart beating in double time. A creature was out there, looking for me. Soon it would surely find me … and then what? I rolled onto my side in an ecstasy of terror, the breathing growing ever nearer. When hot, moist breath caressed my cheek, I thought my heart would stop. Something soft, something powerful, patted my head gently.

Since a human mind can only stand so much before primeval instinct assumes control, I leapt to my feet with a wild cry, running blindly into the night, expecting any moment to feel sharp claws in my soft skin, cruel jaws tearing at my throat. Yet, the pursuit never happened. Within seconds, I was close to the side gate, the glow of sodium streetlights offering safety. Risking a glance over my shoulder, for a heart-stopping moment I glimpsed two flashes of green, surely eyes: cat's eyes. As I blinked in the sudden headlight glare of a passing lorry, something slipped into the woods.

A rough voice yelled. 'What do you think you're doing?'

The park keeper was standing at the gate, a padlock in his hand. 'Don't you know we close at dusk?'

I couldn't even speak.

'What's the matter? Cat got your tongue?'

I nodded, pushing past him into the safety of Hedbury Road, my mind in turmoil again. On the walk home, every shadow, every unexpected noise, spooked me.

I reached Blackdog Street, where Mrs Goodfellow had already

turned in and Hobbes had not yet returned. Dregs was curled up in his basket in the kitchen. Much to his indignation, needing reassurance, I lay beside him. It must have taken a couple of hours before I stopped trembling.

9

Something woke me. I was still lost in a sleep fuzz, surrounded by darkness, confused, my bed uncomfortable and smelling of dog. Recollection slowly returning, I knew where I was, why I had memories of fear. I was on my own, Dregs having deserted me, probably to sleep in my bed, if I was any judge of character. Though I was already shivering, a chilling realisation emerged from the depths of unconsciousness; a door had banged, the sound, I was nearly sure, having come from below. I longed to be under blankets, oblivious and if that meant sharing with the dog so much the better, for something was moving in the cellar.

When the wooden steps creaked, I crawled, without thinking, in a state of panic, across the kitchen floor, huddling into a corner, holding my breath, listening to the slow footsteps coming up, coming towards the kitchen. I'd spent long hours wondering about the mysterious door down in the cellar, the door hidden behind a heap of coal. Hobbes had once tried to deny its existence, making me doubt the evidence of my own eyes, but I knew what I'd seen. Later, when he'd refused to say what lay behind it, putting the fear of Hobbes into me when I'd pressed, I'd surmised, since he had no compunction in exposing me to the most nightmarish of situations, that something beyond averagely horrible was there.

The footsteps drawing nearer, terror rising, I suppressed a whimper and scrambled into the cupboard beneath the sink, lying there on my front, a scrubbing brush pressed into my soft bits. As I pulled the cupboard door to, I knocked over a bottle of disinfectant, the fumes soon stinging my eyes, making my nose run. Though the animal part of my brain was urging the need to make less noise than a sleeping mouse, I was sure my heart sounded like a kettledrum pounded by an enthusiastic gorilla, sure anyone could hear it two streets away. The door from the cellar to the kitchen opened and shut; footsteps entered the kitchen; there was an unearthly grunt as if from a wild beast. Then a dull thud suggested something solid had been dropped onto the kitchen table. I concentrated on not moving, keeping utterly quiet.

A sudden shaft of electric light stabbed through the crack where I'd left the cupboard door slightly ajar and I could see the kitchen floor and the vegetable rack in the corner. Despite part of me being desperate for a glimpse of what was out there, another part recoiled, fearing what would be revealed. Even worse, if I could see out, then it could see in.

'Who's there?' asked Hobbes.

Hearing it, though some of my terrors subsided on the principle of 'better the devil you know', I didn't move, hoping he couldn't have heard me, that the disinfectant would mask my scent.

'I require an answer, and quickly.'

Holding my breath, not moving a muscle, as his footsteps approached my hidey-hole, I wanted to scream.

The cupboard door jerking open, I looked up to see him staring down, scowling.

'Good evening,' I said, forcing a friendly smile.

'What are you doing in there?'

'Umm … I don't know … I …'

'If you're worried about personal hygiene,' he said, wrinkling his nose, 'I'd suggest taking a bath rather than disinfecting yourself. Out you come.'

Squatting down, seizing an arm and a leg, he dragged me out, lifting me, letting me dangle while he examined me, like a butterfly collector with a dubious specimen. Apparently satisfied, he set me down, his scowl holding me as firmly as tweezers grip a butterfly. 'Would you care to tell me what you were doing in there?'

I had no choice but to tell him, my story erupting like pus from a pierced boil. 'I went for a walk in Ride Park but there was a panther, I think, and it patted me on the head and I came home and stayed down here with Dregs, because I was still frightened. I must have fallen asleep and I think he's gone to my bed now. And ... and then I heard something in the cellar and got scared again, scared something was coming for me.'

I felt a little better.

He nodded. 'What did you expect was coming from the cellar?'

'Umm ... I don't know but I thought something had come through ... that door.'

'I used the door. Now, tell me about the panther.'

I told him what I could, feeling powerless, something in his eyes compelling me to talk, though I had no intention of holding anything back.

His scowl relaxed into a frown, though it still held me tight. 'That's very interesting. You see, this evening, I was trailing a panther through Loop Woods and round Bishop's Farm. Since it couldn't have been in two places at once, there must be two panthers out there.'

'Did you catch the one you were after?'

'No, it gave me the slip. I haven't yet worked out how.'

'Did you actually see it?'

'I could smell it and I must only have been seconds behind. It's puzzling.'

His frown releasing me, I became aware that he was trying to stop me seeing whatever he'd lugged into the kitchen.

'But why did you come through the cellar?' I asked, trying, without making it too obvious, to catch a glimpse behind him, finding he was too close, blocking my field of view.

'That's police business,' he said, looking thoughtful. 'I need to examine something urgently and I want to examine it in my own way before anyone can tamper with it.'

'What is it?'

'Evidence.'

'Evidence of what?'

'I won't know until I've examined it. Now run along, you should be in bed.'

I tried to peep under his arm but his bulk blocked me.

His frown beginning to deepen once more, he stared into my eyes. 'You should be in bed. You must be feeling sleepy. Really sleepy.'

I nodded and yawned. Escorting me upstairs, he evicted a resentful Dregs from my bed. 'Sleep well,' he said, closing the door behind him, going back downstairs.

I undressed, put on my pyjamas and got into bed, certain sleep was out of the question, yet unable to keep my eyes open.

It felt as if I'd hardly lain down before I awoke. Getting up, I drew back the curtains, finding it was dull and grey outside, drizzle spattering the window. As usual, clean clothes had been laid out for me. I assumed Mrs G was responsible, though I'd never caught her at it. One day, I thought, I should thank her.

The stink of disinfectant was all over me, bringing the events of the previous night back into my head. I was still haunted by the panther's green eyes, again feeling the helpless terror as it had stalked me through the darkness. Worse memories returned, vague memories, almost as if I'd dreamt them: Hobbes emerging from the cellar, finding me cowering under the sink, questioning me. A horrific image squeezed back from when he'd pushed me from the kitchen and I'd glimpsed a reflection in the shiny bottom of a copper pan hanging on the wall. A man's body was lying on the kitchen table. Hobbes, I feared, had killed again. I wondered who his latest victim was, what he'd done.

Though unable to understand why he'd felt the need to bring the corpse home, it made me think of Whisky, the cat, who'd always done the same, usually keeping a little something for later; I'd once found a half-eaten rat under my pillow. Perhaps, I thought, Hobbes, too, liked to eat at leisure. The idea made me feel quite ill, yet I realised that, if he stored his leftovers behind the mysterious door, it was no wonder he didn't want me to see.

Yet, life had to go on and I was starving. So, steeling myself, rising above the ghastliness, I headed downstairs into the kitchen, where Dregs, bounding towards me with his usual morning enthusiasm, struck me as being a little wary, perhaps fearing I'd hug him again. Mrs Goodfellow, smiling, said 'Good morning', as I took my seat at the table.

Hobbes wasn't there. Neither was the corpse. Everything seemed so normal, I might have believed I'd dreamt the incident, had it not been for the lingering scent of disinfectant, nearly masked by the enticing aroma of the mushroom omelette Mrs Goodfellow was making. When she fed me, I found it as light as a cloud and utterly delicious, my appetite only slightly restrained by a nagging worry that Hobbes might not have scrubbed the table. It occurred to me, as I finished off the last bit of omelette and reached for the marmalade, that exposure to Hobbes had desensitised me. I doubted I'd have been so cool before my life in Blackdog Street.

After finishing breakfast, I helped Mrs G dry up, a rare event, but successful in that I didn't break anything and managed to locate the cutlery draw without prompting. We were chatting about the weather and pork chops when she told me she was going out to visit a dear old friend, who'd broken a leg falling off a trampoline.

'How old is she?' I asked.

'Eighty-eight.'

'Should she have been doing that at her age?'

'Well, dear, she's been doing it since she was sixty. Why stop when she enjoys it? I think her big mistake was jumping out the bedroom window to get a bigger bounce.'

'That sounds dangerous.'

'I suppose it does now you mention it, though it wasn't the big bounce that hurt her, but hitting the shed and landing on a pile of bricks. She's a silly old fool sometimes, I don't know how many times I've told her to get a proper landing mat, but she always knows best.'

As often occurred in conversation with the old girl, I was soon out of my depth. I tried a change of subject. 'Where's Hobbes this morning?'

'At work. He was out very early and had Sugar Puffs for breakfast again. I'm worried he's not eating enough.'

'I'm sure he won't starve,' I said, suppressing a grimace.

'You're probably right.' She sighed. 'Still, I'll get him a good, big, juicy rib-eye steak for his supper. You like a steak, too, don't you?'

I nodded.

'That's alright, then. Thank you for your help and I'd better be off to the hospital.'

Having wiped her hands on her pinafore, she put a lead on Dregs and left me on my own.

Though I tried to think pleasant thoughts, I kept returning to Hobbes and the hidden door. Sitting back at the kitchen table, I realised I had the perfect opportunity to investigate, yet, had no idea what dangers lay behind it, assuming there really were any. One way or another, I needed to confirm my suspicions, or prove them false. I began trembling, torn between curiosity and self-preservation. Standing up, I marched round the kitchen trying to dispel my nervous energy. To my surprise, finding myself holding the handle of the door down to the cellar, the conflict in my head still raging, I decided there could be no harm in merely taking a quick look. I pushed open the door, turned on the light and started down the creaking wooden steps, breathing in air as moist and cool as a cavern, amazed as always by the extent of the cellar. On reaching the bottom, I stood a moment, taking a deep breath, before walking onto the old brick floor, past the enormous wine racks, noticing no dust or cobwebs on any of the hundreds of bottles down there. Mrs G's devotion to cleanliness and order was soothing.

The door, as I'd expected, was hidden behind a pile of coal that gleamed as if it had been polished. I laughed at the very idea, before forcing myself to calm down and to be serious. I could see that, if I really wanted to have a look at the door, heavy spadework would be required, so, picking up the broad, heavy coal shovel propped against the wall, I put my back into the task. Though it wasn't long before I was sweating, taking a moment for a breather, I saw I'd uncovered the top of the doorframe, having shifted about a third of the coal. Taking off my shirt, hanging it on the pedal of a penny-farthing, quietly rusting in the corner, I set to work again. Blisters tingled on my palms and, after another ten minutes, I had to stop to wipe the sweat from my eyes. I gritted my teeth and kept digging.

I was gasping for breath, a little light-headed, by the time I completely uncovered the door. After a moment's triumph, came a horrible moment when, cursing my stupidity, I realised I'd have to shift the whole lot back again. My plan, if I'd had one, was to get the coal out of the way, open the door, take a swift shufti and get the hell out of there, leaving no trace. Things had already gone awry, since I'd lost track of time, having no idea how long the old girl had been away, or when Hobbes would return. However, since I'd gone so far, I reckoned I might as well carry on and open it.

I reached out, taking the cold brass door knob in a shaking hand and turning it. Nothing happened and though I tried pushing and tugging, it was clear the door was locked.

'Bugger it!' I muttered, performing a stamping, fist-shaking dance of frustration, culminating in a wild kick at the door. It didn't help and, as I hobbled away, swearing like a bastard, I was glad Hobbes couldn't hear me.

'Right, Andy,' I said out loud, 'you've screwed this up right and proper. What are you going to do now?'

'Shut up and think,' was the answer.

Sitting on the coal, I thought: if the door was locked, then there had to be a key, a key that, perhaps, Hobbes kept hidden down there. Since taking a few minutes to search for it would make little difference to the mess I was in, since my only other option was to admit defeat, to shovel the coal back and walk away still ignorant, I started looking. The old Andy would no doubt have followed the second option but I'd developed into sterner stuff under Hobbes's tutelage.

I searched everywhere, trying to use my intelligence to work out where anyone might conceal a key. I looked under piles of flowerpots, through a cupboard full of ancient paint tins, even pulled a couple of loose bricks from the wall, without any luck. At last, in despair, making a decision to give up, to abandon my stupid plan, a feeling of utter relief surged through me. Dry of mouth, needing a glass of water, I walked slowly towards the steps, heading for the kitchen, hoping I'd have sufficient time and strength to shift all the coal back, to clean myself up, so no one would be any the wiser.

I didn't quite make it to the kitchen, for, hanging in plain view from a nail beneath the light switch, was a large black key. My stomach lurching, my heart thumping, I reached for it and picked it up. It was as long as my hand, weighty and old-fashioned. Taking it to the door, fitting it in the keyhole, I turned it. Its motion was smooth, silent, well lubricated, unnerving since I was anticipating a gothic creak.

The door being heavy, I had to lean against it, shoving hard until, just as I was about to give up, it swung open. I would have plummeted straight down the narrow flight of worn stone steps had I not grabbed a rusting rail, which supported me until it snapped. Stumbling forward, losing my footing, I landed hard on my bottom and slipped into the darkness, bumping and grazing my elbows on the way. Though I managed to regain my footing before the end of the stair, my momentum carrying me forward, I ran into a wall, knocking the wind out of me, making me fall backwards into a couple of inches of icy water. Gasping as it soaked my overheated body, I stood up, cracking the top of my head on something hard, falling back into the puddle, cursing and nursing what felt like a fine collection of bruises and scrapes.

As the shock and pain receded, I started to make sense of wherever I was. I groped back to where I could stand up safely, the reek of ancient stone and damp all pervasive, the only light, the feeble and distant remnants that made it down the narrow steps from above. I was in a tight, bare passageway, leading, so far as I could tell, towards the town. Since I'd got so far, self-esteem insisted on investigating a little more. I took a few steps forward, my hands held out like a mummy from a horror film.

I was sopping wet, my trousers clinging to my skin, shivering, more with nerves than with cold. Although the floor was smooth and regular, occasional projections from the wall proved dangerous and painful to my elbows. After no more than a dozen steps, finding myself in utter blackness, having gone far enough to satisfy honour, if not curiosity, I glanced back over my shoulder to reassure myself that I could still see the faint light from the cellar.

Unable to see anything, anything at all, my nervousness multiplied. Though reason suggested the passage was not quite straight, or, maybe, that the door had swung shut, I was gripped by a sudden horror that I might wander off into a maze of passages. Turning round, taking a step forward, I smacked straight into a solid wall. Sliding down onto my side, I lay stunned on the rocky floor and, by the time my head cleared, I'd lost any sense of direction.

Since the total silence amid the blackness was oppressive, I spoke out loud to myself. 'C'mon, Andy, stay cool and think. There are only two ways to go: backwards or forwards. If you take about twelve careful paces you'll be back at the steps, or if not, you'll be twelve paces further into the tunnel. If that's the case, all you have to do is turn again and take twenty-four paces and you'll be out. It's quite simple.'

I did my best to ignore the small voice in my head saying, 'What if there's more than one tunnel down here? Then you've had it. It'll serve you right, too; he told you not to come down here.'

The small voice made me forget to count. 'No problem,' I said to myself. 'Just count to twelve and, if there's still nothing, turn around and count up to, let's say twenty and then we'll be out. No problem.'

Having counted out twelve steps, all I could see, or rather, couldn't see, was darkness. The tunnel feeling like it might have widened, I made sure to keep my left hand against the wall. In the distance, a long way off, I thought I could hear running water.

'Oh well, that was the wrong way,' I said in a brave voice. 'About turn and you'll soon be out.'

I turned, groping along the opposite wall, counting out each step with a cheerful boy-scout optimism I didn't feel. I'd counted to fifteen when, reaching a dead end, my heart went into a frenzy of pounding, my breathing growing harsh and rapid. Trying to force myself to stay calm, I tried to think, aware that blind panic was lurking, ready to overrun any remaining good sense.

'There must be another tunnel,' I said. 'If I work my way back, I'll be able to find where I went wrong.' The trouble was, I didn't believe me.

Sometime later, I realised I'd been right not to believe me. Having no idea where I was, or to where I was heading, I just kept walking, on the dubious grounds that, sooner or later, I'd find a way out. The small voice in my head said, 'You've really done it, you've got yourself well and truly lost and I hope you're satisfied. Well done. You're in the labyrinth and you didn't even bring any string.'

Snippets of Greek mythology, learned at school, in particular, something about a Minotaur that lived in a similar place, devouring human flesh, kept flashing into my mind, the sort of memories I could have done without, for my imagination was already in full swing. The thing was, Hobbes, though warning of dangers behind the door, hadn't specified what they might be and I was conjuring up monsters, the sort previously only seen in nightmares, to scare me half to death. Since running was out of the question, I sat down on the hard stone floor, taking a breather, regretting my failure to get that glass of water for, by then, I would have been glad to drink from the puddle at the bottom of the staircase. Even in the midst of my terror and despair, I recognised that was a stupid idea, because, if I found the puddle, I'd be able to go to the kitchen. I listened for the running water I thought I'd heard, however long ago that had been, yet all I could hear was my own breathing.

Sitting there, calming myself, I wondered what on earth, or rather, below earth the tunnels were. I wasn't aware of any mine workings in the area and wondered if they could have been smugglers' tunnels, or part of an elaborate wartime bomb shelter, or maybe I was in one of those places where dead bodies were stored. What were they called? Catamarans? Something like that. Catacombs – that was the word. What a perfect place to hide a body.

I shouldn't have gone down there.

Vile images entered my mind, as bright as if I could really see them, of grinning skulls and heaps of rotten bones, and Hobbes sitting in the middle, chewing on some bit of somebody. Yet, I couldn't smell decay, which was some comfort. All my nose could detect was damp, soil and my own sweat. I was shivering, goose pimples erupting on my skin, teeth chattering, so I got to my feet, needing to keep walking or die of hypothermia. Anyway, I was bound to come across something eventually.

I couldn't stand much more of the darkness and the silence.

In fact, it wasn't quite silent. Something was moving, something I hoped wasn't rats, because there was nothing worse than rats, except for something bigger and fiercer. Whatever it was, it didn't sound as small as a rat: not by a long way.

Surely there wasn't another panther? Was it possible I'd stumbled into their daytime hideaway? But then, Hobbes would have known about it already, unless they were what he was hiding. Nothing made sense in that blackness, in my state of rising terror.

The noise getting louder, sounding horribly like paws, I held my breath, on the edge of blind panic, hearing something sniffing, something not far away. My nerves, or what was left of them, unable to take any more, I turned to flee, knowing it was hopeless.

'Stop! Stop right there!' said a voice that could not be disobeyed. 'Do not take another step. Stay exactly where you are.'

I stopped, terror giving way to fearful, almost tearful, relief.

'I'm lost,' I said, looking back over my shoulder, a futile thing to do in the blackness.

'Of course you are,' said Hobbes. 'Now do as I say, exactly as I say.'

'Alright.' My voice was surprising in its pitch, its feeble lack of timbre.

'Do not turn around. Take a step backwards ... now another ... and another ... one more ought to do it. Now you can turn around, and put your right hand against the wall ... your right hand! That's it. Now walk towards me, and slowly.'

I turned towards his voice, reassured by its calm authority, though the fear of whatever was behind goaded me into a scurry.

'Stop there,' he said, 'do not put your foot down.'

'Why not?' I gulped, keeping it raised.

'Because you'll tread on the dog.'

A cold nose pressing into my left hand, I stroked Dregs's head, safe for the first time since I'd lost my way. Hobbes's hand touched my shoulder.

'You shouldn't have come down here,' he said, 'there are more dangers than you can possibly imagine.'

'Like what?'

'Now is not the time for questions,' he said looping a length of cord around my neck. 'Follow me.'

The cord tightening, I followed, like a small child on a harness and, just like a child, I felt secure, wondering why, though I feared I was in for a severe telling off, I had no concerns about my well-being. There'd been no anger in his voice, only concern, and my suspicion that he'd murdered Henry Bishop and others no longer mattered; he was still my friend, someone I could rely on. It wasn't a ruthless application of logic that led me to this conclusion, it was just a feeling; sometimes feelings are worth more than logic.

Though Dregs's paws pattered quietly as we twisted and turned through the blackness, my feet scuffed and clattered, as I tripped and stumbled in the rear. Of Hobbes, other than a light pressure on my neck and the usual faint, feral odour, I could discern nothing, except on the occasions when he paused to sniff. I didn't care, so long as I got out of that horrible place, where the weight of aeons of darkness was crushing me, the unseen walls squeezing too tightly.

At last, so faint at first I doubted my own eyes, I began to see Hobbes's silhouette. As the outline sharpened, I could make out Dregs, padding to heel, two steps in front. Eventually, I could see my own hands, and then, a moment of bliss, the doorway. Though I longed to rush up the steps, to put the dark behind me, I had to climb up at Hobbes's steady, deliberate pace, until, at last, I was blinking in the dim light of the cellar. The dog yawned and shook himself, apparently sharing my feelings of relief as Hobbes shut and locked the door, pocketing the key.

'Thank you for getting me out of there,' I said, as a thought struck. 'Umm … how would you have opened the door if I hadn't already moved the coal?'

'Quite easily. Now, you'd best get upstairs, get washed and make yourself respectable. We need to have a little chat, but it can wait till we've had some grub.'

Looking at myself, I was staggered how black, streaked and filthy I was.

As he picked up the shovel, shifting the coal back, I climbed the stairs to the kitchen, a flutter of butterflies taking wing in my stomach at the prospect of the little chat. Dregs bounded after me, pushing past at the top.

'Have you been having fun, dear?' asked Mrs Goodfellow, who was slicing bread at the table, apparently unsurprised by my appearance.

'It wasn't fun. I got lost.'

'Well, at least you didn't tumble into the bottomless pit of doom, or worse. Never mind, dear, you'll find clean clothes in your room.'

'Thank you,' I said, turning towards the stairs.

'But you'd better take those filthy things off first. I'm not having you messing up anywhere else. Anyone would think you've been rolling around in the coal.'

'But …'

'But nothing. Hurry up.' She gave me what passed for her stern look.

Hobbes emerged from the cellar without a speck of dirt on him, having taken all of two minutes to put the coal back.

'C'mon, Andy,' he said, 'clean yourself up, and quickly. I'm famished.'

Giving up, I stripped to my underpants, which apparently passed muster for she nodded. 'Now hurry up. Dinner will be ready when you are.'

'Just one thing,' she said as I turned away, 'that young lady of yours called round when you were out.'

'Really?'

'Yes, really. Now move yourself.'

Although I hesitated, wanting to find out more, Hobbes's expression moved me on. My insides had been twisting themselves into knots at the prospect of the impending little chat, yet the mere thought of Violet blew away my immediate fears, as I tried to work out why she'd come round. It was hardly likely she wanted to see more of me, unless I'd misjudged everything. As hope sprouted, so did a sudden horror, for the old girl had said she'd called round, but hadn't actually said she'd left and the idea of her seeing me streaked with dirt and sweat, wearing only a pair of Y-fronts, made me cringe. Adopting stealth mode, creeping like a cat, I peeped nervously into the sitting room, as Dregs pushed past, making a circle of the room, sniffing and acting in an unusually manic way, before rushing back into the kitchen. I wasn't entirely sure if I was relieved or disappointed to find her gone.

I went upstairs and ran a bath. I was amazed how much black muck sloughed off me as I scrubbed away, using Mrs Goodfellow's long-handled back scrubber and a bar of soap. I had to change the water twice before it stayed reasonably clear. Afterwards, having dried myself and made some sort of effort to clean the bath, without completely removing the dark ring, I dressed and went downstairs.

For once, I didn't pay much attention to my lunch, though the crusty ham sandwiches didn't deserve such negligence. The problem was that, as the time for my little chat with Hobbes grew closer, my mouth was becoming as dry as talcum powder, despite the sluicing of a couple of pints of ginger beer down my throat. I wanted it to be all over, even if I really didn't want it to start, and he seemed to be lingering over his meal, as if he had all day. Though part of me wanted to urge him to hurry up, I suspected the waiting wouldn't be the worst part. At last, dabbing his lips with a napkin, he rose to his feet.

'Let's go through to the sitting room,' he said. 'I think some explanation is in order.'

I followed him, quaking. He appeared calm, but that meant little.

'Take a seat,' he said, indicating the near end of the sofa, planting his big backside on the far end. 'Make yourself comfortable.'

Nodding, I attempted a smile as, sighing, he rested his feet on the coffee table, just as Mrs Goodfellow came in with the tea. As she tutted, he shifted his feet onto the carpet with a sheepish grin.

'Thanks, lass,' he said as she returned to the kitchen.

'Now, then, Andy,' he said turning towards me, piling sugar into his mug, 'a few months ago, I told you not to use that door and I believe I suggested you would do better to forget all about it. Is that correct?'

I gulped, nodding.

Having stirred his tea with his finger, he took a long slurp and continued. 'Since it is often dangerous to seek out secrets, my intention was to instil such fear into you that you wouldn't dream of going in there. I thought, as the months went by, that it had worked.'

'It had,' I said, my voice a croak. 'Nearly.'

'I had good reasons, for there are untold dangers down there, dangers it would have been better for you to remain ignorant of. Unfortunately, I failed to take into account human curiosity. It was remiss of me and I apologise.'

I grunted, the little chat failing to live up to expectations.

'It must have been difficult to restrain yourself for so long. Was there something in particular that made you look?'

It was a tricky question and I squirmed before answering. 'Well, it was like this … umm … it was last night.'

'I see. Anything in particular?'

I was too bewildered to lie. 'The body you brought in.'

'I'd hoped I'd concealed it.'

'I saw the reflection.'

'I expect,' he said, 'that you want to know why I brought it back here?'

'Yes.' I nodded. 'Who was it and why?'

'You didn't recognise him?'

I shook my head. 'I only caught a glimpse.'

'It was the late-lamented Henry Bishop.'

'Oh … but why?'

'Because I needed a really close look at the body before the pathologist mucked it up and it was easier to fetch him back here than to conceal myself in the morgue.'

'But how did you get him out of the morgue?'

'The tunnels run right across town and beyond. One of them goes by the morgue and there's a very useful manhole cover in the basement that allows access. Since hardly anyone even knows about the tunnels, I sometimes use them to move about without being observed, something I think is essential at the present.' Finishing his tea in one draught, he wiped his lips with the back of his hand.

'What's so special about the present?' I asked.

'I've sensed someone watching me. I don't know who yet, or why.'

'I see but ... umm ... why did you want to examine Henry Bishop's body?'

'I wanted to know what killed him.'

'Why didn't you have a look when you were at the restaurant?'

I experienced the rare pleasure of making Hobbes start. 'You saw me?'

'Yes and there was blood all over you and ... and when you disappeared, I thought you'd ... well, I didn't know what to think.' I still didn't and my nervousness returned.

'Ah!' he said. 'That explains it; I thought something was bothering you. Alright, I'll tell you what happened. If you recall, I was looking for Henry, following the incident with the Bashem's lad. It turned out he was a surprisingly good woodsman but I got onto his trail in the end and was only a few minutes behind when something crossed his path.'

'What?'

'A big cat that got to Henry before I could. Though he fired both barrels of his shotgun, it was to no avail and it attacked him. Managing to break away, bleeding badly, he made a run for the restaurant. I got some of his blood on me as I followed through the bushes.'

His explanation relaxed me enough that I was able to take a sip of tea. 'Umm ... why didn't you help him?'

'Because I hoped he'd be safe in the restaurant and believed it would be better to apprehend the cat before it caused any more trouble.'

'Shouldn't you have waited for backup? It might have been

dangerous. And what happened?'

He frowned. 'Unfortunately, it gave me the slip, almost as if it had vanished. It was most peculiar and, since then, I've been aware of being watched from time to time. Since I'd venture to suggest such behaviour is unusual for a cat, it must be a person.'

'Why would anyone watch you? And why can't you catch the cat? It can't really vanish.'

'I don't know. It's a mystery.'

I scratched my head for Hobbes rarely admitted ignorance, and asked another question that had been bugging me. 'What are the tunnels for? Who made them?'

'I'll tell you what I can,' said Hobbes, 'but I'm no expert on tunnelling. I discovered them by chance many years ago while searching for a lost farthing. They are, I believe, ancient and, I suspect, may pre-date human settlement in this area. However, there are extensive crypts under the church that may have been part of the tunnels once upon a time.'

'Any idea who did make them?'

'Not for sure, but something still lives down there. I've picked up their scent now and again but I can't categorise it. I just think of them as troglodytes and if I use their tunnels I make sure to leave a gift of meat in payment. It always goes, and goes quickly.'

'Troglodytes? Do you think they're dangerous?'

'Probably, though they've never bothered me and, since they do not, to my knowledge, commit any crimes and, since they evidently don't wish to meet me, I leave them be. They are not the only dangers, though. You were right on the edge of a shaft when I found you. Two more steps and you'd have dropped right in.'

I shivered and, the phone warbling suddenly, spilled tea down my shirt. Fortunately it had cooled.

Hobbes shook his head. 'You'll need another clean shirt and it's still only two o'clock.' Chuckling, he reached for the phone.

'Inspector Hobbes,' he said, 'how can I help you? ... Yes, he is here. Would you like to talk to him? Right you are.' He winked at me. 'It's for you.'

10

Since no one ever rang me, I took the phone from Hobbes feeling confused.

'Hello?'

'Hi, Andy, it's me.'

'Violet?' My heart dancing ecstatically, I broke into a sweat. 'I wasn't expecting you.'

'Who were you expecting?'

She sounded a little hurt.

'No one. I just thought after ... well ... after last time you'd probably want to forget all about me.'

'It was hardly your fault, was it?'

'No ... but I just thought ...'

'I called round this morning, but Mrs Goodfellow said you were out. Didn't she say?'

'Well ... yes, she did. Umm ... I'm glad you've called.'

'Thank you. Did you go anywhere nice?'

'No, I got lost.'

'Where?'

Hobbes shook his head.

'I don't know ... I just found myself lost, if that makes any sense. I'm found now.'

'Good,' she said with a gentle laugh, 'because I was wondering if we might ... er ... meet again. If that's alright with you?'

'Umm ... OK,' I said. 'If you'd like.'

'Oh, you don't have to if you don't want.'

It dawned on me that my response might have suggested a lack of enthusiasm. The only excuse I could make was that I'd still been reeling from Hobbes's revelations when the surprise of hearing her voice had knocked me off balance; it was a good thing I still had the wits to realise in time. 'Sorry, that didn't come out quite the way it should have. What I mean is, I'd really like to see you again.'

'That's good, because I'd love to see you, too.'

My heart leapt. 'That's great ... fantastic. Umm ... when?'

'How about tomorrow afternoon? I finish at four on Fridays so I could come round straight after.'

I paused, as if checking through my varied appointments. 'Umm ... yeah, that sounds fine. What would you like to do?'

'I don't know,' she said, hesitantly. 'What would you like to do?'

'I don't know either ... umm,' I replied, my mind completely out of ideas.

'How about,' said Hobbes in what he evidently meant as a whisper, 'going to the pictures or for a picnic?'

'Good ideas,' said Violet. 'Are you alright? Your voice sounded hoarse.'

'I'm great. It wasn't my voice, but it was a good idea.'

'Which one?'

'Both, I suppose.'

'I'll just check the forecast,' said Violet, clicking computer keys. 'It says the rain's going to pass, so a picnic could be good fun.'

'Yes,' I agreed, 'so long as we steer clear of Loop Woods, with things being what they are.'

'I'll second that. Where would you suggest?'

She had me there. I caught myself 'umming', a bad habit I was occasionally guilty of. I just couldn't think of anywhere suitable.

'How about the arboretum?' said Hobbes.

'Umm ... how about the arboretum?' I said.

'Why not? Where is it?'

'Umm ...' I glanced at Hobbes for inspiration.

'The other side of Hedbury. About a ten-minute drive.'

I relayed the message, including an appropriate adjustment for normal driving. 'It's the other side of Hedbury. That's probably twenty minutes by car.'

'It sounds ideal. I'll come round just after four.'

'Sounds great ... umm ... but what about food?'

'Oh yes,' she said, laughing again, 'I'd forgotten that. I suppose we could just pop into a supermarket and pick up a few things. Anyway, I've really got to go now; I've got emails to send. I'll see you tomorrow. Bye.'

'Great,' I said, 'I'm looking forward to it. Bye.'

Putting the phone down, amazed, I turned towards Hobbes. 'She's going to pick me up tomorrow at four.'

'Who is, dear?' asked Mrs G, coming in from the kitchen, sagging beneath the weight of the sledgehammer on her shoulder.

'Violet is,' I said. 'We're going for a picnic at the arboretum.'

'Good for you, dear. I can make up a hamper if you'd like.'

'There's no need. We can get something from the shops.'

'You could,' she said, shaking her head, 'but I could make up something special.'

'I don't want to inconvenience you,' I said, thinking I ought to put on a little show of reluctance before accepting, for there was no doubt a spread she would rustle up would put any shop-bought stuff to shame.

'It won't be a problem, dear.'

'OK, then,' I said, as if doing her a favour, 'I'd be delighted.'

'I know,' she said, smiling, stumping upstairs, dragging the sledgehammer.

I have no idea what she did with it for I heard nothing after her door shut. I sat back next to Hobbes, expecting to continue our little talk when the phone warbled again.

'Inspector Hobbes,' he answered, 'how can I help you? What? ... I see ... How many? Right, just the one? Are you sure? Yes, I suppose one is enough ... I'll be right over.' Slapping down the receiver, he turned to me and grinned.

'What's up?' I asked.

'It's not so much up as out.'

'Out? What's out, then?' I asked, puzzled by his gleeful expression.

'An elephant.' He rubbed his hands together, sounding like someone trying to grate a coconut shell, and pulled out his car keys.

'What?'

'You heard.'

'I know but I meant "why?" or "where?" I mean why is there an elephant out? Where is it? What's it doing?'

'I'll tell you in the car,' said Hobbes, 'if you'd like to come along ... Dregs!'

Rain pattering against the window, I grabbed my mac as the dog bounded past.

'Come along, and quickly,' Hobbes urged, opening the front door, leaping down the steps, looking like an excited child, if you could ignore his bulk and his hairiness and his large, lumpy head, which I couldn't.

Dregs and I followed, running through the puddles, flinging ourselves into the car as he drove away. Somewhere, a horn blared but he gave it no mind, unlike Dregs who barked at the challenge. As I strapped myself in, hanging onto the seat, I wondered again about the folly that kept me following Hobbes. Time and time again I'd argued with myself that I didn't have to but, whenever the call came, I responded before my brain had a chance to stop me. Still, going anywhere with him usually lead to excitement and, much to my surprise, part of me that had never before manifested itself found it irresistible.

'Right,' he said, twisting the wheel as we screeched into Pound Street, 'about the elephant.'

'Go on,' I said.

'Apparently, it was being transported from one zoo to another. When the driver stopped for a cup of tea at the Greasy Pole it escaped and is now running amuck in the car park.'

'How could it escape?'

'You have as much idea as I do.' The car swerved and speeded up.

'What are you going to do?'

'I don't know, yet.'

'Will there be backup?'

'Oh yes, Derek Poll is on the scene and, of course, I'll have you.'

'Oh, great.'

In a matter of minutes we were screeching to a halt by the Greasy Pole café where thirty or more gawping people had gathered. PC Poll's long arms were holding them back. An athletic-looking young man in a dark suit, towards the front of the crowd, appeared vaguely familiar, though I couldn't place him. Besides, I was more interested in the rogue elephant, which, though I couldn't see it, I could deduce, using the detective skills I'd picked up from Hobbes, had recently been in the vicinity. It had clearly been on the café's patio – all over it in fact – and by the time I was out of the car, Dregs was sniffing at the steaming dung as if at a rare perfume. I suspected, however, that the pile of pooh had not yet registered with Eric Wyszynski, the café's owner, who, dressed in his habitual stained white jacket, his scrawny, tattooed hands clasped to his greasy hair, was staring at what remained of his café, a pile of rubble having appeared where there'd once been a wall. He wasn't taking his misfortune well to judge from the river of obscenities spewing from beneath his nicotine-stained moustache.

The elephant had presumably escaped from the box-trailer in the car park, a trailer that was, in my opinion, far too small to hold one in comfort for any time and, to judge from the state of it, it had been inside for a considerable time. Though I took the scene in within a few seconds, the star of the show was missing.

'Where is it then?' I asked.

In response, Hobbes, wrapping an arm around me, leaped

backwards, completely over the car, landing on the grass verge behind. The shock, knocking the wind out of me, I was still struggling for breath as he set me back on my feet. Then, with a trumpeting and the pounding of heavy feet, the elephant lumbered over the spot where I'd been standing, heading directly towards the onlookers who scattered like dry leaves in the wind. Only one elderly man, standing beneath a black umbrella, didn't move a muscle. It was Augustus Godley, the oldest human in Sorenchester, who was still hale and well, despite the slowness of age.

As the elephant pounded towards him, I thought he'd had it, for I couldn't see how even Hobbes could rescue him in time. Yet, he didn't need to, for the beast, swerving, ran across the road, causing a big blue car to brake sharply and a small white one to run into the back of it. Neither driver got out as the elephant trundled into a meadow by the side of the river Soren.

'Are you alright?' I asked, running towards the old man, who was wearing a strange smile.

'Aye, lad,' he said, 'I'm grand. This takes me back to the time I was in India, when I had to shoot an elephant in my pyjamas.'

'Really?'

'How it got into my pyjamas, I'll never know.' A thin laugh wheezed between his lips.

'C'mon, Andy,' Hobbes shouted. 'And quickly, this is no time for listening to Mr Godley's jokes. There's an elephant to catch.'

'How? Won't you need a tranquilliser gun?'

'Let's hope not.'

'Oh, great.'

He loped across the road and into the meadow. The elephant, standing in the river, drinking, watched, flapping his great ears.

'Now then, my lad,' said Hobbes, approaching the beast, 'let's be having you. By rights you should be in your trailer.'

The elephant, shaking his massive tusks, lobbed a trunk-full of mud.

Hobbes sidestepped it and continued. 'That's enough of your

nonsense.'

'Be careful, sir,' said PC Poll.

Hobbes looked back with a grin. 'Of course, but I'm sure Jumbo will come quietly.' As he reached for the elephant it shook its broad, grey head, seized him around the waist, lifted him high in the air and shook him like a terrier shakes a rat.

'An awkward customer, eh?' said Hobbes, dangling upside down over the river. With a grunt, he took the trunk in his hands, squeezing until, the elephant releasing him, he fell backwards into the river with a great splash and a yell. Jumping up in one fluid movement, grabbing a flapping ear, he half vaulted, half hauled himself onto the elephant's back. Dregs ran towards them, barking.

The great beast, taking fright, bolted along the river bed away from me, sending up curtains of foaming cappuccino-coloured water. Hobbes, somehow clinging to its back, despite the violent bouncing and scything attacks from its trunk, looked surprisingly small and vulnerable.

'Why doesn't he get down?' I muttered.

'He can't get down from an elephant,' said Augustus who, having shuffled to my side, was watching proceedings with a smile.

'Why not?' I asked, puzzled.

'Because, down comes from ducks.' He chuckled.

I groaned, staring at him. Hobbes might be killed any moment and all Augustus, an old friend of his, could do was make stupid, schoolboy jokes.

'I'd move, if I were you, sir,' cried PC Poll.

Dregs, tail between his legs, was rushing towards us, the elephant close behind, with Hobbes still clinging on, the grin on his face making him look like a child enjoying a free ride on the rollercoaster. PC Poll's advice seemed reasonable, so turning away, I fled. I'd only gone ten steps or so when, remembering Augustus, I hesitated, slowed, stopped and turned back. The elephant was again heading straight towards him, and I had no chance of reaching him in time. Since I could no longer see Hobbes, I assumed he'd fallen off. The elephant bellowed and wondering if, perhaps, he wasn't running quite so fast, reckoning I might just have a chance, I sprinted towards Augustus, who was watching calmly, unconcerned by the mountain of muscle bearing down on him. I reached him a moment before the elephant, still bellowing, came to a standstill, almost within touching distance.

Hobbes's voice rang out. 'Are you two alright?'

I still couldn't see him. 'We're fine,' I shouted. 'How about you?'

'A little wet.'

'Where are you?' I asked, peering along the river's sodden banks.

'Here.' His hand waved from behind the elephant, which was standing still, as if in deep thought.

In a slow and stately manner, it turned, stomping up the bank into the meadow, while Dregs bristled and growled from a safe distance. Hobbes, gripping its tail in one hand, seeming to have its undivided attention, guided it towards the trailer. I expected him to force it back inside. Instead, he shouted, 'Who's in charge of this poor animal?'

A stout, little man wearing greasy overalls and a faded denim cap, looking around, as if expecting to see someone, finally raised his hand. 'It looks like I am, guvnor. But I'm only the driver.'

'Alright,' said Hobbes, 'before he goes back, he needs feeding and I want the trailer cleaned out properly and a good supply of clean water and fodder put in. How long was he in there?'

'I don't know, guvnor, but I only picked him up a couple of hours ago.'

'Who was in charge before that?'

'I don't know. A bloke in a suit paid me five hundred quid to take the rig to Brighton Zoo. I only met him this morning.'

'Where did you pick it up?'

'At a service station, the other side of Birmingham. It took us the best part of two hours to get here. The bloke reckoned that, as it would take us another couple of hours to reach Brighton, it'd be a good idea to stop here and get a bite to eat. He said it was pretty good.'

I shuddered. In the past, having eaten at the Greasy Pole, I knew it wasn't good. Furthermore, Hobbes had hinted that he knew something about the place, something too horrible for my delicate ears. The only element in its favour was that it wasn't expensive.

'Where is the gentleman now?' asked Hobbes.

The little man shook his head. 'I wish I knew, guvnor. He hasn't paid me yet. All I know is that I was just sitting down with my burger and my mug of coffee when he says he has to step out, 'cause he's gotta make sure the elephant's alright. A couple of minutes later, all hell breaks loose, the wall comes down, the ceiling caves in, and we has to run for it.'

'I see,' said Hobbes. 'Do you know the gentleman's name?'

'I'm sorry.'

Hobbes sighed. 'Fair enough. Just get the trailer cleaned up and feed Jumbo.'

'Me? It's not my trailer. I'm just moving it.'

Hobbes growling, the little man ran up the ramp into the trailer, grabbed a bucket and shovel and set to work.

'I've got my hands full, Derek,' said Hobbes, turning to face Constable Poll, 'so would you ensure no one's been injured and then take statements from anyone who's got anything useful to say?' He beckoned me. 'Andy, find some food for this beast and plenty of it.'

'Umm … right. What do they eat?'

'Cabbage, bread, apples, bananas, carrots – that sort of thing. Try the kitchen. It looks like some of it's still standing.'

Eric appeared, wiping his eyes as if he'd been crying. 'He can't just go taking what he wants from my café.'

'Yes, he can,' said Hobbes. 'It would only go to waste otherwise. It's not like you're going to be in business for a while.'

Eric nodded unhappily and, oblivious to the rain, sitting on the kerb, sobbed like a broken man. Since I can't bear to see a grown man crying, I turned away and rummaged, finding several bags of white sliced bread, a bunch of browning bananas, a pile of cabbages and a crate filled with carrots, quite surprised to discover Eric could, apparently, have served vegetables with his stodge. Having piled a selection into a box, I hurried towards Hobbes, who was still holding the elephant's tail.

'Well done,' he said, 'but I believe that lot will do more good at the front end. He's quite calm now, but be careful.'

Plonking the box down in front of the elephant, I backed away, although I didn't feel in any danger. Picking up a carrot, it stuffed it into his mouth and, though I wasn't an expert, the way it tucked in suggested it hadn't been fed for far too long. As soon as it was absorbed in feeding, Hobbes released his grip, strolled round and patted its head. I noticed his thick, hairy toes were jutting from the ruins of his boots.

He followed my glance and shrugged. 'I appear to have worn out my boots. It takes a lot of leather to stop an elephant.'

The rain was still falling, Hobbes was soaked and splattered with mud – at least, I hoped it was mud – and I was nearly as wet, having, in all the confusion, never got round to donning my mac. We stood around, waiting until the elephant had eaten its fill, and the back of the trailer was nice and clean. Then Hobbes led it inside.

The stout little man, who answered to the name of 'arry, seemed a decent sort of bloke, who'd just been trying to earn a living and wasn't responsible for what had happened. Unfortunately, he couldn't give a detailed description of the man who'd employed him. All he could say was that his employer was young and fit, that he'd worn a dark suit and a blue tie emblazoned with a golden emblem. No one fitting the description could be seen, which didn't surprise me, for I wouldn't have wanted to take the blame had my elephant demolished a café.

It was one of those extremely rare occasions when I almost wished I was still working for the *Bugle*, for I couldn't yet see any reporters in the burgeoning crowd and wondered, for a moment, whether I might knock off a few hundred words to see how much Editorsaurus Rex Witcherley would pay for it. Yet, the prospect of having to face him again giving me the willies, I abandoned the idea.

Although Hobbes had the situation well under control, several police cars, two fire engines and an ambulance had rushed up, lights flashing. I couldn't blame them for wanting to be there, for it's not every day an elephant creates havoc in Sorenchester. With so many police officers attending, and the elephant happy and under control, there was no longer any reason for Hobbes to be there. So, leaving things in their hands, we left. I was glad to go, for I was shivering, dripping, sodden, and the rain was showing no signs of abating. As we walked towards the car, Dregs shook himself all over me and I was too wet to care. Even so, I was in a better state than Hobbes, for being dragged through a river by a rampaging elephant is one of the most effective ways of ruffling an individual's attire; his clothes had suffered almost as much as his boots.

For once, I didn't much mind his maniac driving, since it got us home quicker. When safely in the warmth, throwing off my soaked clothes, I wrapped myself in a dressing gown and drank hot tea, while he took first go in the bathroom, his roars suggesting he was enjoying his shower. When he'd finished, I took a long, hot and, as far as I was concerned, well-deserved bath. Afterwards, as if by magic, clean, fresh, dry clothes, nicely pressed and neatly folded, had appeared on my dressing table, while my soggy, dripping relics had vanished. Mrs G, I thought, was a marvel.

Going downstairs, I found Hobbes at the kitchen table, looking as clean and fresh as I felt. Dregs, on the other hand, having picked up on the idea of bath time, had wedged himself in the cupboard beneath the sink, and was resisting any attempts to remove him, until undone by Mrs G's low cunning. She dropped a scrap of meat into his bowl and, unable to control his hunger, he emerged, sealing his fate. Seizing him round the middle with her skinny arms, she carried him off to the bathtub of doom. To be honest, I didn't feel sorry for him, despite his hangdog appearance, having become convinced that he only exhibited token resistance for pride's sake and that, secretly, he rather enjoyed it.

I poured a fresh mug of tea and sat opposite Hobbes, who was staring out of the window in a manner suggestive of deep thought, or total paralysis. The rain having finally stopped, a glint of sunlight hinting the clouds were breaking up, a bird singing, I felt warm, relaxed and at peace with the world.

'Do you find it strange,' asked Hobbes, 'that someone would go to the bother and expense of transporting an elephant as far as Eric's café only to abandon it?'

I nodded. 'He must be bonkers – especially if he'd stopped there because he thought it was good. No one thinks the Greasy Pole is good.'

'Yet, according to Harry, the man had not acted at all strangely, other than being in possession of an elephant just outside Birmingham. And there's another thing, why would anyone come this way to get to Brighton? It's miles out of the way.'

'It just proves he's bonkers,' I said and shrugged. It didn't seem important.

'Maybe he is, as you say, bonkers. Yet the combination of events is striking. A mysterious young man offers to pay five hundred pounds, a generous sum for a few hours of work, to transport an elephant from Birmingham to Brighton. He then chooses a route taking them miles out of the way, stops at the Greasy Pole and steps outside for a minute, during which, the elephant, which is ravenous and bad-tempered, somehow escapes from a locked trailer and demolishes the café. By then our man is no longer to be seen. The whole scenario seems most unlikely.'

'Are you suggesting it wasn't an accident?'

'I think so. I asked one of the lads at the station to check who was supposed to be transporting an elephant to Brighton Zoo. He phoned back to say there isn't a zoo in Brighton. What's more, he'd checked round all the zoos within fifty miles of there and none of them was expecting an elephant.'

'That's very strange indeed, unless Harry got muddled up about where he was going.'

'Harry didn't strike me as a man who'd get muddled but, you're right, it is very strange, unless the man had a reason for letting an elephant loose at that particular spot. Perhaps, I'd better have a word with Eric and see if he's got any enemies.'

'He must have – anyone who's ever eaten there.'

Hobbes chuckled. 'I take your point but, really, I think a bad meal is unlikely to make anyone resort to such a bizarre scheme to get revenge, unless, of course, it killed someone. Mind you, that's unlikely. People are surprisingly resilient.'

'Isn't it weird,' I said, 'that this was another incident with a dangerous animal? It's like we've become infested with them.'

He nodded. 'It is unusual, even for Sorenchester, and I wonder if there might be a connection. I can't see any obvious link, but it's worth a little investigation.

'Right,' he said, standing up, 'I'd better go and see Eric. He's in hospital with shock so I'll go on my own; I don't want to alarm him. One more thing, Mr Catt at the Wildlife Park has agreed to look after Jumbo until things are sorted out. He's rather pleased.'

He walked away with a slight hobble. Even Hobbes wasn't entirely immune to elephants.

I sat at the kitchen table, staring into space, until Dregs, frenzied and exuberant, burst in on me. It was a hard job keeping him at a safe distance as he shook himself, trying his damnedest to rub his damp fur against my legs. Ending up in a sort of obstacle race round the kitchen, I found I was enjoying the chase almost as much as he was, and a cackling laugh from Mrs G, who'd appeared with a couple of grubby towels, suggested she appreciated the spectacle.

'Well, dear,' she said when we'd quietened down, 'have you any preferences for your picnic tomorrow?'

That was a poser. My memory stretched back to the rare occasions when mother had packed a picnic for a day on the beach or in the park. It had usually rained, or hailed, forcing us to spend long, gloomy hours in the steamy car, its plastic seats sticking to the backs of my bare legs, a faint aroma of vomit in the air. I'd been sick on the way to Great Aunt Molly's funeral and, although I'd only been sick on that one occasion, if repeatedly and profusely and, over the years, we'd had several cars, some with leather seats, the brain insisted on plastic seats and vomit. It also insisted on white bread and fish-paste sandwiches in greaseproof paper, packets of salt and vinegar crisps, which I didn't much like, and packets of cupcakes, which I loved, the whole lot being washed down with stewed, lukewarm tea from a tartan flask, a flask matching the rug on which we'd planned to sit.

In fairness to the past, I did recall an occasion when the sun had shone for us in a flower-strewn meadow beside a lazy river. I remembered the satisfying, rich, earthy aroma of the water, watching fish splash and jump, the way it all started to go wrong when father, smiling for once, biting down on a chocolate cup cake, was stung by a wasp. His tongue swelling up as big and purple as an aubergine, we had to pack everything away as quickly as possible and get him, groaning, back to the car, which had, in the meantime, been thickly plastered in pungent slurry by a careless farmer. I would never forget father's incoherent grunts of rage and pain as we rushed him to casualty. Since, so far as I could remember, that had been the Caplet family's most successful picnic ever, I began to panic about subjecting Violet to a similar fiasco and fretted, wondering if I should call the whole thing off, before any harm was done.

'Are you alright, dear?'

The old girl, interrupting my pondering, made me jump. 'Umm … yes. I'm alright, but I'm not sure what's best for a picnic.'

'Well, dear,' she said, her face crinkling with thought, 'how about a nice bit of cold beef? And there's some chicken in the fridge. I'll make a nice salad to go with it, and I could bake a veal and ham pie.'

'That sounds pretty good,' I said, my mouth beginning to water.

'That'll do for a start. Then I'll put in a crusty loaf and some biscuits, and I was thinking of baking a fruit cake.'

'Fantastic.'

'And some ginger beer and wine. How about hard-boiled eggs?'

'It sounds rather a lot,' I said, intending to impose some mild restraint, starting to worry about carrying it all. 'And that's without any fish-paste sandwiches.'

'I can do you some fish-paste sandwiches, if you really want.'

'No, please don't, but everything else sounds great!'

'Good,' she said, smiling. 'I haven't made a picnic since my old man went away and there's a nice hamper just gathering dust in the attic. I'll get it down after supper and make sure the mice haven't eaten it.'

'I can do that.'

'That's very kind of you, dear.'

'Not at all.' Since Hobbes had, at last, got round to fixing the loose planks in the attic, I was glad of any opportunity to look around up there, being half convinced that great treasures nestled among the piles of junk. 'I'll do it now, while I think about it.'

'Very good, dear. I think you'll find the hamper behind the trunk, the elephant's trunk that is, not the wooden one. That reminds me, Mr Goodfellow's old summer blazer is in the wooden one and you'll look really smart in it.'

'OK, then,' I said, turning away, heading towards the stairs.

The phone rang as I passed it. Hoping it might be Violet, I

lifted the receiver, my heart pounding.

'Congratulations,' said a disembodied voice, 'you have won a guaranteed major prize in the Lithuanian State Lottery.'

I slammed the phone down, muttering a curse under my breath as I walked upstairs. They'd got me once. Never again.

11

I stood at the top of the loft-ladder besides the enormous stuffed bear, which was either a former resident or something salvaged from a skip, depending on whether you believed Hobbes or Mrs Goodfellow. The stiletto beam of sunlight stabbing through a crack in the grimy window added little to the feeble glow of a naked light bulb; I waited as my eyes adjusted. Since Mrs Goodfellow, regarding the attic as Hobbes's space, rarely visited, there was a sprinkling of dust and dirt everywhere. Most of the floor was covered in tatty piles of clothes, bits of old bikes, nameless junk and a rusty steel rack, concealing dozens of Hobbes's paintings. In my uneducated opinion, he had genuine talent, yet it seemed to embarrass him and he didn't like to talk about it. I found his work oddly beautiful and deeply disturbing in equal measure. Besides the paintings, something else about the attic made me a little uneasy, yet, since he'd never said I shouldn't go up, at least since he'd made the flooring safe, I reckoned I was reasonably safe.

Spotting the old wooden trunk I wanted beneath a large cardboard box, I went towards it. As I moved the box aside, the bottom dropped out and hundreds of photographs fell to the floor. Kneeling down, annoyed, intending to pick them up, to put them back, I made the mistake of looking.

They were in rough chronological order, the early ones showing sepia or faded black and white images of Sorenchester, and it was strange to see horses and carts on streets that had otherwise changed little over the years. Hobbes appeared in some, usually in his police constable's uniform, a splendid moustache obliterating most of his mouth. After I'd shuffled through a few dozen, Mrs Goodfellow made her first appearance, though she wasn't Mrs Goodfellow then, but a small, solemn-faced girl. She'd once told me how Hobbes pulled her from the smouldering wreck of a house after a bomb had killed the rest of her family during the war. I wondered about her family, what her name had been then, where she'd lived, realising how little I knew about her, feeling guilty that I'd never bothered to ask.

Still, time was passing so I pressed on, carrying out a botched repair on the box, placing it on a crate, apparently one containing a magic lantern, and began piling everything back, dropping a large, brittle brown envelope, spilling a pile of colour prints. They were holiday snaps, a little out of focus, faded in the way excessive washing fades summer clothes. Hobbes had barely changed, except that he was sporting a magnificent pair of sideburns and looked very casual in jeans and a t-shirt. Mrs Goodfellow, looking disturbingly young and attractive, wearing a variety of scandalously short skirts and huge straw hats, was with a man in flared scarlet trousers and a paisley-patterned waistcoat, whose shoulder-length dark hair was tied to his forehead with a beaded band. I guessed, although it was hard to make out any distinguishing features behind the mass of facial foliage, that he was Mr Goodfellow. A youngish woman I couldn't identify, with protuberant eyes and a long pigtail, wearing a loose brown kaftan, appeared in many of the prints.

On the back of one, Mrs Goodfellow had written *The old fellow, Robin, Froggy and me – Monterey, California, 1967*. Remembering something about the famous festival there, I giggled at the idea of Hobbes and Mrs G hanging out with hippies. It seemed so wrong.

As I flicked through them, I noticed how Froggy – I assumed that was the young woman's nickname – was usually by Hobbes's side, often with a hand on his shoulder, making him look rather nervous, and couldn't help wondering what sort of relationship they'd had. He'd never mentioned her, being reluctant to talk about his past; I had an idea this was more because he lived his life in the present than because of any reticence. Still, I could ask Mrs G, who was always happy to talk about him; the problem was shutting her up once she'd started.

As I began putting the photos back, I noticed one of Hobbes, messing around in the woods, shirt off, exposing a chest as hairy as a gorilla's. The image, being vaguely familiar, I wished I could remember where I'd seen it before.

I must have been up there for over an hour before I actually got a move on, putting all the photos back, starting the search for the picnic hamper, which, though it wasn't difficult to spot, was a pain to reach because of all the boxes and piles of old-fashioned police uniforms and other obsolete clothing in the way. Hobbes might have made a decent living as a theatrical supplier, if any actors matched his girth and shape. I dug through, shifting wooden boxes overflowing with cups and shields, suggesting he'd been some sort of sportsman in his day and, though he didn't have the physique of a typical athlete, I'd never come across anyone as healthy or so strong.

I struggled with a musty, old canvas tent in my way, hauling it aside, revealing a rusty crate, bound with heavy chains and padlocks. A wave of horror pulsed through me, the hairs on the back of my neck stiffening, my heart racing, because, for some reason, an idea that I'd stumbled across the last resting place of Arthur Crud burst into my head, making me realise I still didn't entirely trust Hobbes. The thought wouldn't go away, even though I was probably being ridiculous, the crate looking as if it hadn't been disturbed for decades. Grabbing the hamper, I turned around, wanting to be downstairs as quickly as possible, nearly forgetting the blazer.

I hurried back towards the trunk and opened it, finding the blazer neatly rolled on top. It turned out to be one of those red, white and blue striped affairs, not my style at all, yet possessing a certain je ne sais quoi, though I wasn't sure quite what it was.

Grabbing it, I shut the lid and hastened towards the ladder.

'Hurry up, Andy,' Hobbes yelled from below, 'supper's ready.'

Catching my foot on something, overbalancing, I fell headfirst through the hatch, dropping my cargo. He caught me by the ankles.

'Thank you,' I said, grateful and uncomfortable if not especially shocked.

'I take it,' he said, flipping me the right way up, 'that you're hungry?' He set me down on the carpet and picked up the hamper and blazer.

'I am rather,' I said. 'I didn't realise I'd been up there so long.'

'Well you have, it's nearly half-past six and the lass is about to dish up rib-eye beef steaks. So wash your hands and come along, and quickly, because I'm starving.'

Doing as I was told, I tried to clear my mind, tried to convince myself I'd been imagining things. After all, why would he keep a body in a crate in his attic when he had all those tunnels? Disgusted with myself because, though he'd just saved me once again, I didn't entirely trust him, I resolved to try to be fair.

The aroma of frying steak and onions percolating upstairs proving far stronger than mere self-disgust, I headed for the kitchen, pondering how, since I'd been staying at 13 Blackdog Street, I'd always eaten so well and so much and yet my waistline had shrunk. I put it down to all the exercise, though nervous terror might also have played a role.

After the truly delicious, succulent rib-eye steaks with onions and wonderful crispy, fluffy chips, with a mug of tea in my hand and a satisfying fullness in my belly, I sat on the sofa, where Hobbes was deep in thought.

'How's Eric?' I asked.

'Eric? He's still undergoing treatment for shock. They tell me he'll be alright but he's not happy.'

'Well, you wouldn't be happy if an elephant had demolished your café.'

'I don't have a café anymore, but I take your point. Apart from swearing, he was almost speechless, yet I got the impression something was worrying him. Yes, I know an elephant demolishing his means of livelihood would worry him, but I had the notion there was more.'

'What d'you mean?'

'He seemed uneasy, as if he might be scared of something.'

'Or somebody,' I suggested, wondering if the reason for Eric's discomfiture might be sitting beside me.

'Or someone,' he agreed. 'What made you suggest that?'

'Umm … I don't know really,' I said, the familiar heat of a blush rising around my ears. It reminded me of the time Editorsaurus Rex overheard me calling him a fat, dozy prat. The consequences still made me cringe.

Hobbes took my remark at face value. 'Oh, well, I wondered if something had occurred to you, too. You see, I have a hunch the elephant incident was deliberate.'

'But why?' I asked, filled with scepticism. 'I can understand anyone getting upset with Eric, but using an elephant to get back at him is ridiculous. It must just have been a bizarre accident.'

'That's what everyone at the station says,' said Hobbes. 'They reckon it would be too complicated, too expensive and too ludicrous for anyone to go to the trouble of transporting an elephant merely to annoy Eric. Maybe they're right, or maybe that's what someone wants us to think. In any case, Eric is refusing to talk and I haven't been able to persuade him: the nurses were keeping too close an eye on me. I need to think.'

I would have liked to ask more but, turning on the television, he sat back, relaxing, apparently enthralled by the black and white cowboy film. I watched for a while until, a cougar attacking the hero, I got the heebie-jeebies and retreated to the kitchen.

Mrs Goodfellow, sitting at the table, having washed and polished bits of cutlery and wine glasses until they glittered, was replacing them in the picnic basket. 'I'm making sure everything's ready for tomorrow, dear,' she said, her false teeth grinning from the yellow duster by her side. They gleamed as bright as the cutlery.

'Thank you. That's very kind.'

'Not at all, it's nice to find a use for the old basket. It brings back such memories; my husband bought it for me when we were in America.'

'Oh, yeah,' I said, 'I found some photos of you in America in the attic.'

'Happy days!' she said. 'At least they were happy for Mr Goodfellow and me, but the old fellow found it tough going.'

'It couldn't have been too bad; it looked as if he'd got himself a girlfriend.'

Mrs G frowned. 'She got him more like, and took advantage of him.'

'Really?' I asked, sniggering at the revelation. 'Shouldn't she have made an honest man out of him?'

'He always was honest. I mean she took advantage of his generous nature.'

'How?'

'She lied to him, making up stories of her hard, tragic life until he felt obliged to take care of her, sorting out her debts, giving her money he couldn't afford to lose. She was a nasty piece of work.'

'Was she called Froggy because of her eyes?'

'No.'

'She wasn't French was she?'

'No, dear, it was because she caught flies with her tongue, a very nasty habit, if quite useful in a field full of hippies.'

'You're having me on. Aren't you?'

She grinned. 'Actually, we called her Froggy because of her voice.'

'Wasn't that a bit mean?'

'I suppose so, but it was what her friends called her. Others called her "the Leech", which was as fitting a name as you could hope for.'

'What was her real name?'

'She said it was Enola-Gaye Johnson, but I think she

was lying.'

'What happened to her?'

'I don't know. When the old fellow's money ran out she ran out too and we never saw her again, for which I, for one, was grateful. She'd left him so low on money he had to get a job.'

'What did he do? Detective work?'

'No, he got into the movies.'

'A film star?'

'He was hardly a star, dear. He was an extra.'

'Was he in anything?'

'Just one film, dear. He played a gorilla in *Planet of the Apes*.'

'Quite a stretch for him, then,' I said. I don't think she got the joke.

'Not so much as you might think, because he had acted before, playing the bear in the Sorenchester Players' production of *A Winter's Tale* in '62 and he was in their production of Frankenstein, though I can't remember what he played.'

'He must be a talented actor.' I smiled. 'And it's amazing he never became a star.'

'Maybe he would have been,' she said, 'if it hadn't been for the incident in the woods.'

'What was that?' I asked.

'It was so hot, we'd been skinny-dipping in a beaver lake,' she said, blushing, 'thinking no one else was around. After a while, the old fellow noticed a racoon rummaging around in our things and ran over to make sure it didn't do any damage, not realising he'd been spotted by a cameraman. Next thing we knew, he was headline news. They thought they'd filmed Bigfoot.'

'They thought Hobbes was Bigfoot?' I said, faking amazement, remembering the snippet of film I'd seen on the telly, understanding why the photo of him in the woods had looked so familiar.

'Yes, dear, which was quite ridiculous, because he looks nothing like Bigfoots. Or are they Bigfeet?'

'So you know what Bigfoot looks like?' I asked, chuckling.

'Of course, dear, we stayed with some for a few days. They're very nice, if a bit smelly.'

Once again my view of the world had widened. Of course, it was possible she was having me on but I didn't think so, being quite astute about such things. I'm not sure which concept my brain found it hardest to accept: Hobbes in a Hollywood movie, or the old girl staying with Bigfoot. Thinking about it gave me a headache and I turned in early.

I was enjoying the picnic with Violet, lying next to her in a sun-drenched clearing, when she stood up, saying she was hot and needed to cool off in the lake, the lake that had mysteriously replaced the trees. As I watched her walking, naked, into the water, wondering where my own clothes had gone, I ran forward, my feet becoming entangled in delphiniums, and fell, splashing and thrashing. When I was able to stand upright, I hugged her, amazed how strong and hairy she'd become, appalled to see it wasn't her anymore. Somehow, I'd got hold of Bigfoot and, pushing the beast away, I fled towards the shore, only running into deep water, where green-skinned girls licked up flies and croaked. Hobbes appeared in the trees riding an elephant, while Dregs snarled as he gnawed on a rotting corpse he'd dragged from a hole in the ground.

I woke up, refreshed if confused by the vivid dream, got up and drew back the curtains. Since brittle sunlight filled the room, it looked as though the weather forecasters had got it right; not that I relied on them, for Hobbes's predictions were far more accurate. Looking out on the day, my stomach lurched as hope, excitement and terror collided, remembering that, in only a few hours, Violet was going to take me on a picnic.

Still, a few nerves, the odd butterfly in my stomach, were not enough to put me off breakfast. Going down, I discovered Hobbes had eaten hours ago, and Mrs G was preparing scrambled eggs for me, scrambled eggs as yellow as primroses, as light and fluffy as … in truth, I doubted I'd ever eaten anything so light and delicious, except possibly her cheese soufflé, which, in my opinion, she didn't make often enough. Mind you, I thought that about all of her meals.

The problem was that, as soon as I'd finished, I began to feel twitchy, unable to work out how I'd fill the time until the picnic. Mrs G was already preparing food but refused my offer of help. Normally, I'd have felt relieved to have asked and got away with it, but I needed something to occupy my mind. I was saved by Hobbes appearing in his smart suit.

'Are you going anywhere nice?'

'Henry Bishop's funeral.'

'Can I come?' I asked, thinking it would at least get me out for a couple of hours.

'If you want to,' said Hobbes, sounding surprised, 'but get a move on, I'm going in five minutes. Make yourself respectable and don't wear the blazer you brought down last night.'

'I wasn't intending to,' I said, running upstairs and scrambling into Mr Goodfellow's dark-grey suit, a suit I'd never worn before but which, as I'd expected, fitted uncannily well. I checked its pockets for money, finding, to my regret, that they were empty, apart from a neatly pressed silk handkerchief, which I requisitioned, even though orange is not really my colour.

'You took your time,' said Hobbes, glancing at his watch, 'so we'll have to hurry, I'm glad to say. Excellent.' Clapping his hands, he grinned like a maniac.

'I wasn't that long,' I said, already regretting what I'd let myself in for.

'Long enough. Now let's move … not you, Dregs, you're staying.'

The dog's ears and tail drooped.

'There's no use you looking like that. You can't go until you learn how to behave with decorum.' Turning away, opening the front door, he led me to the car and drove to Henry Bishop's funeral in the manner of a man hurtling to his own. So much for decorum, I thought.

We arrived in time, parked outside and walked respectfully into the chapel. The funeral turned out to be a cremation.

'Mrs Bishop's taking no chances,' Hobbes whispered, as we took our seats at the back.

Despite, or because of my shock at his lack of respect, I sniggered.

'Now then, Andy,' he said with a frown.

It made things worse. I chuckled. Hobbes, shaking his head, trying to look stern, despite his lips twitching into a grin, failed to prevent a guffaw bursting from me and resorted to clamping his great hairy paw over my mouth. Though it dammed the stream of laughter, the build-up continued, with little snorts escaping from my nose, until that too was blocked. Tears welled up, overflowing down my cheeks, while my body shook with helpless laughter, though, with both nose and mouth blocked, I feared I would die laughing. Fortunately, Hobbes, knowing his stuff, managed to regulate the air supply, keeping me alive and (relatively) quiet.

A man in a black suit, one stinking of mothballs, leaned over the pew. 'Is he alright?'

'He's very upset,' said Hobbes.

'Did he know Mr Bishop well?'

'Not especially, he's just very sensitive.'

The organ music starting, I regained some control and he released me, though occasional titters and smirks still found their way out, some turning into strangled chuckles or broad grins. Several disapproving stares were directed my way, even though I was doing my utmost to avoid eye contact, aware the slightest stimulus might set me off again. As sanity returned, I was astonished how many had turned up to see the end of Henry. Some I recognised as local farmers and traders, yet there was also a number of smart, tough-looking young men in sharp business suits, suggesting Henry had enjoyed a wider circle of friends than I would have believed.

Mrs Bishop, her face concealed behind a black veil, the only representative of her sex, appeared grief-stricken, though I'd have thought she'd have been glad to get rid of the old bastard. Despite the manner of his death, I felt scant sympathy for him. The service began, dragging on, while my grins abated and gave way to yawns. The chapel was small and white, with a purple carpet and wooden pews, a coffin, presumably filled with Henry Bishop, at the front, beside a gold-coloured lectern, from where a bored-looking vicar spouted his stuff.

At length, it was Mrs Bishop's turn. Rising slowly, she approached the lectern and addressed us. 'Thank you,' she said, 'to all of you for coming to mourn my poor darling Henry. Of the people you meet, only one or two enter your life, touching you so deeply that forever after they remain a part of you. Some are but brief candles that flicker and blow out in the storms of life but Henry was like a bonfire, a beacon of warmth and light in my life. I hoped he would burn forever. He was my husband for nigh on thirty years and I don't regret a single day of it.'

My mouth dropped open in disbelief; Hobbes clumped it shut with the back of his hand as Mrs Bishop carried on eulogising her late husband in the same vein for several minutes, almost making me believe we'd gone to the wrong service. She told of meeting Henry in Portsmouth, when he was an able seaman, she a barmaid, saying it had been love at first sight. By the time she finished, I was blinking back tears. Human relationships were obviously far deeper and more complex than I'd have believed. Even so, I was glad when the coffin slid behind the curtains and we'd seen the last of Henry, and even more glad when the service ended.

Hobbes and I made our escape as the congregation began to disperse.

'Alas, poor Henry,' said Hobbes, grinning.

'I'm sorry about sniggering,' I said. 'I think it was nerves.'

'It did suggest a lack of respect for the dear departed, but I wouldn't worry about it; I think we covered it up.'

'What did you make of Mrs Bishop's spiel?' I asked.

'It was interesting and puzzling, yet I'm sure she'll get over him and see him in his true colours. I'd like to hope she'll soon be a merry widow.'

I nodded, wondering whether there'd been a hint of disappointment in his voice. My suspicion that he'd murdered Henry hadn't quite gone away. A puff of smoke billowed from the crematorium's chimney, and a faint whiff like cooking bacon made my mouth water, until a sudden suspicion the two were connected, nearly made me sick. My suit felt suddenly too heavy and restrictive, sweat trickled down my back.

'I wonder,' I said, trying to break my chain of thought, 'what's happened to the panthers. Have there been any more sightings?'

'Not that I'm aware of,' said Hobbes, strolling towards the car. 'Yet, perhaps it's not surprising. They're very good at hiding and it's been raining heavily.'

'Don't they like the rain?'

'I've no idea but people are less inclined to go out in it and so there are fewer eyes to see them.' He paused, staring at something. 'Of course, it's possible they have gone away.'

'I see,' I said.

He shook his head. 'No, you don't, you're not looking in the right place.'

'What do you mean?' I asked turning to where he was looking.

'Mice,' he said, pointing to a rubbish bin where three or four brown mice were scurrying and squeaking over a discarded packet of sandwiches.

'Fascinating,' I said. I've never been keen on rodents since a hamster savaged my ear.

He raised his eyebrows. 'But don't you see what it means?'

'No.'

'While the cat's away, the mice will play.'

'That's just a saying.'

'There's often truth in old sayings.'

'Yeah, I know. But … really?'

He fixed me with an expression of such total innocence I knew he'd been playing with me. Probably.

The congregation was leaving the chapel, heading for the cars. Hobbes, raising his hand to shut me up, watched with hunter's eyes. I watched too, with no real interest, although one of the mourners, one of the tough-looking young men I'd noticed earlier, seemed familiar.

'The man in the dark suit,' I said, 'I've seen him before.'

'Nearly everyone's wearing dark suits, except Mrs Bishop,' said Hobbes, 'and you saw them all in the chapel.'

'That guy getting into the grey BMW – I saw him yesterday at the Greasy Pole and I was sure I'd seen him before.'

'There were many people at the Greasy Pole yesterday, and Sorenchester is such a small town it's not surprising you see the same ones now and again.'

'I know, but I'm sure he'd gone before you sorted it all out.'

'So did others. Some people are busy, you know?'

I didn't think the remark was directed at me, since he'd never hinted that he might consider me a freeloader, but it hit hard. I was probably feeling a little vulnerable, for it had crossed my mind that Violet might think me a loser. After all, she was holding down a responsible job, at least so I assumed, not actually knowing what she did, she was wealthy, she was gorgeous, she was sophisticated, she was intelligent. Surely I thought, she would tire of me, sooner or later and, though I hoped it would be later, I had an idea getting dumped would hurt more as time passed. Perhaps I'd have to enter a monastery to get over her: or an asylum, if such things still existed.

'Where do you go?' asked Hobbes, dragging me back to the present.

'What?'

'Where do you go when that vacant expression appears on your face?'

'Nowhere, really … I was just thinking.'

'About your young lady, I'll be bound.'

I nodded. Sometimes he could be quite astute.

'Right then, now you're back, I'm going to offer Mrs Bishop

a lift.'

Henry Bishop's friends, who obviously held the poor woman in as much regard as Henry, had commandeered all the transport, leaving her stranded. I wondered how she'd react to Hobbes's offer but she smiled, getting into the car as he opened the door for her. 'You're very kind, Inspector,' she said. 'Of course, I didn't expect to be offered a lift by those bastards he called mates, but I'd got my bus fare ready.' She sighed. 'Thank God that's all over. Did you enjoy my performance?' She pushed the black veil from her face.

'It was very moving,' I said, getting into the back seat.

She turned to look at me as Hobbes introduced us. Her eye, though still bruised, was concealed beneath make-up and I was surprised to see no trace of tears.

'Moving?' she said and laughed. 'God knows, I should have been an actress. I might have been, too, if Henry hadn't banged me up. You should have seen him in his uniform, back in the day.'

'Was he good looking, then?' It seemed unlikely.

'Hard to believe, eh, seeing what he turned into, but that's what the drink did to him and he wasn't always so bad. He did do the right thing after getting me in the club. At least, we thought it was right at the time but it's a pity you can't see how things will turn out. We had our fair share of problems, not least poor little Mikey getting run over, and then the foot-and-mouth disease doing for his dad's farm that he was going to inherit. Still, he didn't have to deal with them by boozing and taking it out on me, did he?'

I shook my head, making sympathetic noises. Hobbes, I noticed, was driving with care and consideration, though his teeth glinted in a broad grin.

'How are you coping, since he passed away?' he asked.

'I'm coping just fine without the old devil,' said Mrs Bishop, with a broad smile, 'and I'm glad he's dead and burned. I hope he continues to burn! God knows he deserves to.'

'Will you be alright … for money and stuff?' asked Hobbes.

'I'll be fine. I've got my little nest egg, something I've built up over the years for when I left him. That should see me alright.'

'And you'll inherit his assets, won't you?' I said.

She shrugged. 'I suppose so. I'm seeing the solicitor next week to sort things out, though I doubt the old bugger made a will. He was too selfish to consider what might happen to me if he died. Still, I will probably be alright. He can't have drunk it all away and he's been getting paid pretty well, since he started working for King Enterprises.'

'King Enterprises?' I asked, anything to do with Violet interesting me.

'That's right, lad.'

'Do you know Felix King, then?'

'He's the boss right?'

I nodded.

'Of course not. Henry wasn't likely to be mixing in those circles. He worked for one of King's underlings, a rather unpleasant young man.'

'What did Henry do for them?' asked Hobbes.

'I'm not entirely sure. I think he may have collected rents and debts. Whatever it was, he seemed to enjoy it and got paid well enough – not that I ever saw a penny of it. He reckoned he'd soon be getting very much richer and that we'd be able to move into town.'

Hobbes, having steered into Mrs Bishop's yard, stopped the car and leapt out. He opened the door and offered his hand to help her out.

'You are very kind, Inspector,' she said. 'It's a fine day and it's a wonderful feeling to be coming home and know he won't be around.' She chuckled. 'Still, whatever you said to the old devil worked. He didn't lay a finger on me, though it didn't stop his foul mouth. For that I've got to thank a panther, apparently. Thank you for the lift.'

Hobbes walked her to the front door. 'Are you sure you'll be alright, Mrs Bishop?'

'I'll be better than alright. My sister's coming round this afternoon. I haven't hardly seen her since Henry turned bad. Thank you once again. Goodbye.'

She entered the house, smiling as she closed the door. Hobbes was right about her becoming a merry widow, though the transformation seemed a little rushed to me, possibly a little lacking in decorum. I couldn't blame her.

'Right,' said Hobbes, 'let's get back for dinner. Hanging round crematoriums always gives me an appetite.'

12

The mere prospect of spending more time alone with Violet unbalanced my mind so much that the next few hours were a little hazy; I couldn't even remember what the old girl prepared for lunch, though I'm sure I ate it alone, Hobbes having taken Dregs with him to work. Unable to settle, I kept looking at the clock, standing up, sitting down, walking round the house and garden, watching Mrs G at work and, generally, fidgeting. In the end, having had enough, she bundled me out the front door, saying she wouldn't let me back in until half-past three.

'Umm … but that'll only give me half an hour to have a bath and get ready.'

'That's more than enough,' she said, shutting me out and, although I had my key in my trouser pocket, I didn't try going back inside. She'd looked as if she meant what she said and it would have been quite wrong to try forcing my way back in; besides, I wouldn't have stood a chance.

Instead, having wandered aimlessly around the middle of town in a myopic daze, I came to rest on a bench in the shade of the church, surrounded by a coachload of tourists listening to some history stuff. A problem with my bench was that, even after the tourists moved inside the church, the parapet blocked my view of the clock tower, meaning I had to keep getting up to cross the road, from where I could see the clock's hands' lethargic progress. After repeating the procedure several times, becoming convinced the clock had slowed down, I hurried down The Shambles to a jeweller's shop, where ranks of clocks and watches in the window confirmed the church's infallibility.

Seeing all the shiny stuff laid out before me made me wish I could afford a new watch to replace the one I'd blown up in a microwave accident, though I was usually quite happy to be free of time's tyranny.

So much rushing around in the sun had got the sweat flowing, so, dabbing my face with the orange silk handkerchief, I retreated to the bench and fidgeted for several minutes, trying to keep cool. I was joined by the lanky figure of PC Poll, who, having marched up The Shambles, sat down beside me. Making a pretence that I hadn't seen him, for, despite Hobbes's influence, a uniformed police officer, even one I knew quite well, still made me feel guilty, I sat unusually still.

'So it was you, Mr Caplet,' he said. 'I might have known.'

'Hi … umm … Derek. What's up?' I said, turning to face him.

He smiled. 'You are. We had a report of a suspicious-looking character casing the jewellers. What have you been doing?'

'Nothing … I only looked in to check the time.'

'Wouldn't it have been easier to look up at the one on the church?'

'Well … umm … yes. Actually, I thought it might have stopped.'

'But,' said Poll, giving me a sceptical glance, 'the proprietor reported that you've been staring in his shop every couple of minutes, worrying his staff. He said you looked nervous and shifty, and he's correct. Are you sure everything's alright?'

'There's a perfectly simple explanation,' I said, feeling the blush coming.

'Go on.'

'It's sort of because I've … umm … got a date. I'm meeting a lady at four o'clock but Mrs Goodfellow won't let me back in the house till half-past three and I can't risk being late.'

'You've got a date?' said Poll.

Never before had I heard such doubt in his voice and, having always regarded him as far too nice and trusting to be a policeman, I wondered whether I should revise my opinion.

'Yes,' I said.

'Who's the unfortunate lady?'

There was, I suspected, a hint of a smirk on his face and I didn't like it. 'That's none of your business. And she's not unfortunate.'

'Oh, go on. I was only joking.' He smiled.

'Yeah, sorry,' I said, certain my cheeks must be glowing like a sunset. 'She's just someone I bumped into at the Wildlife Park. Her name's Violet and she's very nice.'

'OK, Andy,' he said, standing up, 'I believe you, thousands wouldn't. Please, just calm down and don't go frightening any more shopkeepers. See you.'

He wandered off along Vermin Street, stopping to chat with half a dozen locals on his way. Despite his long legs, he rarely got anywhere fast.

As he left, I decided a brisk walk around town might work off some of my nervous energy. It worked quite well and I was admiring the way some builders were transforming a near-derelict house into smart flats, when their radio informed me the three-thirty news was starting. I raced home, in a panic, sweating like a racehorse by the time I got in. Opening the front door, charging in, I galloped upstairs, threw off my damp clothes and oozed into the bathroom.

Though not a fan of cold showers, a lack of time and my red-hot body tempted me to make an exception. I hadn't forgotten Hobbes's plumbing but hoped, being prepared, to stand up to it. It was a mistake. Standing beneath the plate-sized rosette, I turned the tap on, producing a pathetic, tepid dribble. Turning it full on, disappointingly, seemed to make little difference, so, deciding I'd better make the most of it, I reached for the soap and lathered up.

The shower burped and an icy torrent struck me in the back with the power of a mountain waterfall, knocking me to my knees, then flattening me against the bottom of the bath. I gasped and squealed, trying to escape, when it stopped as suddenly as it had started. I raised my head, catching my breath and, with no warning, it started again, pressing me against the hard, white enamel. Helpless, I groped for the side, as the gentle trickle returned. I was already dazed, battered and disoriented before the following deluge demolished me again, staying full on this time, sometimes scalding hot, sometimes icy cold. In trying to drag myself clear, I pulled down the shower curtain, the pole striking my head a stunning blow, while the plastic sheet, clinging around me, turned my struggles to futility. Like a drowning man going down for the third time, panic set in, for I couldn't help believing it was curtains for me. When I opened my mouth to cry for help, nothing came out, because of the flood going in.

To my amazement, the inundation ended, the battering ceased, and I was saved. Raising myself on my arms, I rolled from the bath onto the lino, sucking dry air into my lungs, choking a while.

'Don't you go dripping all over the place,' said Mrs Goodfellow, holding out a fluffy white towel.

I pulled myself to my feet, wrapping the towel around my waist, and hugged her, any embarrassment having been swept away in a surge of relief and gratitude.

In all honesty, I was sure her arrival had saved me from a terribly silly end, the sort of bizarre death that makes newspaper readers snort with derisive laughter. At least, that's how they affected my father and one particular story came to mind, one he'd read to us at breakfast. It was about a burglar, who, having used a screwdriver to force open a skylight, had clamped the tool between his teeth while trying to climb down into the shop. When he slipped, he'd fallen on his face, forcing the screwdriver down his throat, choking him. I remembered the incident well for, not only had it been one of the rare occasions when my father had laughed out loud, but also because he'd pebble-dashed me with the cornflakes he'd been masticating.

'Are you alright, dear?' asked Mrs Goodfellow.

'I am now,' I said, hugging her again, grabbing at the slipping towel.

'Good,' she said, as she turned to leave the bathroom. 'I came to let you know it's ten-to-four, so you'd better get a move on. Your picnic's all packed and waiting by the door.'

I did get a move on, drying myself, dressing and grooming in record time, the shower having refreshed me no end, leaving me feeling tingling, alert and lucky to be alive. Examining myself in the mirror, trying my straw boater at various rakish angles, I indulged myself in a complacent smile. With the blue of my eyes matching the stripes on the blazer, my brown, wispy hair looking neat, I didn't think I looked half bad. Confidence rising, I went downstairs.

'Very smart, dear,' said Mrs Goodfellow. 'What lady could resist?'

When the doorbell rang, the lurch in my stomach came not from panic but from exhilaration and anticipation and I nearly skipped to the front door. I opened it. There stood Violet, smiling and divine.

'Hi,' she said and, just for an instant, her eyes widened, as if shocked at what she could see. Her smile stayed in place, but that one look convinced me my Technicolor blazer and straw hat were ridiculous. I wasn't surprised, for, after all, I was the same old, hopeless Andy, not the debonair gentleman I'd hoped to be.

'Hello,' I said.

Though she was wearing a simple red t-shirt and a faded denim skirt that must have seen a few years, even in such simple garments she retained, to my eyes, an air of elegance and sophistication. Yet something about her was different. Her expression showing a hint of stress, or possibly distress, I feared my appearance lay at the root of it.

The conversation exhausted, we looked at each other and squirmed. At least I squirmed, trying to work out if I had time to change into something more appropriate.

'Hello, dear,' said Mrs Goodfellow peering out at Violet from under my arm. 'How are you?'

'Very well, thanks.'

'Good. I've packed a picnic for you. Now, off you go and have a lovely time. Andy, why don't you pick up the hamper?'

'Umm ... right.' I squatted down to pick it up, alarmed, if not surprised, by its weight, as the old girl nudged me outside.

'Goodbye,' she said, 'have fun.'

I nodded, my confidence already shattered, and followed Violet down the steps.

'Where's your car?' I asked, looking around, hoping I wouldn't have to carry the hamper too far.

'It's just round the bend, behind that white van.'

Something in her voice suggested a problem. Stopping abruptly, she turned to face me.

'Look,' she said, 'there's no easy way to say this but my brother wants to come along and I hope it's alright with you. You see, Felix has a terribly stressful job and needs to unwind sometimes. He only said he wanted to come a few minutes ago and I couldn't really say no and there was no time to ask you. Anyway, it'll be a good chance for you to meet him. I hope you don't mind?'

'Oh, I'm sure it will be just fine,' I said, forcing a smile, my spirits sinking into my tennis pumps.

She smiled back, a little crookedly. 'Thanks. Do you think we'll need to get more food?'

I could answer that question with confidence. 'No, the old girl's used to catering for Hobbes so there'll be plenty and, as for cutlery and stuff, there's four of everything. We'll have loads, and there'll still be lots left over for feeding the ducks.'

'Will there be ducks? I like them but I thought there'd just be trees.'

'Umm ... I don't know, actually. I've never been there before, but there always seemed to be ducks when I went on picnics as a boy.' I remembered a flock of the flat-footed, quacking villains creating mayhem, decimating our sandwiches; that had been another unsuccessful Caplet family picnic.

We drew up to her car.

'Andy,' she said, 'this is my brother, Felix.'

I noticed with a mixture of anger and jealousy that he'd taken possession of the front passenger seat, that his clothes, khaki shorts and faded black polo shirt, were as casual as his sister's, yet he, too, looked smart and well-groomed, even if he had rather overdone the aftershave. He nodded at me, grinning, making me feel overdressed and awkward.

'Felix,' she said, 'this is Andy.'

'Hi,' I said, attempting to smile back, feeling like a phoney, a dissembler. 'But this isn't the first time we've met. Your brother helped me out when there was a misunderstanding in the bookshop.'

'Did I?' asked Felix, shrugging. 'I don't remember – but I'm glad I was of service, though I'm sure you were capable of sorting things out for yourself.'

'I expect so,' I lied. Things had a habit of blowing up in my face.

'Right,' he said, indicating the back seat, 'shove that hamper in the back and hop in.' Despite the car being a two-door model, he never offered to move.

My attempted casual vault into the back turning into a trip, I sprawled across the hamper, while trying to act cool. It wasn't easy.

'Let's go,' said Felix.

As Violet started the car, moving off, I struggled into a seat, retrieving my boater from the footwell, trying to look like a man enjoying myself. Violet, concentrating on her driving, didn't speak, Felix poked buttons on his mobile, while I fidgeted in the back, uncomfortable, the hamper pressing into my side. The journey was uneventful, except for my boater blowing off as we rounded a bend. Though I grabbed it, pleased with my reflexes, part of me wished I'd lost the ridiculous thing.

The silence being disconcerting, I was relieved when we reached the arboretum. Yet, I wasn't happy, for though I had reason to be grateful to Felix, I didn't want him there, even when he paid our admission money.

The car coming to a stop, he sprang out.

'Grab that basket, Andy.'

He didn't ask: it was an order.

'We'll find somewhere good to eat. I reckon over there's promising.' He gestured across the valley towards the trees on the far side.

It looked a pretty stiff walk for a man with a hamper.

'Or over there might be better,' I said, pointing in the opposite direction, towards a small meadow between stands of ornamental trees, no more than fifty metres away, 'It's got tables and benches. It looks ideal.'

'Oh, no,' said Felix. 'We don't want to be next to the car park and a brisk walk will do us all a power of good. Besides, while we're getting there I can update Violet on the project.'

He turned, putting his arm around his sister's shoulders. She gave a small, apologetic smile as he led her away down the hill. I struggled after them as best I could, sagging beneath the weight of the hamper, sweat prickling my skin, my shirt sticking to my back. I couldn't make out much of what Felix was saying, though it seemed to be mostly business talk about markets, investments and returns: pretty dull stuff, and not what I would have chosen to talk about on such an evening.

Nature, at least, was on my side. Butterflies dipped and swooped between banks of wild flowers, bumblebees busied themselves in patches of red clover and the air smelled fresh and earthy combined with the scent of warm grass and blossoms. I'm sure I would have appreciated it, had it not been for Felix hogging Violet, leaving me to struggle behind like a pack mule, the hamper seemingly gaining weight with every step. As we reached the bottom of the valley, starting upwards, the path became rough and uneven, the grass slippery, between spiky gorse bushes with yellow blooms. By the time we reached the woods, where roots were conspiring to trip me, my head was pounding with the heat, my breath coming in short gasps. A malevolent twig struck my head, knocking my hat to a ludicrous angle over my eyes, leaving me unable to see the snare of brambles about to hook my leg. I fell to my knees, letting loose an involuntary oath, yet holding fast to the basket.

'Here, let me give you a hand,' said Felix, taking the hamper from my outstretched arms. Violet, smiling, hesitated, as if about to help me up, but followed her brother as he strode away.

'He really is a stubborn fool,' said Felix, 'but he's willing to make a deal now he's seen what can happen, and if we can persuade that buffoon Binks about the need for progress, then we'll be getting somewhere. I'll get Mike to have a few words with him and see if he can't change his mind.'

Standing up, I brushed myself down, appalled how grievously the knees of my trousers had suffered, the crisp white cotton having been stained green from the lush grass, brown from the damp earth, the sharp creases having turned to saggy bags, tiny, bloody dots pointing to where thorns had penetrated. Muttering rude, biting words under my breath, arms and shoulders aching, I followed Violet.

'This will do perfectly,' said Felix, having carried the burden all of twenty steps into a glade.

To be fair, which I wasn't inclined to be, it was a great spot, the deep green carpet of turf beneath our feet as soft as fleece, a multitude of daisies everywhere, bright as stars in the night sky, the fragrance of wild flowers intoxicating.

'What did you do with the rugs?' asked Felix, setting the hamper down in a patch of buttercups.

'Rugs?'

'The ones you were sitting on when we drove here. You haven't left them in the car have you?'

'Me?'

'Yes, you.' He shook his head. 'You didn't expect me to carry them as well as the picnic did you? You'd better go and get them – it'll give me a chance to finish my conversation with

Violet. We'll see you back here in a few minutes. OK?'

'But the grass is really soft,' I said. 'We won't need rugs. What do you think?' I turned to Violet who opened her mouth as if she might agree. She didn't get the chance.

Felix nodded. 'It's soft enough, I'll grant you, but it's still damp after all the rain. You wouldn't want my sister to catch her death would you?'

'No … but.'

'Of course not. Now, run along and get those rugs. The sooner you start, the sooner you'll return, right? If you wouldn't mind getting a move on, I'm quite hungry. By the way, when you're down there, you'll find a camping chair in the boot. You might as well bring that too, there's a good chap.'

Though dazed, confused and furious, for some reason I turned back towards the car.

'Oh, Andy!' He called me back after a few seconds. 'You'll need these.'

Violet handed him the car keys, which he threw towards me, or, rather, at me. Though it was some consolation to catch them cleanly, my mood was black as I stamped back towards the car.

The twig I'd run into earlier, still being up to no good, speared my boater, pulling it from my head. Putting it back on, though it now incorporated a dent and a finger-sized hole, I continued my long trek, muttering savage imprecations against picnics in general and picnics with Felix in particular, wishing I'd stayed at home, thinking about trying to hitch a lift back. Only the fear that no one would stop for a sweaty prat dressed like a dishevelled music-hall comedian and the realisation that I'd be leaving Mrs G's picnic basket behind stopped my escape. So far, Violet had barely spoken to me, while Felix was treating me like a lackey. Despite having known all along that it would go wrong with Violet, the end seemed to be approaching even faster than I'd anticipated, and prior knowledge didn't make the prospect any easier.

Nevertheless, I picked up the rugs and Felix's chair and lugged them all the weary way back. I guessed each trip must have taken me about twenty minutes, so I'd been in the arboretum for an hour and all I'd got was hot, dirty, sweaty, thirsty, angry, miserable and tired. Felix and Violet watched me all the way back. Reaching them at last, I dumped the gear on the grass.

'Good man,' said Felix, 'and now you must have a drink after all your exertions.'

I nodded, speechless, dripping.

'Come on, Violet,' he said, 'get the man a drink. He deserves one.'

She opened a bottle of ginger beer, filled a glass and handed it to me.

'Thank you,' I said, taking a swig, delighted it had stayed cool in its stone bottle, enjoying its spicy, sweet flavour.

She smiled. I smiled and took another pull at my glass. A drop going the wrong way, I started choking and gasping for air.

'Are you alright?' she asked, her hand on my shoulder.

'Does he sound alright?' said Felix. 'Take his glass. I'll sort him out.'

As soon as she took it, a blow between my shoulder blades felled me as if I'd been pole-axed. Sprawling in the grass, I groaned, forcing myself to stop choking for I couldn't have endured a repeat performance.

'Is that better?' asked Felix.

I nodded and he reached down, pulling me to my feet. He was much stronger than he looked.

'Good. Now spread those rugs and let's eat.'

Violet did as commanded and, as I helped her lay the food out, he erected his chair, sitting back into it with a sigh. Her hand brushing mine gently, deliberately, I hoped I'd been premature in pronouncing the death of the affair, if that's what it was.

'Excellent job, you two. Thanks,' said Felix, smiling as the last of the meal was set before him.

Somehow, those few simple words nearly made everything alright. I grinned up at him, repenting my evil thoughts, for though his earlier bulldozing had reminded me of Rex Witcherley, Felix could display a charm the Editorsaurus never would.

Nevertheless, I still felt like a dog at his master's feet, hoping for scraps. Not that there was any danger of being left with scraps, for the old girl, as usual, had excelled herself and I was delighted to see that, as well as ginger beer, she'd packed a couple of bottles of wine.

Violet picked them up. 'Red or white?'

'Red,' said Felix and I in unison.

'Just as well,' she said, 'they're both red.' She uncorked a bottle, pouring a glass for each of us, and handed them round.

Felix sniffed and took a sip, his eyebrows rising in appreciation. 'This is good,' he said, 'where did you get it from?'

'Umm …' I said, scratching my head, 'I think they're probably from Hobbes's cellar. He keeps a few down there and enjoys a drop now and again, when he's not working, of course.'

'Well,' said Felix, staring into the glass, 'this is truly excellent. Is it all as good as this?'

'Well … umm … it all tastes good to me. I don't know much about it, though I think this is the normal stuff. He's got a lot more that he keeps for special occasions.'

'The Inspector knows his wine, then. I'm surprised after what I've heard about him. Does he keep a large cellar?'

'Umm … pretty large, probably. Several hundred bottles I'd say.'

'Then he's a lucky man,' said Felix taking another sip. 'I don't suppose you know his supplier?'

'I don't. I've never actually seen him buy any; it's always just been there.'

'Well, it must have come from somewhere.' Felix leant forward, picking up the bottle. 'I don't recognise the label. What d'you make of it?' He glanced at Violet.

She sniffed the glass, rolling a drop round on her tongue, inhaling. 'It's like drinking bottled sunshine. This is beautifully balanced, elegant, sensuous, spicy wine. I've rarely tasted anything to equal it.'

'Me neither,' said Felix. 'And you say he's got hundreds of bottles of this? And keeps better ones? That's amazing.'

'Is it?' I asked, surprised. 'I mean I … umm … like the stuff, but I didn't think it was anything special.'

'It is very special,' said Felix, holding his glass up to the sky. 'I'd like to get hold of a few crates of it myself. Would you mind asking him from where he gets it?'

'No, of course not.'

'Good, man,' said Felix pausing. 'Still, I can't help wondering how an inspector can afford such quality. Police pay must be better than I thought.'

'Do you reckon it's worth a bit?'

'It should be. The only wine I recall coming close to this in the last few years was a vintage Burgundy from Domaine Chambourge. I think that one retailed at around five hundred pounds a bottle, if you could get it.'

I was stunned to learn anyone would spend so much on a bottle of wine. The most I'd ever paid had been ten pounds for a bottle of some white plonk I'd bought from a bloke in the Feathers, intending to impress a girl at a party. It hadn't worked and I could still remember the way she'd pursed her lips on realising I hadn't chilled it, the way she'd rolled her eyes when I drove a corkscrew through the screw-top, the way she'd clicked her tongue when I spilled a drop down her front, the way she'd walked out without a word after the first sip. I'd thought her overly judgemental until, taking a gulp to console myself, I felt as if the wine was stripping the enamel from my teeth, forcing me to drink about a gallon of water to douse the burning in my mouth and throat. Since then, I'd been happy to knock back any wine that left my teeth intact. Even so, I had enough palate remaining to have realised that Hobbes's stock was rather nice, without enough to realise it was exceptional. For a moment I wondered if they were having me on, yet their expressions as they sipped the stuff reminded me of one of the windows in the church, one depicting Saint somebody-or-other ascending to heaven, convinced me they meant it.

To me, the food, though no better than I'd expected, was even more impressive than the wine. As for Felix and Violet, after their first bite of one of Mrs G's cheese sandwiches, they ate in awed silence. Yet the sandwiches were the least of the delights, for she'd packed bite-sized meat pies that self-destructed in the mouth, leaving just a wonderful savoury taste, a crispy salad with a dressing that made me want to cry for joy, succulent cold meats and so many wonderful things that six of us could have dined with no hardship. As it was, I think we all rather stuffed ourselves, leaving little.

Felix sighed as he finished the last slice of fruit cake, refilled his glass and raised it. 'To Andy, who knows how to picnic. I haven't eaten so well in years.'

'It was no bother,' I said, truthfully, 'except that it was heavy to carry.'

'No problem,' he said, 'I'll carry it back. In the meantime, would you care for a top up?'

After he'd filled my glass, I stretched out on the rug.

'That was lovely,' said Violet, placing her hand on mine, giving it a squeeze, 'thank you.'

Feeling very full, very satisfied and very relaxed, as the shadows lengthened, I sprawled at Violet's side as we chatted about art and literature and business. In truth, Felix and Violet did the chatting, while I, trying to look intelligent, grunted occasionally to express agreement. Yet, when Violet leaned back with her head against my thigh, I felt as happy as I'd ever been.

'Isn't it a glorious evening,' I said.

'It is,' said Felix, 'and, of course, it's the solstice.'

'Oh yes,' said Violet, raising her head, 'I nearly forgot.'

'What is it?' I asked.

'The summer solstice,' said Felix, with a snort of derision, 'the longest day, the shortest night.'

'Oh, yes … of course … when the nutters prance round the stones on Hedbury Common.'

'So the local rag says,' said Violet, smiling, 'though I wouldn't go so far as calling them nutters; they're probably just having fun. After all, Midsummer's traditionally a time of celebration.'

'That's not how my father saw it,' I said, reflectively. 'He used to reckon it was all downhill towards winter from now on.'

'Sounds like a cheery soul.'

'Not really,' I said, about to relate an amusing anecdote from my childhood.

Felix's mobile phone chirruped, just as the evening sun disappeared behind a cloud.

'Excuse me,' he said, getting up, pulling the phone from his pocket. 'Felix King … Oh, it's you Mike … I said I wasn't to be disturbed … I see … Right, I'd best see to it at once … I'm at the arboretum, just past Hedbury, with Violet and her … friend, so pick me up in the lay-by in front of the kiosk as you come in …' He glanced at his wristwatch. 'I'll see you in about twenty minutes.' He pushed the mobile back into his pocket.

'Must you go?' asked Violet.

'I'm afraid so, something's come up,' he said and grinned. 'It's about time we had some good news on the project.'

Though I tried to look suitably sad at his imminent departure, my heart felt as if it were turning cartwheels of delight. Admittedly, things had improved considerably since we'd started the meal, but the food and drink, superb though they were, were not the real reasons for the picnic. What I wanted was to have her to myself, and it was beginning to look as if I might get my way. The affair was back on and, with the sun escaping the cloud's embrace, warmth flooded my soul.

'Actually, Andy,' said Felix, stretching, slicking back his hair, 'I was hoping to have a word with you this evening and, since I really must get a move on, I'd appreciate you walking back with me. It will give Violet a chance to pack up.'

Annoyed that he expected me to jump at his command,

angered at his assumption that Violet would pack up on his say so, I should have just refused. Perhaps I would have, had I not been so polite, had Felix not been the sort of man who expected obedience and always seemed to get it. Without knowing quite why, I found myself walking with him.

'That was a splendid picnic and an excellent wine,' he said, 'and I'd really appreciate it if you could source it for me.'

'Sauce it?'

'Find out from where the Inspector obtains his supplies. Or you could ask him if he'd mind selling me a few crates. Money won't be a problem once this project comes to completion, and it's starting to move, so I won't quibble about the cost. Would you do that for me, Andy?'

'Umm ... yes. I expect so,' I said, thinking his request not sufficiently important to drag me away from Violet, although the distant rumble of thunder suggested the picnic would have been curtailed soon anyway.

'Good man,' said Felix, pleasantly. 'And now there's something else I'd like to say, so you'd do well to listen.'

His voice had changed. All hint of friendliness had vanished, along with the commanding, yet reasonable, tones of a leader of men. In an instant it had grown cold, the tone reminding me a little of Hobbes when having a chat with a miscreant.

'I make a point,' he said, 'of taking a long, hard look at Violet's male friends. As her older brother, I've always looked out for her, always wanted what's best for her.'

'Good,' I said, wondering where he was going, fearing I could guess, 'I'm ... umm ... pleased to hear that.'

'She's very attractive, don't you agree?'

I nodded.

'But there are some, hangers-on, toadies, rogues and parasites, who find her wealth more attractive. Do you know what I mean?'

'Umm ... yes. I suppose so.'

'So, which category do you fit into, Mr Caplet?'

'Me? None of them ... I just like her and ...'

'You say that, yet know nothing about her, except that she is rich. I, on the other hand, know rather a lot about you: you have no job, no home and no prospects. Am I right?'

'Well ...'

'You live on Hobbes's charity and I have learned that Violet has already bought you an expensive meal. Is my information correct so far?'

'Sort of ... umm ... but ...'

'It appears to me that you are a chancer and a parasite. She is smart, successful and cultured; you are a worthless waste of breath. Would you agree that a worthless waste of breath is not a suitable man for Violet?'

'Yes ... but I'm not ...'

'You seem to have taken her in for the moment but, in all honesty, I can't see what she sees in you. However, I do not intend her to be hurt again.'

'But ... I ... I'd never do that,' I said, feeling a chill run through me, shivering, despite the evening still being so warm.

'Men such as you have hurt her in the past and it has resulted in breakdowns. I will not go into the details. Suffice to say, I will not allow you to be the cause of such unpleasantness. When my car arrives, you will return to her, help her pack and carry the picnic and rugs back to her car. Afterwards, you will ask her to drive you straight home and you will not see her again. Understood?'

'Yes, I understand what you're saying, but surely it's her choice.'

'No, Mr Caplet. I expect you to do as I say, or you will regret it. Now, do you understand?'

'Yes ... But ...'

'Enough. I hope you know what's good for you.'

As he said this, we reached the car park and a glossy black Jaguar turned into the arboretum and stopped. As Felix marched towards it, a fit young man, who looked as if he might play rugby or some other manly sport, emerged, opening the back door for him.

'I'm glad we understand each other,' said Felix with a pleasant smile, his menace dissipated, 'because I really wouldn't want anything nasty happening to you. You can't help the way you are.

'Thank you so much for a delightful picnic and don't forget to ask the Inspector about his wine. Here's my card.' He pressed it into my hand, nodded and slid into the back of the car.

'Thanks,' I said, stupidly, standing there bemused as the young man, closing the door, climbed into the driver's seat and drove away.

I had much to think about while trudging back to Violet.

13

With the sun sinking and reddening, heavy clouds creeping up on the horizon, the heat and humidity seemed to be on the rise, the air feeling as thick as golden syrup. The gentle breeze that had maintained a little freshness in the air was growing fretful and capricious as the evening lengthened. Everyone else was heading for the exit and the birds had stopped singing. Not that I cared.

My legs were heavy, as if encased in concrete, and, although it was my fifth trek of the evening, it wasn't physical tiredness causing my weakness, for Felix's threats had knocked the stuffing out of me. I'd thought we'd been getting on tolerably well or, at least, that any animosity was on my side; he'd been saying nice things about the picnic and the wine, so his attack, shocking in its unexpectedness, had hit me like a punch to the jaw. Yet the threats weren't the worse of it, his brutal dissection of my character having really struck home, since I couldn't really refute his accusations: I really was out of work, reliant on Hobbes for shelter and food; I really was penniless (though not literally so, as I'd picked one up from the gutter); I really was useless. Such a realisation, hurtful though it was, was not nearly as painful as the prospect of ending it with Violet, for despite knowing our relationship was doomed, bound to smash into an uncharted reef sooner or later, it was still agony now the reef was just ahead and I had no means to steer away.

Yet, deep within, I felt a resistance movement stirring, my anger building, for her money meant nothing to me and I'd never have dreamt of hurting her. Who was Felix to tell me what to do or, for that matter, to speak for his sister? It had to be her decision to say when she was fed up with me.

I was in a dilemma, unsure whether to meekly give in or to damn the consequences and stand up to him, wondering if, perhaps, he'd just been testing me, giving me the chance to be a man, to prove myself worthy. Yet, I couldn't make myself believe he hadn't been deadly serious, or rid myself of the fear that he might not stop at cutting words the next time we met, unless I'd done what he'd asked. Even so, I could hardly bring myself to think that he, a respectable businessman, would really do anything to me, at least nothing violent. Yet if I was wrong and he did attack me, I was sure, his brief display of strength coming to mind, that I'd stand little chance of beating him. Even if I did get lucky, perhaps punching him out, I doubted Violet would be happy with me and running away from him would probably impress her even less than fighting.

There was another consideration: Felix might not have to do his own dirty work for Mike, his driver, had looked more than a bit handy.

He'd also looked familiar.

When I reached the clearing, Violet's smile drove away depressing thoughts.

'You took your time, slowcoach,' she teased, stretching out on the rug, back arched, slim arms behind her head. Her t-shirt, having pulled up to reveal an inch of soft, smooth belly, was tight across her breasts. 'I've packed everything away, apart from the drinks. I thought you might want something.'

'Yes … it's a long walk.' My throat was dry.

'You do look hot. Wine or ginger beer?'

'Both, please.'

As she sat up, reaching for the bottles, I sat down beside her, knowing with absolute certainty that I really did not give a damn about her wealth or what her brother thought of me. What I wanted was her, and I didn't mean physically: at least not just physically. Before anything, though, I needed a drink. As she handed me a glass of ginger beer, I gulped it down in one, glugging a glass of wine straight after it.

As I sat there, my thirst quenched, I came to a firm decision that, whatever Felix might do later, I was going to kiss her. I would, definitely, without hesitation, should an opportunity arise, in the fullness of time, kiss her. Finishing off the last bottle of ginger beer, throwing back the last dregs, I gazed into her gorgeous eyes.

Her face was just a few inches from mine and, taking myself by surprise, seizing the opportunity, I leaned forward and held her gently by the shoulders. Reassured by her easy sway towards me, I puckered my lips, looked deep into her dark eyes … and burped.

'Oh, God,' I said, recoiling, ashamed, 'I'm so sorry! I didn't mean it, it was all the fizz.'

Without trying, I'd blown it, done what Felix wanted, leaving me embarrassed, feeling like a total klutz.

However, she seemed to be taking it rather well. Rolling back onto the rug, she lay there rocking, little gasps of amusement soon becoming helpless laughter, continuing for what seemed like ages. When, at last, it looked as if she might be regaining control, she glanced up at me, catching my eye, starting again and setting me off. I collapsed on the rug beside her and, next thing I knew, she was lying half across me, her face buried in my blazer. Eventually, our laughter subsiding, she pinned me to the rug and kissed me full on the lips, making my head swirl as if I was on a fairground ride, the kiss lingering until, far too soon, she pulled away, sitting up abruptly. My lips still tingling, I reached for her hand.

'What was that?' she said, pushing me away.

'Just a kiss,' I said, deflated, disappointed. It had been good for me, the first real one I'd enjoyed in years, since Jenny Riley had pounced on me in the playground during a game of kiss chase; I'd been running away very slowly.

'Not that. Something's out there, didn't you hear it?' Wild-eyed, she stared into the woods.

'What do you mean?'

'An animal I think.'

I sprang to my feet, genuine dread gathering in my stomach. 'What sort of animal?' I asked, a big, dangerous cat springing to mind. 'Where?'

'I don't know.'

Taking my hand, she pulled herself to her feet, her body trembling as she snuggled against me. Suddenly alarmed, I put my arm around her shoulders, which certainly comforted me.

'We should probably go,' I said. 'What do you think?'

She nodded and, releasing her with regret, I threw the last odds and sods into the hamper, piled the rugs on top, and picked it up. Grabbing Felix's folding chair, she held it like a weapon, urging me back to the car, while I concentrated on keeping as close together as possible, feeling sure she was making a real effort not to run. At last, reaching the car park, hurrying towards her car, she rummaged frantically through her little hessian bag, her eyes as big as headlights.

'I can't find the keys,' she said, her voice shrill, on the edge of panic.

'It's alright,' I said, panting and sweating, resting the hamper on the bonnet, catching my breath.

'It isn't!' she said, shaking her head. 'I must have dropped them. I'm not going back to look. I'll call Felix and get help.'

'Don't worry,' I said, trying to be reassuring, 'I've still got them.'

'Thank God.' Her face was as white as a fridge door and her hand was trembling. 'Give them here.'

'They're in my pocket. I'll just put this down and …'

Thrusting her hand into my trousers, she grabbed the keys, the touch of her warm hand in such an intimate spot like an electric shock through all my nerves, though not at all unpleasant. Even so, it paralysed me for a second or two, by which time she'd opened the car doors, sat down and was scrabbling to get the key in the ignition. Chucking the hamper into the back seat, I threw myself in beside her as, the engine bursting into life, we drove away in a plume of dust.

'Let's get out of here,' she said, through clenched teeth.

'Yeah, let's. But … umm … what was it? A panther?'

'No.' Shaking her head, turning the steering wheel, tyres screeching, she drove into the main road.

'What then?' I asked, the acceleration pinning me back.

'I don't know.'

'Do you think,' I said, noticing the speedo creeping up to ninety, 'we might be going a little fast?'

'We've got to get away.'

'But we're safe now,' I said, trying to calm her, worried that she was driving like Hobbes in a hurry, but without his reflexes.

Shaking her head, she leaned forward, hugging the wheel, as if urging the car ever faster.

I held my breath and the edge of my seat as we screeched round a bend. 'We must be miles away by now. It can't possibly catch us.'

Her manner, even more than her driving, scared me while Felix's remark about breakdowns made me doubt anything had been out there, for her change of mood had been so swift, she could easily have been mentally unstable, no doubt explaining why she'd taken a fancy to me. Perhaps my kiss had driven her over the edge.

'Please, slow down,' I said. 'You're starting to frighten me. This road's not very …'

'Sorry, Andy. We've got to get away.'

'But I don't understand. What did you see? A fox, maybe?'

'It was no fox,' she shouted, her face flushed and angry.

Hitting a pothole, the car swerved, for a moment looking like it would veer into a tree, before she regained control.

'You must have seen something … umm … what was it?'

'Something in the woods.'

'Can you describe it?' I asked. 'Careful!'

We rounded a bend too close to the verge, the back tyres

bumping.

'I didn't *see* anything,' said Violet, 'but something was there.'

'But what?'

'You wouldn't believe me.'

'I might but, please, slow down, for God's sake, we're coming to a village.'

Taking a deep breath, she nodded, slowing quite a lot as we approached the first house, a stone cottage with scruffy garden and leggy hollyhocks round the front. Bright yellow light was pouring from its open front door and a white pig with stuck up ears hurtled out, demolishing the garden gate, stopping in the middle of the road, sniffing something that had been squashed.

As Violet stamped on the brake, only my seat belt stopped me from kissing the windscreen. The tyres squealed. The pig looked like a goner. As we swerved, missing it by a grunt, we hit the kerb and lurched off the road. For a moment there was darkness, and then greenery, a thump and evening light. The car stopping at last, I turned towards Violet, who was slumped forward, still gripping the wheel.

'Are you alright?'

She didn't move.

Unbuckling my seat belt, I leapt from the car and ran round, pushing through a jungle of bamboo canes and clinging plants until I could pull the door open. 'Are you alright?' I asked again, reaching for her hand.

She turned towards me, blood oozing from her mouth and nose. 'I think so but my lip hurts. You?'

'I'm fine,' I said, leaning over, turning off the ignition, pulling out the key.

'Good,' she said. 'And the pig?'

'We missed it.'

She nodded. 'I'm so sorry, Andy.'

'Don't worry about me,' I said, 'there's no real harm done, that's the main thing.'

'No real harm done?' a man shouted. 'You've ruined my hedge and destroyed my runner beans.'

A hefty, bald-headed, middle-aged man in a checked shirt and olive corduroy trousers was striding towards us from an old stone cottage, his face, red and contorted with rage, complementing his voice. We'd crashed into a country garden, one that might have been idyllic before our arrival, with roses blooming around the cottage windows, a vine clinging to its walls and raised vegetable beds that were lush and green.

'I'm ever so sorry,' I said, holding up my hands in apology, the keys jangling, 'but a pig ran across the road and ...'

'Sod the bloody pig!' the man bellowed, 'you were probably speeding. I know you lot with your flashy clothes and expensive motors, tearing up the countryside, wrecking people's gardens. Just look at my hedge! My great grandfather planted it a hundred years ago and you've just ruined it. I'll have the law on you, just see if I don't. You're going to pay for it and for what you've done to my runner beans. Now get off my bloody spuds!'

'Sorry,' I said, making sure to place my feet where they would cause least harm, making a big play of causing no further damage. Unfortunately, my attempted leap onto the path falling short, I stumbled backwards.

'Get off my bloody carrots!' the man screamed.

His face turning almost purple, his meaty hand seized my collar, dragging me off his precious vegetables onto the garden path. I was convinced he intended pulverizing me until Violet groaned. Turning my head, I watched her slide from the car, collapsing, lying still on the ground. The man, dropping me like a bit of litter, ran towards her. I couldn't help noticing that he went right through his carrots and potatoes.

'Are you hurt, my dear?' he asked, rolling her onto her back with surprising gentleness.

She didn't reply.

'What's wrong with you?' he bellowed. 'Why the hell didn't you tell me there was an injured woman in the car?'

'I was going to …'

'Shut up,' he roared at the top of his voice. 'Maureen!'

A stout, little woman with permed white hair and sallow skin hobbled from the cottage, looking confused. 'Yes, Tom?'

'Call an ambulance. Tell them there's been a road accident and that a woman's unconscious.'

'Yes, Tom,' she said, retreating.

Running towards Violet, I knelt at her side, feeling useless and terrified she was dying, holding her hand, shocked by how clammy and cold it felt.

Then I remembered my ABC.

A was for airways. Wiping blood and soil from her mouth and nose with the edge of my shirt, I made sure everything was clear.

B was for breathing. It was alright, her chest rising and falling, though faster than I'd have liked.

C was for circulation. Placing two fingers against her neck, finding the pulse, I was relieved beyond joy to feel how strong and regular it was.

The only blood was coming from a small split on her lower lip and from her left nostril.

'What's going on?' asked a tall, angular woman standing where the hedge had been.

'This idiot,' said the angry man, 'has crashed his car through my hedge and badly injured the young lady. Maureen's calling an ambulance but I fear it's too late.'

The woman stared at me through dead fish-eyes. 'I bet he's been drinking. They've always been drinking.'

'His breath stinks of it,' said Tom. 'They'll put him away this time, if there's still any justice in this country.'

'And good riddance,' added another spectator, an owl-faced man, peering at me.

Several people were soon at the gap, staring at me with contempt. Ignoring them as best I could, taking off my blazer, I laid it gently under Violet's head, trying to decide whether I needed to put her into the recovery position, longing for the ambulance to turn up. When at last her eyes opened, she stared up at me as if I were a complete stranger and tried to sit.

'No,' I said, placing a hand on her shoulder, 'it's best if you lie still until the ambulance gets here.'

'Where am I?' she asked, clawing my hand away roughly, sitting up anyway.

Though my hand stung, four little bleeding scratches showing where she'd made contact, I forced myself to ignore it. 'You're in this gentleman's garden,' I said.

'Felix?'

'No, it's me, Andy.'

'Are we having a picnic?'

'It's no bloody picnic,' Tom muttered.

'Did we catch many this time?' she asked, staring as if she thought she should know me, but couldn't quite place me.

'How many what?' asked Tom.

Her eyes suddenly coming into focus, she threw her arms around my neck. 'What happened?'

'You ... umm ... fainted after the accident.'

'Accident? Oh, yes ... stupid pig!'

'Don't you go calling me names,' said Tom, standing over us, grumbling. By the smell of him, I wasn't the only one who'd been drinking.

Violet, letting go of me, glanced up. 'Do we know him?'

'No,' I said, 'but unfortunately we crashed into his garden and did a bit of damage.'

'A lot of damage,' said Tom, 'which someone's going to pay for.' He kicked a pebble savagely.

'Are they?' asked Violet, smiling, 'well, that's good news, isn't it? ... I think I'm going to lie down again, I'm feeling a little woozy. Why is all that stuff on my car?'

'That's my hedge and beans,' said Tom.

'Just so long as we know.' Lying back, she closed her eyes.

A minute or two later, to the delight of the onlookers, several of whom seemed disappointed Violet wasn't dead, a police car arrived and a police officer strode towards us. To my disappointment, it was one from Hedbury, not someone I knew.

'What's going on here, then?' he asked.

'This idiot,' said Tom, jabbing his finger into my chest, 'crashed through my hedge and ruined my garden, not to mention injuring the young lady, who is lucky to be alive. I think I should point out that he's drunk.'

'I'm not dru ...,' I began and stopped, realising Violet had taken a drink. So far as I knew, she'd only had one small glass of wine and a little ginger beer, which was only slightly alcoholic. Though she should have been fine, I hadn't been with her all the time and, if she'd had more than I thought, I'd be dropping her right in it.

'I was driving,' she said, making my hesitation redundant.

'Is that correct, sir?' asked the officer looking at me as if at a rat.

I nodded.

'Are you injured, miss?' he asked, squatting beside her.

'I don't think so. I hit my lip and bumped my head but I'm not really hurt ... I just feel a bit funny.'

'I think she fainted after the accident,' I said, trying to be helpful. 'She's had a stressful evening.'

'Been out with you had she, sir?' asked the officer, standing up. 'Now, miss, just stay where you are while I ascertain a few facts.' Reaching into his shirt pocket for a notebook, he turned to me. 'Would you mind telling me what happened, sir?'

I did my best, with Tom interrupting and bemoaning his wrecked garden, judging it sensible to avoid mentioning Violet getting spooked in the arboretum, putting all the blame on the pig and whoever had let it out.

When I mentioned the house from which the pig had erupted, Tom nodded. 'That'll be Charlie Brick's place,' he said. 'He keeps pigs round the back.' He pointed. 'That's him by what's left of my poor hedge. Just look at it! Someone's going to pay for it.'

'I'm sure they will, sir,' said the police officer soothingly, beckoning over a little man wearing dirty white overalls.

Charlie Brick, dark, curly whiskers surrounding a pink face that made me think of a very intelligent monkey, loafed towards us.

The officer got straight to the point. 'Did a pig run from your house a few minutes ago?'

'It might have done, sir,' said Charlie in a slow drawl. 'The bugger, if you'll pardon my French, slipped through my fingers in the kitchen.'

'This gentleman alleges that it caused the young lady to swerve and crash.'

'Well, I'm sorry to hear that, but I expects she was driving too fast. Them's always driving too fast through our village.'

'Was she speeding, sir?' asked the officer, looking at me searchingly.

'I don't think so,' I lied. 'I'm not a driver myself, but I could tell she was slowing down before the accident, and I'm sure she wasn't driving any faster than anyone normally drives me.'

'I see.' The officer, making a note, turned towards Charlie. 'What happened to the pig?'

'I don't rightly know, sir,' said Charlie, scratching his head in a simian fashion, 'but I expects he'll be back when I feeds the others.'

'Where are the others?'

'In the sty, sir.'

'So what was that one doing in your kitchen?' asked the officer, looking confused.

'That's where I does my slaughtering – in the kitchen, if you understand me.'

'You were about to slaughter him?'

'Yes, sir, only he took fright when I started sharpening the knife and, well, sir, there ain't too many places to hold onto a pig. But he'll be back, the daft bugger … excuse me, and then I'll have him. There's nowt like home-cured bacon, sir.'

'Thank you,' said the officer. 'I must warn you that you may have committed an offence by allowing the animal to stray onto the public highway. You may not have heard the last of this.'

'Well, sir, I didn't exactly allow him to stray. I begged him to come back, but he wouldn't listen. That's pigs for you all over. Wilful they are, sir, wilful.' Charlie wandered away, shaking his head, scratching his ribs with a long, hairy hand.

The following flurry of activity left me quite bemused. The police officer kept asking questions and speaking into his radio. Violet groaned and was sick. The ambulance arrived at last and the paramedics, after a quick assessment, carried her away. Although I tried to go with her, they shut the doors in my face, leaving me at the roadside, watching her go, until a blaring horn made me jump out of the way. It was a tow truck. Tom's face turned an even deeper shade of purple as the car, attached to cables, was dragged from his garden, trailing a thicket of bamboo canes and bean plants through the hole in the hedge. As soon as the truck drove away, so did the police officer and, the show being over, the spectators went about their business, leaving Tom and I on our own. He wasn't very good company.

'Umm … could I use your phone?' I asked, realising I'd been left without transport, hoping Hobbes wouldn't mind picking me up.

'What?' asked Tom, his face attaining a darker tinge than I'd have believed possible. 'Use my phone? You think I'm going to let you into my house after what you've done to my garden? Not a bloody chance. There's a pay phone by the green. Now, get lost before I lose my bloody temper.'

As he stepped towards me, cracking his knuckles, I grabbed my blazer and fled, running until clear he wasn't following, stopping to take stock of my situation. It wasn't great, for I had an idea Blackdog Street was a weary walk away; a nearby signpost saying 'Sorenchester 14 miles', without any apology, concurred. Completely broke, apart from the penny I'd picked up, the pay phone was useless, even if it happened to be working, and it never occurred to me that I might be able to reverse the charges.

Though there would, presumably, have been plenty of telephones in peoples' houses, I doubted anyone seeing my filthy white trousers, my ludicrous blazer, my soiled and bloody shirt and my battered and holed straw hat would let me in. In despair, I tried to calculate how long it would take me to walk home but, having little idea of my walking speed, my best answer was a long time.

My hand was sore, four long scratches beading blood where Violet had slapped it. Sucking it away, I sighed, starting the trek, realising within a few minutes that it had not just been Tom's face that had darkened; everything had darkened and not only from the advancing evening. A rumble of not-too-distant thunder hinting at what was to come, my mood dipped even further.

Even worse than the prospect of getting soaked and exhausted, was not knowing how Violet was, though I could take some comfort from the fact that she was in good hands. Although I was nearly sure she'd only fainted, that her injuries were trivial, my mind kept throwing up all sorts of what ifs that deepened my gloom and despondency. Furthermore, Felix's threats still haunted me, leaving me unsure whether I even dared check up on her. Thinking that, perhaps it was the right time to break things off, I still had to know she was alright.

I hurried on, trying to get as far as possible before the storm hit, though it was clear the mile or two I might put behind me would make little difference; I was in for a soaking.

The storm continuing to rumble with malice, I reached Hedbury, finding it battened down for the night, except for the pubs, which were doing good trade. As I passed the Jolly Highwayman, I looked in through the big bay window, seeing it full of jovial, happy people, wishing I could join them, even entertaining the possibility of begging for a drink, or the use of the phone. Yet pride or, more likely, an unwillingness to be seen in the state I was in, exerted itself and I pressed on.

I was just passing a sign saying 'Sorenchester 11' when the first heavy raindrops struck. Coming individually at first, as if the storm was still making up its mind whether to unload its cargo, they made little difference to me since I was already damp with sweat. Within minutes, however, I was immersed in a downpour. Turning up my collar, huddling into my blazer in a futile attempt at shelter, I trudged on, rain ricocheting off the tarmac up to my thighs, passing cars dousing me in a heavy mist. That was when I was lucky. When I wasn't lucky, sheets of water skimmed across the road from lorry wheels, drenching me. With none of the drivers showing any inclination to stop and pick up a suffering human being, I had to leap onto the verge many times when they didn't appear to even notice me. In fairness, I doubted they expected to see anyone out on such a night.

The roadside was thick with grass, thistle-infested and slick with mud. When I slipped, I slid into the ditch. Though it wasn't deep, it was swampy and even worse was a selvedge of stinging nettles that spitefully attacked my poor hands as I pulled myself out. The rain, though not a constant torrent, came and went with great persistence as the storm rumbled near and far. To start with I made an effort to avoid the puddles, but it wasn't long before, being as wet as a frog, I couldn't have cared less. My clothes clung around my body, making every movement a struggle and, in spite of the effort, my teeth started chattering. As black night engulfed everything, all I could do was to keep walking.

It seemed like hours had passed when, at last, I made out the faint glimmer of electric light from what had to be the town, as an oncoming white van forced me into a puddle, which turned out to be a pothole, turning my ankle. Sitting on the verge, I hugged my leg, trying to comfort it and, despite the pain, the cold and the wet, I laughed; the picnic had lived up to – and exceeded – the disasters expected of Caplet outings. Then I cried.

After several minutes, during which not a single vehicle passed, I wiped my nose on my blazer sleeve, stood up and limped on, nearly crying again when I realised the lights I'd seen were shining across the fields from Randle, a village not even on the same road, and that there were another four miles to go before I reached the outskirts of Sorenchester, and then the best part of another mile after that. The idea of curling up in the ditch and letting life slip away began to have its appeal, yet, before I died, I had to know Violet was safe. I kept going. My tennis pumps, limp and sodden, rubbed my feet, particularly the one attached to my good ankle and, discovering how extraordinarily difficult it was to limp on both sides, my progress was painfully slow. A stick poking from the hedge jabbed into my calf, tearing my trouser leg. Though I swore at it, it made a passable walking stick until, when it snapped, I fell hard, lying for a while in the road, winded, exhausted, sore, aching and shivering. Only a vast expenditure of willpower got me back to my feet. A lightning flash and simultaneous roll of thunder making me jump, I drew a deep breath.

The next flash, seeing, exposed in stark black and white, a figure staring at me from the other side of the road, my blood would have run cold had I not already been so chilled; the muscles in my legs would have turned to water had they not already been so weak and wobbly. I tried hard, really hard, to convince myself my imagination was playing tricks, that, on such a dark and stormy night, a mind could easily wander from reality, especially one weakened by fatigue, shock and pain.

It didn't work for I knew I really had seen a creature from nightmares, a creature with dark hair, glinting white teeth and reflective eyes, though nothing like a panther. The thing was, it had been standing upright. I wished Hobbes was with me.

I wished I hadn't just seen a werewolf.

When the next flash split the night, it had vanished. I couldn't decide if that was reassuring or not. If it had gone, then all well and good, but how did I know it wasn't stalking me? What if it was already behind me, preparing to spring and tear me apart? Was that a twig cracking? Was that heavy breathing?

Out there in the dripping darkness all my being turned to fear and I learned what a sudden dose of adrenaline can do to a tired body. I ran like an Olympic champion, oblivious to the pain in my ankle, the rawness of my feet, my weary legs, only slowing when the streetlights of Sorenchester surrounded me, cocooning me in the safety of civilisation. When I looked back I was sure something dark slipped into the shadows. Yet, knowing it hadn't got me, the elation of survival spurred me on.

I hobbled through the deserted streets, the storm receding into distant rumblings, the rain turning to a light drizzle. It stopped completely when I reached Blackdog Street.

The house was quiet when I let myself in. I dragged myself upstairs, filled the bath with hot water, stripped off my filthy, sodden clothes and lowered myself in with a groan. Though my chilled skin protested, my feet stinging and throbbing, it was glorious to feel the warmth ooze back into my body. I would have fallen asleep had I not dropped the soap with a splash. I got out, dried myself, wrapped a towel around my middle and stumbled towards my room. Too tired to worry about anything, even Violet, I must have fallen asleep as soon as I'd got into bed.

14

On waking, I wished I hadn't. My head was throbbing with the power of a ten-pint hangover, my armpits had apparently been fitted with painful lumps, as big as golf balls, and my ankle kept going into agonising spasms on every heartbeat. Everywhere hurt and, weak as a newly-hatched chick, I was shivering, presumably because all my bedclothes had fallen off. Blindly groping on the floor failing to find them, I opened my eyes and whimpered, for even my eyeballs ached. The door clicked open.

'Good morning,' said Mrs Goodfellow. 'How are you today?'

Shaking my head in response proving a big mistake, my groan sounded as pathetic as I felt.

'Are you feeling poorly?'

'Yes,' I said through chattering teeth.

'You must be cold, dear, without any bedclothes or pyjamas,' she said, pulling the blankets over me and touching my forehead. 'You feel like you're burning, but I'll fetch you a hot water bottle.'

She left, returning a few minutes later with a grey rubber object that appeared to have been moulded in the shape of a deformed hippopotamus. I hugged it, enjoying the warmth, and snuggled down.

'Were you caught in the storm, dear? I thought you must have been because of the state of your clothes. I'm having 'em laundered and Milord should be able to fix the trousers and the blazer, but your pumps have had it and there's such a big hole in the straw hat I doubt there's any chance of fixing it. Now, can I get you something to eat?'

'No.'

'A nice hot drink, then?'

'Please … and some aspirins.'

'Aspirins? I don't think we've got any, though I do have a tincture that should make you feel as right as reindeer.'

As her footsteps receded, having an urgent need to relieve my bladder, I pulled myself into a sitting position, fearing any delay might prove disastrous and, though I hardly dared get to my feet, I had no choice. Wrapping a soft blanket around me, I hobbled to the bathroom, making it with seconds to spare, finding it a long way back.

The storm having passed, the sun shone painfully brightly through the closed curtains, as I curled up in bed, blankets piled high, the warm rubber hippo on my stomach, still shivering when the old girl returned with a mug of steaming something. Fluffing a couple of pillows, slipping them under my shoulders, she helped me sip the concoction. I'm not certain what was in it, though there might have been lavender. Finishing it, I lay back, feeling disconnected from the aches and pains in my body.

A scuffling woke me, or I think so, because everything was vague and fuzzy, almost as if I was dreaming or hallucinating. The curtains having been drawn back and the window opened, I could hear the Saturday bustle of the town as I lay a while, blinking, fascinated by the scintillating patterns swirling in the sunlight. Trying to work out what was causing the peculiar misshapen shadow moving across the carpet, I looked up, seeing Hobbes's face upside down outside the window, winking at me from beneath a broad grin.

Puzzled, I closed my eyes. When I looked again, he'd been replaced by Milord Schmidt, hunched on a small stool, stitching a tear in my blazer.

'Good afternoon,' he said, peering over the top of his half-moon spectacles, stretching out his long, thin legs.

An unfamiliar middle-aged woman, smelling of disinfectant, was leaning over me, poking various tender places, shaking her head and frowning. When I opened my mouth to ask what she was doing, she popped in a thermometer, continuing the prodding occasionally saying 'um' or 'aah'. The 'ooh' came from me; her hands could have been warmer.

Retrieving the thermometer, she peered at it. 'You did well to call me in,' she said, ignoring me. 'He's certainly got a high fever, so it's no wonder he's feeling poorly. He would appear to have picked up a rather nasty infection, almost certainly a bacterial one, though I'll take a blood sample to make sure. In the meantime, I'll prescribe him a course of antibiotics. He should start it as soon as possible. I must say it's peculiar how the illness happened just like that, but I'd be surprised if it wasn't connected with the scratches on his hand.

'I almost think he should be in hospital, but I've an idea he'll be better off here. Make sure he has plenty to drink and he can eat a little when he feels up to it. Call me if he gets any worse, or if there's no improvement in the next two days.'

'Now,' she said, swabbing my arm with alcohol, 'you'll feel a little scratch.'

When she thrust the needle into my arm just below the elbow, I whimpered, nearly fainting as the little glass tube filled up with my blood. As she straightened up, turning away, I felt a momentary resentment that I hadn't been involved before drifting off.

Now and again Mrs Goodfellow shook me awake to pop some foul-tasting pills down my throat, washing them down with cool drinks. Sometimes I sweated, kicking off the bedclothes; other times I shivered, clutching them around me. The long night let loose dreams, leading me down nightmare alleys, where big cats with glowing eyes prowled, oblivious to something darker, something worse than panthers, lurking in the shadows. It was something looking like a man, except it was all wrong, though not in the way Hobbes was wrong. It was stalking Violet and I tried to warn her, only for Charlie Brick to release a herd of grinning pigs that ran squealing through a hole in the hedge, getting in my way. Unable to get close, I screamed for her to run.

'It's only a nightmare, dear,' said Mrs G.

I opened my eyes, blinking in the morning light, my chin rasping against the white sheets. I found it was surprisingly bristly.

'How are you feeling?' asked Mrs Goodfellow.

'Not so bad,' I said.

'That's good. You've been rather ill and Doctor Procter was quite worried – we all were – but the antibiotics seem to be working. Would you like any breakfast?'

'Umm … yes. Yes, I would. I really fancy scrambled eggs. I'm starving.'

Smiling, she walked away. After a few minutes, I sat up abruptly, feeling something terribly wrong around my waist. I put my hand beneath the sheets. Appalled at what I touched, I threw back the blankets and stared in absolute, horrified disbelief. Someone, and I didn't need to guess who, had encased my nether regions in a nappy.

A tray appeared at the bedroom door, followed by Mrs Goodfellow.

'Why,' I asked, pointing, 'am I wearing this?'

'To keep you dry.'

'But …'

'You needed it, dear, to stop you wetting the bed.'

'I did what?'

'Sorry, dear. It was for the best. You weren't able to get to the bathroom.'

'Oh, God,' I muttered, cringing, covering myself up, disgusted and ashamed, 'I'm really sorry.'

'You couldn't help it and, anyway, I saw a lot worse when I was nursing. Don't worry. Enjoy your breakfast.' Handing me the tray, she left me to it.

I shrugged. What had happened had happened, and didn't

alter the fact that I was ravenous. She'd made scrambled eggs on toast and I wolfed them down at first, desperate to fill the emptiness. Only towards the end, the edge having been smoothed off my hunger, did I begin to appreciate their wonderful fragrance and fluffiness, though my taste buds didn't seem quite up to scratch. Even the tea tasted odd, though I still gulped it down.

I'd just finished eating when she returned with the *Bugle*. 'I brought you this. Would you like anything else, dear?'

'Yes, please. Could I have some toast and marmalade?'

'Of course. Would two slices do?'

'Better make it four … and some more tea would be great. Thanks.'

The headline was intriguing.

'Publican struck by lightning on battery charge.'

Underneath was a photograph of Featherlight Binks, wrestling with six police officers in front of the Feathers. I wasn't surprised, knowing how often he'd been arrested before.

What confused me was seeing it was in Monday's paper, which made no sense. The picnic had been on Friday evening, after which I'd walked home and gone to bed. It must, therefore, have been Saturday morning when I'd woken up feeling poorly, and now, somehow, it was Monday. Sunday had apparently come and gone without trace, which was weird, almost as if I'd been time travelling, skipping over a day of my life. Still, there was no point fretting. All I could do was to resume life where I'd rejoined it.

I forced myself to read the story. 'Leonard Holdfast Binks,' it said, 'landlord of the Feathers public house, was arrested on Sunday lunchtime, following allegations of a serious assault. According to Mr William Shawcroft, an eyewitness, when officers informed Binks, widely known as Featherlight, that he was under arrest, he adopted an aggressive stance, letting slip a tirade of foul and abusive language before attempting to absent himself from the premises via the back door. He was arrested after a struggle during which six officers received minor yet spectacular injuries.

According to Mr Shawcroft, Binks would probably have made good his escape had he not been under the weather, having been struck by lightning during Friday night's storm. Binks, he reports, is frequently struck, possibly on account of a metal plate in his head. Mr Shawcroft stated that Binks, who has several previous convictions for violence and cooking, is normally at his most placid following a lightning strike and that his behaviour was out of character. As Binks was dragged into the back of a police van, he denied assaulting anyone over the weekend and threatened anyone who disagreed with him with "a good shoeing".

'The victim, an as yet unnamed businessman, remains in hospital, where a spokesman reports that he is critical but stable.'

I'd just finished the article when Mrs Goodfellow returned with the toast and marmalade and more tea.

'I see Featherlight's in trouble again,' I remarked.

'It seems so,' she said, adjusting my pillows. 'Yet the old fellow has his doubts.'

'But, he injured six policemen,' I said, pointing at the photo. 'You can see what he did. There can't be any doubt.'

'He did that, but denies the original assault.'

'Well, he would, wouldn't he?'

'I doubt it. The old fellow reckons Mr Binks is honest. That is, though he may be involved in a multitude of nefarious schemes, he doesn't actually tell lies. Of course, what he perceives as the truth might differ from how you or I might see it.'

I laughed. 'You might be right, I'm sure he really believes he is a purveyor of fine ales and good food.'

'That's true, dear. Anyway, the old fellow believes him.'

'I still don't get it. If he didn't attack the businessman, then who did?'

'I have no idea, dear. Now, enjoy the rest of your breakfast and then you can tell me all about your picnic.'

After breakfast, while Mrs Goodfellow tidied up, I told my tale, though leaving out Felix's threats and the werewolf. I was still trying to come to terms with it all. When I'd finished, fearing the worst, I asked whether Violet had been in touch.

'No, I'm afraid not. I did wonder when she didn't call, if you two had fallen out.'

'I hope she's alright,' I said, a flock of worries fluttering round my stomach like frightened pigeons.

'I expect she is, dear. Otherwise we'd have heard something. Her brother would have let you know, wouldn't he?'

'Maybe,' I said, without feeling reassured. Still, I had an inkling that if anything really bad had happened, then Hobbes would have known and told the old girl. I still wasn't happy but the feelings of panic took wing.

After a bath, I brushed my teeth, removing a triple dose of morning breath, and went back to bed for a couple of hours. Waking just before lunch, I was strong enough to hobble downstairs, where Mrs Goodfellow had prepared chicken soup especially for me, Hobbes and Dregs having gone out for the day. Though I'd guess it was up to standard, my taste buds were still numb, for which I blamed the antibiotics, hoping the effect was temporary.

'The old fellow's supposed to be having the afternoon off,' said Mrs G, 'but he said he'd better take a close look at Loop's Farm.'

'Loop's Farm?'

'That's right, dear. The festival's on next weekend and those cats still haven't gone away – he says he nearly caught one on Saturday night. What's more, he believes something else is on the prowl, though it seemed to intrigue him rather than worry him.'

I nodded, coming to a decision. 'That's interesting,' I said, 'because I think I saw something when I was walking home, something odd.'

'Did you, dear?'

'Yes, it was when the lightning flashed. I saw it and it scared me so much I ran away as fast as my legs could carry me, and further than I'd have thought possible.'

'What did you see?'

Screwing up my eyes, I tried to pick out the image from a mess of memories. 'It was about man-sized and shaped, not as big as Hobbes or Featherlight, but big enough and it was sort of standing upright, yet kind of hunched, and it looked like it had hair and eyes. And teeth.'

'All the better to eat you with, dear.'

I laughed. 'But the crazy thing is I'm sure it was wearing trousers.'

'So you're telling me you saw what looked like a man wearing trousers? Extraordinary!'

'Yes,' I said, feeling slightly foolish, 'but it wasn't a man, I'm certain.'

'You haven't been very well. Perhaps the fever made you imagine things.'

'Maybe … but I don't think so. I don't think I was ill then.'

On reflection, I didn't believe I'd been hallucinating, remaining convinced something frightening had really been out there, something that was almost certainly a werewolf, though I didn't want to admit it, not even to myself. Once upon a time, before Hobbes, I'd have found it impossible to believe the evidence of my eyes, but I'd learned that strange folk lived among us, strange folk that went unremarked for the most part.

Still lethargic and tired, it was all I could do to slump in front of the telly, watching a heart-warming made-for-TV movie about a woman's brave fight for life and love after a horrific car crash left her with a collection of rather photogenic scars. Climaxing in a spurt of sickly sentimentality, it nearly turned my stomach, leaving me deep in melancholy.

Desperate for news of Violet, I could have kicked myself for not having thought to get her phone number, an obvious move, yet one that had never occurred to me, since she'd been the one to get in touch. I wondered if I'd been a little passive, whether some assertiveness would have been to my benefit, perhaps even impressing Felix. Realising that, if I'd shown any sign of being a man, I wouldn't have been me, I spent some time wallowing in a mire of self-indulgent misery. Yet, eventually, I roused enough to call the hospital. The woman I spoke to refused to answer any questions about Violet on the grounds that the law forbade it, refusing to budge even after I'd told her what I thought of the law.

I moped, having run out of options. Though, in truth, I knew I hadn't, I indulged my feelings of helplessness, unwilling to admit the most obvious course of action; I had Felix's card and could phone him, if I dared. I fretted and dithered and, though it was a close call, my need to know won out in the end. Finding his card, dried out and creased, on the dressing table in my room, I took it to the phone and dialled the number.

'Mr King's office,' said an efficient female voice. 'Carol speaking. How may I help you?'

'I umm … I'd like to talk to Felix.'

'Mr King is out of the office. Can I take a message?'

'Umm …' I said, having failed to anticipate this contingency, 'yes … or perhaps you can help me? I want to know how Violet King is.'

'I'm afraid Miss King is off work. She was involved in a car accident.'

'I know. I was with her. How is she?'

'May I take your name, sir?'

'Yes, it's Caplet. Andy Caplet.'

'I thought it might be; Mr King informed me of the possibility you would call. He said anyone with a modicum of decency would have followed her to the hospital.'

'But I couldn't …'

'Mr King,' Carol continued, 'asked me to let you know that you are a self-centred, money-grubbing bastard.'

'I'm not …'

'And you are to leave his sister alone. Should you persist in importuning her, steps will be taken. That is all.'

'But is she alright?'

'That is all, Mr Caplet.'

'But please, I must know how she is.'

'You could have asked her yourself if you'd been bothered enough to visit her in hospital.'

'But I was seriously ill.'

'Were you?' she asked, the faintest hint of feminine sympathy in her voice.

'Yes ... I've had a terrible fever and have only just risen from my sickbed,' I said, laying it on a bit thick, making my voice sound weak and feeble.

It worked.

'Alright, then,' she said, lowering her voice to a whisper, 'and don't tell anyone I told you, but Miss King is fine now. She had a mild shock with a few minor cuts and bruises and is taking a break until she feels better.'

'Thank you,' I murmured, though I don't know why I, too, felt the need to lower my voice. Things were going so well that I thought I'd push my luck. 'Umm ... I wonder if you could let me have her address? Or her phone number?'

'Don't push it,' said Carol, 'I've already said more than I should have.'

'Please!'

'Sorry.' Her voice returned to normal. 'Thank you for calling, sir. Goodbye.' She put the phone down.

My first feeling was of relief that Violet was alright for, although, I'd had no reason to believe she wouldn't be, it was a great weight off my mind to be certain. My second feeling was of outrage. How dare Felix try to order me around? How dare he tell his secretary to insult me? The third feeling was of slow, cold fear. What if Carol told Felix I'd called? The fourth feeling was more familiar: total bewilderment. I didn't know what to do next.

As afternoon rolled into early evening, I caught myself laughing at children's cartoons, feeling better the sillier they were, for they stopped me having to think. The early evening news put my problems into perspective, though other people's tragedies didn't make me feel any better about my own.

The front door bursting open, I was pounced on by Dregs who seemed delighted to see me downstairs and, though my battle to keep his tongue at a safe distance ended in an abject rout, his enthusiasm cheered me.

'Good to see you up,' said Hobbes, striding into the room, baring his great yellow teeth in a smile. 'How are you feeling?'

'Not too bad. I'm ready for my supper, though.'

'Me too,' he said as he bounded upstairs to wash his hands.

At supper, I was, once again, a little disappointed at the lack of response from my taste buds, despite Mrs G having cooked a magnificent shepherd's pie with Sunday's leftover lamb. Still, it filled me up perfectly and I would have been a relatively contented Andy, had Hobbes not poured himself a goblet of wine and drunk it with such evident enjoyment. Mrs G wouldn't allow me any alcohol while I was on antibiotics.

The wine reminding me of what Felix had said, I wondered if he'd regard me more favourably if I sorted something out for him.

'Violet's brother, Felix, asked me to ask you where you got your wine from.'

'And you've asked me,' said Hobbes with a chuckle. 'Well done.' He took another sip and sighed.

'The thing is, Felix reckons it's quality stuff and wants to buy some.'

'He's right about the quality, but he'll not find it on sale anywhere.'

'Why not?'

'Because it's a gift.'

'Who from?' I asked, resentful that no one ever gave me valuable presents.

'A friend.'

'Oh, well, in that case, Felix wanted to know whether he might buy any off you. He said you could name your price.'

'What price can you put on a gift from a friend?'

asked Hobbes.

That stumped me, though I knew what price you could put on a gift from a mother. It was £5.99 in the sale – she'd left the price tag on the jumper she'd given me for my birthday. 'I don't know but I reckon he'd pay … umm … a hundred pounds a bottle.'

'As much as that?' asked Hobbes, raising his eyebrows. 'Doesn't he know he can pick up a drinkable wine from the supermarket for less than a tenner?'

'I doubt he'd consider drinking anything in that price range.'

'Why not?'

'Umm … I think he regards himself as a connoisseur, liking only the really good stuff. That's why he's so interested in yours.'

I felt I was really in there, fighting for Felix, doing exactly what he wanted me to do, though I wouldn't have been had I not wanted a chance with Violet. I still couldn't accept it was any of Felix's business what I did with his sister, as long as she wanted me. Of course, she hadn't called me and I seemed to be losing any chance of getting the wine for him.

'I'm sorry,' said Hobbes firmly, 'I can't sell the wine, though, since he's a friend of yours, he can have a crate as a gift.'

'What? Really?' I said, staggered by his generosity.

'Of course.' He drained his goblet. 'If he's a friend of yours, then he's a friend of mine. Right, I'm off to bed. I'm getting too old for all these nights out on the tiles. Thanks, lass for a delicious supper.' Yawning, he rose from the table and strode upstairs.

I sat back, feeling like a hypocrite, for, though I hadn't actually said Felix was my friend, I'd let him think it. Worse, I didn't care to think on my reason for helping Felix: getting him the wine in order to buy his favour, hoping he would then allow me to get off with his little sister. I didn't feel at all good about myself, despite my intentions being, more or less, strictly honourable. The whole episode had acquired a sleazy taint.

Mrs Goodfellow, materialising at my elbow, nudged me, resulting in a vertical take-off. 'A penny for your thoughts,' she said.

I landed back on my chair, shaking.

'You were looking very thoughtful, dear.'

'Yes ... umm ... I was just wondering where he gets his wine from.'

'From an old friend,' she said.

'Yeah, but which old friend?'

'It's from the Count.'

'His friend's a Count?'

'Yes, they met during the war, when the old fellow was able to do him a small service. They became friends and the Count sends him wine in gratitude.'

'Which war?'

'The Great one, dear. The First World War, you know?'

'I know,' I said, having seen the Victoria Cross in a tin in a drawer in his desk at the police station. Besides, Mrs Goodfellow had occasionally told me small details of his heroics, something he never spoke of. Though, somehow, I'd grown comfortable with the idea of his participation in a war a century ago, I was puzzled by his friend. 'I suppose the Count must be pretty ancient then?'

'I suppose he is, but he never forgets to send the wine.'

'Felix said he'd drunk a similar wine that cost five hundred pounds a bottle and the Count must send crates of it every year.'

'That's right, except during the Second War, when transport was a problem. He always sends half a dozen crates of the ordinary and one of the good stuff.'

'He must be very rich if he can afford to send all that, and generous.'

'He is very wealthy. He has a chateau perched on a hill with magnificent views all along the river – you should see it – and he is generous to a fault. Mind you he wouldn't have been either if it hadn't been for the old fellow.'

'Why? What did he do?'

'I'll tell you what I know,' she said. 'Years ago, when the old fellow had a week's leave and we visited the Count, he told me something of what had occurred. The Count is a charming fellow, by the way, with lovely white teeth; you'd like him. During the war he was a French Army lieutenant and was marching back from the front with his section when a shell struck the duckboards, throwing them all into liquid mud. Men would often drown if they fell in and that would probably have been their fate.'

'It must have been horrible,' I said, shuddering.

'It must have been, and all of them would probably have died had the old fellow not been passing and pulled them out. Afterwards, an officer reprimanded him for losing his boots.'

'That's typical!' I said, clicking my tongue.

'It wasn't really; he only lost them once. He seemed to hit it off with the Count, who ever since has expressed his gratitude with wine. That's about as much as I know, dear.'

'Thank you. I sometimes wish he'd talk more about the war.'

'He won't. He hardly ever says much about it these days. He reckons there's too much going on now to waste time on ancient history. Even so, he did once try to trace his ancestors but gave up.'

'He was adopted, wasn't he? Did he find anything?'

'Not that I know. Well, I can't stand round here all evening; I've got my Kung Fu to get to. We'll be looking after security during the festival. See you later, dear.'

She walked away, leaving me with Dregs who, having taken a leaf out of Hobbes's book, was lying on his back in his basket, an idiot grin on his face, emitting gentle snores. Leaving him to it, I hobbled through into the sitting room, wishing my feet weren't so sore, wondering if I could really let Hobbes give Felix the wine. If he did, I might yet have a chance with Violet, though, I couldn't help thinking that Felix would still detest me. In that case, he'd be the only winner.

I sat watching telly until the old girl got back, her face pink and shiny. Then, after a cup of cocoa and yet another antibiotic tablet, I went up to bed, sleeping as if I hadn't already slept for most of the weekend.

Next morning at breakfast, I sensed, once I'd filled my stomach enough to take notice of anything other than bacon and eggs, that Hobbes, the *Bugle* open but unread before him, stirring his tea and sucking his finger, was lost in thought. He stared at the ceiling apparently finding great interest in its network of cracks as I launched an attack on the toast and marmalade.

'There'll be no moon tonight,' he said.

'Won't there?' I asked, brushing crumbs off my chin.

'No, and furthermore, there'll be heavy cloud cover.'

'That's no good,' I said. 'It'll probably rain.'

'Yes, and it will be very dark in the woods.'

'I suppose so.' I wondered where he was heading.

'Which means those cats won't be able to see so well, which might give me a chance to nab them.'

'Are you sure? I thought cats could see pretty well in the dark.'

'They can, but it will be very dark tonight, which might be to my advantage.'

'Might it? Won't it be dark for you, too?'

'Of course, but that will not be a problem.'

'They'll still be able to hear and smell you, won't they?'

'Yes, and I'll be able to hear and smell them.'

'So, what are you going to do?'

'Think about it. By the way, I think something else is out there, something that might interest you.'

Something in the way he said it made my skin crawl. I could still see the creature in the lightning flash. 'What?'

'Something rare and rather exciting, I think.'

'Yes, but what?' My nerves tightened.

'Though I'm not entirely sure.'

'Please tell me.'

'I think we have a werewolf.'

'No!' I said, unwilling to believe him despite what I'd seen.

'Yes. Right, I'm off to work.' He rose from the table, leaving me open-mouthed and shaking.

'But what are you going to do about it?'

'Nothing, unless anyone makes trouble. Goodbye.' Calling Dregs, he left me to my thoughts.

I sat at the table, shaking, convinced he should be doing considerably more than nothing. Perhaps I was prejudiced, and he had insisted werewolves weren't dangerous, but I couldn't help feeling he should be raising a mob with flaming brands and pitchforks to destroy the monster. The merest glimpse had filled me with dread and I'd discovered how easily fear could turn to hatred. I wanted the thing dead so I would feel safe. Whether there was a genuine threat didn't matter.

15

Mrs Goodfellow took a break from washing the dishes to stand beside me and look sympathetic. 'Are you feeling poorly again, dear?'

'No,' I said, trembling, 'he thinks there's a werewolf.'

She smiled. 'Yes, isn't it exciting?'

'Exciting? It's terrifying.'

'Oh no, it's wonderful news. It would be lovely if they could make a comeback round here. I miss them; we used to have such fun.'

Either the old girl and Hobbes were quite mad, or I was.

'Yes,' she said, 'we used to have great times with old Wolfie. I wonder who the new one is? Wouldn't it be funny if it was someone we know?'

'Hilarious,' I said, grimacing, the very idea giving me the creeps.

'They've probably just moved into the area.' She chuckled. 'How long have you been in town, dear?'

'Long enough. I'm no freak.'

'Of course you aren't, dear,' she said.

'Umm … good. So long as that's clear.'

'We ought to go out one night, see if we can find it and make friends.'

'Well, not tonight, then. He said there'll be no moon.'

'That might make it a bit tricky for the likes of us, but it won't be a problem for him.'

'What I mean is there won't be any about. Don't werewolves

only come out when there's a moon?'

'Of course not, dear. People believe such silly things and I think this myth came about since werewolves were most often spotted when the moon was out, so people assumed they only came out then.'

'Well, what's wrong with that?'

'The thing is, dear, if you're going to see anything at night it's likely to be under the moon, ideally the full moon – because of the light.'

'So they do come out at other times?'

'Of course.'

'So, one might be out tonight?'

'Yes.'

I decided I wouldn't be out that night.

It came as some surprise to find myself trailing through Loop Woods, a few hours later, wondering why I'd changed my mind so easily. I'd made my first mistake after finishing supper when I'd mentioned to Hobbes that Dr Procter had been round and pronounced me fit and well, so long as I was careful.

'In that case,' he said, 'do you fancy coming out tonight and having a go at nabbing those big cats?'

Though the sane bit of my brain, stunned for a moment, did not fancy it at all, my crazy mouth had already made my second mistake by saying, 'I'd love to'. The third mistake had been when the sane bit of brain, trying to get me to change my mind, wanting me to say no, had discovered that my crazy mouth was still refusing to cooperate. I could blame no one but myself.

It was already getting gloomy, an occasional fine drizzle a hint of what was to come. Anticipating heavy rain, I was wrapped up in an old mac and a flat cap, both Mr Goodfellow's cast-offs. Dregs led the way, his thick, dark hair a match for any weather. Hobbes sauntered at my side, wearing his tatty old raincoat, carrying a canvas bag and a chair from the kitchen. I was still more than mildly miffed he hadn't let me take one as well.

'Why couldn't I have a chair?' I asked. 'It might be a long night and I don't want to be sitting on damp ground.'

'Don't worry about that, I know a tree that'll give good shelter and be an excellent vantage point.'

'So what's the chair for? To give you a step up into the tree?'

'No. What I'll do is give you and Dregs a hand onto a safe branch and scramble up afterwards.'

'So what is it for?'

'For the cats. I've seen how lion tamers do it.'

'But you've never tried?'

'There has to be a first time for everything.'

'And what's in the bag?'

'A bullwhip. Lion tamers apparently use them, though I'm not sure why.'

I was getting a bad feeling about this venture and perching in a tree in darkness was no longer top of my worry list. 'But after you've successfully tamed it ...'

'Them,' corrected Hobbes.

'Or them ... What are you going to do then?'

'I've put a couple of dog collars and leads in the bag, so I expect I'll be able to work something out.'

'Have you actually thought this through?'

'No, improvisation is half the fun.'

Shaking my head, thinking it was more like madness, I kept with him, though it seemed that even Dregs, who was keeping within touching distance, was nervous. Hobbes loped through the quickly deepening gloom, his chair and bag slung across his back, his knuckles brushing the leaf mould, stopping now and again to sniff the air. A bird fluttered to its roost, giving a low warble, and that, besides the scuff and stumbling of my feet and the rustling of Dregs's paws was all I could hear. As usual, I was amazed how Hobbes, even with his great clumping feet, could move as silently as an owl when he wished. The breeze strengthening, the sun nearly down, I wished I'd put on a jumper. Pausing to get my bearings, I tried to come to terms with being there, thinking that, although on a warm, sunny afternoon I wasn't averse to a gentle stroll in the woods, with the night falling, hard, heavy clouds threatening torrents, dangerous animals about, I'd rather have stayed at home.

'Keep up,' said Hobbes, 'or you might get lost.'

I put on a spurt, having no intention of letting that happen.

Hobbes, stopping abruptly, held up his hand. 'Come here,' he whispered, 'and quietly.'

As Dregs stiffened and bristled, Hobbes reached out and grabbed his collar. My mouth felt dry, as if I'd been force-fed cream crackers; I couldn't even gulp, a sick feeling of cold fear filling my stomach.

'Shhh!' Hobbes murmured, 'over there, by the fallen tree.'

A giant tree trunk, moss covered and cracked, lay in gentle repose, gradually returning to the soil. Hearing what sounded like a cough and something purring, my mind said run, but my legs just shook. A grunt, as if from a man, was followed by a series of chattering squeaks and I suppressed a gasp as a sleek, grey animal with a black and white striped snout and small white-tipped ears gambolled into sight. Another launched itself over the tree trunk and the pair of badger cubs conducted a play fight, rolling and scrabbling in the leaf mould, driving away all of my fear. I'd never before seen wild badgers, apart from dead ones by the side of the Pigton Road, and hadn't realised how much I wanted to. A few moments later, a larger animal, the mother I supposed, ambled into view, rooting under the dead tree with powerful paws, grunting and coughing.

Though I would have been happy to stand and watch for hours, Dregs whined in a tone that meant he wanted to play, Mother Badger barked a warning, and all three trundled into the undergrowth.

'Oh well,' said Hobbes, smiling, 'we'd best get on'.

He loped away, leading us into denser woodland as the evening turned to night-time, any starlight being smothered by the trees and a sodden blanket of cloud. When an owl hooted, I felt Dregs jump. Raindrops pattered into the silent woods; I heard them long before I felt them.

'Here we are,' said Hobbes, patting the trunk of a tree that was barely visible in the darkness. His bag rustling, he squatted on his haunches, spreading something on the ground.

'What are you doing?' I whispered.

'Putting down some bait; Mrs Goodfellow bought me some marrowbones.'

'Will they work?'

'We'll see. Right, you two need to be out of the way.'

Before I could even think of objecting, he grabbed me round the waist, launching me upwards. Though I flailed in panic, I landed gently on something broad and solid. Groping around, I felt how a couple of sturdy, horizontal boughs, having interlocked, had formed a sort of small platform. I didn't know how high I was, what was above or what was below. All I knew was that I was up a tree and that I might just as well have been blind.

'Hold on,' said Hobbes, 'here comes the dog.'

'You can't throw him into a tree,' I said, reaching for some sort of handhold.

I was wrong. Dregs, landing beside me with a surprised yelp, sniffed around and proved he was made of sterner stuff than I by curling up as if to sleep.

'Where are you?' I called down to Hobbes.

'Up here,' he said.

'Eh? What?' Jerking back, staring blindly into the canopy, I nearly lost my balance.

His hand grabbed my shoulder, steadying me. 'I told you to hold on. Do as I say, and keep quiet. We may be here for some time.'

Finding a twisted cable, some sort of creeping plant that felt solid, I looped it round my left hand and sat still, as the rain started for real with a sound like a thousand tiny drummers and, though the leaves sheltered me and my cap kept off the worst of it, heavy dollops would, from time to time, explode into my face. My trousers, growing soggy, clung coldly around my legs. Though Dregs sighed every now and then, Hobbes might have sloped off minutes or hours earlier and I wouldn't have known; the concept of time seemed meaningless. Huddling against the rain as best I could, I wished again I'd stayed at home, deciding that almost anywhere was more comfortable than halfway up a tree in the rain. My bottom growing numb and wet, I wriggled in an effort to find a more comfortable position, letting out a soft groan.

'Shhh!' Hobbes hissed by my ear, clamping his hand across my mouth to stifle the gasp rising to my lips. 'Something's coming,' he whispered and was gone.

I held onto my precious creeper, waves of fear crashing through my body, scared that he hadn't said what was coming, giving me no clue as to whether it might be panthers, or a werewolf or just the badgers returning. Those next few moments rated well up my top ten most terrifying experiences. I couldn't see, all I could hear was rain, I was perched God knew how high up a tree, and all I could smell was the earthy scent of leaf mould and the stink of wet dog. When Dregs, all of a sudden, pressed his cold nose into my neck, I jumped, losing my grip, plummeting. In such a crisis, my brain must have worked faster than normal, because it had time to remember Hobbes's warning, to suppress a shriek, and still wonder how much I'd hurt myself when I hit the ground.

Instead of actually hitting the ground, I landed astride something soft, if not as soft as a man in my position might have wished. The thing snarled, twisting away from me and, despite the shock, all I could do was whimper, clutching my delicate parts, dropping to my knees. Two green eyes flashed and, by some trick of the light or of my imagination, I could see it clearly: it being a big, black cat. Judging by the way it was thrashing its tail, I'd annoyed it; judging by the way it was limping, I'd hurt it.

Strangely, I wasn't quite as scared as I had been in the tree.

Perhaps the pain had something to do with it, but my fear of the dark unknown proved even worse than what was before me. It wasn't rational, of course, for anything has more potential for harm than nothing, and a big cat has more potential than most things. Neither was it rational to kneel there thinking such thoughts when I should have been fleeing for my life.

At last, I legged it, though not for long as I ran headlong into a spiky bush. Disentangling myself, I turned to face the panther. It was poised to spring.

'Whoa! Here, kitty, kitty,' Hobbes shouted from a distance: too great a distance.

As the panther leapt, I dropped and curled into a ball, my hands covering my face, an instinctive reaction that I doubted would help, yet the panther never touched me. Its great paws landed by my head and it ran. A moment later, something dark, hairy and heavy hurtled past, followed by Dregs, barking, with Hobbes bringing up the rear, bounding after them, almost silently.

I climbed back to my feet, trembling, sore, feeling horribly out of place. Not far away, something angry was growling and spitting and I wondered how many panthers infested the woods. The sounds of the chase were receding into the distance when an animal yelped in pain, a piteous sound, but it wasn't Dregs or Hobbes.

Though my first instinct was to run towards it and help, I didn't dare turn my back on the growling, spitting thing, hoping Hobbes had trapped it, fearing he hadn't, that the panther was winding up its fury before tearing me into little pieces. The tree I'd been in felt like sanctuary, though I doubted any panther would have trouble climbing it.

If I'd only had a light, I wouldn't have felt quite so vulnerable, yet the darkness had returned. I could see nothing. As a genius idea popped into my head, I plunged deep into the spiky bush, convinced nothing would be able to get at me, besides the wicked, scimitar thorns that raked my hands and face and stabbed through my trousers. It was fortunate my heavy mac, as impenetrable as chain mail, protected my vital organs. Despite superficial scratches, I was safe, but stuck.

The woods suddenly becoming uncannily quiet, except for the steady drip of rain-rinsed leaves, I tried to control my breathing, listening as hard as I could. Something was panting to my right and not far away I made out the faint rustling of furtive footsteps, heading to my left, towards where I'd heard the growling. I stayed put, the thorns giving me little other choice, all my senses on alert, as minutes rolled by like aeons and my nerves stretched.

'Are you alright there?' asked Hobbes from above.

My taut nerves snapping under the shock, I shrieked like a girl in a horror film until his hand clamped on my mouth to shut me up.

'It's only me,' he said, 'calm down and relax, alright?'

I nodded and he released me.

'What are you doing in that there briar patch?'

'Trying to get out,' I said, breathing hard, yet acting cool, until, an incautious movement resulting in a scratch on my neck, I yelped.

'I'll give you a hand.'

Grabbing my wrists, he lifted me straight upwards, so that I could just see his face, which being upside down, led me to believe he was holding onto a tree branch with his legs.

'Just hang in there a moment,' he said, 'until I find somewhere to put you down.'

I felt a swift, smooth motion as if he was sliding along a branch.

'This'll do,' he said, swinging me to one side and letting go.

Anticipating a long drop, I braced myself, rolling like I'd seen gymnasts do when I hit the ground, realising I'd only dropped a few inches and was lying on a soft litter of leaf mould and moss. Hobbes gave me a hand up.

'What just happened?' I asked, 'I mean … I don't get it, it was confusing.'

'OK,' he said, 'I was just arresting the first panther when you threw yourself onto the second one. Though it was brave, and I didn't think you had it in you, it was also a bit foolish.'

I tried a devil-may-care shrug.

He continued. 'I'd just got mine tied up, which it didn't seem to appreciate, when I realised the other one had the better of you. I came back to help, but there was no need; the werewolf got there first.'

'So that other thing was a werewolf?' I asked, shivering.

'Yes, which was lucky for you, because I might not have made it in time.'

I gulped, imagining hot, rank breath on my face, teeth tearing into my soft flesh. It didn't take much imagination, after what had happened to Henry Bishop. 'But what cried out? Was it the ... umm ...?'

'The werewolf,' said Hobbes, 'caught his foot in a wire snare. I'm going to have to have another word with Skeleton Bob about his poaching.'

'Is it ... he ... alright? The werewolf?'

'I expect he's got a sore leg but he managed to release himself and limped away. Dregs went with him.'

'Will Dregs be safe?'

'I expect so. The two of them seemed to be getting on very well.'

'Good ... umm ... Can I see the panther you caught?'

'I'm afraid not. It escaped.'

'How? Weren't your knots any good?'

'My knots,' said Hobbes, 'were fine. Unfortunately, someone cut them.'

'How?' I asked, intelligently.

'With a knife, a very sharp knife.'

'Who would do such a thing?'

'Someone with a sharp knife who wanted to release it. Now come along, we ought to investigate.'

'What about Dregs?'

'He'll find us, but if you're worried you can look for him. He went that way.'

Though I suppose he pointed, it was still too dark to see, yet, possibly, not so dark as it had been. I weighed up my options: I could search for Dregs, who was quite capable of looking after himself, on my own, in a wood full of werewolves and panthers, or I could stay where I was, on my own, in a wood full of panthers and werewolves, or I could follow Hobbes. Though none of them really appealed, the latter meant I'd at least have Hobbes with me.

'I'll come along,' I said. 'Just don't go too fast.'

'I'll try not to. Follow me.'

The rain returning, showing ambitions of becoming a deluge, I pulled up my collar and set out after him, a hopeless task, since after a few moments I couldn't see or hear him anymore. At first, I jogged in the direction in which I guessed he'd gone but after banging my knee on a fallen log, I resorted to slow walking. After a tree stump had barked my shin, I decided I might as well use it as seat.

A twig cracked, leaves rustled and something was breathing heavily. I sprang into an alert crouch, facing – I hoped – whatever was approaching. After a few minutes, my knees starting to hurt, I had to stand up straight as something solid smacked into the backs of my legs, knocking me headlong into the ground with a soggy thud. Shocked and winded, raising my hands for protection, I felt a soft, wet tongue lick them and hugged Dregs's soggy fur, nearly crying with relief.

'Good dog,' I said, clambering to my feet with difficulty on account of the exuberant licking. When he shook himself, showering me, I didn't care and grabbed his collar as he bounced about me, feeling safe, which was foolish.

'Stay!' I said in my best commanding voice. 'The two of us might as well just hang around here until Hobbes gets back.'

Unfortunately, on hearing Hobbes's name, he set off to find

him, his lunge taking me unawares, the collar tightening around my fingers, dragging me behind. Though I managed to keep up for a few steps, I soon realised it was extremely difficult to run in a crouch. How Dregs managed to keep going without choking, I had no idea. At last he stopped running and, groaning, muttering what I'd like to do to him, I managed to wrestle my hand from his collar.

'I thought you were supposed to be following me,' said Hobbes.

Though I ought to have been used to such shocks, I wasn't. 'I tried,' I said. 'I thought you were going to be slow.'

'I was, but you were slower. You'd have been faster if you hadn't stopped to play with the dog.'

'I wasn't playing … umm … did you find the panthers?'

'No, I lost them by the road. I don't know how they got away, but something very strange is going on.'

'You're telling me?'

'Yes. It's puzzling, because it's not difficult to track large animals through woods.'

'I know,' I said.

'And it should be even easier on a road, but they just vanished. I think there must have been a human with them but the scents were confusing.'

'Perhaps the human put them into a van and drove away.'

'That's plausible,' said Hobbes, 'because a vehicle had been parked by the roadside not so long ago.'

'Why,' I asked, 'would someone take panthers into the woods? It could be really dangerous.' Puzzled, I scratched my head, dislodging a number of leaves, as well as something soft and wriggly that made me shiver. Something smelled really bad.

'For exercise, maybe,' said Hobbes, 'but something smells wrong – and I don't just mean you. For future reference, rolling in fox dung is not effective with cats, who hunt mostly by sight and hearing. Smell is secondary.'

'I'll try to remember that,' I said, assuming nonchalance,

trying to rise above the stink, which seemed to be all over me, stomach-turning and disgusting.

'Well,' said Hobbes, 'the lass won't allow that sort of fragrance into the house, but I know somewhere you can wash. Follow me .... Is this slow enough?'

'Umm ... a little slower might be better.'

He took us through the woods as the rain clouds drifted away and the stars twinkled. With the prospect of a wash and going home to bed, I began to feel more cheerful, until I caught another whiff of myself. Dregs, on the other hand, finding me a source of delight, danced around, sniffing and whining with excitable good humour.

'What about the werewolf?' I asked, trying to divert my attention from the stink. 'Was it badly hurt?'

'No,' said Hobbes, 'I don't think so. They're as tough as old cow tails.'

'I wonder who it is?'

'I have a pretty good idea.'

'Who?' The night sky, glimpsed through a gap in the canopy, was definitely less dark.

'That would be telling. I'll let you know when I'm sure.'

'When will that be?'

'Soon ... now mind this stile. It's slippy.'

He vaulted over while Dregs squeezed between the old planks of a tumbledown wooden fence. I scrambled after them, jumping down into the soft grass of a meadow, the woodland scents soon replaced by the great smell of sheep, at least when the fox dung wasn't overpowering everything.

'Where are we?'

'This is the edge of Loop Farm,' said Hobbes, striding forward. 'Henry Bishop's, or, rather, Mrs Bishop's place is just over there to the right.'

'Where can I wash then? Isn't it too late, or too early, to disturb people?'

'You won't disturb anyone, unless you yell too loudly.'

'Why would I yell?' I asked, more than a little wary.

'Because the water will be cold.'

'What water?' I asked, wariness turning to worry. I hung back, but not far enough.

'This water,' he said, seizing my shoulders, lifting me above his head and throwing me.

The water was cold: bloody cold. Going in backwards, I rose, gasping, to the surface, where he allowed me a couple of indignant breaths before dunking me again. I came up spluttering, seeing that he'd chucked me into a big, metal trough.

'Now let's have your coat,' he said, 'and I'll give it a good scrub.'

'But …'

I never had a chance to argue, for he unbelted and unbuttoned my coat, whipping it off, dunking me again before I could react. Grabbing the side of the trough, I tried to haul myself out, still gasping.

'One more time should do it.'

The last thing I heard before going down for the third time was his chuckle.

'Well done,' he said as I emerged, puffing. 'Give yourself a good rub down.'

'Do I have to?'

'I'm afraid so. I'll try to get some of the pong out of this.'

He began scrubbing and beating my coat against the metal sides of the trough. The water, once I was over the initial shock, didn't feel so bad, so I stayed put, rubbing at any dubious areas on my clothing, as Dregs joined in the jolly romp; cold water possessed none of the terrors of a warm bath.

'That'll do for now,' said Hobbes, lifting me onto the grass.

Dregs leapt out and delighted me by shaking himself all over Hobbes, who, shrugging it off, wrung the water from my coat. While Dregs rushed about, rubbing against the grass, I stood and dripped, seeing the distant blue-grey outline of hills standing out on the clearing horizon, hearing the birds chorusing from the woods and hedges.

'It's all very well,' I said, 'but how am I going to get dry?'

'Like this,' said Hobbes, his grin bright and clear, as he grabbed my wrist and ankle. 'Your very own spin dryer.' The world turned into a blur and I became aware I was yelling, with a mixture of indignation and exhilaration.

When, at last, he set me down, I tottered sideways for several steps like a drunkard, fell over and lay laughing in the grass. Hobbes sat next to me, Dregs flopping on my feet, as a pink glow over the hills heralded the dawn. Within minutes we were bathed in brittle, golden light, a fluffy mist lending an air of softness to the farmland. Across the glistening fields, I could see the festival stages had been set up. If the weather held, it looked like we'd be enjoying a great festival, despite the music.

'That,' said Hobbes, in a thoughtful voice, 'was a great night out.'

Looking at my sodden, grimy clothes, the scratches on my hands, I thought of how I'd been bruised and terrified.

'I wouldn't have missed it for anything,' I said, intending sarcasm. It didn't come out that way and I realised, I really wouldn't have missed it. Nevertheless, as the sun's warmth touched me, a great tiredness settled in my heart. I yawned, my head nodding, Hobbes's voice seeming very distant.

'C'mon, Andy, grab your coat, it's time to go home.'

Forcing myself to stay awake, I got to my feet and followed him, smiling as Dregs scouted ahead, his tail wagging happily, knowing just how he felt.

16

With a yawn and a stretch, I came awake, my hands sore, the rich aroma of oxtail soup pervading my room. Since I was in bed, with no memory of getting home, I guessed Hobbes must have put me there. Sitting up, I examined a selection of scratches that mapped the events of the previous night.

'Good afternoon,' said a heavily accented, guttural voice.

'Bloody hell,' I squeaked.

Milord, back-lit by sunlight, half-moon spectacles glinting, sat hunched on a three-legged stool by the window, a pile of my clothes at his side. He nodded.

'Is it afternoon already?' I asked, hoping a show of normality would mask my bemusement and shock.

'Yes, it is past noon.'

'Gosh, I must have slept like a baby.'

'No, this time you were not wearing a nappy.'

Bemusement turning to embarrassment, I tried to camouflage it behind a weak laugh and a question. 'How come you're always repairing my clothes in here?'

'Because you are always damaging them. You have become a great source of employment, for which, I thank you.'

'You're welcome. I mean to say … umm … why do you do it in my room? Haven't you got a workshop?'

'Of course, but Frau Goodfellow does not provide for me when I work there.'

'That is a good reason.'

Leaving him to it, for the soup was demanding my attention, I got up, dressed in the bathroom and trotted downstairs.

The old girl was cutting bread. 'Hungry, dear?'

'Ravenous,' I said, sneaking a slice of bread when she turned for a plate.

'Good, but we'd better wait for the old fellow.'

'Is he at the station?'

'No, he's at the hospital.'

'Is he alright?'

'He's fine, apart from some nasty scratches on his hands.'

'I've got a few of those and they don't half sting,' I said, holding up my hands, showing them off.

'They look like gardening scratches,' she said, peering. 'The old fellow's came from a panther's claws.'

I was ashamed of trying to play up my pathetic collection of injuries.

'I gather you boys had some fun last night?'

'Yes, I suppose it was pretty exciting, or was when it wasn't terrifying. But, if his scratches aren't serious, what's he doing at the hospital?'

'You remember Mr Binks was arrested for assault?'

'Yes, of course.'

'Well, the man he is alleged to have attacked died in hospital, so now it's a murder and the old fellow's on the case.'

'Oh no! Does that mean he'll be late for lunch?'

'Not likely,' said Hobbes strolling into the kitchen.

Dregs padded after him, flopped into his basket with a sigh, and was asleep within seconds. Late nights could obviously be too much for dogs, as well.

'Glad to see you up,' said Hobbes. 'D'you know you sleep like a baby?'

'Only when I was ill. I don't always wear nappies, you know.'

He laughed. 'I mean you suck your thumb.'

'Umm ... it was probably scratched. But do you know what's happening with Featherlight?'

Hobbes, taking his place at the table, sighed. 'He's in a real pickle. I'll tell you after I've had my dinner.'

We feasted on the magnificent soup and fresh crusty bread before adjourning to the sitting room. Hobbes, having taken a slurp of tea, rested his mug on the coffee table.

'Featherlight,' he said, 'has been charged with the murder of the unidentified man who passed away in hospital this morning.'

'Does he still deny it?'

'Yes, though the evidence appears to be against him.'

'What evidence?'

'To start with, no fewer than twenty-three people witnessed an altercation between Featherlight and the deceased gentleman at the Feathers on Saturday evening. All agree that Featherlight punched him, put him in an armlock and dragged him outside. Approximately five minutes later, he was discovered unconscious in the alley by the side of the pub.'

'That would appear to be pretty conclusive.' I said. 'So why does he keep denying it?'

'He denies assaulting the man, who he says called himself Mike, or Mickey, but admits punching him.'

'What's the difference?'

'He claims the punch was in self-defence. He also admits putting him into an armlock and escorting him from the premises.'

I snorted. 'Escorting him from the premises? Is that what he said?'

Hobbes chuckled. 'Remember, he had been talking to a lawyer. What he means is that he thumped the man and threw him out.'

'In front of twenty-three witnesses.'

'Most of them entirely credible. They include Kevin Godley and Billy Shawcroft. They'll all stand up in court, if it goes there.'

'How will anyone be able to see Billy in the witness box?'

'Steps will be taken,' said Hobbes.

'But it sounds like Featherlight's not really got a case.'

'On the face of it, no.' He stroked his chin. 'However, there are some points that may be in his favour. Firstly, all the witnesses agree that he only punched the victim once when inside the pub, yet the man had received a thorough beating when he was found.'

'But he could have dragged the poor guy down the alley and done it.'

'True, though he'd have had to be quick and Billy is sure he was only outside for a matter of seconds. Of course, Featherlight can be surprisingly fast, in short bursts.'

'I know, I've seen him in action once or twice and he can be quite frightening.' I paused, as if to think and, to my surprise, a thought occurred. 'Who found the victim? If they found him only five minutes later, they might have seen or heard something.'

'Excellent,' said Hobbes, 'you're thinking well. A group of lads out on a pub-crawl found him and appear to have acted quite responsibly, despite being inebriated. One of them called for help on his mobile while the others did what they could to assist until the ambulance turned up.

'The strange thing is that we received another call about the incident a few seconds after the first.'

'Why was that strange?'

'Well, the caller, who wouldn't give his name, claimed to have witnessed Featherlight beating a man.'

'So, why didn't he stop him?'

'He said he tried to, but Featherlight attacked him and he had to run.'

'That sounds likely,' I said. 'I know I wouldn't like to mess with him. I reckon he did do it and is lying to save his skin.'

'That is possible,' said Hobbes, 'though he denies hitting anyone else.'

'Well, he would, wouldn't he?'

'Maybe, yet I've always known him to tell the truth, or at least the truth as he understands it. Still, I can't rule out the possibility that he is lying, especially with the charge being so serious. However, one of the lads who found him claims to have seen someone running away down the alley. Unfortunately, he couldn't give a description, other than that he thought it was a man. None of the others saw anything.'

'The guy was pissed, so how reliable is he?'

'I don't know,' said Hobbes, with a shrug, 'though I don't think he was as intoxicated as all that. Nevertheless, I might have agreed with your assessment, had it not been for that second phone call.'

'Which said Featherlight did it,' I said. 'I don't see how he's going to get out of this one. He's been close to going to jail for a long time and I can't see him keeping out of it again.'

Hobbes poured himself another mug of tea. 'He probably does deserve to go to prison, if only for his cooking, but I'm not convinced he's lying and wouldn't be surprised if the second phone call gets him off the hook. I think it would be very helpful if I could find whoever made it. There was one other thing, you know, that was extremely odd.'

'What?'

'Dregs. When we got there he refused to go down the alley. He stood at the entrance, trembling and bristling. The only time he's been like that before was at the Wildlife Park. What's more, I understood what was bothering him, because I sensed something wrong.'

'You were scared?' I couldn't believe it.

'No, not scared ... stimulated more like .... I don't know ... I'm still thinking about it.'

'But why?'

'I can't say for certain. There was something in the air, a scent, but it was strange, not exactly animal, and not exactly human.'

'Like a werewolf?'

'Not really. Besides, Dregs likes werewolves.'

He sat in thought for a few moments, the house silent, apart from Dregs snoring in the kitchen, until a car drove past, its occupants kindly sharing their music with the world.

'Of course,' said Hobbes, 'this case would be simpler if we knew the victim's identity. Unfortunately, he had no wallet, or keys, or anything that might identify him. That fact could be in Featherlight's favour, as he had nothing like that on him when he was arrested.'

'He could easily have hidden stuff.'

'He could, but I searched the area and found nothing. We are assuming, of course, that the victim had some personal effects to take and it's possible he didn't, though his expensive suit and shoes suggested he was well-off; in my experience, prosperous people usually have some identification about their persons. In addition, there was a white mark on his wrist, indicative of a watchstrap, but no watch. Again, Featherlight hadn't got it. Furthermore, he's never before robbed anyone he's thumped.'

'But there's got to be a first time for everything,' I said, 'and isn't it most likely that he did bash the poor guy and left him for dead in the alley? What if somebody else found him first, a tramp maybe, robbed him and then called the police because he had a bit of conscience.'

'It's one of the scenarios the CID lads are considering. It probably wasn't a tramp, though, since the second call was also made from a mobile.'

'You know,' I said, a thought occurring, 'I wouldn't be so sure that Featherlight has never robbed anyone. I saw him once thump a bloke called Lofty Peeke and take money from his pocket.'

'Ah yes,' said Hobbes, 'I remember the Lofty Peeke incident and, you're right, Featherlight did take money from him. In mitigation, he only took what he believed he was owed after Lofty had complained about his meal and refused to pay.'

'That's not much of an excuse.'

'No,' said Hobbes. 'But, there is another factor that must be taken into consideration: Billy says the Feathers has had considerably more awkward customers during the last month or so than is usual, all of them large, burly men, all of them looking for trouble. He reckons someone's trying to intimidate Featherlight.'

'I can't imagine him being intimidated by anyone – he's not

even frightened of you.'

Hobbes held me in a disconcerting frown for a few seconds before laughing. 'You're right, he's not even frightened of me and, evidently, he wasn't intimidated by the victim, who was a large, burly man. Featherlight claims he'd attempted to be friendly, but that the man had, I quote, been a complete tosser.'

I shrugged. 'I can't imagine him being friendly with anyone, unless his idea of it is to knock someone's teeth down his throat.'

'True,' said Hobbes. 'He is not the most genial of hosts. By the way, I made a sketch of what the dead man might have looked like without two black eyes, a broken nose and a cracked skull.' Digging into his trouser pocket, he pulled out a crumpled sheet of paper.

Staggered, as always, at the dexterity of his massive fingers, I saw the image of a thickset young man with hard eyes and square jaw, an image that reminded me of someone.

'I think I know him,' I said.

'Really? Who is he?'

'Umm ... I don't know.'

'So, in what sense do you mean you know him?'

'I've seen him around. His name's Mike.'

'So Featherlight said,' said Hobbes.

'Yes, but the thing is I think I saw this guy on Friday evening. He looks like the driver who picked up Felix after the picnic.'

'Are you sure?'

'Yes, if your drawing is accurate.'

'It's only a quick sketch, but, I flatter myself, it's a reasonable impression.'

I nodded, hot with excitement. 'What's more, I'd seen him before; I'm nearly sure he's the guy Featherlight knocked out when they were playing tennis and, come to think of it, his kit bag had a King Enterprises logo. It didn't mean anything at the time.'

Hobbes sat up from his habitual slouch. 'That's very interesting. How sure are you that it's the same man?'

'Quite sure ... umm ... I think. I wouldn't swear to it but I'd bet a tenner that it was, if I was a betting man and had a tenner.'

'That's good,' he said, 'though I'll need positive identification. How would you like to see the body?'

'Not at all,' I said, shuddering at the horrible thought, as an even worse one came to mind. 'You're not going to bring it back here are you?'

'Of course not. We'll go and take a look tonight, after supper, and make sure no one sees us.'

Something aroused my suspicions. 'We will go by way of the front door, won't we? That is, it will be an … umm … official visit, won't it?' Goosebumps were springing up all over.

'I wasn't thinking so much of going through official channels as going through the tunnels.'

'Why? Wouldn't it be best if I made an official ID?' I asked, not fancying going back underground, even with Hobbes.

'All in good time,' he said. 'For the moment, I think it would be better to keep what you said between ourselves.'

'But why?'

'Because, I don't want Felix King to know we've discovered the dead man's identity. I'm sorry he's a friend of yours but I suspect him of … not being entirely straight and don't wish to get his guard up.'

'He's not exactly a friend,' I said, 'not really. Not at all, in fact. He sort of … umm … threatened me if I continued to see Violet.'

'Go on,' he said, slouching back onto the cushions.

I told him the entire story, including why I'd felt the need to ask about the wine. When I'd finished, he patted me on the shoulder quite gently. In fact, he barely left a mark.

'Never mind,' he said. 'I thought there might be a problem between you and that young lady. I now understand why you haven't seen her since the picnic.'

'It's not because I'm scared of Felix,' I said, 'although I am a bit, it's because I didn't get her telephone number or address. I can't believe how stupid I was.'

Smiling, he raised his eyebrows.

'Anyway, I got Felix's number off the card he gave me and called to check how she was getting on, but when his secretary realised who I was, she passed on his message that ... umm ... steps would be taken if I kept on importuning Violet. She did though, let on that Violet was alright but taking a few days off work.

'I wasn't importuning her. At least I don't think so; I'm not sure what it means. I just hoped the two of us had got, I don't know, something.'

'I would suggest,' said Hobbes, 'that you speak to her as soon as possible. I have observed that time can drive a wedge between friends who stop talking.'

'I'd love to, but don't know how to get hold of her. I was thinking of hanging around her office to see if I can talk to her when she gets back.'

'You could do that, or I could find her address for you. Besides, I think I'd enjoy a little chat with Mr King – concerning wine, you know? I might also try to find out about his driver, Mike.'

'When?'

'Right away. Would you like to come?'

'Me? Is that alright?'

'Of course, you can introduce us. Get dressed like a man of means, and quickly.'

Dashing upstairs, I put on a light-grey suit, a white silk shirt and, a rarity in Mr G's collection, a sober tie. It was only when I was adjusting the tie that I remembered Milord. He'd vanished, leaving behind a neat pile of perfectly repaired clothes.

'Very respectable,' said Hobbes, with an approving nod as I came downstairs, 'though I'm not quite sure about the slippers.'

Turning back, I put on a pair of glossy black brogues.

He was waiting by the door with two bottles of wine in his hand. 'Let's get going,' he said.

'Where to?'

'Mr King's offices, of course.'

'Where are they?'

'Didn't you look at his card?'

'Only at the phone number.'

'Go and get it.'

I ran upstairs, a bead of sweat trickling down my face. On reaching the top step, I remembered leaving the card next to the phone and, turning too fast, slipping, I bounced downwards with a series of undignified yelps.

'No need to rush, I've found it,' said Hobbes, handing me the bottles. 'Take these and let's go.'

Picking myself up, I hobbled after him and, since Dregs was still sleeping like a dog, I enjoyed the rare privilege of the front passenger seat and the feelings of terror and despair that came with it. I tried not to panic as he hurtled down The Shambles. The placard outside the *Bugle's* offices read, *Murdered Man Dies in Hospital. Police Suspect Homicide.*

'Where are we going?' I asked.

'Mr King's offices are in that new building off the Amor Lane Estate,' he said above the wailing of the brakes. 'Why is that Muppet slowing down?'

'Because he's approaching a busy roundabout,' I explained.

'Ah, a responsible driver.'

As we sped past the car, its driver, green-faced, goggle-eyed, stared, making me wonder why he was dressed as Kermit the Frog. I didn't wonder for long since Hobbes, taking the short, anti-clockwise route around the roundabout, despite the coach bearing down on us, drove everything else from my mind. Of course, we made it unscathed, leaving no casualties.

Within a few minutes, a sign for King Enterprises directed us towards a glistening, new steel and glass edifice, in a row with four similar buildings, adrift in a sea of car parks, grass and ornamental shrubs.

'I can't see any free spaces,' I said, looking around.

'This will do,' he said, driving onto a patch of lawn and stopping, 'but try not to trample the daisies. Follow me.'

He sprang from the car, slamming the door, marching towards the front of the building. As I scrambled after him, I dropped one of the bottles. Fortunately, my reactions were fast enough to catch it on my big toe. Picking up the bottle, I limped after him.

The door, one of those electronic ones that should open only after the correct code has been entered, gave way after one tug from Hobbes. Holding it open, he ushered me inside and up two flights of stairs; he didn't approve of lifts and I was just glad there were so few high-rise buildings in the area. At the top, we found ourselves in a shiny reception, smelling of newness, with potted plants, hard seats and a young woman with poodle hair and big glasses. She looked up, huge-eyed.

'Good afternoon, miss,' Hobbes boomed, 'we're here to see Mr King.'

'How did you get in?' she asked, her voice high and squeaky.

It wasn't Carol; I hoped her little kindness to me had not cost her.

'Through the door and up the stairs,' said Hobbes, advancing with what I assumed he meant as a friendly smile.

'Do you have an appointment?'

He waved his hand dismissively. 'I never bother with nonsense like that. Could you tell him Hobbes is here? It's about the wine.'

I held up the bottles.

'I'll see if he's available. Are you a wine merchant?'

'Just a friend,' said Hobbes, with a chuckle that turned her face white, despite the crust of make-up.

'And the other gentleman?' she asked, sticking to her guns.

'Is another friend.'

'Please, take a seat,' she said, leaving us at a brisk walk that became a rather undignified scurry as she exited the room.

Ignoring the seats, Hobbes followed her, so of course I followed him. The girl, hastening down a corridor, noticing we were on her tail, squeaked like a frightened mouse and plunged into a side room. When we got there, two burly security guards in black trousers and short-sleeved white shirts were waiting at the door. The girl was behind a table strewn with dirty mugs and even dirtier magazines.

'Excuse me, sir,' said the first guard, a tall man with a shaven head and a deep scar beneath one eye, 'I don't believe you have authorisation to be on these premises.' Stepping forward he placed his hand on Hobbes's shoulder. 'I'm going to have to ask you to leave.'

The other guard, shorter but broader, the possessor of an eternal stare, reached for Hobbes's other shoulder. I felt a weird mixture of relief that they weren't going to manhandle me, combined with indignation that they hadn't even appeared to notice my presence.

'Ask me then,' said Hobbes, smiling.

'Would you mind leaving the premises, sir?' asked the tall one, trying to push him back.

'Of course I wouldn't,' said Hobbes, 'after we've had our chat with Mr King.'

The guards, exchanging glances, pushed in unison. They had as much chance of moving him as the church tower. Adopting a different approach, they seized his arms, trying to drag him out, finding an old tree could not have rooted more firmly than he had.

'Please, leave the premises, sir,' said the tall one, red in the face and puffing, 'we wouldn't want to resort to force.'

'I wouldn't want you to either,' said Hobbes, pleasantly, 'because it wouldn't be worth it. As I believe I mentioned, we're not leaving until we've seen Mr King.'

In response, the shorter guard punched him in the stomach before spinning away, cradling his fist and groaning.

'Can we see him now?' asked Hobbes.

The taller one, adopting a karate stance, launched into a jumping kick, which might have looked quite impressive had the strip light hanging from the ceiling only been a couple of inches higher. As it wasn't, his leap being cut short by his forehead striking the fitting, his legs continuing forward with the momentum, he pivoted in mid-air, plunging down amidst a kaleidoscopic shower of splintered glass and would have landed flat on his back had Hobbes not caught him. Brushing the glass from the table, Hobbes laid the man, who was swearing, yet semi-conscious, on it.

Hobbes turned to the girl. 'Really, miss, wouldn't it be much easier if you just showed us into Mr King's office?'

She gulped, nodded and scuttled out like a nervous rabbit, while Hobbes busied himself with picking up the shattered glass and placing it in a bin.

'Did you have to do that?' I asked, feeling a certain sympathy for the security men, who'd only been trying to carry out their duties.

'Do what?'

'Umm ... whatever you just did.'

'I didn't do anything, did I?'

'No ... I know but ... umm ... couldn't you have not done it differently?'

'If I hadn't wanted to not do it in my own way.'

The conversation becoming tangled, I shook my head, giving up, sitting on the edge of the table, listening to the tall guard's incoherent cursing as a trickle of blood meandered down the side of his face into the shaven hair of his temple. The other guard paced up and down, rubbing and shaking his hand, avoiding eye contact.

Felix appeared at the door in a cloud of aftershave, the poodle-haired girl bobbing nervously behind him. I felt a little sorry for her, though not a lot, being unable to waste too much sympathy on anyone who would choose such a hairstyle.

'Andy, what a pleasant surprise,' said Felix, stepping forward, shaking my hand like a friend. Though his mouth smiled, there was no smile in his eyes, especially when they lighted on his two stricken guards. 'And this must be Inspector Hobbes.'

Hobbes nodded.

Felix, stepping forward, shook his hand without flinching. 'I'm delighted Andy has brought you to see me and I'm dreadfully sorry about the mix up. Had I known you were here I would, of course, have invited you straight in. It's not often I receive such a distinguished guest, but it's my secretary Linda's first day and she wasn't to know. She knows now of course and I trust she will prove more reliable than Carol, who let me down rather badly.' He glanced at me.

Though I felt incredibly guilty about Carol, I hoped she'd soon find a better employer.

'But enough of my business,' said Felix, 'let's go to my office.' He glanced towards his men. 'Get this place sorted out. I'll speak to you later.'

He took us from the side room, along a glass-walled corridor, past a rubber plant, a water dispenser and a number of cringeworthy inspirational pictures, to his office. Full of daylight and gleaming metal, it dwarfed the reception and might have been considered a pleasant, airy room had his aftershave, or cologne, or whatever it was, not been so overpowering. Inviting us to sit on a soft, white leather sofa, he pulled up a matching chair for himself as we made ourselves comfortable.

Touching his fingertips together, Felix leaned back. 'It's very good of you to come. I appreciate you taking time out of your busy schedules to visit.'

I assumed he was having a dig at me.

'It's no trouble at all,' said Hobbes. 'I'm always glad to make the acquaintance of a fellow wine buff, and Andy reckons you are something of an expert.'

'Well, hardly an expert,' said Felix with a modest smile, 'merely an enthusiastic amateur.'

'If you say so,' said Hobbes. 'I thought you'd appreciate these. The '63 is reckoned to be an especially fine vintage. Andy, have you got the bottles?'

I placed them on the table in front of Felix.

Picking them up, he studied the labels. 'I expect he told you how much I'd like to get hold of a few crates of this. The thing is,

I'm planning a celebration for when my current project is completed. In addition, I thought I'd like to market it. There would be, I'm sure, a great demand for a wine of such quality. We would, of course, split the profits equitably and, if it's all as fine as the bottle we enjoyed at the picnic, I think we would be in for a tidy sum. We'd have to make the label snazzier, of course, but, with a little advertising in select magazines we'd be onto a winner.'

Hobbes, shaking his head, looked sorrowful. 'Sorry but the wine is a gift from a friend and is not for sale.'

'But think of the money.'

'My friend has more than sufficient for his needs. He produces just enough wine to meet his own requirements and has no desire to expand his hobby.'

Felix sighed. 'A shame, but no matter, I respect his restraint. There are far too many people in my line of work who are only interested in accumulating money, even when they already possess far more than they could run through in a lifetime.'

'So, what is your motivation?' asked Hobbes.

'I can't deny that property development is a lucrative business, and I've made many killings over the years. Though I am a wealthy man, money is merely a means to an end.'

'And what is the end?'

'A better world, Inspector. I intend to play a role in the eradication of certain evils, evils that have plagued mankind since the dawn of time. That's my motivation.'

'What sort of evils?'

Felix's eyes gleamed. 'I intend to use my money to eliminate genetic mishaps.'

'That's a massive task.'

Felix nodded. 'I know. It's too much for one individual. I can't possibly rid the world of all its evils, but I might be able to make an impression on one or two of them. And, of course, it's not just me. A corporation such as this can achieve so much more, though it won't happen overnight. I'll have to see what I can do over the weekend.' He laughed, the gleam fading from his eyes.

'Philanthropy is a marvellous way to use your money,' said Hobbes, with great approval. 'I wonder ...' he paused, '... if it's not a bit cheeky, whether you might be able to do me a favour this weekend?'

'A favour?'

'Yes. You may be aware that there's to be a music festival? Well, a charity I'm involved with looks after underprivileged nippers, and I was wondering whether you might spare a car and driver to deliver them in the mornings and take them home afterwards. Andy mentioned that you have a driver ... Mike was it?'

It was the first I'd heard of any charity.

Felix shook his head. 'Alas, I can't help. Any other weekend, maybe, but I'm going to be busy.'

'You don't need to be involved at all,' Hobbes pointed out, 'other than by lending us a car and Mike – assuming he's willing, that is.'

'I'm afraid Mike Rook is no longer in my employment. I gather he inherited a plantation in Borneo, or some such place. He'd worked his notice, and was planning to fly out there last Saturday. I imagine he's there by now. It means, alas, that I am currently without a driver, which is inconvenient.'

'Not to worry,' said Hobbes. 'I can make other arrangements.' He glanced at a clock on the wall by Felix's desk. 'I say, is that the time? I'm afraid I have police business to attend to. I do hope you enjoy the wine and, if you do, I can let you have a crate for your party: as a gift of course.' He rose to his feet. 'Nice to meet you Mr King, but time and criminals wait for no man. Come along, Andy.'

Felix stood up and, to my regret, shook my hand again. 'Delighted you could visit. I hope we will meet again.'

'So long as it's not in my professional capacity,' said Hobbes with a pleasant laugh. 'Goodbye.'

'Goodbye, Inspector ... Andy.'

17

As Hobbes and I walked back to the car, a small grey cat shot past, ears flat against its skull. It was lucky to escape the wheels of a reversing van.

'Stupid animal,' I muttered.

'No doubt she had a reason for her behaviour,' said Hobbes, opening the door.

'So,' I asked, 'what do you make of Felix?'

Resting his arm on the car's roof, he thought for a moment. 'Mr King struck me as a good man. He's obviously an intelligent businessman with a laudable vision of what he wishes to achieve and it's clear he has nothing to do with any of the recent funny business. Of course, I never thought it likely that he had. Sorenchester could do with more like him.'

As we got into the car, I was annoyed how Felix had fooled him so easily. Yet, when we were driving away he chuckled.

'What's so funny?'

'Mr King is. I hope I didn't overdo it, but flattery is like cream on a trifle; you can never lay it on too thickly.'

'What d'you mean?' I asked, confused.

'Mr King is not quite what he appears to be. I don't suppose you noticed him hiding in the shrubbery as we left? He got there extremely quickly and gave the cat a fright – it's lucky she wasn't squashed. I thought, since he was listening, I'd say something flattering.'

'He was listening? How? We weren't talking very loud.'

'He's got sharp ears.'

'Do you mean they're a bit pointed?'

'You noticed that did you? But I mean he has acute hearing.'

'Has he? ... Umm .... How did you know he was behind the bush?'

Hobbes's nose twitched. 'His aftershave is distinctive.'

'So, do you ... umm ... think Felix is actually involved in ... umm ... funny business? Did he attack Mike the driver?'

He shrugged. 'I don't know, yet, but I do know that he lied when he claimed Mr Rook was planning to leave; his name was still on the duty roster for next month.'

'What duty roster?'

'The one on the wall by his desk.'

'I didn't notice.'

'No, but I observe my surroundings. By the way, Miss King is now staying in London but will be returning on Friday.'

'How can you possibly know that?'

'There was a sticky note on his desk. But enough of that. Mr King worries me.'

'Me too.'

'There's something odd about him. Did you notice his scent?'

'I could hardly miss it.'

'No,' he said, shaking his head and slotting us into a minuscule gap between two cars, 'I don't mean his aftershave, I mean his own scent.'

'Are you saying he's smelly? I didn't notice but I think I know what you mean. One of my mother's larger friends didn't shower too often but slapped stuff on to cover it. The combination of perfume and stale sweat was overwhelming.'

'I don't mean that at all. The opposite rather ... I couldn't pick up any scent from him. That stuff he wears seems to block everything.'

'Perhaps it's deodorant?' I suggested, having learned not to question his sense of smell, his nose seeming to match Dregs's.

'If so, it's a very effective one and he must use it all over, even on his hair. I wonder what he's hiding?'

'Perhaps he's embarrassed by body odours. Some people are.'

'Perhaps, but that's enough speculation. Hold tight.' He steered onto the dual carriageway, overtaking a convoy of lorries by driving along the verge.

I held my seat as tightly as I could, teeth rattling, until, having passed them all, we veered onto the road. 'Where are we going?'

'To have a word with Skeleton Bob, to tell him to be much more careful where he sets his snares. He might have hurt someone last night.'

'Some werewolf, you mean?'

'Werewolves are someone, too. Here we go.'

As he spun the wheel to the right, the car skipped through a gap in the crash barrier, straight across the opposite carriageway, dodging a petrol tanker bearing down on us. We made it, pursued by the discordant blaring of horns. Hobbes had once told me that if someone had time to sound the horn, he'd already decided there was no danger and was merely giving vent to his temper. I almost believed him.

We bumped off the carriageway onto the verge, up a steep slope, the engine straining and whining, across a patch of scrub and into the lane leading to Bob's place. The spherical Mrs Nibblet, glowing in a bright orange shell suit, reminding me of the space-hopper I'd had as a boy, was apparently picking nettles. She straightened up and frowned as we stopped.

'Oh, it's you again is it? What d'you want this time? Can't you go and arrest some real criminals instead of hassling us poor folk as is only trying to make a living?'

Hobbes, climbing from the car, bowed. 'Good afternoon, Mrs Nibblet. I'm not here to cause any unpleasantness; I just need a word with your husband.'

'Well, you can't. He's out. Goodbye.'

'Out you say? Then, that must be his identical twin peeking from the shed.'

'Oh, you bloody fool,' said Mrs Nibblet, rolling her eyes and shaking her head. 'You might as well come out now, why don't you?'

Skeleton Bob, emerging from the lopsided wooden shed by the house, scratched his head, smiling, displaying a set of coloured and disfigured teeth that even Mrs Goodfellow couldn't love. I wondered whether he'd ever visited a dentist.

'Hello, Bob,' said Hobbes.

Bob nodded, his eyes as wary as those of a hunted animal. 'What d'you want?'

'Just a pleasant little chat.'

Hobbes's smile didn't seem to reassure him.

Mrs Nibblet scowled. 'He's hardly left the house this last week. Don't you go nicking him for no good reason.'

Hobbes's eyebrows expressed shock. 'I wouldn't dream of it, madam. I'm not going to nick him, I'm here to offer a little friendly advice.'

Bob, his trousers heaving and writhing, as if containing a ferret, looked both suspicious and hopeful. Yelping, twitching, doubling up as if in pain, he reached into his pocket. 'Excuse me,' he said, pulling out a wriggling ferret by the scruff of the neck, walking towards the cage and dropping it inside. He turned back to face Hobbes. 'What do you mean?'

'All I want to do is to warn you …'

Mrs Nibblet sniffed. 'Threaten, more like.'

Hobbes beamed. 'I want to warn … no … encourage Bob, to take more care where he sets his snares.'

'They're nothing to do with me,' said Bob, trying to look innocent.

'Well you know best,' said Hobbes, raising his hands in mollification. 'I'll just say that one of those snares of yours might have caused a serious injury to a rare animal last night.'

'How do you know it was one of mine?'

'Oh, you fool!' Mrs Nibblet groaned. 'Just admit everything, why don't you?'

Hobbes tapped the side of his nose. 'I know many things. What do you set them for? Pheasants?'

Bob, with a glance at his wife, shook his head. 'No, I only set them for rabbits. When I want pheasants, I dazzle 'em with my lamp and catch 'em in my net.'

Mrs Nibblet slapped her forehead. 'Bob!'

'Oh, lawks,' said Bob. 'Now you've gone and snared me with all your clever words.'

Mrs Nibblet looked on the verge of tearing her hair out or punching her husband.

Hobbes, noticing my incredulous look, rolled his eyes. Skeleton Bob would never make it into Mensa. His name was on a long and varied criminal record, though he'd never been jailed, partly on account of the pettiness of his misdeeds, but mostly because the fines he paid far exceeded any harm he did. Though Hobbes tolerated his activities with just the occasional chat if he ever pushed his luck, more ambitious police officers, interested in meeting targets, took a less liberal view, with the result that Bob appeared in court every couple of months. It wasn't difficult to catch him or to get a confession.

'It doesn't matter, madam,' said Hobbes smiling. 'I know he's a poacher. You know he's a poacher. Even Andy knows he's a poacher. We also know he's not good at holding onto gainful employment and that money and food would be in short supply without his evening job. I also happen to know that he sells game to the milkman, who cheats him, and to the curate, who doesn't. Bob's not greedy, though, and doesn't take more than he needs.'

'That's true enough,' said Mrs Nibblet. 'He's soft in the head and I must be, too, for marrying him.' She smiled at her skinny spouse, who was hitching up his trousers again.

'No matter,' Hobbes continued. 'We were having a stroll through Loop Woods last night.'

'Did you see them?' asked Bob, looking as excited as his ferret, which was running bounding circuits of its cage.

'See what?'

'The big black cats. They were out.'

'Yes, we saw them.'

'I reckon,' said Bob, 'they may be dangerous, but they weren't the only things out. There was something else.'

'Bob!' cautioned Mrs Nibblet, shaking her head.

'I know there was,' said Hobbes, 'because it was that something else that got caught in your snare. I'm glad to say, it wasn't much hurt.'

'You see, Fenella?' Bob grinned. 'It's not just me. Mr Hobbes saw them as well and he's a policeman. Would you like a cup of tea?'

'That would be nice,' said Hobbes.

'We've only got nettle tea,' said Mrs Nibblet, 'we can't afford the shop stuff at the moment.'

'You can't beat a cup of nettle tea,' said Hobbes, smacking his lips.

I wasn't so sanguine. Nettles in my experience were horrible, nasty, vicious weeds that inflicted pain on the unwary. My worst memories came from a boiling hot day in the school holidays when, having sneaked from the garden I was meant to be weeding, I visited a little stream at the back of the playing fields. Since no one was around and since I was hidden by the weeping willows fringing the stream, I stripped to my pants for a paddle, making strenuous attempts at catching the wildlife that wiggled and darted through the muddy waters. I'd come close to landing some tadpoles and a stickleback when the sun's going in forced the goosebumps out. While trotting up and down the bank to dry off and warm up, a brilliant idea occurred: I could become Tarzandy, King of the Jungle. Though I had to contend with a scarcity of lions and a lack of creepers, it seemed to me that if I grasped a handful of the weepier branches, I could swing over the water and return safely to dry land.

It all worked beautifully, apart from the return safely to dry land part. Though I swung out in fine style, I'd failed to appreciate that my weight would bend the branches down. Despite my best efforts, my feet splashed up the water while my momentum was hurling me, at increasing pace, into the bank but not onto the bank. Raising my legs in desperation, I slid onto solid ground, cutting a path into the centre of a patch of stinging nettles. The more I struggled to get clear, the more they stung my bare skin, and by the time I got out, running home, howling and crying, I looked like a smallpox victim. I went off Tarzan after that.

When I came back to the present, Hobbes, seeming to know a great deal about the subject, was advising Bob how to set humane snares in rabbit runs where they would only be a danger to rabbits, thus sparing less-edible wildlife. They'd perched on a pair of discarded beer kegs that served as stools in the rickety, bramble-infested lean-to that pretended to be a porch. I joined them.

'I'll strive to be more careful in future,' said Bob.

Fenella waddled from the cottage bearing four non-too-clean mugs of nettle tea on a rusty tray. 'Here you go, lads,' she said, handing them round, lifting her ample backside onto a keg, which, being solidly made, groaned, but did not buckle.

My tea was in a cracked mug celebrating the coronation of Edward VIII, which seemed wrong somehow, though I couldn't work out why. Half thinking it might be a joke the others were in on and of which I was the butt, I sniffed the steaming liquid, a strange aroma reminding me of cut grass. Yet, as the others appeared to be drinking it, I risked a sip, finding it scalding hot, though not at all stingy, with an earthy, robust flavour that was quite pleasant.

Hobbes, taking a gulp, turned to Bob. 'So tell me about the other thing you saw in the woods?'

'Promise you won't laugh?'

'I promise.'

'Well, I'm not sure, but I think I saw … something I haven't seen before.'

'Go on.'

'Look, I've kind of felt something out there before, but last night was the first time I saw it proper. I was out setting my traps, trying to get 'em done before the rain came down, 'cause I could see we was in for a stinker.'

'And you were right, but what did you see?'

'I was coming to that,' said Bob, taking a slow sip and sighing. 'This is a lovely cuppa, love.'

Mrs Nibblet smiled.

He continued. 'I'd just got going when I felt the wood was … watchful, a bit like it is when the big cats come out, but not quite the same. It was sort of like the feeling when a fox is out, except this seemed more like curiosity than fear. I knew something was up, so I hid in a culvert and waited. I could feel it coming and then I saw it by a tree, cocking its leg like a dog.'

'What was it?' I had to ask.

'A werewolf.'

'Stuff and nonsense,' said Mrs Nibblet.

'No, really.' Bob glanced at Hobbes. 'You saw it too, didn't you?

'I did, and so did Andy. The creature saved him from the panther, only it got its paw snagged in one of your snares.'

'You see, Fenella?' Bob turned to her in triumph. 'They saw it too. Now what do you say?'

'That you're all soft in the head.'

Hobbes nodded. 'Unfortunately, that's the reaction you'll get if you tell anyone. They'll never believe you.'

'I know,' said Bob, his head nodding as if on a spring, 'I had enough grief when I told the boys down the pub about the big cats, and I was right about them an' all.'

'So it's best to keep things like this under your hat, then,' said Hobbes.

'That's the first sensible thing you've said,' said Mrs Nibblet. 'Perhaps you're not as daft as you look.'

'No one could be as daft as he looks,' I quipped, regretting my loose tongue as Hobbes's frown bored through me. 'Sorry.' I laughed nervously.

Then he chuckled, the Nibblets smiled, and I'd got away

with it.

'We'd best be on our way,' said Hobbes, getting to his feet, 'or we'll be late for our suppers and it's cauliflower cheese tonight. Thank you for the nettle tea and your hospitality, Mrs Nibblet, and, Bob, remember what I said about snares. C'mon Andy, drink up. And quickly.'

I took a sip or two from my mug, though it was still scalding hot, and handed it back three-quarters full. Mumbling my thanks, I got back in the car. As we drove away, I was puzzled, if pleased, that Hobbes was driving with care and consideration, keeping within the speed limit. As we parked on Blackdog Street, the front wheel dropped off.

'I'll get Billy to fix it,' said Hobbes, getting out, bounding up the steps to the front door.

'Does he know about cars?' I asked, as I followed. 'I thought he was only a barman.'

'Only a barman? No, if you want anything mechanical fixed, Billy's your man.'

As soon as the door opened, Dregs, having obviously slept off last night's exertions, his delight in seeing us evident, overwhelmed me. Though I appreciated the welcome, I wished he hadn't knocked me down the steps and, though I assumed he hadn't meant to do it, he made a noise very much like a snigger as I sprawled in the gutter, before dancing around me with a toothy grin. Every time it had happened, I'd made mental notes to be more careful, but events nearly always erased them.

Picking myself up, slapping the dust from my jacket, I entered the house, showing as much dignity as I could muster with a party of excited camera-wielding Japanese tourists for an audience.

Still, all my woes fell away as we sat down for supper, for, having finished my course of antibiotics, my taste buds had returned to life. Their resurrection, combined with Mrs G's cauliflower cheese, outstanding even by her standards, was almost like a religious experience and brought tears to my eyes.

'Too hot for you?' Hobbes grinned. 'If I were you, I'd let it cool. Now, is there any more, lass?'

'It's fine,' I said, as the old girl refilled his plate. 'In fact it's perfect. A perfect end to the day.'

'Not quite the end of the day. You've got to identify a body first.'

I felt like a man who, clinched in a slow smooch with the most beautiful girl at a dance, has just realised the large, muscle-bound, tattooed hooligan approaching him is her boyfriend. I had once been that man and Leticia, for that had been her name, had used me to make her man, Crusher, jealous. Though things had worked out very well for Leticia and Crusher, my evening had ended in a skip.

'Do I have to? I'm tired and I don't want to go down those tunnels again.'

'Oh yes,' said Hobbes, 'the tunnels – I was joking but, since the car's out of action, the tunnels might be the easiest way of getting there.'

'What about a taxi?'

'I don't think that's a good idea; I can never bring myself to trust taxi drivers. No, you've convinced me, the tunnels are the best way.'

I had long ago realised that he didn't like being driven, perceiving most drivers, other than Billy, as dangerous. He had a point, I supposed: other drivers had accidents but, when he crashed, it was deliberate, or so he said.

We sat on the sofa watching a lousy film and, despite all my efforts, yawns kept breaking loose. I hoped Hobbes would regard them as a symptom of extreme fatigue and have pity. During a particularly wide and extended yawn, he turned to me.

'I see this film doesn't interest you. I'm not surprised. Anyway, the morgue will be as quiet as the grave now, so it's a good time to visit.'

I shivered. 'I hope it's quiet all the time. Do we really have to go?'

'Yes.'

'Can I take a torch?' I asked, fighting to stay calm.

'If you want. The lass keeps one in the drawer in the kitchen and it might have batteries. Grab it if you want; she won't mind; she uses it when she's cleaning the cupboards. Let's go.'

He got up, heading towards the cellar with Dregs at his heels.

Although the torch did contain working batteries, I'd have felt considerably happier had it been bigger and brighter than a cigarette lighter. I took it anyway, even if it provided more reassurance than light. When I reached the cellar, the coal pile was not in place and Hobbes was standing with his ear to the tunnel door, listening. So was Dregs. The hairs on my neck bristled.

'What's up?'

'Shhh!' He stepped back, a hairy finger pressed to his thick lips.

Dregs whined, standing alert in front of us as the doorknob slowly turned. Something was trying to get into the cellar and I felt a desperate urge to get out, though my legs, in a display of reckless loyalty, refused to leave Hobbes.

As the door swung back, I could hear shuffling footsteps, while cold, damp air seemed to be crawling around my feet. Shivering, I gulped, wanting to scream, to run, baffled as to why Hobbes was smiling and Dregs was wagging his tail. When something small and brown appeared in the doorway, I gasped; the last thing I'd been expecting was a shopping basket.

A small, skinny figure stepped into view.

'Hello,' she said. 'Can someone give me a hand with my baskets?'

Hobbes, took the basket from the floor, reached into the darkness for another and carried them upstairs. One contained a pair of steam irons and the other a large, bony-looking fish. I assumed she'd bought them somewhere, though I couldn't quite let go of the idea that she'd merely taken them for a walk.

As I watched Hobbes, Dregs and Mrs Goodfellow leave the

cellar, I realised with a chill of horror that I was alone, standing with my back to the open door of the tunnels. Turning, I peered into the blackness below, fearing something was coming. The feeling was too much to bear, so, running forwards, wary of the steep steps, I grabbed the knob and pulled the door shut. A metallic chink came from behind it, repeating several times, diminishing like a fading echo. I was puzzled until I tried to lock the door.

'Sod it!' I muttered, clenching my fists, the fear of troglodytes, and God only knew what else, having access to the house, forcing me to act, to go below, to retrieve the key. After all, it would only be at the bottom of the steps; there would be no need to go any further, and I had a torch. What's more, Hobbes knew where I was and would, no doubt, follow in a matter of seconds. Though I could have waited, I had to prove something to myself.

Taking a couple of deep breaths, setting my jaw in a rugged, determined grin to underline my resolve, I turned the knob, pushed open the door and faced the void. My torch gleaming faintly, I stepped down, finding that, as the darkness deepened, its beam strengthened, revealing strange, intricate patterns carved into the dripping stone. I didn't dare spare any time examining them. Walking down took much longer than falling down and I had to force myself to continue. When I reached the bottom, the torch fading quickly, flickered and died. Though I shook and banged it, it was a goner. I became aware of a faint, distinct stink, like a combination of sour milk and day-old cabbage water.

In the dimness, I could just make out the key, lying in the puddle. I wondered whether the puddle was permanent, or just a result of heavy rain, and imagined it growing into a lake during the depths of winter. Bending down, groping for the key, I found the water so cold it hurt. The bad smell was growing stronger; I tried not to breathe it in.

As my hand closed round the key, there was a noise like the suckers on a rubber bath mat being pulled up, something plopped into the puddle, and the water swirled. I fled, taking the steps two or even three at a time. On reaching the cellar, I yanked the door closed behind me and locked it, though I didn't feel safe until I'd run upstairs into the kitchen.

The old girl was scaling the fish in the sink. 'Are you alright, dear?'

I nodded, panting too hard to speak, and slumped onto a chair. Hobbes was on the phone in the sitting room.

'So,' he said, 'we have a positive identity? Well, that saves me a job ... Thank you ... Goodbye.'

The receiver clicked down and Hobbes returned to the kitchen.

'That,' he said, 'was the station. The lab has confirmed the body is that of Michael Peter Rook. He'd served time for GBH, among other things, and they were able to match his fingerprints. Furthermore, he didn't die of his original injuries. He'd been smothered in his hospital bed. That's good news, eh?'

'Good news?' My voice was shaky. 'Why?'

'Well, firstly, it means Featherlight couldn't have been responsible for his death and, secondly, you don't have to identify the body. Thirdly, it's going to be fun finding out who did kill him ... and why.'

'I see.' I could have punched the air at my reprieve. To be honest, I'm not sure I could have forced myself back down the tunnels, though I bet Hobbes could have.

'I'll just lock up,' he said.

'I've already done that.'

'Well done.'

'Thanks. Umm ... I dropped the key and went to get it and I think something was clinging to the wall. It dropped into the puddle ... I don't know what it was.'

'Nor do I,' said Hobbes, 'but those suckers stink.'

'They certainly do. Are they dangerous?'

'I expect so, but they've never done me any harm.'

Though he didn't reassure me, the relief of not having to go to the morgue made me euphoric, almost as if I'd downed a couple of bottles of wine. When Hobbes returned to the cellar to replace the coal, the existence of the extra barricade made me feel even better. I slipped across the kitchen floor and landed a kiss on the old girl's cheek, as warm and as soft as velvet.

'Thank you, dear,' she said and surprised me by blushing. Then she inserted a thin knife blade into the fish and its guts fell out, stinking and slimy.

'Fish tomorrow?' I asked.

'No, dear.'

I pointed at the mess in the sink. 'So, why are you gutting it?'

'It's something to do while I think.'

'What are you thinking about?'

'The festival. I'm just making sure I haven't forgotten anything. Ensuring the punters are safe and have a good time is very important.'

'I'm sure it is,' I said, smiling, thinking she wasn't a typical security guard.

'Ah, yes,' said Hobbes stepping back into the kitchen. 'I'm planning to go there first thing in the morning to make sure everything's safe before the crowds turn up. I thought I might turn in early tonight, as I doubt I'll be getting much sleep over the weekend. And Andy, make sure you pack a bag.'

When he went to bed, it was only nine o'clock. Though it seemed very early, after pushing a few clothes and other essentials into the old canvas kit bag that had been left by my bed, I too turned in.

18

When I awoke, it hardly seemed a minute had passed.

Despite the scent of frying bacon making my mouth water, the comfort of warm blankets, for a few minutes, was even more alluring. Even in my drowsy state I knew this to be unusual, the old girl's cooking having proved far more effective at getting me up than the alarm clock I'd relied on back in the days when I'd had a job. I couldn't understand why I was so heavy with sleep that I didn't want to move. Still, in the end, the bacon won. Sitting up, opening my eyes, I found it was so dark I feared we must be in for a storm, like the ones that had afflicted so many festivals I'd seen on the telly.

I dragged myself from bed, yawning across the room, and pulled open the curtains, surprised the street lighting was still on, as if in the middle of the night. Dazed, I washed, dressed and fumbled down the dark stairs to the kitchen, where I stood blinking in the doorway, fluorescent light battering my bleary eyes.

The old girl was at the cooker, sizzling bacon in a pair of blackened cast-iron pans that I struggled to lift. When she raised one in each hand to shake them, I feared her skinny wrists would snap, but she seemed as unperturbed as Dregs, who was still sprawled in his basket, emitting gentle snores. Hobbes, dressed alarmingly in his blue striped pyjamas and kitten slippers, leant across the table, slicing slabs of bread from a vast white loaf.

'Good morning,' he said.

'Is it?' I asked, too dozy to argue, sitting down at the table and yawning.

'You're up early,' said Mrs G by way of greeting.

'So are you. Why?'

Flipping a rasher, she examined it for defects and, finding none, flipped some more. 'Well, dear, it's going to be a busy day, so we thought we'd best make an early start. We weren't planning on waking you yet.'

'Thanks ... but what are we going to do?'

'Keep people safe,' said Hobbes, waving the bread knife a little too close to my nose. 'The lass and her team will be ensuring there's no trouble with the festival-goers, while I'll be undercover, mingling, being inconspicuous.'

I tried not to laugh.

'And I'll keep an eye out in case other things cause trouble,' he continued.

'You mean the big cats?'

'I do in part, but I'll be policing as well, seeing that nothing goes on that shouldn't.'

'What can I do?' I asked, feeling like a spare part.

'You can enjoy the music ... but keep alert and let me know of anything you think I should know. In the meantime, would you care to saw this bread while I get changed? When you've finished this loaf, there are three more in the pantry; that should be sufficient.' He handed me the bread knife.

'Sufficient for what?' Since he'd already carved a small hill of slices, I reckoned it might not all be for us.

'For you two and for my security lads,' said Mrs Goodfellow. 'They'll be getting to the farm for seven and I think it's only right and proper that they start the day with a decent bit of breakfast in their bellies.'

'And when do we get ours?' The aroma having wakened my stomach, it was grumbling and groaning quietly like a disappointed audience.

'When we get there.'

'So ... umm ... what time is it now?'

'Nearly four o'clock.'

I sighed, glancing out the window where a brittle, monochrome light was becoming apparent and a chaffinch began to sing. Twice in three days, I'd witnessed the sunrise and, much as I appreciated it, I hoped it wasn't habit forming.

I set to work, building a tottering tower of sliced bread, which the old girl, butter knife in hand, jar of home-made chutney chinking, converted into bacon sandwiches, hiding them away in a succession of brown paper bags. To my regret, not a single sandwich finding its way to me, I had to make do with a handful of the crumbs from the breadboard. Fortunately, there was a pot of tea and a couple of steaming mugs provided temporary respite. Still, I couldn't say I wasn't jealous when Dregs woke up and she treated him to a selection of bacon scraps.

I sat, watching as she scrubbed the dishes. She was wearing her normal checked skirt, a brown cardigan and, as a concession to the event, a pair of green wellington boots, very much down-at-heel.

'Shouldn't you have a uniform or something?'

'I have, dear,' she said, turning round, pointing to a badge pinned to the middle of her cardie. 'All the lads have them. Miss Pipkin typed them for us on her computer and Billy Shawcroft had them laminated. Nice aren't they?'

The badge read 'Festical Sexurity'.

'Shouldn't that be 'Festival Security'?'

'Yes, dear, but old Miss Pipkin's eyesight is not so good these days and I didn't want to upset her. Anyway, it might have been worse.'

'Much worse,' I said, smirking, 'though they won't do much for your authority, will they? Won't everyone laugh at you?'

'They might, if anyone notices. But that's not such a bad thing.'

'Isn't it?'

'No, dear. Laughter can dispel tension.'

'I suppose it can,' I said, thinking that not all laughter was well meant.

Hobbes's reappearance drove out such thoughts, replacing them with horror and a large dollop of amusement. Dregs, growling, retreated under the table, barking at Hobbes's hairy feet, which were enclosed in an ancient pair of leather sandals. I averted my eyes.

'It's time to load the car,' said Hobbes. 'Would you give me a hand?'

'Umm ... yes.' I said, controlling myself, following him to the sitting room, wondering where the hell he'd found his clothes. Though I'd have been the first to admit my ignorance of things sartorial, even I knew the summer of love had run its course in 1967. I'd heard rumours of maroon velvet, flared trousers, but had never truly believed such things existed. He was also wearing what might have been an orange kaftan; if so, it was one for a much shorter person, barely covering his belly, the sleeves cut off at the elbow. His rectangular, blue-tinted sunglasses might have looked cool were they not beneath a stained, broad-brimmed, brown-suede hat, and I was sure his psychedelic glass beads would have been a bad idea at any point in history.

Even so, his clothes weren't the worst of it; even more alarming were the long, black, snaggly wig and the immense, droopy moustache. He was going to be as inconspicuous as a bull in a boudoir, though, in fairness, I doubted anyone seeing him would immediately think police officer.

I wondered why there was a pile of poles and tattered khaki rags on the floor.

'Right,' said Hobbes, 'let's pack the tents first.'

By the looks of them, he'd got them from Army Surplus at some point between the wars.

'I'll carry this lot if you open the boot. Take these.' Tossing me the keys, stooping, he scooped the whole lot into his massive arms.

Within a few minutes, we'd packed the car, all four of us

squeezing into whatever space remained. I ended up with Dregs sitting on my lap, since he'd also been relegated to the back seat to make way for Mrs Goodfellow. Only when we were hurtling towards the festival site did I remember the front wheel, guessing Billy had fixed it overnight. I hoped he'd not been too drunk and, since we made it without any problems, I guessed he hadn't been.

As we arrived at Loop's Farm, Bashem and Bullimore, leaning on the gate in the same pose as when I'd last seen them, directed us towards a large, flat, grassy field where we parked in the farthest corner, beside a crumbling stone wall. The next field along, glinting green in the morning sun, sloped gently down towards a pair of stages between towering cliffs of speakers, awaiting the crowds. I had to admit it, everything looked surprisingly professional.

I got out of the car, clutching myself and groaning, for Dregs was never careful where he put his great paws when excited, and he was very excited. Racing across the field, he bounced around the farmers, as if they were old friends.

As Mrs G went to liaise with them, Hobbes and I carried the tents to a suitable spot. Truthfully, I only carried a tent peg that he dropped but I think my moral support was invaluable. His method for pitching tents involved a great deal of grunting and reminded me of Jonah being swallowed by the whale. I helped where I could, running round, lifting and pushing wherever it looked useful. Hobbes appeared to have gone down for the third time, when, emerging briefly, he handed me two lengths of twine.

'Hold tight and don't let go,' he said.

Only when both structures were up and he was battering the last pegs in with his fist did I realise I was holding both ends of a length of baler twine, with no connection with camping whatsoever.

'Well done, Andy, thanks,' he said, grinning through his new-fangled moustache, and pointing. 'This one's ours and that's for the lass and Dregs. Now, let's get the bedding inside.'

Whereas I'd hoped for camp beds and sleeping bags, we had a

pile of rugs and blankets. The ground looked hard and lumpy.

We'd just finished when I was delighted to see the security crew turn up, which meant Mrs Goodfellow could dole out the bacon butties. She had, of course, prepared plenty for everyone, and there was enough left over to feed the pack of young Bashems who'd emerged from the farmhouse in great excitement.

After a couple of sandwiches, Hobbes, taking Dregs, vanished in the direction of Loop Woods, leaving the security crew to stand around trying to look important, giving the impression of being nervous. They weren't the big, rough lads I'd been expecting, apart from one hulking yet wobbly youth called Arnold, who was there with his dad, a slight, balding man with a paunch exaggerated by a knitted blue cardigan. The rest of them weren't much to look at either, being, for the most part, friendly, middle-aged blokes. One was actually wearing a red bow tie. Yet, the old girl, as she issued orders, exuded an air of quiet confidence that almost reassured me. Trucks and vans started arriving from nine o'clock, carrying caterers and stallholders onto the site.

I was free to mooch around, the only drone among the workers, a most pleasant sensation. The sun was warm, the scent of cut grass soothing, my belly full, as I stretched out in a patch of tiny, aromatic yellow flowers, watching the swifts and swallows swooping and soaring in the forget-me-not blue sky. Yawning, I shut my eyes, awaking to the strumming of an imperfectly tuned guitar.

I sat up, bleary, heavy-limbed, blinking in the bright summer sunshine, to see a line of cars and vans blocking the lane onto the farm, along with a mass of pedestrians. Mrs Goodfellow and Arnold's dad were at the gate, collecting tickets, letting the punters in and, since hundreds of tents had already sprouted like toadstools across the field, it took me a few moments to work out where ours were.

People were everywhere, talking, eating, strumming guitars

and dancing. A spotty-faced troubadour, leaning against the wall, his hair like a failed experiment by a drunken basket-weaver, was twanging his instrument and chanting in a nasal monotone. Though a great believer in self-expression, I couldn't help thinking there should be limits.

I went towards the gates, looking for Mrs Goodfellow, hoping for food, finding only Arnold's dad addressing a group of hard-faced, shaven-headed, tattooed, young men.

'Sorry, gentlemen,' he said, 'I'm afraid you can't come in without a ticket, but I believe Mr Bullimore still has a few left, if you wish to purchase them.'

'We're not,' said a nightmare figure with a spider's web tattooed across his face, 'going to buy any tickets. Now, it's bloody obvious there's no way a fat, old git like you is gonna stop us getting in, so step aside and no one gets hurt. Right?'

'Sorry, my friends. No tickets, no entry.'

The men muttered and swore, bunching together, leaning over Arnold's dad.

'I'm not getting through to you, am I?' said the man with the facial tattoo, shoving Arnold's dad in the chest before dropping to his knees, moaning. 'Ooh, that hurt ... that really hurt. What did you do that for?'

'I'm sorry to inconvenience you, sir, but I was merely ensuring my message got through to you and your friends. We have a rule: no tickets, no entry. I didn't make it, but I will enforce it.'

The group helped their sobbing friend back to his feet and led him away. He was walking slowly, with extreme concentration, and none of the rest seemed inclined to argue. Arnold's dad, smiling, continued to collect tickets, chatting to people as if nothing had happened.

As I wandered around, I caught up with Hobbes, sitting cross-legged on the grass, pounding a bodhran amidst an impromptu bunch of drummers before a crowd of admirers. That the crowd was mostly young and female both surprised and irritated me, though I had to admit he had a mean sense of rhythm.

'The big guy can't 'alf play,' said a skinny girl with too much eye make-up.

'Ah, but you should hear him sing,' I replied, which was nasty.

'Give us a song,' she cried, and the chorus joined in.

'Right on,' said Hobbes, screwing up his face, closing his eyes and bursting into a rendition of 'Puff, the Magic Dragon'.

Those nearby clamped hands to ears and fled, even his fellow drummers. Those further afield stopped whatever they were doing and looked stricken. It wasn't that he sang out of tune, which he didn't, or that he mangled the lyrics, which he did, it was the sheer, gut-tearing volume. Finishing, he opened his eyes, looking up as if anticipating applause and I think I detected a hint of surprise, or maybe disappointment, that I was the only one left.

He grinned. 'Hi, man, where've you been?'

'Sleeping in the sun, but I guess it must be lunchtime now. Do you fancy getting a bite?'

'Why not? There's a stall selling hot roast pork or beef rolls, how about one of them?'

'That sounds perfect.'

'Come on then.'

We strolled to the food zone, from where the most delicious smells arose, and bought a couple of enormous pork rolls with apple sauce.

'Thanks,' I said, taking mine. 'Umm … I didn't know you could drum?'

'Yeah, man, though I haven't played much since I left the Army.'

We leaned against a mossy, old stone wall, munching, keeping it all together with difficulty, for the rolls were full to overflowing.

'Have you seen any signs of the panthers?'

'No. At least, no new ones. I did find some spoors, but they were at least two days old, which might suggest the cats have moved on. Then again, it might not. Still, I think everyone's likely to be safe. The sheer number of people here, not to mention the noise, should keep the creatures away.'

'What about … umm … the werewolf?'

'If he's around, he'll be no trouble, unless something upsets him.'

'What's going to upset him?'

Hobbes shrugged, pushing the remains of his roll into his mouth, chewing slowly, observing the crowd. Finishing my last piece of pork, I wiped my mouth with the serviette, which seemed to spread more grease than it absorbed.

'Right,' he said, walking away, 'I'm off to patrol. I'll see you later.'

I mooched about, listening, watching and absorbing the atmosphere. A couple of hours later, Hobbes reappeared.

'All seems well,' he said, with a smile. 'Hullo, something's about to happen.'

'Ladies and gentlemen,' said Bernie Bullimore, sporting a sparkling red waistcoat and a battered top hat, his voice booming over the sound system, 'welcome to the First Annual Grand Sorenchester Music Festival. I'm delighted so many of you are here and hope we've got a programme with something for everybody. Though we don't officially kick-off until five o'clock, we've had a young band turn up and they're desperate to play. I thought we'd given 'em a chance.'

Like many others, Hobbes and I headed towards the stage, passing an oddball bunch of hippie types, among whom even Hobbes would not have stood out too far. They were sitting cross-legged, facing the stage.

'Oh, no,' said one as Hobbes stepped round him, 'it's the Pigs.'

Bernie's voice roared out across the fields. 'Ladies and gentlemen, please give a massive Sorenchester welcome to the Pigs.'

To give the crowd its due, there was a spatter of cheering and even one or two whoops but, mostly, it clapped politely, as five lads shambled onto stage and picked up their instruments.

A tall, skinny youth grasped the microphone. 'Good afternoon, we're the Pigs. One, two, three … er …'

'Four!' prompted a loud mouth in the crowd, to much laughter.

The singer counted the band in again, punching the air when he reached 'four' and the song would probably have been more impressive had the sound system worked. We could hear the tinny, un-amplified drums and the guitarist's aggrieved moaning before the crowd's guffaws drowned it out. The Pigs slouched off stage, returning ten minutes later, when the problems had been rectified. An hour later, I think most agreed their first set had been the better one. Still, the lads had tried and, as they trooped off, fists clenched, they generated a smattering of applause, which, taking as a sign of approval, encouraged them to come back for an encore.

'Thank you, Sorenchester,' the singer bellowed and, something striking him on the forehead, collapsed face first onto the stage.

Having seen nothing, I was reluctant to point the finger at Hobbes, who, chuckling, wiped his hands on his velvet trousers as the band trudged off, bearing their stricken leader.

'Rock and roll,' said Hobbes. 'Who's on next, man?'

'Umm ... It's the Famous Fenderton Fiddle Fellows at five. What time is it now?'

Hobbes, with a glance at the horizon, answered, 'Half-past four.'

I wondered how he knew, until I realised he'd been looking in the direction of the church clock, at least four or five miles away. I was impressed, though, for all I knew, he could have been lying. People were still arriving and I'd guess there were several thousand on the site, their tents as many and as close together as zits on a teenager's chin. Hobbes wandered off to make sure Mrs G was alright, although, with Dregs at her side, I didn't expect she'd have had much trouble, even if anyone had felt inclined to try anything. Besides, with the exception of the bunch Arnold's dad had turned away, everyone seemed in a friendly mood, gathering in small groups, chatting, laughing and occasionally singing. Queues snaked across the field towards the catering vans, beer tents and toilets.

I went over to watch a young man in motley garb juggling a handful of assorted cook's knives before a fascinated audience. We gasped with astonishment when, spinning a cleaver in a high loop, he bounced it off his forehead, carrying on as if it had been part of the act. Only when blood dripped into his eyes did he lose control, receiving several spectacular stab wounds and fainting as the knives responded to gravity. A team of St. John's Ambulance carried him away, along with the capful of small change he'd earned for his pains.

I wandered through the crowd seeing other, more successful, if less spectacular, jugglers, along with magicians, buskers and face-painters, narrowly avoiding getting my face painted by a hefty, determined lady in dungarees, escape only becoming possible when she discovered I was broke. I've tried to suppress memories of how she found this out, but it involved some pain and a loss of dignity. A number of brawny young blokes, their arms adorned with tangles of fantastic tattoos, laughed at my plight before heading towards the beer tent, which was doing a roaring trade.

To my surprise, when the Famous Fenderton Fiddle Fellows took to the stage, they'd transmuted from the drunken shambles I remembered into a good-time band, quite matching the spirit of the occasion. The crowd danced and sang and even I found my feet tapping. Hobbes was on the far side, apparently attempting to fit waltz steps to a rock beat, alternately smiling at the people around him and apologising when he stepped on them.

Towards the end of the set, a girl with long blonde hair and big hazel eyes, catching hold of my wrist, dragged me, protesting slightly, into a space where we and several others bobbed and gyrated to the music. The way she was smiling at everyone made me suspect the lager I could smell on her breath was not the only substance she'd taken. At the end, hot and sweaty, heart thumping, I dropped to the grass, my new friend, sprawling across me, kissed me hard on the lips.

I responded with a squeeze that made her giggle, until,

pushing herself up on her arms she stared into my face with a look of disgust. 'You're not Wayne,' she said, getting to her feet, leaving me.

'Hello, Andy,' said a familiar voice, 'I'm glad to see you're enjoying yourself.'

Felix King, dressed in an immaculate linen suit, was looking down on me.

I sat up. 'Umm … Hello … I didn't know you'd be here.'

'It's always good to meet the locals. I'll see you around.'

He strolled away towards the camping field, a pair of large, intimidating young men in dark suits following and, to my horror, Violet walking in front. She was stunning in a diaphanous pale-green sundress, showing off her slim, tanned shoulders and I realised with dismay that she must have walked past when I'd been rolling in the grass with the strange girl. I wanted to run and explain myself, to tell her that what she'd seen wasn't what it looked like, but Felix, having caught up with her, putting his arm around her, glanced back at me, shaking his head.

My spirits plummeted. I feared I'd blown it and lost her forever. I pounded the turf with my clenched fists.

'What's that poor grass ever done to you, mate?' asked a bloke in a baseball cap, watching me with an infuriating grin. He walked away when I ignored him.

Getting back to my feet, I came to a decision that, whatever the risk, I was going to talk to her and explain. If she then told me to shove off, I was done for, yet there was a chance she'd listen and understand. As for Felix and his heavies, I didn't care; they could do their worst. Not that they were likely to do much in a packed field.

The crowd was swelling in anticipation of the next act, which I assumed, because of the cries of 'Come on Tim', was Tiny Tim Jones, who'd been released on parole. When at last I pushed my way through and out the other side, there was no sign of Violet, or Felix and his merry men. I walked around for a while, disconsolate.

Mrs G and Dregs were still by the gate. She was counting the ticket stubs out onto a table and frowning.

'Hello, dear,' she said, as I approached, 'are you enjoying yourself?'

'Yeah, I am,' I said, stroking Dregs's head. 'Umm … you look worried. Is something the matter?'

'Well, dear, the thing is, Mr Bullimore said he'd sold three-thousand tickets, but I've got more stubs than that.'

'Forgeries, maybe? At thirty quid a ticket, someone might have thought it worthwhile.'

'I fear you may be right, dear, but they all look genuine. I'll ask the old fellow when he turns up; he's good at spotting things. Have you seen him?'

'Yes, he was dancing.'

'I'm glad. He's good at it.'

'Umm … I'm not sure good is the right word, he was treading on people.'

'I expect it's because of this modern music and the grass. He can do a wonderful foxtrot on a sprung floor.'

'He looked more like a fox with the trots.' I smirked.

The old girl gave me her 'stern' look. 'Did you do any better?'

'Sort of. I danced with a young lady.'

'Good for you, but why are you looking so glum?'

'Because Violet saw me.'

'Well, a dance can't hurt.'

'Umm …' I said, squirming and blushing, 'we weren't actually dancing when she saw us … we were sort of rolling around in the grass.'

Mrs G's eyebrows rose and her eyes twinkled behind her glasses. 'I see.'

'No, you don't … I didn't mean it to happen … in fact, I'm not sure how it did happen and I wish it hadn't … At least not when she could see me. I want to explain it was all a mistake, but I can't find her and I don't know what she'll say if I do … and I'm not sure what Felix will do to me if … when I speak to her.'

'He won't do anything while I'm around.'

'Thank you. I'm going to talk to her whatever happens.'

'Well, take care, dear and don't do anything too foolish. I suspect millionaires won't be spending the night in a tent; if I were you, I'd check those camper vans on the edge of the site.'

'Thanks, I will, though I thought they were heading this way. Perhaps they're staying in the farmhouse?'

'I doubt it, dear. There can't be much room inside with six children, not to mention Mr and Mrs Bashem and Mr Bullimore.'

'Six? I thought there were an awful lot of them. Oh well, I expect they're all out enjoying the music.'

'I expect so, dear. Anyway, here's young Arnold come to take over the gate.'

Arnold wobbled towards us, a large paper cup of cola in one hand, an even larger burger in the other. He nodded with a greasy grin. Though, since living at Hobbes's, burgers had lost much of their appeal, the sight of it, combined with the scent of fried onions, made me realise I was quite hungry. I wondered what I could do about it.

'Well, unless anything happens, I'm off duty until midnight,' said Mrs G. 'I'll go and make supper. I expect you'll be hungry; I know the old fellow will be.'

'I was starting to feel a bit peckish,' I admitted. 'What are you going to do?'

'Chicken in the bucket.'

'Can I help?'

'No, dear, it's all prepared. I just need to mix it up and get it on the heat. It'll probably be ready after the next act.'

'Umm … did you really say chicken in the bucket?'

'Yes, dear, though it's not really in a bucket; it's in a Dutch oven. You go and enjoy the music. I'm sure you'll find your young lady later.'

Taking Dregs with her, she walked away, and I headed back towards the stage in time for the end of Tim's short set, a complete racket. However, afterwards, we were privileged to witness a bizarre set from a lunatic calling herself Mad Donna. Though, when she started, some complained that she was not quite what they'd been expecting, her crazed antics and weird gibberings exerted a trance-like fascination, soon overriding any objections. She had a five-piece band, yet the music was strangely irrelevant. We finally cheered her off after three encores. I thought she'd be a hard act to follow, until I was strolling back to the tent and the scent of Mrs G's chicken in the bucket struck me.

The old girl, sitting cross-legged on the ground, was stirring an iron pot with a large wooden spoon or possibly a small paddle, with Hobbes squatting beside her, whittling a whistle from a small stick. Despite, or possibly because of, his weird costume and behaviour, I had to admit he'd done an amazing job at fitting in. No one would suspect him of being a policeman: he was quite obviously a nutter.

I sprawled on the grass next to Dregs while the old girl dished up, pulling in quite an audience. Sad people with hungry eyes swallowed, gazing at the steam swirling from the gurgling pot, the pot that was sending out such enticing aromas. When, at last, they turned away, trudging towards the burger vans, I had never before felt so privileged and lucky. When she handed me a bowl, with a hunk of fresh, crusty bread and a spoon, I could barely wait for Hobbes to say grace. Hunger, fresh air and exquisite cooking had given me an appetite and I regret I rather stuffed myself, fearful any might go to waste, or be offered to the passing throng. Though undoubtedly selfish, I'd challenge anyone to resist another bite of the old girl's cooking. A bottle of the good wine added extra zest to the meal.

When we'd finished, I asked if I could help with the washing up.

'Oh no, dear,' she said, smiling. 'Why don't you boys run along and enjoy yourselves.'

Sometimes, I thought, she had all the right answers. We sat watching Simon and Garth Ingle perform a set of whimsical folky songs, Dregs howling and, in my view, improving the performance. However, some people seemed to want to listen, so eventually we led him away, paying a quick visit to the beer tent.

'A pint of lager and two quarts of "Old Gutbuster" please, man,' said Hobbes to the barmaid.

Taking our drinks, we sat in the evening sun. Though Hobbes gulped down two pints in a matter of seconds, I sipped at mine, feeling far too full to take on copious amounts. My thoughts kept returning to Violet and, halfway through my drink, I came to a decision.

'I'm going to find Violet,' I said.

Hobbes nodded. 'Good idea. Would you like me to come with you? In case Mr King starts anything?'

'Thanks,' I said, 'but I'd rather do this on my own. I'll be alright. See you later.'

I got up, searching the crowd, examining every face, as bands came and went, some of them rather good, making me wish I could share them with her. I didn't see her, or Felix, or any of his men. In the end, when darkness had fallen except for the stage lighting, I gave up and watched No One You've Ever Heard Of. Their music was noisy with a pounding beat and the band, giving the performance of a lifetime, almost revived my spirits, making me cheer along with all the others. Hobbes joined me for a short time and then wandered off to ensure there was no trouble. I didn't think there would be; everybody seemed intent on enjoying themselves.

The band finishing, I returned to the tent, removing my shoes and crawling under the blankets. To start with, Dregs lay across my feet, welcome warmth, on a clear night with a steady breeze. I lay, yawning, trying to sleep, the ground even harder and lumpier than it had looked, people far too noisy. It became apparent that, despite exhaustion, I would never drop off. My fidgeting disturbed Dregs, who, sighing, wandered out into the night. After about half an hour, remembering I hadn't brushed my teeth, I dragged myself from beneath the covers, found my toothbrush and a towel and headed for the washrooms, shivering in the night air.

Just about everyone had moved away from the silent stage, now lit only by starlight and the crescent moon. Small groups of people, sprawling in the grass, sitting on stools, laughed and talked, as if no one else planned on sleeping that night. An assortment of teenagers were attempting rudimentary cooking on an open fire, impaling sausages on sticks, but the bottles and cans surrounding them suggested why they were not enjoying much success. As another sausage flared up in a blaze of glory, they roared with laughter. I doubted they'd get much to eat; they didn't appear to mind.

Finding the washrooms, I blinked under the strip light until, a basin becoming free, I brushed my teeth, made a brave attempt at washing in cold water, and headed back across the field. I paused to watch a bare-chested tumbler's wobbly one-man display. When he collapsed amidst great cheers, I turned away, bumping into a woman. Her perfume was powerful and heady.

'Oops … umm … sorry,' I said.

'Andy?'

'Oh … umm … Violet … Hi.'

19

'Well,' said Violet, 'I suppose I should be grateful you've remembered my name.'

'Of course I have,' I said. 'I'm so glad I bumped into you – I've been ... umm ... looking for you all night.'

She glanced at my towel and toothbrush. 'Have you?'

'Yes, really.'

Even in semi-darkness, she looked stunning, her eyes reflecting the crescent moon, her dark, lustrous hair gleaming over her shoulders. Another whiff of her perfume reached my nostrils. 'I've been trying to see you ever since the accident ... I really have.'

'Oh, yes? I was in hospital; I assume you know where that is?'

She wouldn't look me in the face, despite my best efforts.

'Yes ... but ...'

'You couldn't even bother to get in touch when they released me. A token interest would have been polite.'

'I wanted to talk to you. I did try.'

'Did you? How hard is it to pick up a telephone?'

'But I hadn't got your number,' I said, realising how utterly useless I must be presenting myself.

'Ever heard of directory enquiries? Anyway, you could have asked Felix.'

'I did, but he wouldn't ...'

'Wouldn't what?'

Her voice was harsh and cold and it hurt to hear it like that. I hesitated, wondering if I should just tell her what he'd said, fearing she wouldn't believe me.

'Umm … he … umm … suggested it might be better if I … we didn't see each other again.'

'And you didn't think it worthwhile to ask me?'

'Yes, I did … but …'

'Is this man bothering you?' asked one of Felix's men, tall, burly, with a head as smooth as a pickled-onion, approaching from the darkness.

Before she could answer, before I could think, but not before I could squeak, he frogmarched me across the field.

'It would,' he said, politely enough, had he not been crushing my shoulder, 'be an excellent idea for you to stop hassling Miss King. If you are tempted, resist it. If you don't, you are likely to find yourself in deep shit. You know what I'm saying?'

When I nodded, he released me.

'Good night,' he said, turning back the way he'd come.

Unable to see Violet anymore, I realised she might have been almost anywhere in the darkness, so all I could do was return to the tent and reflect on our chance meeting. It had not been a success and, although, the interruption hadn't helped, I couldn't fool myself that it had been going well before that. Knowing she believed I hadn't wanted to see her, hadn't even wanted to make sure she was alright, hurt as much as her cold voice. More painful though, was my shoulder, which, I suspected, would be displaying a hand-sized bruise by the morning.

My response to the henchman must have impressed her. If she'd been thinking 'what are you, Andy, man or mouse?' then my pathetic squeak would have confirmed her suspicions. I wished I'd had the guts to take Mrs Goodfellow's martial arts classes. If I had, I might not have been such a wimp.

It was too late of course, so, crawling back into the tent like the mouse I was, curling up under the blankets, I lay awake for what seemed like hours, futile regrets churning through my brain. I didn't expect to drop off.

Hobbes shook me from deep sleep. 'Wake up!'

'What's happening?' I asked, snuggling deeper into the blankets.

'Trouble.'

'Oh, right. I don't suppose you'll need me.'

Though my nose, my only exposed part, was cold, my bedding was warm and, to my astonishment, comfortable.

'Get your boots on,' said Hobbes, 'and quickly.' He tugged the blankets off me, except for the one I was clutching to my face.

I sat up, bleary and cross. He bundled me from the tent, sitting me down in front with my shoes. People were running backwards and forwards, making panicky noises as I struggled with my laces, the brisk breeze making me shiver and wrap my blanket around my shoulders. In the distance, a girl screamed, a faint orange glow became an intense red flame and I became aware of the stink of burning plastic. Something bad was happening.

'They're setting fire to tents,' said Hobbes. 'Follow me.'

Unable to make sense of shoelaces, I stumbled after him, shoes flapping, trying not to trip. When another tent flared up, his easy lope became a sprint and, on reaching it, he dived head-long into the inferno, as if into a swimming pool. Smoke and flames, bursting high into the night sky, rolled and twisted in the wind, casting shifting, fractured, red light over the crowd. People were coughing as the smoke billowed around the field.

The tent erupting with sparks and flaming fragments, Hobbes burst forth like a rocket from the launch pad, a limp body beneath each arm. I was still running as he laid them on the grass and, without thinking, pulling the blanket from my shoulders, I threw it over the nearest figure, beating out the smouldering patches, realising it was a young woman cocooned within a sleeping bag. Despite the smoke and fumes, I could smell the alcohol on her breath as she started to come awake.

'What the hell d'you think you're doing?' she asked, 'Get off me.'

An arm emerged and dealt a stinging slap across my face.

With no time to explain, ripping the blanket from her, I spread it over the other figure, patting out any smoking bits. On looking up, I saw Hobbes rolling on the ground, his head ablaze. I grabbed the blanket but before I could get to him, he tore off his head and tossed it to the ground.

I screeched, an incoherent outpouring of horror, feeling sick, staring stunned and uncomprehending, as he leapt to his feet, stamping out the blaze. Only then did I realise that he'd simply torn off his hippie hat and wig.

'Are you alright?' I asked.

'Never better,' he said, 'though I was, maybe, a little hot-headed diving in like that, if not as hot-headed as I was getting out. I appear to be a little singed. It'll pass.'

Despite everything, I chuckled, before spluttering, the swirling, acrid smoke catching the back of my throat.

Hobbes, still smoking slightly, patted me on the back. 'You did well. It was good thinking to bring that blanket.'

He turned away and attended to the two he'd rescued. I knelt beside them as the girl, who looked familiar, unzipped herself.

'You!' she said, looking up at me and frowning.

'I'm still not Wayne,' I said.

'I'm sorry,' she said. 'I mean, I'm sorry I hit you, not that you're not Wayne.'

'Don't worry about it. I'm alright. You didn't hit me hard. Are you hurt?'

'I'm OK.' She coughed. 'Your lip's bleeding, I'm sorry; I thought you were Wayne trying it on. And I'm really sorry I stitched you up this afternoon.'

'What d'you mean? That was on purpose? Why?'

She looked away. 'Some bloke gave me twenty quid to jump on you.'

'Who?'

'I don't know. A tall guy in a suit … quite old: older than you, anyway. He said you were a bastard who was trying it on with his sister and I was to show her what you were like. I'm sorry.'

'Don't worry about it,' I said, despite seething – not at her, not much, but at Felix. Turning towards the other casualty, who was lying very still, I asked Hobbes how he was.

'He appears to be dead …'

The girl screamed, clapping a hand across her mouth.

Hobbes held up his hands, shaking his head. 'I was trying to say that he appears to be dead drunk. Otherwise, he seems alright apart from his hair. He'll not be needing a cut for a while.'

'Fetch water!' he roared at the crowd, getting to his feet, tearing down burning tents, three of which were already ablaze, others being in imminent danger as the breeze whipped up sparks and flame.

A few individuals, getting past the gawping stage, set up a chain from a standpipe, hurling containers of water onto the conflagrations. I joined them and, under the command of Mrs Goodfellow's team, with Hobbes's demolitions providing a firebreak, it wasn't too long before we were in control. When the fire brigade turned up, at last, there wasn't much left to do, other than damping down the remaining hot spots.

When, shortly afterwards, an ambulance arrived to take him away, Wayne had sobered up enough to realise his hair was a blackened frizz, and was seemingly more concerned about that than the loss of his tent and near immolation.

As order and calm gradually reasserted themselves, Hobbes took me across the field.

'It was very brave,' I said, 'to throw yourself into a fire. You were lucky you weren't hurt.'

'I was just doing my job.'

'But,' I continued, 'how did you know there was going to be a fire?'

'I didn't, but I had smelt trouble.'

'What sort of trouble.'

'Two panthers.'

'Won't the fires have scared them off?'

'Possibly.'

'Where did you see them?'

'I didn't see them,' he said, tapping the side of his nose.

'So, where didn't you see them?'

'Near the stage, heading towards the farmhouse.'

'OK, so what are we going to do?' I asked, with as much bravado as I could, worried he'd want to involve me in the trouble. Why else would he have woken me?

'Find them, if possible.'

'Will you need me?'

'Need? Probably not, but I thought you might be interested.'

'Interested is not the word,' I said, thinking terrified might be more appropriate.

'Good. Now follow me, keep close and keep quiet.'

I jogged behind, hoping the panthers had fled. As we reached the gate into the lane, he stopped suddenly.

I didn't. Bouncing off him, I sat down heavily. 'Oof!'

'Shh!'

'Sorry.'

'Shh!'

I used the gatepost to pull myself up, trying to see why he'd stopped, unable to see much at all, and certainly nothing to worry me, apart from Hobbes, of course.

'That's odd,' he murmured, sniffing the air.

'What's odd?'

'That scent. I know it. But from where?'

I couldn't smell anything, except for burned tent and a faint whiff of manure. The dark outline of the farmhouse stood out on the other side of the lane.

'It's familiar and strange. I noticed it at home recently. Just faintly. It'll come to me. In the meantime, duck.'

'You what?' I asked, puzzled.

He dragged me to the ground behind the wall as a spear of light stabbed through the darkness with a deafening retort.

'What's happening?' I asked keeping my head and voice low. 'Is someone shooting us?'

'No, someone shot at us. There's an important difference.'

'OK. But why shoot at us at all?'

'We'd better find out and stop them doing it again.'

'Can I do anything?'

'Yes, you can scream, as if you've been hit.'

'What?'

'Go on.'

'Agh,' I cried.

'No, like this,' he said, grabbing my wrist and pressing.

'Aaagh!' I screamed, writhing, until he released me.

'Much better. Now do that every few seconds.'

'OK, but for how long?'

He'd already vanished, so I lay where I was and screamed. A few seconds later I screamed again and then again, making sure it was a really good one, proud of its length, volume and pitch. A light flashed in my face, dazzling me.

'What's up with you?' asked a man.

'Nothing ... but I have a good reason.' There was no sign of Hobbes and a number of people were staring at me, while keeping at a safe distance.

'What reason?'

'Umm ... I don't know, exactly.'

'You're a dickhead,' said the man, and the group trudged away.

Once again, I screamed.

'Nutter!'

On the far side of the lane, someone's yell was stifled. I peeped over the wall to see Hobbes standing by the farmhouse, holding some poor devil by the collar, dangling him with his feet just scraping the ground. A shotgun with a broken back lay in the dirt until Hobbes booted it into a ditch, if he could boot anything with sandals on. Keeping my head down, creeping from the field, I went to see what was happening.

As he turned the man round, I saw it was Mr Bullimore, shaking like a man on the gallows.

'Good evening, sir,' said Hobbes. 'Perhaps you'd explain why you fired at us?'

'If I'd known who it was, I wouldn't have.'

'You shouldn't,' said Hobbes, 'be firing at anyone; it's against the law.'

Bullimore's voice shook. 'I apologise … I thought it was them again.'

'Them?'

'Yes, them.'

'Right,' said Hobbes, 'I think we should go inside and have a little chat. Don't you?'

'No,' said Bullimore, shaking his head, 'we've got to find them.'

'Whom,' asked Hobbes, 'do we need to find and why?'

'Them!' Bullimore screamed, his scream far more convincing than any I'd managed.

Hobbes shrugged. 'Calm down, sir, let's go inside and then you can explain. Let's be having you, sir.'

Setting Bullimore back down, keeping a firm grip on his collar, he marched him round the side of the house to the front door, a great, solid, iron-studded creation, yet battered and cracked, as if it had withstood a siege. When he tried the handle it didn't turn. He knocked; a few moments later, he thumped it.

'Is anyone in?'

'Yes … I hope so,' said Bullimore. 'I do have the key, though. There's only this one door.'

He stepped forward and tried to open it.

'I'm afraid,' said Hobbes, 'that it appears to be bolted, which suggests someone is in.' He pounded the door so that it shook, with a rhythm and volume that must have made people suppose another band had come on stage. When it stayed shut, he raised his fists as if contemplating demolition, hesitated and let his fists drop to his side. 'You two stay here,' he said. 'I'll let myself in.'

I leaned against the gritty, old farmhouse wall in a state of hyper-nervousness, waiting with Bullimore, who might have been paralysed. Hobbes disappeared round the back of the house, glass shattered and, soon afterwards, the bolts on the door squealing, he reappeared in a blaze of electric light. As Bullimore rushed past him, I followed, stepping over a scattering of various-sized wellington boots, finding myself in an old-fashioned house, with a large plank table, a number of worm-eaten wooden chairs and very few modern comforts.

Mr Bullimore shouted, 'Helen? Les? Kids?'

No one replied. I knelt to tie my shoelaces hearing him running from room to room. As I got back to my feet, I became aware of a faint background odour, not dissimilar to Hobbes's feral scent, and noticed him sniffing the air and frowning while looking around.

Bullimore, white-faced and panting, pounded down the shiny, dark-wood stairs back into the front room. 'They're not here!'

'Someone must have bolted the door,' I said. 'So where are they?'

'I don't know,' he said, slumping heavily onto a creaky wooden stool.

Hobbes was crawling, toad-like, around the front room, sniffing, staring intently at the threadbare rug on the timeworn flagstones. Stopping, poking at a spot, he licked his finger. 'This is blood and it's fresh.'

Bullimore, groaning, held his head.

'Though,' said Hobbes, 'it's not human.'

Bullimore gave another, longer, groan.

Hobbes, quivering like a terrier in a barn full of rats, reached the back window. 'There are fresh scuff marks here … and dried mud. Someone has gone out through the window.'

'When?' I asked.

'Within the hour, I'd say.'

Bullimore looked up, his eyes hopeful.

'Hello, hello, hello,' said Hobbes, pointing to the peeling cream paint on the woodwork, 'this is interesting.' Holding a long, thick, brown hair between thumb and fingernails, he examined it.

'Never mind that,' said Bullimore, despondent again, 'the window is locked and can only be locked from the inside. What you say doesn't make sense.'

Hobbes, standing up, pushed at the sash window, which moved easily and silently, sliding back into place when he let it go. 'The lock,' he said, peering at it, 'is broken. It appears to have broken a very long time ago.'

Bullimore groaned again, his face tinged grey.

'Now, sir,' said Hobbes, sounding urgent, 'I think it's time you told me what's going on. I want the truth, mind, no matter how peculiar.'

'I don't know how to tell you; you'll never believe it.'

'I'm very good at believing things. Try me. And quickly.'

Bullimore sighed, rocking backwards and forwards. 'I'm not sure where to start ... it's rather complicated and I really shouldn't tell you this.' He hesitated. 'In fact, I can't unless you promise not to tell anyone. You won't believe it anyway.'

'I said quickly,' Hobbes growled, 'and I meant it; we may not have much time. Perhaps it would help if I told you that I already know about Mr Bashem? I already had a strong suspicion, but the blood and the hair confirm it.'

'What d'you know about him?' asked Bullimore, staring, looking nervous.

'That he's your son-in-law, that he's thirty-eight, that he and Mrs Bashem have six children, and that he's a werewolf.'

Bullimore's mouth dropped open, mimicking mine. I was stunned Hobbes would think Mr Bashem was the werewolf; he seemed such a nice man. Maybe he was a little hairy and, perhaps he could have done with taking a bath but ...

'How did you know?' asked Bullimore.

'It's my business to know,' said Hobbes. 'Now, please, tell me what's going on, before it's too late.'

'I'll try,' said Bullimore. 'Do you know anything about werewolves? Anything at all?'

'A little.' Hobbes smiled. 'I was friends with one many years ago. He lived in a werehouse in town, next to the railway station.'

'There isn't a railway station in town,' I said.

'This was before your time, Andy. So, Mr Bullimore, I am familiar with the type.'

Bullimore sighed, looking relieved. 'That's good, because I didn't know how to start. You're absolutely right, Les is a werewolf. He's a good lad, though, or I wouldn't have let him near my daughter, being very protective after her poor mother died. I admit to being unsure about him to start with, and took steps to keep the wolf from the door when some of his behaviour struck me as barking mad. He'd scratch himself in public and wolf down his meals and, though I tried to put him off, he was dogged and one night he collared me and won me round. Of course, he'd long ago won Helen's heart.

'Well, to cut a long story short, they got married, with my blessing, and moved into a council house in Wolverhampton where, unfortunately, there were allegations about inappropriate use of lampposts and a misunderstanding over a cat that resulted in bad relations with the neighbours. A very unpleasant situation arose and Les was hounded by vigilantes. When he complained to the council, he was howled down and in the end they had to do a moonlight flit.

'They tried other places but similar things happened. It seemed that someone was always telling malicious tales to their new neighbours. Though they were lies or gross distortions the result was always the same; people weren't prepared to tolerate him, or Helen, or the young 'uns when they came along. They were spat at in the street and it began to get increasingly violent. In the end, in despair, they turned to me for help. As it happened, I'd long had an ambition to settle down in the country.'

'So you all moved here,' said Hobbes. 'Why?'

'Because Loop's Farm is mine. It's been in the family for generations and I inherited it from my grandfather, though he never lived here. It was always rented out in my time until the old boy who was the tenant passed away and we moved in. We're not great farmers, though the young 'uns have learned how to herd sheep, and money has been tight. That's why we came up with the idea of the festival. We thought it would make a bit of cash while, hopefully, getting people on our side. Things seemed to be going well until a couple of months ago. It all started with our neighbour, Henry Bishop.'

'I saw him die,' I said.

Bullimore stared at me, puzzled.

'This is not the time for idle chitchat,' said Hobbes. 'Please continue, sir.'

I didn't feel he was being fair. It wasn't chitchat; I had seen the man die, it had been horrible, and I'd suspected Hobbes. Though part of me still did, I began to wonder if Mr Bashem might actually have been the culprit.

'Did Les kill him?' I blurted out.

Hobbes scowled. 'If you don't keep quiet, I'll send you outside.'

Bullimore, ignoring me, carried on. 'Though Bishop was grumpy and miserable, he wasn't too bad at first and seemed harmless. Then he offered to buy the upper field, the one next to Loop Woods. We refused to sell, though the money would have been handy, but you don't just sell your heritage to get over being broke. Besides, it was such a ridiculously low offer, we reckoned he must have found out we were in a mess and tried to take advantage. It wasn't nice, it was business.

'After we rejected his offer, he turned nasty, objecting and complaining about everything, even the festival, though he'd made no complaint when we first told him. Not that it was anything to do with him – it wasn't going to have any impact on him or his land.

'Things took a turn for the worse when he took a pot shot at Les, though he claimed it was an accident and he was only after rabbits. We almost believed him until he had a go at the young 'uns. We had to ban them from anywhere he could see them.'

'I see,' said Hobbes nodding. 'You should have told the police.'

'We didn't want any more trouble. They aren't all like you, Mr Hobbes.'

'You're absolutely right there,' I said.

'Thank you,' said Hobbes, baring his great yellow teeth in a grin that would have terrified anyone without my experience.

'Things have been getting really bad, lately,' Bullimore continued. 'We've had tough men in suits come round here, causing trouble.'

'That'll be the Mormons,' I said, trying to lighten the mood.

'I warned you,' said Hobbes, grabbing my collar and the seat of my trousers, shoving me out the front door into the farmyard and shutting me out. Only by pressing my ear to the keyhole, could I hear.

'They've been offering a pittance, trying to force us to sell up. They said if we didn't accept their terms and get out there'd be trouble.'

'Do you know who they were?'

'Hired muscle, working for a bloke called Felix King, a developer, apparently.'

'That,' said Hobbes, 'doesn't entirely surprise me.'

'You know him? He's got a sister who's nearly as bad as him, a pity because she's a fine-looking lass. They say her name's Violet. We think it's short for Violent.'

Feeling a rush of fury that the fat, old farmer dared talk about her like that, I stood on the doorstep puffing, clenching and unclenching my fists. Though I knew my reaction was stupid, and despite being sure it was all over between us, I couldn't just stand there and let her be insulted. Actually, that was all I could do. That and fume.

Bullimore carried on. 'We hoped things would be better after Bishop died, assuming at first he was behind it; he turned out to have been just a pawn and the threats got worse. The truth is, Mr Hobbes, that we became suspicious of you, or, rather, of your friend. Les was trying to find out what they were up to and, having seen him with her at your house, followed them to the arboretum, where he hid in the woods, watching and listening. Your friend seemed very pally with them at first but it soon became very clear he was not one of King's cronies. In the end, Les, feeling sorry for him, kept an eye on him when he was going home after the accident.'

'So it was Les,' said Hobbes. 'I suspected so.'

'How did you guess?'

'I'd been hunting the panthers when I picked up a trail I didn't recognise. I was a little concerned when I became aware it was closing in on Andy, until I remembered the scent of werewolf.'

'Did you find the panthers?'

'No. I keep coming across their scent but it's usually blocked by something and, more puzzling, it often just stops. I think someone must be transporting them.'

'That's possible. I heard King used an elephant to break the guy who owns the Greasy Pole. He wants his land as well.'

'I'd suspected that. Mr King's driver was in the crowd when it happened and fitted the description of the man who'd released the creature. Unfortunately, he was murdered before I could interview him.'

'I'll bet King did that … or his sister. They're ruthless.'

'It's likely,' said Hobbes. 'Anyway, I think that's enough history. What's been going on tonight?'

'King and his henchmen came round this afternoon, when I was on stage. He made another offer, worse than previous ones and, when Les told him where he could stick it, he received a beating for his trouble. I hope that's why you found the blood on the rug. When King left, he said Les would regret not getting out when he had the chance.'

Someone screamed. Across the field I could see people running.

Bullimore was still talking. 'They said they'd be back after dark. Les was going to bolt the door – it's really strong – but I feared it was only a matter of time before they tried the windows. Although they're not easy to reach, they're still the weakest part.

That's why I went out with my shotgun. I thought I'd scare them off. I didn't mean to shoot at you.

'But now my family has gone, I've got to find them.'

At that point, I sort of forgave Mr Bullimore for shooting at us.

Something was happening in the field. Another tent flaring up, people were panicking and shouting, though I couldn't see what the problem was at first, for the fire brigade was still on site and could easily cope with a burning tent. I made out Mrs Goodfellow and Arnold's dad on the edge of the crowd, brandishing big sticks, for some reason. Then, I understood. Silhouetted, in the glare of yet another burning tent, I caught a glimpse of the dark, heart-stopping shape of a panther.

I banged on the door, yelling for Hobbes.

20

The door opened and Hobbes stepped out. 'What's up?'

'There's trouble again,' I said. 'I saw a panther and I think it's setting fire to tents.'

'Panthers aren't known as arsonists, but someone is out to cause trouble.'

An idea came to mind. 'Do you think it could be Felix?'

'I wouldn't be surprised. Violet, too, I'm afraid.'

'No, she can't be; she's not like him.' I still believed in her, despite what I'd heard.

'I hope you're right,' he said, gazing into the field. 'I'd better find the Bashems before it's too late.'

'Why? What do you think will happen?'

'Nothing good.'

'But what about all that?' I pointed to where chaos reigned.

'The lass is in charge and will sort it out with her boys – that's what they're here for – and the fire brigade can deal with the fires. I expect someone has thought to call the police by now.'

'Umm ... can I do anything?'

'Stay with Mr Bullimore, and don't let him out of your sight. You should be safe here.'

'OK,' I said, thinking it didn't seem a very heroic role but, then, I wasn't feeling very heroic. One glimpse of panther had turned my muscles to water.

Hobbes was already loping down the lane, shoulders hunched, knuckles nearly grazing the cobbles, the twisting light of the fires casting a monstrous shadow on the stone wall. Though I almost wished I'd gone with him, I wouldn't have kept up with his pace for long, and the thought of being alone in the darkness with panthers and werewolves prowling, chilled me to the core. Shivering, I stepped into the house.

Mr Bullimore, still slumped in his seat, looked up through reddened eyes and I felt sorry for the old guy.

'Where's Mr Hobbes?' he asked.

'He's gone to look for your family.'

He nodded. 'He's a good man. There's something about him though …'

'You're right there.'

'He reminds me, well, of us. In a way.'

'What d'you mean by us?' I asked, suddenly wary.

'I mean he's not the same as other policemen, or other people. He's not like you.'

'That's true. But why did you say us? What are you trying to say?' My nerves were jangling.

'Les,' said Mr Bullimore, with a strange smile, 'isn't the only werewolf in the family. I'm part werewolf myself, on my mother's side. Maybe that's why I'm such a son of a bitch.'

'Oh yes?' I said, trying to ignore the urge to back away.

'Yes, though I can't change like Les can. About all I can do is to grow hair where I don't want it and fetch sticks. Not much use really.'

'But what about your daughter?'

'Just the sticks, but the young 'uns take after their dad; they're as fine a pack of werepups as you'll ever see. I hope Mr Hobbes finds them.'

He sniffed, looking at me with such a hangdog expression that it made me say something silly. 'Umm … I suppose we could go and help him.'

'He told me to stay here, but you're right, I can't just sit around when they might be in danger. Let's go.'

'OK,' I said, 'if you're quite sure. Or perhaps it would be better to wait? In case they come back. What d'you think?'

'Let's go.' He stood up, looking resolute and strong, putting on a battered tweed jacket, and striding towards the front door. Opening it, he glanced back. 'Are you coming?'

'I suppose so,' I said, already regretting my careless talk, hoping it wouldn't cost lives, particularly my own life, 'though I think we'd better stick together.'

As he stepped into the night, he nodded, which was some comfort as we marched along the lane, following in Hobbes's footprints – if he'd left any.

'Any ideas where to look?' I asked when Mr Bullimore halted by the gate.

'It depends if they're free or if King has kidnapped them.'

'Isn't the word dognapped?' I said unthinkingly, cringing as soon as the words were out.

Mr Bullimore stared hard as I apologised, before drawing a deep breath. 'We'll try the woods. Werewolves feel secure in woods.'

He stepped into the fields, walking quickly, not like Hobbes when he was in the mood, but fast enough to get me panting as I struggled to keep up. Ahead of us, deep within the shadow, loomed Loop Woods, and who knew what lurked within? A twig cracked and, at the same moment, catching my foot on something and stumbling, I thought I saw a movement on the edge of the wood. By the time I regained my balance, I'd lost sight of it.

'What was that?'

'What was what?' asked Mr Bullimore, walking on regardless.

'I … umm … think I saw something. Perhaps we should go back to the house and get torches?'

Turning back, he pushed an object into my hand. 'Take this. I always carry a couple in my pocket, just in case.'

For all its diminutive size, the torch had a powerful, if narrow, beam. Though it provided some reassurance, I'd much rather have returned to the farmhouse, despite it not feeling nearly so safe once Hobbes had left. However, it had thick, stone walls, a stout door and, most importantly, electric lights.

'Hurry up,' called Mr Bullimore.

All of a sudden his voice was too far away. Running towards it, I found I was on the edge of Loop Woods, becoming aware of a strange sort of stillness, as if someone was hiding, holding their breath, waiting to leap out with a yell and scare me half to death.

I glanced back over my shoulder seeing that the fires appeared to have been extinguished and that hundreds of torches were flashing, looking as far away as the stars. The headlights of a fire engine were reflecting on a stone wall, illuminating the still-smoking remains of a tent, as a bulky, dark-suited man appeared in the beam, brandishing a baseball bat at the frail, skinny figure advancing on him. It was Mrs Goodfellow, wagging her finger, as if telling him off. I felt sick and entirely helpless as he raised his club, yet, before he could bring it down, she, darting forward, appeared to tap him on the chin. As he toppled over backwards and Arnold sat on him, I felt enormously proud of the old girl.

'Did you see that?' I asked Mr Bullimore.

There was no reply, just a flicker of his torch beam between the black trunks. Hastening towards it, I realised I was entering a quite different part of the woods to where Hobbes had taken me, for, where there'd been wide spaces between massive trees, soft leaf litter beneath my feet and the odd thorn bush to break up the pattern, this place was crammed with massive, old conifers with few paths. Though I struggled to catch up, I was always being forced out of my way, my torch beam seemingly feeble beneath the dark ceiling, as if the thick, resinous carpet was absorbing all light. My feet sinking into the litter, sharp needles found their way into my shoes, forcing me to stop, take them off and shake them out. When I'd finished, having no idea where Mr Bullimore had got to, I gave up following him, concentrating instead on not getting lost, reasoning that I couldn't go far wrong so long as I didn't lose sight of the glimmer of light seeping in from the edge of the wood behind me.

Something rustled.

'Mr Bullimore?'

There was no reply.

I was trying to convince myself it had only been a rabbit or something, when I received a tremendous blow between the shoulder blades. Falling forward, my torch flew from my hand like a rocket, clattering into a tree, the light going out.

I came to, sprawled on my front, wondering if I'd gone blind. My head was throbbing, my back sore, and I could taste blood. Noticing a familiar, unwelcome smell, I groaned.

'Welcome back,' said a cold voice.

'Felix?'

His laugh made me shiver.

'Where are you?'

'Over here.'

Though I couldn't see him, as I pushed myself into a sitting position, it sounded like he was in front of me. I didn't feel too scared, being oddly reassured that I wasn't alone, not really believing he'd do anything too serious. I hoped Mrs G had already taken care of his henchmen.

'I think something hit me,' I said.

'Like this?' he said, from behind, as something thumped into my back, knocking me face first into the pine needles. I sat up rubbing my neck.

'Pain in the neck?' said Felix, which sounded more like an accusation than a question.

'That hurt.'

'It was meant to.'

'Why did you hit me?'

'Why do you think *I* did it?' His voice now came from my left side.

'Because there's only you here with me.'

'Are you sure?' he asked, now on my right.

'Where are you?'

'Here.'

A blow to my chest sending me crashing onto my back, I

gasped with the shock and moaned.

'Shut your mouth! You're pathetic, and the fun's hardly started.'

As I rolled over and got to my knees, a stunning blow to the back of my neck sent me sprawling, a galaxy of spinning stars filling my head. Hot blood pumped from my nose, pooling in my mouth, and my only consolation was that I couldn't see it, as I attempted to staunch the flow.

I couldn't even try to fight if I couldn't see him. Screaming for help was an option but, before I could give it a go, a clout to my ear knocked me against the rough bark of a tree, leaving me dazed. By then I was filled with cold, hard fear.

'I thought I told you to shut your mouth? Did I tell you to shut your mouth?'

'Yes,' I said, spitting blood.

'So shut it before you make me angry.'

Something growled behind me. My heart was thumping, my breathing was too rapid, I felt sick and everything seemed distant. A cuff across the back of my head made pretty lights dance to the throbbing pulse of pain and all I could do was curl up into a ball like a hedgehog, wishing I had a hedgehog's sharp spines.

As I lay there stunned, my mind fogged with fear, a memory resurfaced of a holiday long ago. I was barefoot, playing in a sunlit garden, blotched with the long, dark shadows of enormous trees, a big, old house in front of me, with a patio on which my father, sitting on a stripy deckchair, was reading a newspaper. I must have been about six or seven, because my sister was there in her pushchair. A shiny blue and red ball lay in the long grass at the edge of the lawn and, as I ran to kick it, my sister's unexpected scream distracting me, I missed and felt a sudden pain. I fell down crying, blood oozing from several little holes in my foot, my father hurrying to see what was wrong. He picked me up, laughing, and pointed out the small, spiny creature curled up next to my ball.

'You know something, Andy?' Felix hissed, 'I don't like you.'

I'd already guessed as much.

'You won't do as you're told. I say, leave Violet alone and what do you do? You get her into a car crash, wait until she's recovered and try it on again. I might have respected you a little if you'd had the balls to stand up to me, or even if you'd visited her in hospital, but you haven't.'

'I would have visited if I could.'

'Shut up. What's more, you hang around with that freak Hobbes, which is not right. You should not associate with his sort. Even worse, you keep company with the vermin from the farmhouse down there and it makes me sick to the stomach to think someone like you has been with my sister, has touched her and shaken my hand.'

'I haven't "been with" her, whatever that means. I just want to be friends,' I said, sitting up, trying to get to my feet against the tree. Despite my fear, my anger was rising, until a thump to my solar plexus folded me up like a penknife.

'Did I give you permission to speak? No, I don't believe I did.

'What sort of person are you? Do you actually enjoy mixing with vermin? It's disgusting and shows you're no better than they are. If anything, you're worse, because that mongrel scum has no choice; they were born like it and they'll die like it, and the sooner the better.'

Spitting out another mouthful of blood, I tried to catch my breath, hoping my head would clear, groping for a stick, or anything to try defending myself, though, unless I could see, I doubted it would be of any use. His ranting, seeming entirely unhinged to me, was even more terrifying than the actual violence.

Although I thought I couldn't see a thing, I noticed there were two small, greenish glints, apparently hovering close together in mid-air just about where I guessed Felix might be. I stared at them, fascinated, while he continued his insane, though precise and articulate, diatribe against Bashem, Bullimore and Hobbes, until, when they blinked, I realised they were eyes, though human eyes wouldn't glint in the dark like that. Knowing Felix had a panther with him reduced me to a quivering jelly of a man, for even a beating had to be better than being mauled. I concentrated on being as still as I could, on keeping quiet and on controlling my breathing.

Felix stopped talking as distant shouts were followed by cheers. I guessed he was listening.

I tried to see things from his point of view: his not liking me was, perhaps, understandable, his protectiveness towards Violet was admirable, in a way, and I could see why anyone might regard Hobbes as a freak, since he often appeared pretty freakish to me. However, I could see no reason for hating the Bashems so much for, although they were undoubtedly werewolves, the mere fact making me nervous, despite all Hobbes's assurances, they'd done nothing, so far as I knew, to deserve the loathing Felix had heaped on them. Yet, since he was no longer spouting his nonsense, I hoped he might have calmed down, and risked opening my mouth.

'Why do you hate the Bashem family so much?' I asked, my voice sounding thin and shrill.

'Because,' he said, apparently in the mood to talk, 'those half-breed werewolves are nothing more than vermin that pollute the good earth.'

'But they don't … umm … cause any harm, do they?'

'They exist. What more harm can they do? Werewolves are an abomination and their mongrel spawn are even worse. It was one of them that frightened Violet and caused the crash. She might have been killed. Doesn't that mean anything to you?'

'Yes … but she didn't have to drive like that.'

'She had to get away from the filth. She was disgusted and knew you'd be no defence. You're not on their side, are you?'

'No … of course not. I didn't even know they were werewolves until Mr Bullimore told me tonight.'

'Yet you still stayed with him? Did it not disgust you?'

'I wasn't … umm … disgusted – not really. I don't know much

307

about them but Hobbes says werewolves are shy and pretty harmless.'

'And you always believe what that hulking freak says?'

'Well, not necessarily,' I answered truthfully, still finding the whole werewolf concept deeply and fundamentally alarming. Yet it was the way Felix talked about Hobbes that disturbed me most. I wasn't sure why at first, since I'd thought much the same often enough, though not in the same words. Anyone might regard him as a freak – any police inspector who wasn't human was certainly abnormal. At length, I realised: most people just accepted him at face value, as a police inspector. He might make them uncomfortable or scare them, but hardly anyone recognised he wasn't human, at least not until they knew him well, and few knew him as well as I did.

I risked another question. 'Umm … why do you think Hobbes is a freak?'

'Because he is.' Felix laughed, though without any humour. 'He's degenerate, he stinks like a bear, he sniffs like a dog and he looks more than half like an ape. I don't know what he is but he's not human, though he seems to have you fooled.'

'Oh, no.' I shook my head. 'I worked that out long ago.'

'Well, then, since you're so clever, perhaps you'd explain what he is?'

'Umm … I don't really know. I just know he's … umm … unhuman.'

'And yet, you continue to share a house with him and that crazy old woman. How do you stand it? It makes me ill to think of it.' The noise he made, indicative of disgust, almost sounded like a growl.

'I've got used to it. He's not so bad when you get to know him … umm … most of the time he isn't. Anyway, he's nowhere near as strange as some of the other people round here.'

'There's truth in that,' said Felix. 'When I came to this backwater it was purely for business reasons; there was money to be made in developing this place. Parts of the town look like they haven't changed for centuries. It needs modernising and I'm the one going to do it.'

'By fair means or foul?'

That produced a genuine laugh. 'You're right there, Andy. I might occasionally break the rules, or someone's legs, but you've got to be ruthless to get on in my profession. I can't afford to let niceties get in the way of progress.'

'You got an elephant to demolish the Greasy Pole.'

Another laugh. 'Sometimes a flamboyant gesture pays dividends. Eric and I have since come to an arrangement that is mutually beneficial. I get his filthy café, for which I should get a medal, and he gets to keep his looks, such as they are.'

'And what about Featherlight?'

'That fat, filthy bar keeper,' said Felix, allowing a tone of grudging respect into his voice, 'is proving more difficult. He's a stubborn man and as tough as his steaks, though he's got no brains; that runt who works for him does the thinking.'

'Billy?'

'Yes, but that drunken dwarf won't be a problem much longer.'

'Why? What are you going to do to him?'

'Me? I'm not going to do anything but the poor little chap really should check his brakes more often.'

'That's despicable.'

'Thank you.'

A thought occurred. 'Umm … was it you killed Henry Bishop? And why?'

'I'm afraid the dear departed Henry got greedy and thought it might be a good idea to blackmail me, since I'd employed his skills on a couple of little schemes. He had to go.'

'So you set a panther on him?'

'If you like. I regret the incident spoiled Violet's evening. It was sheer bad luck you picked that place.'

'It was Hobbes's idea. He told me it was a good restaurant.'

'Hobbes, eh? He's behind all the problems round here.'

I shook my head. 'No, that's not true. Whatever you think of him, he's the one doing most to keep the peace. If it wasn't for him there'd be a lot more trouble. In fact I know some people choose to live here precisely because they've heard he's fair and won't let anything happen to them because of what they are.'

'That's just my point. Don't you see? If not for him, the weirdoes wouldn't keep coming here and, if any did, the decent folk could kick them out and good riddance. But Hobbes's days are numbered, like all the other freaks. After I've rid the area of the filthy werewolves, I'm going to drive all the weirdoes and deviants out, and make it a place fit for decent people.'

His voice, determined and utterly terrifying, boomed through the woods as if he were addressing a rally of his supporters. Furthermore, the pale eyes kept staring at me, adding an even darker dimension to my fear, though I knew one thing at least was good: so long as he was talking, he wasn't hitting me or setting his panther on me. It appeared that he appreciated a captive audience, and I suddenly realised his words might be evidence, especially should a few intelligent questions prompt him to reveal more than he should.

'What d'you mean drive them out?' I asked.

'I intend to clean out the filth by whatever means necessary and if that means by force and fire, so be it.'

'And if they still won't go?'

'They'll go. I have my removal men.'

'Like Mike Rook?'

'Mike?' He laughed. 'Mike was merely my driver, though he had other uses until he started going soft, reckoning my plan to burn out Binks was a step too far.'

'Is that why you killed him?'

'I had him killed when he threatened to inform Hobbes.'

'He sounds like one of the decent folk you were making Sorenchester fit for,' I said, gulping, in case I was provoking him.

'Decent? He was only going to tell Hobbes if I didn't buy him off. He was nothing but a lousy blackmailer, like Henry Bishop.'

He chuckled. 'Still, Mike did have an inventive mind, and his elephant scheme was a classic. Unfortunately, when he was no longer an asset, he had to go.'

'How did you get at him in the hospital?'

'Through a window. It wasn't difficult. Right, I've answered some of your questions and now it's your turn to answer some of mine. What do you know about the tunnels?'

'How do you know about them?'

'That drunken runt, Billy, told me after I bought him a lot of drinks, and Hobbes's sudden disappearances and unexpected re-appearances proved he hadn't been lying, though he knew little more than that they existed and ran as far as Blackdog Street. I expect one connects to Hobbes's wine cellar. Am I right?'

'Why do you want to know?'

'I'm just curious, like you are, Andy. I expect you'd like to know why I've been telling you all about my business affairs?'

'No, not really.'

'You really are stupid aren't you?'

'Umm …'

'Just accept it, man. Has it not occurred to you that everything I've told you could get me into serious trouble? If you told anyone that is.'

Though he still sounded calm, his voice had grown cold again. I shivered.

'But I won't tell anyone.'

'Promise?'

'Umm … I promise.'

'Do you know, I think I believe you. In fact, I know you won't tell anyone.'

His voice had grown louder, or was he closer? The eyes had disappeared.

'Can you guess why?'

The shock of his voice just next to my ear, his hot breath on my neck was too much. Giving in to terror, lurching to my feet, I ran.

'Come back,' said Felix. 'It'll be easier on you.'

Putting my head down, I fled, longing for light, unseen branches whipping my face, roots and logs trying to trip me, stumbling forward, breathing through my mouth. After a while, the fear he'd set the panther on me forced me to slow down and listen. My head was throbbing and I could feel blood congealing over my face and hands.

'You didn't answer my question.' His voice was in front of me. 'Go on, guess why I believe you.'

Green eyes and white teeth glinted where a hint of moonlight seeped through the heavy canopy. Putting my hands in my pocket, so he wouldn't see how much they were shaking, trying to be cool, unprovocative, I found my penny, hoping it was a lucky one.

'Alright, I'll tell you anyway. I trust you not to tell anyone because I'm going to kill you.'

The eyes approaching, I hurled the coin but I guess my aim was off, because it was Felix who cried out. Turning away, I ran, blindly, desperately.

It might have been a great escape had I not tripped and rolled into a hollow.

'You shouldn't have done that,' said Felix. 'You've made me angry. I was intending to make it quick and painless – well, quick anyway, but now you're going to die like Henry did.'

'Please, no!'

A shadow, even darker than night-time, was approaching and I feared I was going to die. Curling into a ball, I lay still, knowing I was trapped, that I was going to experience pain. The panther growled and I felt a thud as it landed at my side. Rank breath blew in my face, sharp claws raked my side. I cried for help, though my nose being stuffed with clotting blood, my scream sounded more like a duck call.

There was a sudden slight breeze, as if something had leapt over me, an angry hiss, as though from an infuriated cat, and I passed out.

Soft hands were stroking my forehead as I came to. 'I'm so sorry,' said a gentle voice.

'Violet?'

'Yes, you're going to be alright.'

'What happened?'

'You're safe, but I've got to go.'

'Don't leave me, please.'

'I must. They're coming to help you. Goodbye.'

As she moved away, I heard voices. Torch beams flashed between the trees.

'I'm over here,' I croaked.

'Are you alright, dear?' Light was around me and Mrs Goodfellow was peering into my face.

I blinked. 'Not really.'

'You are a mess, dear. We'd best get you back to the farm and clean you up. Can you walk?'

'I don't think so.'

Very soon I was being carried on a stretcher. The woods were left behind. In front was the comforting light of the farmhouse.

21

I didn't half feel ill when my eyes opened.

'He's in shock,' said a woman with a penetrating, brisk, no-nonsense voice that hurt my head.

Although I thought I recognised it, I struggled to work out why the ceiling looked familiar and why something was pressing on my mouth and nose.

'I thought so,' said Mrs Goodfellow.

'Indeed. He's displaying many of the classic symptoms: a rapid, weak pulse, shallow breathing, low blood pressure, clammy skin, blue lips ...'

Raising myself on one arm to see what was happening, realising I was wearing a face mask with a plastic tube, I tore it off. 'Oh. Hello, doctor,' I said, seeing Dr Procter smiling down at me. Then, having vomited into a bucket that appeared in the right place, I slumped back onto my bed.

'Nausea is, of course, another classic symptom,' said the doctor, 'but the oxygen has taken care of the cyanosis and his lips are back to normal – the colour I mean. The swelling will go down, in time. He's evidently had a traumatic experience, but I gather he's quite used to them and, fortunately, he appears to have suffered no major physical injuries. His symptoms are already showing distinct signs of improvement and he should recover quickly. Nevertheless, he has taken quite a beating and it seems a cat's had a go at him again. I wonder what he does to annoy them. I'll write him a prescription for antibiotics; we wouldn't want him to catch whatever he had last time.'

'Is there anything else?'

'Not really. Keep him warm and quiet and give him plenty of fluids. You may notice some strange moods and behaviour as the psychological effects work themselves out.'

Mrs Goodfellow laughed. 'Strange moods and behaviour? How will I know?'

If I'd had the energy, I would have snorted with disdain, but, the blankets being warm, my bed feeling soft, I let myself drift back to sleep. Mrs Goodfellow woke me a couple of times to pour liquids into me or to thrust antibiotics down my throat. Though I'm sure they did me good, what roused me in the end was the pungent aroma of curry.

I got up, limping to the bathroom for a wash, shocked at the unfamiliar face looking back at me from the mirror, for, where there would normally have been pale, smooth, pinkish skin, there were lumps and purple marks, red eyes and a bottom lip, swollen as if someone had inserted half a saucer into it. Yet, my body showed no evidence of wounds or bruises at all, having been covered in bandages, like a mummy. A tentative poke suggested tentative pokes should be avoided.

After dressing, a slow, painful process, I hobbled downstairs towards the kitchen. When Dregs bounded towards me, I cringed, expecting the worst, but, seeming to understand my delicate state, he contented himself with licking my hand.

Mrs G, stirring a vast black cauldron, from where the delicious, enticing, smells were emerging, looked up from the stove. 'Hello, dear, I wondered if this might tempt you. I take it you're feeling better?'

'It did and I am, though I'm starving. Umm … when's supper ready?'

'At half-past six, as usual.'

'When's that?'

'In about twenty minutes, dear.'

'So long?'

'I'm afraid so. The old fellow will be back then.'

'Why isn't he at the festival? And ... umm ... shouldn't you be there, too?'

'It's been called off.'

'I'm not surprised,' I said. 'It was getting rather out of hand, though your boys did quite well ... in the circumstances.'

'Thank you, dear. That's kind.'

I thought I ought to give her some support for, after all, it hadn't been her fault there'd been so much trouble and, in the circumstances, she really hadn't done badly. 'I saw you wallop the guy with the club. That was great.'

'No, it was regrettable, but I had to take him down when he wouldn't listen to reason and threatened to hurt people. The old fellow reckons he was acting under orders.'

'That's no excuse.'

'No, dear, though it is a reason. By the end of the night, we'd detained thirty young men, who were all acting under orders. Though most of them tried to put up a fight, a few ran and are being picked up by the police.' She looked glum for a moment, until a gummy smile broke through. 'On the bright side, I obtained six new teeth for my collection. Unfortunately, one was gold and another had a diamond in it, quite ruining it.'

'That is sad.' I grinned, my face hurting and giving rise to a worrying thought. 'Umm ... I'm not sure I'll be able to eat properly. Just talking hurts enough and I'll never be able to chew.'

'Don't worry, dear, this is mulligatawny soup, so I'm sure you'll be able to manage.'

She wouldn't say any more about the events of the previous night, except that I should ask Hobbes. I tried to be cool and managed to sit quietly, with the exception of my stomach, which grumbled egregiously until he returned and took his place at the table. He looked tired and morose and, besides saying grace, didn't speak until we'd finished. I didn't mind, despite my curiosity, for I was fully engaged in the process of eating the thick, rich soup and, though my swollen mouth barely opened wide enough to let the spoon in, everything was chopped so finely

I had no other problems eating.

Afterwards, while the old girl made tea and washed up, Hobbes and I sat on the sofa. He began twitching and growling, the overture to another bone-crunching episode I feared, until, after a short while, he turned to face me.

'I'm happy to see you up and recovering,' he said, 'and you'll be glad to hear I found the Bashem family safe and sound. They'd hidden in the crowd, which was sensible, and had taken Dregs, which was also sensible. They showed far more intelligence than you; you really shouldn't have gone out. I'd hoped you and Mr Bullimore had the brains to stay put.'

'Sorry, it was my fault; I thought we might be able to help find them. Is Mr Bullimore alright?' I was ashamed I'd never given him, or his family, a thought until then.

'Though he was mauled quite badly, he's a tough old dog and is getting better. He thought the panther was going to kill him, but, for some reason, it simply stopped the attack and ran off.'

'That's odd,' I said, 'because Felix set a panther on me and I think another one turned up and drove it away, which saved me.'

'That sounds like unusual behaviour for a panther,' said Hobbes, looking at me as if expecting more.

'Umm … I expect it was unusual. But …'

'But what?'

'But I think … umm … Violet brought the second one. I'm not sure quite what happened but, just after the first one ran off, she talked to me and stroked my head.'

'So, she was there, too? That is very interesting.'

'Yes and she said she was sorry, though I'm not quite sure why.'

Hobbes grinned. 'I suspect she has rather a lot to be sorry about, but that can wait till later. I think you may just have provided me with a vital clue.'

'Have I? That's great … umm … talking of clues, Felix told me quite a lot during the attack. I thought it might be evidence.'

'Tell me,' said Hobbes.

I told him everything Felix had said, or, at least, everything I could remember.

When I'd finished, Hobbes shook his head. 'I'll get Billy to check his brakes, but why do villains need to gloat and boast about their cleverness and ruthlessness when he could just have killed you and slipped away? That's what I'd do if I ever became villainous.'

I flinched at his casual attitude.

'Your evidence would be useful, should the case ever go to court, but, unfortunately, I doubt it will: not the real one. The lass and her boys have detained most of Mr King's henchmen, who are currently stewing in the nick, awaiting questioning. They will no doubt be prosecuted, yet, they weren't behind the events. Mr King was and he's vanished.'

I nodded, coming up with a phrase I'd once used in an article for the *Bugle*. 'You could say his men were just the cat's paws.'

I cringed, as memory pointed out that my article had not been a great success. It started with a lunchtime lager in the Feathers where, despite furious bellows from Featherlight, who was in dispute with some unfortunate customer, I'd overheard talk from a gang of shoplifters who'd just arrived in town. Having managed to identify the brains of the outfit, and where they were going to strike next, I rushed back to the office and typed up a couple of hundred words. I'd been extremely proud of the article and even Editorsaurus Rex had seemed pleased, until it turned out that my shoplifters had really been shop-fitters. Following a painful and unnecessarily prolonged interview with the Editorsaurus, I was rarely assigned to report anything other than pet shows and fetes.

Still, Hobbes chuckled. 'Cat's paws! That's a good one.'

'I still don't understand what's going on,' I said, feeling even thicker than usual.

'But I'm beginning to.' He smiled. 'Yet, I fear I've been slow; I had all the evidence and still couldn't fit it together, though, in fairness, it is an unusual case.'

I waited, puzzled, as he sat, eyes closed, as if in a deep trance.

'I couldn't understand,' he continued, 'why, though I could track the cats, their spore would suddenly vanish. I have an idea now.

'Are you absolutely certain both Mr King and Miss King spoke to you last night?'

'Yes.'

'Excellent. You see, I was stumped because having examined the place we found you, I found no trace of Mr King.'

'But he was there, honest.'

'I believe you. I did, however, find signs of two big cats and some tufts of fur that might suggest a fight, which agrees with your information. What I found really baffling was coming across clear signs a human had been there, though only around where you were lying. From the size of the footprints, I was almost sure it had been a lady, and I'm now confident it was Miss King. Strangely, she had bare feet and left no apparent trail either approaching or leaving.'

Having great faith in Hobbes's tracking skills, I was puzzled by such a failure. 'She must have done. She couldn't just appear out of thin air, unless she swung through the trees like Tarzan.'

'I did, in fact, check the trees and found nothing to suggest she'd been climbing. However, I think you may have provided the key to explain it all.'

'Go on,' I urged, unable to think of anything I'd said that was important.

'Right. Consider this. Both Mr King and his sister spoke to you, yet he, apparently, left no marks at all, while she only left them near where you'd fallen.'

'I still don't understand.'

Hobbes grinned. 'Yet, there were two distinct sets of big cat prints. Both had approached you and gone away.'

'Weird.'

'Precisely what I thought, so I had a word with Mr Catt at the Wildlife Park this morning. I showed him the fur I'd picked up and some casts I'd made of the paw prints and he was adamant they weren't from a panther, or any cat he's aware of.'

'So, what are you getting at?' I asked, starting to get an inkling, though my brain was having difficulties.

'There is an explanation that fits the evidence.'

At the moment an unearthly cackle announced that Mrs Goodfellow had brought in the tea and, had I not been so sore and stiff, I'd have jumped into orbit, as usual. Setting down the tray, she filled two mugs. Hobbes chucked in a handful of sugar, stirred his mug, sucked his finger and took a great swig. He sighed, the sigh of a contented police officer.

'Thanks, lass,' he said.

She nudged me and grinned. 'Well done – you've cheered him up again.'

'I'm not sure how,' I said, 'but I think I'm going to find out.'

As she headed back towards the kitchen, I took a sip of tea, squealing as it parboiled my split lip. Hobbes poured himself a second mug, giving me a few seconds to think. It didn't help.

'So,' he said, 'have you got it yet?'

'Umm … I'm not sure. You say Felix wasn't there but a panther, no … umm … some mysterious big cat was? So was it a talking cat?'

'You might say that.'

'Really?' I let the idea settle in my brain. 'And you reckon Violet also got there without leaving a trace, though she was there, and there were signs of two cats.'

'That's right. Do you get it yet?'

'No … not unless Violet and Felix could turn into cats!' I laughed.

Hobbes wasn't laughing.

'Come off it,' I said. 'It's bad enough the Bashems turning out to be werewolves, but now you're saying my girlfriend is a cat?' I shook my head. 'It's ridiculous.'

'Is it?'

'Of course. Look, if she was a cat, I'd know and would have taken cat food on the picnic and, what's more,' I felt myself blush,

'I have ... umm ... kissed her, and, I can tell you, she's a real woman.'

'What I mean,' said Hobbes, 'is that she and her brother are werecats.'

'You really mean she can change into a cat?' I asked, trying to maintain a front of scepticism, even though what he was suggesting made sense, in a thoroughly nonsensical way. 'You're saying she can somehow – what's the word? – wolfifest into a cat?'

'The word we use with werecats is transmogrify,' he said, 'though, apart from that, you've got it. Of course, they can revert to human form whenever it suits them.'

By then, I was too full of conflicting thoughts and swirling emotions to cope. Shaking my head, staggering upstairs, I collapsed onto my bed and curled up into the foetal position, my mind squirming with confusion, horror and doubt. After about ten minutes, feeling no better but still with an urge to know, I returned to the sitting room, where Hobbes had taken advantage of my absence to squeeze a third mug of tea from the pot. Dregs was dozing at his feet.

'You'd better tell me everything,' I said. 'Just take it that I believe you.' Though I wasn't sure I did, nothing else made sense.

'I will,' said Hobbes, finishing his tea and taking a deep breath. 'To start with, the big cat sightings only started after Mr King moved into the area, which, I admit, is purely circumstantial evidence. Then, as you know, they vanished whenever I tracked them and, since I often came across tyre tracks close to where I'd lost the trail, I assumed someone was transporting them. I now think it likely they drove themselves. Another thing which may be significant is that Mr King wears an overpowering aftershave or cologne, which I suspect he uses to mask any animal odours. Otherwise, I'm certain I'd have noticed something.'

'It put you off the scent?'

'Or, the scent put me off. And Miss King uses perfume, does she not?'

'Yes, though that's not unusual, is it?'

'No, not in itself, but she does use rather a lot. Furthermore, we only became aware of two big cats after she joined him here. There is one point, though: has she ever met the dog?'

Dregs, opening an eye, wagged his tail.

I thought for a moment. 'No, never. Except … umm … nearly that time at the Wildlife Park when something frightened him when he went inside …' I ground to a halt, seeing what Hobbes was getting at.

'Dogs have excellent noses and aren't easily confused by artificial perfumes. I suspect her animal scent scared him. Of course, my nose wasn't all it should be that day, with all that camel hair. You know something? I've a feeling Mr King might have got away with his intimidation of Eric and Featherlight and, I suspect, others who've sold property to him recently, had he not become aware of the Bashems. His schemes were overturned by his hatred of werewolves.'

'But why does he hate them? Aren't werecats and werewolves equally cursed?'

'It only becomes a curse if they let it become one. The Bashems are perfectly happy with their heritage. As for Mr King's hatred, I can only speculate that it started out as the usual cat and dog thing, but it seems to have grown out of all proportion. I fear he may be somewhat unbalanced.'

'He's stark raving mad,' I said, remembering his tirade in the woods and shivering, 'but what about Violet? She was nice to me.'

'I'm sorry, but I fear she used you to get information about me. I was obviously a threat, being what I am.'

'What are you?' I asked, hoping for insight.

'A police officer.'

'Of course. But, Felix sounded like he hated you personally.'

'He wouldn't be the first.'

Though it was hard to accept, I was starting to believe him. Once upon a time I wouldn't have, but, since being with Hobbes, I'd come to realise the world had more in it than I ever could have imagined.

When we'd finished talking, Hobbes took Dregs out, leaving me to struggle with my confused feelings for Violet. I'd believed she was special, though, in all honesty, I hadn't had much to compare with her. Without doubt, she'd brought glamour and yearning into my life and there'd been days when I'd barely been able to think of anything except her and, furthermore, there'd been whole hours when I'd dared to hope she was mine. Now it all boiled down to one fact, and there was no escaping it: she was a cat. I'd actually fancied a cat.

The realisation, especially since it was more than mere fancy, for even when she'd greeted me so coldly at the festival, I'd still warmed to her, left me utterly bewildered and bereft. I think I had really loved her and part of me still did, while another part couldn't help recoiling at the thought of what she was. Even so, such disasters just seemed to happen to me, my relations with women seemingly cursed. Then, at the back of everything, I was struggling to come to terms with one really odd fact, a fact that didn't make sense: when Felix had seemed certain to kill me, she'd come to my rescue, as if she'd really cared for me, and her last words in the woods still haunted me. I sat for a long time, brooding.

As the evening darkened, Mrs Goodfellow brought a cup of cocoa. Thanking her, I took it to bed and, after forcing my bruised body into a pair of clean, stripy pyjamas, I sat by the window, sipping my drink, still lost in a sea of baffling thoughts. As the lingering fronds of the day slipped away, I stared down into Blackdog Street, glinting silver beneath the glare of electric lights, seeing groups of people wandering past, no doubt on their way between hostelries. One guy, swaying down the centre of the street, collapsed with his head on the kerb, his legs stretched into the road, fortunate that no cars came by. Eventually, his mates lugged him up and dragged him away amidst ribald comments. The town settled into its usual background noise. Thuds nearby suggested someone was working hard at their DIY. In the distance, a dog barked and a plane flew high overhead, flashing red and green lights in the clear sky.

I was just about to turn in when, fancying I'd glimpsed a greenish flash from the roof opposite, I stared into the night, seeing nothing. Dismissing it, I got into bed. After only a few seconds, jumping back out, I shut the window and drew the curtains. Though it was silly, the flash had reminded me of the glowing eyes of the previous night and, stupidly, I blushed; if it had been Violet's flashing eyes out there, she might have seen me undressing. Not that I really believed anything, least of all her, was out there; it had certainly been a trick of the light, or of my imagination. Though I lay down and tried not to think, it didn't work as I needed time for my twisted thoughts to untangle.

The church clock struck eleven as someone sang an enthusiastic, if inaccurate, version of *The Green, Green Grass of Home*. Sometime later, the silence in the street outside suggesting the revellers and DIYers had called it a day, although I could have sworn I'd not slept, I jerked into full wakefulness and sat up.

My skin was crawling with goose pimples. I couldn't see anything, other than faint shadows cast by whatever light made it through the curtain, and couldn't hear anything beyond the hiss of my breathing and the tattoo drummed out by my heart. I tried holding my breath, listening, hoping not to hear whatever had alarmed me. My hope was fulfilled, which frightened me almost as much as if I had heard something.

The thing was, something felt wrong and, though I tried reasoning with myself, arguing against the likelihood of anything being in my room that shouldn't, I was scared, really scared. Grabbing the sheets, I pulled them tight around me, though why I thought that would help was beyond me. Then, at last, on the edge of hearing, yet distinct, I heard a faint sound, a little like Velcro being pulled apart. It came again ... and again. It was close, very close.

'Hello?' I said with quavering voice that tended to falsetto. 'Is somebody there?'

'Yes,' purred a soft voice by my head.

'Violet?' I gasped, knowing instantly what had been wrong: I could smell her perfume. It was too dark to see her. 'What are you doing here?'

'I came to make sure you're alright.'

'I'm OK. That is, I'm not too bad ... nothing's actually broken ... I'm a bit sore though. And you?'

'I'm fine. I'm glad you're alright.'

'I'll turn the light on,' I said, moving as if to get out of bed.

She pushed me back.

'That would not be a very good idea. It will be best if you stay where you are.'

'Why?'

'Trust me.'

'Alright,' I said and almost did, though a strange confusion of terror and elation was swirling through me. 'It's ... umm ... nice to see you again. I mean to say, I'm glad you're here. I've missed you.'

'I've missed you, too. I hoped you'd call after the picnic. Why didn't you?'

'I did try when I was better.'

'You were ill? What was the matter?'

'I got a bad fever, after I'd walked home in the rain.'

'Sorry about that ... I had to get away from the arboretum ... Something nasty was in the woods.'

'Ah, yes,' I said, 'the werewolf.'

There was a sharp intake of breath. 'You know about them?'

'Only what I've picked up recently. They still scare me.'

'Poor Andy, I really wish you hadn't got involved in all of this.'

'In all of what?'

'Our war against those vile, filthy abominations.'

'Well ... they're a bit dirty, maybe, but Hobbes reckons they're alright.'

'He would do, but he's quite wrong. Felix thought you were

one of them.'

'Me? A werewolf? That's crazy.'

'Not a werewolf, but a collaborator, which is almost as bad.'

'You're talking like him.' I said, not liking it at all, for she didn't sound like my Violet. Though I'd loved hearing her voice, always sounding soft and sweet, even when she'd been frightened or angry, the new, fanatical harshness scared and repelled me even more than what she was saying. I hoped, she hadn't meant it.

She continued. 'Felix talks a lot of sense. No one wants those freaks polluting our world.'

'They don't do any harm.'

'That's not the point. They exist. Therefore, they must be annihilated.'

'Why? Hobbes reckons we can all live together.'

'You are starting to sound like a collaborator and I thought you were one of the good guys ... I liked you, despite what Felix said, but perhaps he was right, like he was with Arthur.'

'Who's Arthur?' I asked, suddenly, unaccountably jealous.

'Arthur Crud. He was my fiancé. Felix warned me about him.'

'Arthur Crud? The rapist?'

'That's him. He was like you, nice and harmless on the surface but a monster beneath.'

'He didn't ...' I felt sick.

'Not me. Some other poor girl who worked for us. He'd be banged up in prison right now if your friend Hobbes hadn't got him off.'

'Hobbes did that?' The idea was appalling.

'Yes. And yet you admire him. I don't understand you.'

I felt like I'd fallen into an ocean of confusion. That Hobbes had his bad points, I'd have been the first to admit, though I found it hard to believe he'd help a rapist escape justice. It wasn't what he did and, whereas I knew he had his own take on the law, in my experience, he'd always aimed for justice, even if it might have been a rough sort of justice.

'But I thought Hobbes had killed Arthur Crud,' I said.

'Killed him? Felix would have had him killed if Hobbes hadn't interfered.'

'What?'

'Hobbes got Arthur away when Felix sent round some of the boys to deal with him.'

'Oh. But I'm not like Arthur Crud.'

'No? I saw you throw yourself onto that poor girl.'

'I didn't. She threw herself onto me!'

Though she laughed, it was a cold laugh. 'Don't flatter yourself, you're not that good looking. Actually, you're not bad. What lets you down is being friends with Hobbes, who's responsible for all the nastiness in this godforsaken town. You really should get away from here, and get away quickly.'

'I'm not really his friend,' I said, regretting it immediately, feeling a real traitor. Yet, he wasn't exactly a friend, for friendship implies a sort of equality and I didn't believe I was his equal in anything. Even so, there was something between us and I did care for him and his good opinion. In fact, it occurred to me that I often felt almost like a son, who needed his father's approval. The idea shocked me, though the time was not right for thinking about it. 'I'm only here because I've got nowhere else.'

'I'm glad to hear that,' she said, her voice softening again. 'My advice is to get out of here, to get out of here tomorrow. Then you'll have a future to look forward to, a future untainted by association. But time's getting on and I must say goodbye now. It's been interesting knowing you.'

'Has it? Good. Umm … are you going somewhere?'

'We're leaving. We can't stay after what's happened, can we?'

'I suppose not, but why come to see me? Why not send a note? Surely, this is dangerous.'

'Yes, but I really wanted to see you again. I'd hoped, just for a few days, that you might be the special one because there is something in you … I don't know what. The thing is, in the beginning, Felix asked me to befriend you as a way to get at

327

Hobbes but I actually found that I liked you. You seemed different to other men and I hoped I might get you away from him and that I'd have you forever.'

Her voice was so gentle and sad I sat, entranced, quite forgiving her unforgivable behaviour.

'I'd hoped, too,' I said.

'Did you? It's such a shame. If those stinking werewolves hadn't turned up, it might have worked out. Given time, I would have convinced you to think and act right and saved you. I wish I still could. Maybe, Felix would have accepted you. Still, it can't be helped. Felix has done what had to be done and we've got to move on. Maybe, we'll be able to come back when the fuss dies down and people can see that we acted for the best.'

'You don't always have to do what he says.'

'My interests are his interests.'

'Are you sure?'

'He's my brother.'

'Did he tell you to attack Mr Bullimore?'

'He doesn't tell me what to do. That half-breed stinks of werewolf and had to be destroyed. I'm only sorry I failed.'

'Because you came to help me.'

'Yes.'

'Against Felix.'

'Yes.'

'You don't have to go with him. If you stay, I'm sure we can work something out. You're not like him.'

'I am very much like him. Sometimes we have to be ruthless, even if it hurts. We must always see the bigger picture. But you could come with me.'

'But what about Felix?' I asked, almost ready to risk his wrath, just to be with her. I was too late.

'Hobbes is coming,' she hissed. 'I must go. Goodbye, darling. I am truly sorry.'

Something soft and velvety brushed my cheek. There was a faint sensation of movement and a dark shadow before the curtains flapped and she was gone. Everything was quiet.

I sat, as if her leaving had turned me to stone, knowing I still loved her.

The front door opening, heavy feet pounded upstairs.

Hobbes burst into my room, turning on the light. 'Are you alright?'

'Yes,' I said and astonished myself by bursting into tears.

22

I would, no doubt, have found the next few minutes excruciatingly embarrassing, had I been capable of anything other than gut-wrenching grief. Though grown men weren't supposed to cry, I couldn't have cared less.

'Whatever is the matter?' asked Hobbes, raising his hand as if to console me, hesitating, and scratching his head.

I couldn't force out much intelligible in the gaps between the sobs. He stared and looked uncomfortable. Dregs hurtled upstairs, stopping just outside my room, and, picking up the mood, threw back his big black head and howled.

Mrs Goodfellow, shrouded in a voluminous white nightie, her thin grey hair coiled in rollers, arrived. 'What have you been doing to him?'

'Nothing,' said Hobbes. 'I sensed one of those big cats up here when I was coming up the street, so I thought I'd better make sure it hadn't eaten him.' He sniffed. 'It seems Miss King has been to see you.'

'She has,' I said, squeezing out words in the intervals between upheavals of my chest. 'She said she's got to go away from here.'

I don't think I'd ever felt such a cutting, debilitating sense of loss, at least not as an adult. Unable to help it, I cried, while Dregs bristled and howled.

After several seconds of mayhem, Hobbes roared, 'Be quiet!'

It shut us both up. Dregs, tail between his legs, mournful eyed, fled, while I sat up, blowing my nose on the tissue Mrs G had pulled from her pocket.

'Thank you,' said Hobbes, frowning. 'Now, maybe you'll explain what she was doing here?'

Though I did my best, it wasn't my most coherent narrative and yet he listened, appearing to understand my ramblings.

'Did she give any hint where they might be going?'

I shook my head. 'No. Not today ... She did once mention a house in France, but I don't know.'

'Oh well,' said Hobbes, looking eager, 'I'd better look for her. I'll see you in the morning.'

Loping towards the open window, he vaulted out.

'I'll make you a cup of cocoa,' said Mrs G.

Dregs crept into the room as she left, laying his head on my hand. I stroked his rough hair, which comforted us both so much that, when the old girl returned a few minutes later, carrying a steaming mug, I'd more or less recovered from the crying fit, while Dregs was back to his normal self, though avoiding places where I guessed Violet had been.

'Your eyes are red, dear,' said Mrs Goodfellow, handing me the mug. 'It's hard when a loved one goes away.'

'I'm not sure I ... umm ... loved her.'

'I think you did, dear.'

She was right, though my feelings were too tender to admit to. Only much later did it occur to me that she knew what she was talking about, her husband having left her to find himself in Tahiti. I supposed she'd probably found his desertion hurtful.

'Drink it all up,' she said. 'It'll help you sleep.'

While I sipped, she went to her room for a hammer and nails and made the window secure. Though I was convinced Violet and Felix had gone forever, that it was unnecessary, it did make me feel safer to know he couldn't get in, even though I'd still have welcomed her. If only, I thought, I could have got her away from his malign influence, I could have loved her. I smiled, feeling a little better, wondering if I might be able to tame the wildcat. Though it was a silly thought, it made me giggle. The cocoa had an aromatic aftertaste.

'You put something in this, didn't you?'

'A little something to make you feel better. You'll sleep well.'

'I am feeling a little woozy.'

Waking to sunlight pouring into my room, I enjoyed a few moments of comfortable, hazy dozing until memories of the night's events dropped back into my mind like junk mail, filling it with confusion and a sense of utter loss. I made a decision to lie where I was forever, to refuse all sustenance and comfort, to allow my life to quietly slip away. It seemed the best course or, at least, the one with the least pain. Of course, my death might result in a small amount of grief for a few: Hobbes and the old girl, Billy, maybe, my parents, possibly. As I imagined their tears at my funeral, I hoped that maybe, just maybe, a mysterious, elegant woman, dressed all in black, would linger and drop a single flower on my grave.

I indulged this fantasy until a whiff of frying bacon put things in perspective, persuading me not to pine away.

A quick inventory suggested my injuries were getting better: my lip, though still sore, had shrunk to almost normal proportions, my bruises weren't quite so tender, and the scratches I could see looked clean and well on their way to healing. Getting up, I washed, dressed and made my way down to breakfast, finding Mrs Goodfellow alone with a frying pan. Dregs had been shut out. Occasionally, his head would bounce up at the window.

'Good morning, dear.'

After the usual enquiries, she fed me bacon and eggs, delicious, despite the lingering numbing effect of antibiotics. I felt surprisingly well, and even better after topping up with toast and marmalade.

'Where's Hobbes?' I asked, pushing my plate aside.

'He's still out hunting. It's not like him to miss his breakfast.'

'That's true. Do you think he's caught them?'

'I'm sure he'd be back if he had.'

I half hoped he had caught them; that is, I hoped he'd caught

Felix and slung him in a cell, or a cage. At that moment, Hobbes, looking dishevelled and filthy, walked in, without saying a word, slouched across to the sink, picked up the washing up bowl and poured in a full box of Sugar Puffs and two pints of milk, before putting it on the table. Not bothering with a spoon, he simply shovelled the mess into his mouth with his hands, hands crisscrossed by deep cuts. Finishing the last Sugar Puff, lifting the bowl to his mouth, he poured the remaining milk down his throat.

'That's better,' he said. 'Is there any tea, lass?'

The old girl handed him a steaming mugful, which he drank in one gulp. She refilled it and he repeated the procedure.

'Thank you. It's been a long night.'

'Did you catch them?' I asked, desperate to know about Violet. 'No.'

'So, why are you all scratched?'

'Oh, that,' he said with a glance at his hands. 'There was a fire at the Feathers, which I suspect was arson carried out by Mr King or his sister, possibly in revenge, or to keep me occupied and out the way. Whatever the reason, I had to abandon the hunt, break in to the Feathers and extinguish the blaze, finding, unfortunately, that Featherlight had just installed razor wire around every possible entrance. I had to tear it up to get in and it was lucky for Billy that I did; he was fast asleep behind the bar and drunk.'

'He must have been relieved when you turned up,' I said, memories of my terror and despair, when I'd burned down my flat and been pulled out by Hobbes, returning.

'He will be, when he sobers up.'

'Did you put the fire out?'

'Yes, though I had to shake up a couple of beer kegs and punch holes in them, since all the fire-extinguishers were empty.'

'Featherlight should be prosecuted for that,' I said, virtuously.

'No one was hurt.'

'Umm … apart from you, no one was hurt, and Billy could

have been killed.'

'Yet, I'm fine and so is Billy, so why add to Featherlight's problems?'

'Fair enough. Umm … is he still banged up?'

'No, the murder charge was dropped, due, in no small part, to your evidence, and he's been released, which is just as well as we needed all the cells for Mr King's boys. Most of them, I'm glad to say, are inclined to talk, and their boss will be in a heap of trouble if we catch him. So, I'm afraid, will Miss King.'

'She only did it because he made her.'

Hobbes shook his head. 'Sorry, Andy, that might have been true once, but she had no cause to attack Mr Bullimore.'

'But she stopped attacking him to save me. That's got to be worth something.'

'I'm glad she did and, though there's obviously a better side to her, she murdered Henry Bishop.'

'No,' I said angered at the accusation, 'that's ridiculous. I was with her. She didn't do it.'

'I believe she killed Henry when he went into the restaurant.'

'But surely it was Felix who attacked him. She was having a meal with me.'

'True, but dead men don't open doors. Henry was still alive, badly wounded admittedly, but alive when he got through the door. Who was the first to react?'

'Violet: and she tried to save him.'

'That's what it must have looked like. You said the first thing she did was check his pulse?'

'Yeah.'

'That, I fear, was her cover for tearing his carotid artery, thus killing him instantly.'

Putting my head in my hands, I tried to think back. Henry had certainly been alive when he'd fallen at my feet, and Violet knelt beside him. I remembered her hand, such a pretty little hand, reaching out to his neck, my feeling of nausea as he haemorrhaged over that same hand. Could it have been as

Hobbes was suggesting? I had to admit it; it could.

'If she did do it, she was trying to protect Felix,' I said, as if that excused her.

'I'm sure she was, though I have little doubt she administered the coup de grace after Mr King did the initial damage. Henry's sudden demise struck me as odd at the time, but I was led astray, taking her at face value.'

Mrs G, chuckling, poked him in the ribs with a bony finger. 'You always do where young ladies are concerned.'

Hobbes smiled and returned to his serious look. 'I'm also convinced Miss King murdered Mike Rook. I picked up a trace of her perfume in the room, though, unfortunately, since it was very faint and masked by all the hospital smells, I didn't recognise it until much later. Mr King was undoubtedly responsible for the initial attack, trying to ensure Mr Rook wouldn't speak to me. Since Mr Rook was a tough lad and showing signs of recovery, he arranged for his sister to finish the job.'

'But,' I said, unwilling to give her up without a struggle, 'she can't be a killer, she's too timid and gentle. What about when the werewolf frightened her at the arboretum? If she was like you say, wouldn't she have attacked it?'

'I suspect,' said Hobbes, 'it wasn't Les Bashem who frightened her. Even in werewolf form he offered no threat. He was merely keeping an eye on you two.'

'What then?'

'She was more concerned about her own reaction. Her instinct would be to transmogrify and attack. Yet, since you were there, she couldn't, because you wouldn't have been favourably impressed had she changed into a cat before your eyes. She didn't want to lose you.'

'But why not? I'm nothing special.'

'True ... but you must have been something to her. I can't, for the life of me, understand why. Can you?' He turned to Mrs G.

'No. Not at all, though he does have excellent teeth.'

I was somewhat deflated by their opinions. Yet, when I looked up they were both grinning.

'Cheer up,' said Hobbes. 'You're not so bad, really.'

He raised a hand and, though I cringed, he patted me quite gently and I didn't cry out.

'Thanks,' I said.

'Don't mention it. I'm off for a nap before lunch.' Standing up, he belched. 'Pardon me; it's all the puff in the Sugar Puffs.'

'Before you go,' I said, as a thought occurred, 'what happened to Arthur Crud?'

'Mr Crud? The poor chap was maliciously accused. He's a gentle, bumbling, young fellow, not unlike you. Though the evidence I uncovered totally exonerated him and he was found not guilty, I had to hide him when someone, Mr King I now believe, whipped up bad feeling because he'd taken his sister to lunch on a couple of occasions. Mr Crud is living safely in Cornwall for the time being.'

'Did you know the girl who accused him worked for Felix?'

'I did, though she was only a temporary assistant at his London office. At the time it didn't seem important.'

'Did Felix force her to accuse Arthur?'

'Possibly, but it's more likely he paid her. Apparently, she went missing a couple of weeks afterwards. The London boys couldn't find her and I fear Mr King disposed of a potentially dangerous witness. Right, I'm off.' Yawning, he stamped upstairs.

There were a couple of hours before lunch, which the old girl was just starting. It was going to involve chicken pieces. She could do wonderful things with chicken pieces, though why she was attacking them with a mallet was beyond me.

'I think I'll take the dog out,' I shouted over the thumping.

'Righto, dear. It's a lovely day. Enjoy yourself, if you're well enough.'

'I'm OK, I'll not go far.'

When I left the house, it felt great to be in the sun again, despite a fierce wind whipping up stinging dust from the dry streets. I was glad to reach the soft greenery of Ride Park. As I let

Dregs off his lead, he ran free with a joyous bark and I wished I could enjoy such simple pleasures. Though I'd never expected my relationship with Violet to last, I had hoped.

Dregs, ran back with a long stick, dropped it at my feet and bounced and barked until I threw it, while I struggled to understand my feelings, for even after everything I'd learned about her, I was going to miss her. Though she might have been a murderer, she'd been good to me, and I still couldn't really believe that a woman so sweet and lovely had liked me, maybe even loved me. It was just my luck her turning out to be a cat.

Still, on reflection, I had always been a little afraid of her and, though it had never been the debilitating terror Felix had caused, it had been more even than my normal nervousness in the presence of an attractive woman. I couldn't help myself: I wanted her back, even if she was going to maul me.

As Dregs rushed back towards me, a harsh voice yelled.

'Oi, Caplet!'

Seemingly distracted, Dregs forgot to stop and his stick rapped my shins, making me hop and mutter. Someone laughed.

I turned to see Featherlight, standing on the edge of the woods, a can of beer in his hand.

'You make me laugh, you do.'

'Do I?'

'Yes. Now, when you see your mate Hobbes, tell him I said thanks for rescuing Billy and for putting the fire out and getting me out of the nick. And tell him he owes me for the two kegs of lager he used for putting out the fire.'

'What?' I said, outraged, 'that's not fair.'

'You tell him,' he said, displaying his horrible, big, yellow teeth in a grin, 'he'll understand.' He lumbered away, chuckling, a ring of pale flab flowing from beneath his vest, like a part-inflated rubber ring.

I guessed he'd been joking, though his usual attempts at humour involved pain and humiliation for whichever poor customer he'd picked on. I had, on several occasions, been that customer.

When Dregs was limp and panting, we returned home to find Hobbes was up, washed, groomed and back to normal. I passed on Featherlight's remarks.

He snorted. 'He was in a good mood, I suppose.'

'Well, you did get him off a murder charge, rescued his barman, stopped the Feathers burning down, and got rid of the crook who was trying to force him from his home.'

'I was only doing my job. Now, let's enjoy lunch.'

After he said grace, Mrs Goodfellow served a fantastic gazpacho, a real gazpacho, so very different from my disaster. I could hardly believe only three weeks had passed since then; life with Hobbes moved at a hectic pace.

'Would you like a bottle of wine?' asked Mrs G, as we were savouring the soup.

'Good idea,' said Hobbes. 'I intend to take it easy this afternoon.'

'Excellent,' said I.

'Sorry, dear,' she said, heading towards the cellar, 'you can't have any until Doctor Procter says so.'

She returned, holding two bottles, tutting. 'I really must clean down there. There's coal dust all over these.'

Having wiped them with a damp cloth, she opened one and poured it into a glass big enough for an adequate goldfish bowl. Placing it in front of Hobbes, she served the main course.

'What is it?' I asked, salivating. 'It smells fantastic. Is it Chinese?'

'That's right, dear, bang bang chicken.'

'I didn't know you could make Chinese food.'

'I do sometimes. I nursed there once.'

'When?'

'When I was a nurse.'

'Right ... anyway ... umm ... it looks great.'

'Thank you, dear.'

It was, as I expected, excellent, aromatic, savoury, piquant and served with a refreshing simple salad, just perfect for a hot afternoon. Though, as usual, we ate in silent homage to the old girl's genius, unusually, not all of my attention was focussed onto the meal, part of it still being with Violet. I kept going back to her words about Felix having done what had to be done and, though I'd assumed she'd been referring to his business dealings, I wondered if there was more to them.

The old girl's remark about the coal dust on the bottle puzzled me for she normally kept the cellar as spotless as a surgery. Hobbes, raising his glass, sniffed the contents, making me realise how much I would have enjoyed a glass or two. I tried to concentrate on the bang bang chicken, thinking it was a funny name for a dish, though appropriate, considering the bashing she'd given it. It made me think about the banging I'd heard before Violet turned up.

Hobbes, opening his lips, tilted the glass, my own taste buds anticipating his pleasure.

My next move surprised both of us. Leaping up, my chair falling, clattering, to the ground, I shoved the glass from his hands, the wine splashing over us, the glass shattering onto the kitchen floor. He stared at me, then at his stained shirt front and then at the stem of the glass, still in his great fist.

'Have you recently joined the Temperance Movement?' he asked.

'No ... I think ... umm ... that is ... the wine might be poisoned.'

'No!' He roared.

I cringed, expecting storm-force anger, but the shout was directed at the dog, who was licking at the spillage. Dregs backed away, assuming his martyred look.

'Why do you think that?'

'I don't know. It might be.'

'It never has been before.'

'No, but I think ... umm ... Felix broke into the cellar last night. Someone was banging and I think it was him knocking the door in, because Mrs Goodfellow says there's dust down there and there shouldn't be any. I reckon he's poisoned the wine. Violet said he'd done what had to be done and I think she meant getting you out the way.'

'It smelt alright,' he said, dipping his finger in the mess and touching his tongue, 'and it doesn't taste as if anything's wrong with it.'

'Perhaps he used an odourless, colourless, tasteless poison.'

'Ah yes, one unknown to medical science. There are a lot of them about.'

'Are there?'

'No. Anyway, Dregs seems fine.'

Dregs, wagging his tail on hearing his name, was not the sort to hold a grudge.

'But Felix,' I said, 'might have poisoned some other bottles.'

'Let's take a look.'

Hobbes and I went down the steps. When Dregs stopped at the top, refusing to come any further, I gave Hobbes a significant look that he ignored. On first glance, nothing seemed wrong. However, as we passed the wine racks, we could see the tunnel door's lock had been smashed, a sledgehammer had been discarded in the corner, and the coal pile had been shoved aside. I had no doubt who was responsible. Hobbes, growling, looked around. The wine appeared untouched, except for several bottles of the best stuff having disappeared.

He was totting up how many, when we discovered the bomb.

Sniffing at it, pointing to the electronic counter wired to a number of off-brown sticks, he looked thoughtful. 'I suppose that shows how long we've got before it goes off.'

'Umm ...' I replied, hypnotised by the flashing digits, 'I guess so. Is it counting in minutes or seconds?'

'Seconds by the looks of it.'

'So we've got thirty seconds. What are you going to do?'

'Twenty-five seconds now. Let me think.'

'OK.' Oddly, I felt quite calm.

It read twenty seconds when, grabbing the bomb, tucking it under his arm like a rugby ball, he charged across the cellar, and plunged down the steps into the tunnels.

Time seemed almost to slow down, though I was horribly aware it was running out far too fast. I hesitated, torn between wanting to help Hobbes, realising I couldn't, wondering whether I should make an attempt to get Mrs G and Dregs out of the house, though there was no time, and an urge to save myself.

Before I'd made up my mind, Hobbes bounded back into the cellar. On landing, he turned, jamming the door into place.

He'd got rid of the bomb. 'What did …?'

A tongue of hot red flame hurled him and the door across the cellar and, though it all happened so fast, I'm sure he whooped just before he slammed into the back wall. There was a deafening roar, a flash of heat and a rumble.

I picked myself up, coughing in the dust haze.

'Well,' said Hobbes, standing up, rubbing his elbow, 'that would have been more fun if the wall hadn't got in the way.'

Dregs rushed downstairs, barking and sneezing, Mrs Goodfellow close behind. Looking around, she shook her head. 'Look at the mess you've made.'

'It was a bomb,' I said. 'A great, big, bloody bomb!'

'Language, Andy,' said Hobbes, his face blackened like a coal miner's. 'I'll clean myself up and finish my dinner. Maybe you'll let me enjoy my glass of wine in peace this time.'

I stood there dumbfounded until Mrs G, setting to with dustpan and broom, chivvied me out the way. She didn't appear at all concerned that we might all have been killed.

That was pretty much the end of it, as far as we were concerned. We never heard any further news of Felix or Violet, but every time I read a story about a mysterious big cat sighting I wondered and, though Hobbes reckoned they'd probably gone abroad to continue their horrible schemes, I had a sneaking hope I'd reformed her.

The Bashems and Mr Bullimore, having picked up a small fortune in insurance money for the disastrous festival, continued to live on Loop's Farm. Though we became friends, I never felt quite comfortable if left on my own with them, especially after dark. Some fears were fundamental.

One lasting outcome was that the tunnel leading from the cellar collapsed. I was glad nothing could use it anymore, but I think it upset Hobbes. Another effect was that a section of Blackdog Street subsided, leaving a hole three metres deep. Although the council and gas board looked into it, they never got to the bottom of the mystery. They did, eventually, fill it in.

The day after the explosion, I began writing this memoir, thinking it might help me come to terms with losing her. It didn't.

Also available

Inspector Hobbes and the Blood
unhuman I
Wilkie Martin

When the hapless Andy Caplet, then an inept local reporter, is first assigned to Inspector Hobbes he has no idea what horrors his future holds. Besides coming to terms with Hobbes's weirdness and with the bizarre eccentricities of Mrs Goodfellow, he soon realises that not everyone is what they appear to be.

Who is behind the crime wave in town? Is it possible to catch vampirism from false teeth? And why is the secret to the mystery in the blood? These are just some of the questions Andy must answer as he struggles to make sense of this new world he's been plunged into.

'Odd, inventive, and genuinely very funny indeed'
Katie Jarvis, Cotswold Life.

The Witcherley Book Company
ISBN 9780957635104 (paperback)
ISBN 9780957635111 (ebook)
ISBN 9780957635166 (ebook)
ISBN 9780957635197 (hardback)

Scan QR code to view book sample and shop
(tinyurl.com/unhumanI
or book2look.com/book/ZrFHGPVxgR)

Inspector Hobbes and the Gold Diggers
unhuman III
Wilkie Martin

Andy, Hobbes and Mrs Goodfellow are surprised by the unexpected arrival of a large, disruptive American woman, invoking memories of Hobbes's past. Gold robberies, a skeleton and a vampire come together, to create a puzzle for Hobbes, one in which he needs help from some unexpected sources.

What is Sir Gerald Paynes's secret? Why does Hobbes think a collection of ordinary rocks is so significant? And has Andy found true love at last?

'Inspector Hobbes is back in his greatest adventure yet!'
Jo Ann Hakola (bkfaerie.blogspot.co.uk)

The Witcherley Book Company
ISBN 9780957635142 (paperback)
ISBN 9780957635159 (ebook)
ISBN 9780957635180 (ebook)
ISBN 9781910302071 (hardback)

Scan QR code to view book sample and shop
(tinyurl.com/unhumanIII
book2look.com/book/o8I6rbXQPo)

Inspector Hobbes and the Bones
unhuman IV
Wilkie Martin

There's going to be trouble. Andy Caplet's wife goes away, someone is out to get him, and he loses nearly everything in a storm. Amazing both himself and his unhuman friend Inspector Hobbes, he heroically rescues flood victims and uncovers something shocking.

Is Andy being set up for blackmail by the apparently charming young woman who attempts to seduce him, or is something even more sinister afoot? Hobbes certainly believes so, and he's getting worried.

This is the fourth in Wilkie Martin's unhuman series of cosy comedy crime fantasies.

The Witcherley Book Company
ISBN 9781910302026 (paperback)
ISBN 9781910302033 (ebook)
ISBN 9781910302040 (ebook)
ISBN 9781910302057 (hardback)

Scan QR code to view book sample and shop
(tinyurl.com/unhumanIV
book2look.com/book/6EJ4xgUg5Z)

Acknowledgements

Once again, I would like to thank the past and present members of Catchword for their support, guidance and encouragement: Geoffrey Adams, Gill Boyd, Liz Carew, Jennifer Cryer, Jean Dickenson, Rachel Fixsen, Susan Gibbs, Richard Hensley, Rhiannon Hopkins, Nick John, Sarah King, Dr Anne Lauppe-Dunbar, Dr Rona Laycock, Peter Maguire, Jan Petrie and Susannah White.

I would like to thank Kelly Owen at Ultimate Proof Ltd for copy-editing and for proofreading, and Mark Ecob of Mecob for the series covers.

Writers in the Brewery and the members of Gloucestershire Writers' Network have also provided much appreciated support.

Finally, a huge thank you to my family, to Julia, and to The Witcherley Book Company.

WILKIE MARTIN

Wilkie Martin's first novel *Inspector Hobbes and the Blood*, also published by The Witcherley Book Company, was shortlisted for the Impress Prize for New Writers in 2012 under its original title: *Inspector Hobbes*. As well as novels, Wilkie writes short stories and silly poems, some of which are on YouTube. Like his characters, he relishes a good curry, which he enjoys cooking. In his spare time, he is a qualified scuba-diving instructor, and a guitar twanger who should be stopped.

Born in Nottingham, he went to school in Sutton Coldfield, studied at the University of Leeds, worked in Cheltenham for 25 years, and now lives in the Cotswolds with Julia, his partner of 30 years.

(wilkiemartin.com)

(inyurl.com/WilkieMartinFacebook
or facebook.com/pages/Wilkie-Martin-AuthorPage/112466502150620)

A Note From The Author

I want to thank you for reading my book. As a new author, one of my biggest challenges is getting known and finding readers. I'm thrilled you have read it and hope you enjoyed it; if you did I would really appreciate you letting your friends and family know. Even a quick Google+ or Facebook status update or a tweet really can make a difference, or if you want to write a review then that would be fantastic. I'd also love to hear from you, so send me a message and let me know what you thought of the book. Don't forget to sign-up to my newsletter to get details of my next book. Thank you for your time.

Wilkie, November 2016

Scan QR code to share this book
(tinyurl.com/unhumanII
book2look.com/book/NqlwpcMhNm)

Wilkie's Newsletter

(wilkiemartin.com)